DUNWICH

DUNWICH

PETER LEVENDA

IBIS PRESS
Lake Worth, FL

Published in 2018 by Ibis Press
A division of Nicolas-Hays, Inc.
P. O. Box 540206
Lake Worth, FL 33454-0206
www.ibispress.net

Distributed to the trade by
Red Wheel/Weiser, LLC
65 Parker St. • Ste. 7
Newburyport, MA 01950
www.redwheelweiser.com

ISBN: 978-0-89254-180-5
Ebook: 978-0-89254-675-6

Library of Congress Cataloging-in-Publication Data
Available upon request

Book design and production by Studio 31
www.studio31.com

[MP]

Printed in the United States of America

Are the senders or their descendants still alive? Or have the hazards of 4 billion years been too much for them? Has their star inexorably warmed up and frizzled them, or were they able to colonise a different Solar System with a short-range spaceship? Have they perhaps destroyed themselves, either by too much aggression or too little? The difficulties of placing any form of life on another planetary system are so great that we are unlikely to be their sole descendants.

> — Francis H. Crick and L. E. Orgel "Directed Panspermia," *Icarus* 19, 341-346 (1973)

Despite the great suffering Jerry's abduction experiences caused her, she, like many other abductees, holds to the view that there was something of great value, a creative dimension, "a definite reason," for the abduction process—perhaps the creation of a new race of beings in which she was participating.

> — John E. Mack, *Abduction: Human Encounters with Aliens*, Ballantine, New York, 1995, p.128.

Lavinia Whateley had no known husband, but according to the custom of the region made no attempt to disavow the child; concerning the other side of whose ancestry the country folk might—and did—speculate as widely as they chose. On the contrary, she seemed strangely proud of the dark, goatish-looking infant who formed such a contrast to her own sickly and pink-eyed albinism, and was heard to mutter many curious prophecies about its unusual powers and tremendous future.

> — H. P. Lovecraft, "Dunwich"

PROLOGUE

October 12, 2014
Providence, Rhode Island
Home of Gloria Tibbi

IT WAS HAPPENING AGAIN.

Yes, okay, life would go on as usual. Waking up in the morning. Getting the boys ready for school. Making breakfast. Walking the dog. Going to work at the supermarket. Busy days, endless little details, the distractions of modern life. But it was modern life itself that seemed like a fantasy, a vacation on some tropical isle, compared to the rest of her secret existence: the part she couldn't tell anyone, or they would take her kids away from her for sure. Child Services. It had almost happened before. Before she learned how to keep the door closed between the real world and her world. As if she was an unfit mother. As if she was crazy or a druggie or something. If she talked … wow. It would ruin her life. All their lives. She was a hostage to the demands of the things that came in the night and spirited her away for their nocturnal … ministrations. "Spirited her away," was as good a description as any for it appealed to her religious nature. Somehow they turned her into a spirit and made her walk through walls and float into the air above her home, her town, her planet.

And it was happening again.

She felt like some kind of call-girl, or a nurse on duty during the night shift at some horror show hospital in Hell. They wrenched her from her bed—her two kids asleep in the next room—and transported her to some other place while she remained frozen, paralyzed, and unable to move or speak. Unable to refuse.

She looked it up. "Night terrors," it was called, or "sleep paralysis." Very common. Nothing to worry about. Move along.

And then she was nude. Naked, shivering—not with cold, but with anticipation—and flat on her back on a metal table or slab. It was so like how she got pregnant the first time. And the second time.

7

Flat on her back on a slab in the middle of the night as something poked her, prodded her, penetrated her.

That something, though—whatever it was—wasn't remotely human.

Sometimes they would show her a foetus in a jar, being fed nutrients through a transparent tube that pulsed with different colors. And they would indicate it was *her* foetus. From *her* egg.

"But how ..." she tried to ask, with a mouth that could not form words. "How was it fertilized?" She would get no response. Blank stares, if those eyes could be said to do anything but stare.

She would try again.

"*How* did this happen? *Who* fertilized my eggs?"

And then screaming.

"*Who is the father?*"

It always ended that way, with her screaming. She would wake up in bed, drenched in perspiration, hands clutching the sheets, only to find herself still naked and trembling and with no idea of where she'd been or how she got back home. She could hear the dog barking somewhere—had she let him out? She never let him out at night—and the kids' room was silent. *The kids!*

She threw a sheet around herself and—like every other time this happened—raced to her kids' bedroom and looked through the open door. They were sound asleep, twisted in their covers, oblivious to everything, even to the barking dog.

Not for the first time, she wondered at her kids. She knew their father—a useless drunk, now living in another state with another woman, God help her—but still could not help wondering.

I mean, who was their *father? Really? Was it my ex-husband? Or ...?*

And not for the first time, she let that thought sit where it lay. She turned back to her room, exhausted, and examined herself for the marks.

There they were. In the old days, they would have been called "witches' marks" and her disappearance into the night air over

Providence a witch's flight to the Sabbat. The beings that messed with her body, using it as a kind of incubator for their evil seed, would have been called demons. Incubi. It would have been enough to have her hanged at Salem. No matter that she had a crucifix hanging over her bed and holy water in a bowl near the front door.

She was sore, down there. She stepped into the bathroom and relieved herself, feeling the burning sensation that she knew would dissipate in a few hours. As she sat there, she felt the need for a cigarette even though she had stopped smoking when she became pregnant with her first child, her son Mikey. That had been seven years ago, and little Bobby had followed ten months later. But her nerves were shot. That would go away, too, in a few hours. Or days. That part was never the same.

Then there was the thing that she could never admit, not even to herself. It was the part of the whole experience she pushed furthest from her mind, even as it was happening. She knew if she said it aloud, or thought it straight through, she would be damned. She would go to hell while still alive, no matter that her children needed her. She would surely go to hell.

The part. *That* part. She knew that even rape victims experienced it, but if they admitted to it in the old days the cops would figure they weren't really raped.

That part. The part about her reaction to the penetration, to the whole experience beginning with the abduction from her home. The fear mingled with sexual feelings she tried to suppress. She knew it was biological, neurological, whatever. She shouldn't blame herself for those feelings. It was natural, even if the circumstances were sickening and vile. And she didn't want to give those … those *things* … the satisfaction of seeing her orgasm so shamelessly in front of them. She didn't want to give them the idea that what they were doing was somehow okay, because it *wasn't*. *No way*. And it wasn't like Stockholm Syndrome. Not really. She was a captive, in a sense, sure. They could pick her up and rape her anytime they wanted, so she might as well be their prisoner. She even tried moving, once when Mikey was only two and Bobby was only fourteen months old, but they came for her anyway.

But *was* it rape? They didn't actually sit on top of her and plow away. It was all very clinical, if obscene. And it seemed as if getting her off was not the actual purpose of the process, only a kind of side effect. It's just that she was so sensitive down there, very orgasm-prone as her ex used to say. She couldn't help it.

She stood up, flushed, and looked at her face in the mirror as she washed her hands. Eyes bloodshot. Cheeks flushed. She looked tired, bedraggled. Older than her thirty-five years.

Maybe it was all in her head. Maybe she was a little psychotic or neurotic or whatever they called it. She couldn't prove anything. She wasn't a danger to her kids.

Her kids.

It was at the back of her mind. She almost forgot about it.

She had sent away for some of those genetic testing kits, the kind they advertise on TV all the time. She got one each for her kids and one for herself. They had to spit into some little tubes and then send them back to the lab. It was expensive on her supermarket salary but she was curious. She only had the briefest ideas about her own ethnic background and almost nothing for sure about her ex. She was some kind of Scot-Irish mixture, she was sure. Maybe a little Portuguese or Italian mixed in. The neighborhood she grew up in was like that, and her parents had died when she was little so she didn't really have a lot of data to work with. The genetic test would help clear up some of that confusion. When it finally turned up.

Why was she thinking about it now? She made a conscious effort to block the idea from her mind. She shook her head as if to clear the information away. She didn't want *them* to hear what she was thinking about her kids, learn what she was doing. She slapped her hands over her ears as if to keep her thoughts from leaking out of her brain. The thought came to her, unbidden, from that place deep inside her where her most desperate fears were buried:

She didn't want their "father" to know.

She heard the dog barking again, its unmistakably unique squeaky yelp, and got up to go and let him in. She padded down the hallway to the front door when the barking suddenly stopped.

That was when she realized, with a sickening feeling in the pit of her stomach, that their dog had died a year ago and was buried in the back yard.

She dropped to her knees, her arms wrapped around her abdomen, and wept softly so her kids wouldn't hear her. *What is happening to me?* she asked herself.

And why is it happening *again?*

Same day
Somewhere in Inner Mongolia

The evening meal was simplicity itself.

In the open air in front of the tent a large brass bowl was set over a charcoal flame. Inside the bowl, a hearty broth made from animal bones and scavenged vegetables into which fistfuls of dried chilies had been boiling. Arrayed around the bowl were paper-thin slices of mutton on chipped and cracked porcelain plates, various offal of the sheep similarly sliced, cakes of lamb's blood, and mountains of lettuce leaves, bean sprouts, and *bai cai*, what Cantonese speakers call *bok choy*. The diners would pick up pieces of mutton or vegetables or the blood pudding cakes and dip them into the broth, allowing them to cook briefly before lifting them out again with their chopsticks, dipping the cooked ingredient into a small personal bowl of paste made from sesame and other condiments. Each diner was responsible for his own meal this way, cooked the way he liked it. At the end of the meal, the small bowl of sesame paste had become a kind of soup in its own right due to all the dipping of boiled ingredients, and was slurped appreciatively.

Gregory Angell, one-time tenured professor of Asian languages and religious studies at Columbia University, was indistinguishable from the other nomads sitting around the large brass bowl of broth and Szechuan chilies. He was dressed as they were, in a padded cotton coat and a round, fur-lined hat. His cheeks were red from the cold blowing in across the dunes on its way to Beijing where the grains of Gobi Desert sand would dust the streets of the Chinese capital with a fine grit, mixing with the clouds of soot sent up by the belching, coal-fired power stations and the open-air cook stoves on the balconies of a thousand apartment blocks in the city. He was in Mongolia, in a tribal encampment outside Hohhot, and was briefly at peace.

The events that had propelled him to this station in life had been intense and excruciating. Angell was not by nature a man of action, but a man of books and languages and academic study. But he had been sent to a Kurdish refugee camp in Turkey and from there to Iraq, Iran, Pakistan and eventually to Nepal in search of a sacred (or blasphemous) book around which an entire underground cult had been organized. He had risked his life, running from ISIL, the Taliban, the Iranian Revolutionary Guard, Pakistan's ISI, and God only knew who else, all with elements loyal to a cult named variously after Dagon—a Mesopotamian deity of frightful appetites—or after the great high priest of the cult since ancient times, dread Cthulhu or Kutulu himself, of whom Dagon was a pale avatar. In the process he had been involved with the Yezidi (who were even now in danger of being wiped out by Daesh at Mount Sinjar), the "kafiris" of Kafiristan or Nuristan, and the Kalashas of Pakistan. Most people in the west didn't even know these groups—and many more like them—existed, even though they hold many secrets necessary for human survival.

He thought back on Fahim, who worked at the Baghdad Museum and who was a Yezidi and in charge of keeping the Book away from the cult, and the young and beautiful Jamila who very nearly channeled the forces of Cthulhu in a dramatic ritual in a secret chamber beneath the Himalayas until Angell himself aborted the rite. Was Jamila even alive? Were any of them alive?

He knew that most of those who had helped him get to that

chamber were dead. He had watched them die. Even fabled Jason Miller, the US government's own remote viewer who had used Angell as a stalking horse all over Central Asia in a desperate effort to find and destroy the Book, had died in that miserable cavern.

Miller wanted the Book destroyed. This was a reasonable and logical goal for someone who wanted to see the human race spared the hideous depravities the Book seemed to promise. The Book *should* have been destroyed.

But Angell could not bring himself to do it.

The first usage of the term "holocaust" in modern times was employed by the Nazis and it wasn't for what you might think. The *first* Nazi "holocaust" was the burning of *books*, books considered incompatible with the political and racist agenda of the regime. The destruction of a book, any book, was not something Angell could accept regardless of the book's contents. After all, the Great Library of Alexandria had been destroyed by fire, caused by Caesar's troops in 48 BCE. This ancient holocaust had robbed the world of a great many important texts and classical works, and remained an open wound in the literary history of the period. Could Angell do the same, even if it was only one book, and a book so evil that hordes of terrorists and cultists were ready to kill in its name?

In a knapsack made of blue-dyed sheep's wool and dirty white cotton, and wrapped in layers of black silk, Angell guarded the Book that had caused so much misery and so many lives. He had waited as long as he could in the beautiful yet desolate wastes of Mongolia, hoping he could blend in with the tribes and forget all about the Book and its contents and his own tortured history.

But it was seeing the rock, the grey carven stone with its mysterious couplet, revealed by a wind in the dunes of the Singing Sands of the Badain Jaran desert west of Hohhot, that decided his fate for him. He had seen the rock paintings on Mount Mandela in the Yinshan, and the strange temples that were half-Tibetan and half-Mongol, but this rock was far from the mountains and the temples. The singing of the sands had captivated him, and he listened to the booming and droning for a long while, as if in a trance, before realizing that the sliding sands that caused the eerie sounds had revealed a kind of monolith that had been buried beneath them for centuries.

The words were arcane and strange, written in the Mongolian script, the rock older than Genghis Khan. But once translated they were an exact match for the couplet he had seen written on a Baghdad Museum inventory list in a Kurdish language known as Kurmanji when he first began this mission months ago:

That is not dead which can eternal lie
And with strange aeons even death may die.

Fucking Monroe, thought Angell, thinking back on the mysterious, unseen puppet master who had sent him to Turkey because of Angell's ancestry and his knowledge of the Central Asian languages, religions, and peoples. The spy master of all spy masters. A man so old he could have retired twice by now. A man who was still hunting him from one end of the Earth to the other.

Fucking Aubrey, who was his chaperone as far as the Iraq-Iran border and who then cut him loose among the Zoroastrians and the Revolutionary Guard. The man who had seduced him into this plot by appealing to his better nature and to his need for a God. Any God.

And Howard Phillips fucking Lovecraft, who started this whole mess almost a hundred years ago with his damned story about the Angell family and the Cthulhu Cult.

Him, and that book of his nestled safely if sinisterly in Angell's knapsack:

The fucking *Necronomicon*.

Same day
Lasserre, Ariège
France

At the same moment, but halfway between Providence and Angell's location in Mongolia, Alexander Grothendieck—the undisputed greatest mathematician in the world, now a recluse—was sitting at his home in the Pyrénées in the south of France. He was only eighty kilometers west of Montségur, the famous enclave of the Cathars and site of much speculation concerning the Knights Templar, their mysterious treasure, and the Holy Grail itself. Otto Rahn had been through the region in the 1930s looking for just that artifact. Later, the dreamy-eyed philosopher of alternate history would find himself in the SS, a member of Heinrich Himmler's personal staff. Grothendieck, however, was not a Nazi.

His father had been murdered at one of the camps during the war. Grothendieck and his mother survived the conflict, the young Alexander often living hand to mouth and hiding in the woods. Alexander would come to find solace in mathematics and particularly in algebra: that form of mathematics named after its Persian incarnation: *al-Jabr*. Al-Khwarizmi and even Omar Khayyam were its main exponents in the eighth and eleventh centuries, respectively. However, algebra really had its roots in ancient Babylon, just as geometry had its roots in ancient Egypt. This difference in approach to the mathematical structure of the world—the algebraic and the geometric—resembles the worldviews of their respective originators, with the Egyptians (the builders of the pyramids) focused on geometry and the Babylonians (focused on the manipulation of numbers and their magical properties) on algebra. It was Grothendieck who created a form of algebraic geometry, a combination of both, that constituted a paradigm shift in the world of mathematics.

It was early afternoon in the Languedoc, and Grothendieck was in the midst of a trance. Years earlier, he had abandoned traditional mathematics—and all of academic society for that matter—for a pursuit of the spiritual, He had filled thousands of pages with complex and virtually incomprehensible theories describing the nature of the universe, the interpretation of dreams, and the characteristics of God. He had a flirtation with Buddhism, with free love, and with theosophies of various types. He was mad, driven, and obsessed. But with what, exactly, no one could tell. The man who had single-handedly revolutionized algebraic theory—again and again over the years—was so deep within the algebra of consciousness that he found himself unable to communicate his thought to anyone else on the planet. Still, he wrote and scribbled manically, creating huge manuscripts that would not see the light of day in his lifetime.

A lifetime that was coming to a close, for he would be dead the following month: the tuberculosis that would kill him already sneaking around the edges of his organs looking for an opening, an unlocked door, a virtual Gate.

It all started for him—this journey away from algebra to alchemy—in April of 1974.

In his notes, he wrote:

1-7 avril 1974: "moment de verité," entrée dans la voie spirituelle
April 1-7, 1974: Moment of truth. Entering the spiritual path.

On April 1, 1974 the Ayatollah Khomeini called for the creation of an Islamic Republic of Iran.

On April 5, 1974 the World Trade Center in New York City was officially opened.

On April 7, 1974, Grothendieck wrote that he "entered the divine" with his introduction to Nichiren Buddhism.

Forty years later, he is isolated in a small house in a tiny village in the south of France, only ninety minutes from both Montségur to the east and the Spanish border to the south. In that time Iran has become an Islamic republic, and the World Trade Center is no more. Along the way, Grothendieck abandoned traditional Buddhism as well. But not spirituality. Or his version of it, anyway.

Beneath his hand, on a small round table next to his chair, is his study of what he calls "mutants."

There are, he insists, exceptional people on the planet who are so unique, so advanced in their thinking, that they can only be considered mutant forms of human life. He includes in this list Freud, Darwin, Walt Whitman, Rudolf Steiner (the founder of Anthroposophy), Gandhi, Teilhard de Chardin, and Krishnamurti, among others. What he does not say—even though the thought haunts him, day and night and especially in his sleep—is the obverse of that theory: that there are exceptional people on the planet who are so unique, so debased in their thinking and depraved in their actions, that they also can be considered mutant forms of human life. He has met some of them. His father died at their hands, certainly, and he himself suffered under the Nazi regime. But there were others, more recent, who frightened him even more.

Like the man who came to see him that day.

Grothendieck was careful not to let people know where he lived. He valued his privacy, and the blessed silence that was his environment. He valued his train of thought, a train that went on for days at a time, and any disturbance of that thought was unbearable. He had his writings, his manuscripts, his blend of philosophy, religion and mathematics, and they represented thoughts at once delicate and robust. Any interference could be disastrous, and leave him annoyed and in a foul mood for days as he desperately tried to recoup what thoughts he had lost.

This time, though, someone had found him. A man who was pleasant enough in appearance but to Grothendieck's inner eye—his psychic sense honed to a needle's sharpness over the decades since his embrace of Buddhist meditation and even earlier, beginning in his escape from the Nazis and his life living rough in the woods— the man harbored within himself a core of darkness that seemed to swallow any residual light emanating from Grothendieck's own heart. It wasn't life that was being sucked away from the mad mathematician, but joy.

"Professor Grothendieck?" It was a question for politeness, one that masked an impolite certainty.

"I was not expecting visitors, Monsieur ...?"

"You may call me Aubrey."

Grothendieck smiled.

"Is this some sort of joke?"

"Pardon?"

"Aubrey. It's not your real name, is it?"

It was Aubrey's turn to smile.

"Whatever do you mean, sir?"

"Aubrey. The name is a venerable Anglo-Saxon one. From Alberic. It means 'King of the Elves.' Are you such a king, my lord?"

"Your command of languages is well-known, to be sure. In fact, I do command the allegiance of a number of individuals, *Professeur*. But I work for another, one even more ... venerable."

"I thought as much. There have been others, before you. They have tried to ... what is the word? ... 'weaponize' mathematics. They failed."

"We do not wish to weaponize mathematics, Professor. We believe that, hidden within your equations, is a profound secret. Something to do with the arrangement of space and time, the identification of a flaw in the arithmetic of consciousness perhaps, and that evil persons may already be aware of this flaw and may be attempting to exploit it."

"If you were to repeat that statement to most of my colleagues you would be laughed out of the country. You realize that, don't you?"

"Of course. But your colleagues have not dabbled in the psychic sciences as you have. They have not received Buddhist initiations or studied Theosophy."

"True."

"And you alone of all others have abandoned academia and devoted yourself full-time to the study of subjects that would be considered an affront to scientists and mathematicians everywhere.

Like the American helicopter engineer, Arthur Young, you abandoned your chosen field in favor of a life spent examining the spiritual. And the paranormal."

"You are making me uncomfortable, King of the Elves."

"That is not my intention. But the rumor is that you have been covering thousands of pages of manuscript with writings that can only be considered the ravings of a lunatic. Yet we both know that you are no lunatic, and that your manuscripts are not the ravings of one. As the most distinguished and brilliant mathematician on the planet, moreover one who has understood the inner workings of the psyche, your work these past twenty years or more has been to discover and to elucidate a truth far more profound than even pure mathematics can provide."

"More profound, yes. But also more frightening. I cannot explain these things to you. You are not a mathematician. You don't have the tools. This is far more complicated than a high school algebra conundrum like the square root of minus one. This goes to the very heart of algebra and geometry, of time and space and the flaws in our measurements of both."

"And of the possibility that we humans may exploit these flaws, to travel to distant stars or even other dimensions?"

"No."

"No?"

"No. Not humans. No."

Same day
Dharamsala
India

The young woman with the penetrating blue eyes sat at the feet of the old monk. Outside the temple the headquarters of the Dalai Lama could be seen: a hive of activity as dignitaries and religious leaders of all faiths scurried in and out, looking for an audience with the head of the Tibetan Government-in-Exile: a title the Dalai Lama had relinquished a few years earlier in order to concentrate more deeply on his religious mission.

The Dalai Lama's role was not without its opposition from other Tibetans, particularly those who reverenced the patron protector deity of the Gelugpa school: Dorje Shugden. The Dalai Lama proclaimed Dorje Shugden to be a demonic spirit, a violent protector who attacked those who mixed Nyingmapa practices with Gelugpa practices. To an outsider, this type of conflict seemed almost supernaturally (if not theologically) obscure, but to those who made offerings to Dorje Shugden their whole lives, the sudden ban on his worship was nothing less than an assault.

The young woman had approached this old monk specifically to learn more about Dorje Shugden. She had a reason for doing so, and since Dharamsala was near enough to Kembalung—the beyul or "hidden country" she had just left—nearer, anyway, than her "lost country," the land around Mosul in Iraq, she decided that learning more about this peculiar deity would enable her to gain more insight into what was happening to her and to her people.

She had made the two thousand kilometer journey partially on foot from the Khembalung Valley of Tibet, heading west, and then managed to hitch a ride on a flatbed truck making its way to the Indo-Nepalese border. It had taken a few weeks, and she was heading in the right direction back towards her home in the refugee camp in Kurdish-controlled Turkey, but she still had many thousands of klicks to go before she could rest.

If ever she could rest.

The images of the secret tomb beneath the mountains—and her fractured memory of spirit possession and violence—haunted her nights and hollowed out her days. She would fall asleep, lulled by the rhythm of the truck's motion, only to jerk awake when she felt the hands of some unspeakable being wrapping itself around her soul.

Someone had told her about Dharamsala. And about the Dalai Lama. And about the peaceful religion of Buddhism. So she decided to make her way there after learning that an army calling itself the

Islamic State had amassed troops around her sacred mountain, Sinjar, and was threatening to execute her entire race. After seeing what she had seen at Kembalung, she knew that she needed more than the answers politicians and generals would give her. If a spirit could possess a young woman like herself, what about an entire country?

India was the land of peacocks she saw. This gave her hope, and made her emotions swell with anticipation. After all, her god— Melek Taus—was a peacock. The word "melek" meant "king" in the language of the Arabs. He was the Peacock King, although he also was called the Peacock Angel, and some even called him Shaitan or Satan. Melek Taus would be the first being to be welcomed back to Heaven after the Last Days, to be followed immediately by her people, the ones they called Yezidi. This she knew, as surely as she knew her own name.

Jamila.

She made her way to the first temple she saw, a building resplendent in reds and golds and replete with statues of smiling, benevolent beings. She found a monk who could understand her broken English but more importantly could communicate with his mind. The way she did. He seemed to understand her in a way that even Fahim could not, although Fahim did his best when he was around her.

From the Tibetan monk she learned of Dorje Shugden. He was a *gyalpo*, a fierce warrior god of South Tibet who was the being who possessed the Nechung Oracle, the State Oracle of Tibet. The Dalai Lama had forbidden anyone to worship this being, who was considered demonic and difficult to control except by the Oracle. Something about this situation resonated with her: a strong, powerful, even violent supernatural being who was considered evil but at the same time was prized for its ability to see the future. Dorje Shugden possessed the State Oracle the same way another Being—a High Priest of an ancient race—possessed *her*. Except the Being she knew as Kutulu did not possess her to predict the future but to use her as a Gate into this dimension, into this World.

But if the Dalai Lama could control Dorje Shugden, then maybe she could learn how to control Kutulu.

For his part, the old monk recognized that the young woman before him was a *kuten*: what the Tibetans call a "material basis" for the possessing spirit. A *kuten* for *Kutulu*, then. He understood that her barbaric pronunciation probably was meant in the Tibetan language to be *kusulu*: the spirit of a dead shaman. He was therefore afraid for her, fearful that such a malicious and malevolent demon, a refugee from one of the Bön hells certainly, would use such a pure vessel as this girl as a way of wreaking destruction all around her and of eventually destroying her mind.

He had no idea.

Same day
New Orleans
NOPD

Cuneo, the homicide detective of African-Italian ancestry, sat at his desk and stared at the photos in front of him. It was a case that unofficially was considered closed, not because they had found the perp but because the circumstances were so weird that no one was willing to proceed any further with it. A subterranean vault in the Ninth Ward with two corpses tied to a metal pole in the middle: the centerpiece of what appeared to be a Faraday Cage. Strange diagrams painted on the walls. A psychotic old lady with a library full of grimoires and a pedigree in a generational secret society. Photographs of a man from a hundred years ago: the same man who showed up looking not a day older than his photo warning him off the investigation.

There was no way to solve a case like this using normal police procedures. You had to know other stuff. You had to piece together bits and pieces of voodoo, spirit possession, sick rituals, and old money. He was out of his depth, and almost out of his mind. He had fallen in love with New Orleans after his career in NYPD, and now he was wondering if the honeymoon was over. This wasn't the New Orleans of the French Quarter and Mardi Gras. This was the New Orleans of Hurricane Katrina, dead neighborhoods, and ancient families hiding behind the moss-covered elms on their vast estates and the gator-infested bayous that served as their moats. This wasn't the New Orleans of *The Big Easy*, but the New Orleans of friggin' *Angel Heart*.

And he didn't want what happened to Mickey Rourke's face to happen to his.

From beneath the pile of photos—some of them dating back to 1907—and the inspector's files from the investigation of the cult that performed human sacrifice out in the bayous, he withdrew the book he purchased at one of the last actual bookstores in New Orleans that didn't smell like sandalwood incense and John the Conqueror Root. It was a fancy new edition of *The Sixth and Seventh Books of Moses*, all hardcover and academically-footnoted. He had seen the same book, in poorly-printed pamphlet form, in every botanica and voodoo supply shop in the Quarter and that didn't help him much. He couldn't make heads or tails out of it. The Latin and Hebrew were bowdlerized messes, and the instructions made no sense. This version cost a lot more, but he trusted that the footnotes and the introductory material would enable him to penetrate the mysteries of just what the hell was taking place behind closed doors and open swamps in the Big Uneasy.

He knew he shouldn't be wasting time on a case no one wanted solved. NOPD was notoriously under-staffed. But every cop had one case that wouldn't go away, no matter how hard he or she tried. This one was Cuneo's, for better or for worse.

He opened the book at a random page and began to read.

Same day
Fort Meade

Monroe had been hitting the bottle a lot lately. He had been abstemious for most of the past few months as the chatter surrounding the Book increased and he was compelled to enlist the aid of Gregory Angell in his attempt to obtain it before the others did. He was sorry to hear of the death of Jason Miller, his prized remote viewer who had gone rogue once he divined the existence of the Book, and of the deaths of the other agents who had made the ultimate sacrifice both in Iran and in Nepal.

And he was especially sorry to have lost Angell himself, a man he had exploited in the most shameful manner and then lost somewhere in the Himalayas. Along with the Book.

So Monroe—ordinarily dapper in dark blue or charcoal grey pinstripe suits, thin, urbane, and with a head of shocking white hair— began to drink. Single malts, it was true, and only after sundown. But it was a steady ritual that dulled his senses. His operation had averted a global catastrophe and vindicated everything he had been working on for decades. He should have been proud. But there was a bad taste in his mouth at the way it had ended.

In his drawer he had the Glock that Angell had surrendered to Aubrey before the trip to Turkey had begun. In a glassine evidence bag he had the bullet that had killed a man known as Adnan, the spook who had accompanied Angell as far as Nepal before he lost his life in a shootout at a hidden tomb. The bullet did not match the Glock, but that was not a problem for Monroe.

In another glassine envelope he had a bullet that was test-fired from the Glock. It would be a simple matter to replace one bullet with the other and thereby pin Adnan's death on Angell. It was a fall-back option, in case they needed Angell again. Something to hold over him.

Because, really, Angell still had the Book. The one that had started this whole mess so long ago. Monroe knew that Angell had not destroyed the Book. Angell was a scholar. A reader. A lover of books. He could no more destroy a book—any book—than a drunk could empty a bottle of whiskey down the kitchen sink.

That was the reason no one had heard from Angell since those events in Nepal. He had become the next Keeper of the Book. Find Angell, and you find the Book.

Find Angell, and you find the *Necronomicon*.

"So," Monroe said aloud, to himself. "Let's find Angell."

BOOK ONE

The classical method of making the homunculus is to take the fertilized ova of a woman and to reproduce as closely as may be, without the uterus, the normal conditions of gestation therein.

—Aleister Crowley, *Of the Homunculus: A Secret Instruction of the Ninth Degree*

But know this: that which is received in the matrix through unnatural works tends towards becoming a monster and a freakish growth. Also, though it may go inside again, that which has contact with the air is no longer a seed, but a *materia homunculi*.

—Paracelsus, *Liber de Homunculis*

She turned away, not wanting to see.
Those eyes! Like an animal's, a tiger's, not like a human being's!
He *wasn't* a human being, of course. He was—some kind of a half-breed.

—Ira Levin, *Rosemary's Baby*

CHAPTER ONE

MOST PEOPLE THOUGHT HARRY had the worst possible job at NSA. He sat in a small room—his own office, at least—in a sub-basement at Fort Meade with a powerful computer that was protected by multiple layers of security and a door that had three different locks: one was a keypad lock, one used fingerprint recognition and the other was iris recognition. All three had to be employed in a precise order which changed every day. You would think he had the nuclear launch codes in there. He didn't. All he had was porn.

Harry's job involved porn analysis. And not just any porn. There were other analysts who did that type of grunt work, using specialized algorithms to go through millions of digitized images to detect embedded code in the odd pixel. It was called steganography, after the father of modern cryptography—the occultist and priest Abbot Trithemius—and his seminal work, *Steganographia*. There were indications that Al-Qaeda used this method to communicate secretly with its members worldwide. That was probably an urban legend, but considering how much porn was discovered at Osama bin Laden's bunker in Abbottabad it was not that far-fetched.

Harry, though, was not examining just any kind of porn. His specialty was kiddie porn.

There was a booming industry in images of young girls (mostly girls) under the age of 15. While the most heinous of the images involved nude girls and girls performing sexual acts with grown men, there was a secondary market in the distribution of images of young girls dressed in swimsuits as well as in school uniforms and sleepwear: images that could not be considered x-rated, but which many countries had declared pornographic nonetheless. The girls were posed provocatively, as if they knew precisely what they were doing and the type of reaction they wanted to provoke. Girls as young as nine or ten—and many even younger—were exploited this way, with professional production quality lighting, sets, clothing, props, etc. These girls originated from Eastern Europe and Russia for the most part, with a large Japanese contingent as well (these images were not considered illegal in Japan until recently, and even then the ban has not been strictly enforced).

Harry was involved in the analysis of images and video captured from sites specializing in *kawaii* ("cute") and *imouto* ("little sister"): Japanese versions of borderline child porn. The girls who pose in these photos and video display no other talents than sitting, standing, walking, and laying down in a variety of costumes with innocent and not-so-innocent expressions. They would age out of this industry by the time they were sixteen or seventeen. For that reason, the websites advertised them as U15, or "under 15." In Japan, the industry was above-ground and huge, with devoted fan bases, multimedia packages, collectible DVDs, and the like. In Eastern Europe, the industry was just as large but mostly underground, accessible only through the dark web but occasionally leaking out into easily available websites that advertised "child models": sites that were shut down almost as quickly as they went up.

Harry was looking for embedded code in these images, like his counterparts upstairs, but he had another agenda as well. Some of the girls used in these sites were products of a human trafficking ring that had tentacles within several organized crime families as well as with some kind of macabre cult of devil worshippers. Or something. That there was a Yakuza connection to the Japanese sites was beyond doubt, but there were hints at a Chechen Mafia link to the Eastern European sites and that is what made his superiors nervous. The possibility of a link to jihadist terror groups could not be ignored.

Harry himself was something of a womanizer. Everyone seemed to know that about him. It was as if he went overboard trying to prove that he wasn't stimulated by the images he trolled and deliberately went after women who were *older* than he was. This was getting more difficult every year, since Harry was already over forty and showing every minute of his age. The last thing Harry wanted to hear, though, was that he was "robbing the cradle." That phrase had very different implications for someone in his line of work.

The images he was working with that day had already been analyzed by the experts in terms of embedded code. What he was looking for was something quite different, something that would be overlooked by your garden-variety pervert.

He paid close attention to electrical faceplates, for instance. These were dead give-aways as to the geographic location where the photos were taken. Every country seemed to have its own version of electrical outlet, and Harry knew them all. Some countries, like China, often had two or three different types of outlets in the same room. He could tell at a glance if a photo was taken in Japan or Ukraine, England or somewhere in the United States. The grounded three-prong outlets were usually the easiest to identify.

Then there were the magazines, books, etc. Some of them were too easy. If they had Cyrillic lettering, Harry would analyze them and determine if he was looking at Russian, Ukrainian, perhaps something from Central Asia, etc. There were French, Italian, Polish, Czech publications in some of the photos. This enabled some cross-checking with known child trafficking and international pedophile rings, always keeping in mind that another task of his was to determine when a given photo was taken. Sometimes he only got them when they were already two or three years old, and his job was made that much more difficult.

Today, however, he had noticed something else and this is what he was concentrating on. He lost track of time as he raced through image after image, sometimes loading a video file and going through it frame by frame. The pictures of young girls in swimsuits had ceased to distract him long ago. He had gotten over his disgust at how they were being exploited because it didn't do them, or him, any good. His brief was to isolate the traffickers and their channels, and this he was very good at doing. Today, though, he spotted an anomaly that nagged at him. Something else was going on here.

There it was again. Harry stopped and enlarged the image in front of him. It was of a young blond girl, probably Russian or Ukrainian, maybe Czech. She was pretty well-known on the dark web and went by a variety of names, such as Amber or Danielle. She could not have been more than thirteen when her most famous photos were taken, but her eyes told a story that was much older. She was wearing a two-piece swimsuit and was posed provocatively resting on her stomach on a beach towel, her eyes looking at you over her shoulder in what would have been an unmistakable invitation from an older woman.

The bottom half of her suit was pulled down just enough to reveal part of a tattoo. This is what had grabbed Harry's attention.

He printed out the photo and put it with a few others he had been collecting the past week. All of different girls, but all of the same tattoo.

The girls in this file ranged in age from about ten to about fifteen, according to Harry's practiced eye. Some were Asian, one or two were Latina, and at least three were Eastern European. This kind of multi-ethnicity is what raised red flags for Harry, for they all sported what had to be the same sort of gang or organized crime symbol. If they were branded by the same group, that meant he was looking at an international gang of child abusers that stretched across continents.

The websites that specialized in this material usually kept to a single race. The Japanese had their own *kawaii* and *imouto* sites and boasted much higher production values than those from Eastern Europe. There was virtually no similarity of style in the final media—but the identical tattoo was evidence that the girls were being trafficked by a single source.

Porn stars had a lot of tattoos, generally. Some were the inevitable Chinese characters, others were phrases in Latin or Spanish. There were bear paw tattoos, tiger paw tattoos, scorpions, barbed wire, infinity symbols, cartoon characters … some of the Asian porn stars even had full color dragons, usually on their backs, but now increasingly on the rest of their bodies. Tattoos were becoming highly visible throughout the pornographic world, in inverse proportion to disappearing pubic hair it seemed.

But not where the kids were concerned. For the most part, the material Harry was looking at stopped short of out-and-out porn. This was the area that some sites called "child erotica": images of children that did not involve adults and which did not include any overt sexual contact or display. Some jurisdictions did not prosecute possession of "child erotica," although that was changing as the laws began to catch up to the possibilities offered by high-speed internet, virtual private networks or VPN, and anonymous browsers like Tor. There was a rage of controversy over what constituted "child porn" versus "child erotica," but the general attitude among law enforcement was that any image that focused on the bodies of young girls (or boys) constituted exploitation and abuse regardless of whether or not the bodies were naked. It wasn't hard to understand: why were the children being photographed that way, in seductive positions that imitated those of adult women, if the photographers were not going for sexual stimulation? And who knew if the children in the photographs were not being trafficked or subject to much greater abuse off-camera?

This tattoo, however, was like nothing he had ever seen in child erotica before.

Normally, those girls were not tattooed or otherwise marked. The pedophiles that went in for this sort of thing were usually turned off by anything that suggested the girls were not "pure" or "virginal." A tramp stamp would be a definite turn off. But in these cases the tattoo was small and innocent-looking, about the size of a quarter, like those temporary markings little kids used to get on wax paper from cereal boxes.

It was in two colors. The most prominent color was a dark shade of pink and it was used for a floral image, like pink roses—feminine and childish—an overlay on the base image which was in a darker color ink, a shade of blue, and which was much more sinister.

Harry had seen something like it before, in an intelligence briefing that had been conducted by that old guy a few months back. What was his name? Madison ... Moriarty ... no, Monroe. That was it. Monroe. Some ancient spook who haunted the halls of Fort Meade like a real-life ghost. Everyone was so deferential to him, but no one seemed to know why. Every Director over the past two decades that Harry had been there had seemed to inherit Monroe from his predecessor, like the key to the executive washroom. Or a particularly stubborn virus.

And yet Monroe wasn't really NSA. He was just *there*, seconded to the NSA by some other agency. No one would say which one. (At least, *he* wasn't cleared high enough for that information.) But it was Monroe who gave them all this briefing some time ago when it seemed that there was an increase in terrorist chatter around the world. There were rumors of dead agents and a missing teacher or something. Probably some do-gooder on a junket to Baghdad is the way Harry saw it. But that's all they were. Rumors.

Until now, maybe, because at the moment Harry had in his hands proof that at least some of what old Monroe was talking about had some basis in reality.

He took the elevator up a few floors to see his supervisor. He kept the photos in a folder with classification markings, tucked under his arm. He remembered the last time he had dropped a folder full of child porn onto the gleaming hallway floor outside the office of NSA's general counsel, Rajesh De, who had his own hands full with the Snowden affair. He still felt the embarrassment and humiliation of that incident burn his cheeks.

This time, however, passed without incident. His supervisor was expecting him.

"Hello, Harry. I got your message. What's up?"

Sylvia Matos sat behind her government-issue metal desk and somehow made it look like the Oval Office. She was impeccably dressed, as usual, and wore her trademark glasses on her trademark chain around her neck. There were a handful of credentials and photographs on the available wall space that reinforced the impression that Sylvia Matos was a political animal as well as an experienced cryptanalyst with two degrees in computer science. She was also fit and attractive, with a vaguely olive complexion and straight, still-black, hair cut in a short and easy-to-manage do. At fifty-three, she could have passed as Helen Mirren's younger, albeit Portuguese, sister.

Matos was a good ten-to-fifteen years older than Harry, which meant he had once tried an ill-advised, if somewhat lackluster, pass on Ms. Matos during last year's Christmas party. It was water under the bridge, however, and there was no discomfort in their relationship at this point. At least none that Harry could notice.

"Ms. Matos, I have an anomaly here that I think you should look at."

"What kind of anomaly?" She was suddenly all business, putting on her glasses and holding out her hand for the folder.

"It's a series of tattoos."

"Tattoos?" She knew the type of material that Harry worked with and suppressed a shiver of distaste as she gingerly opened the folder.

"Well, the same tattoo. But on different victims. Some as young as ten, I think, and from all over the world."

"Gang related? Yakuza?" The Japanese crime gangs used tattoos as a form of identification, but only on their own members and not on the girls.

"No, and not the Russian mafia either. This is a very distinct mark and it reminded me of something I saw during the Monroe presentation."

She looked up to stare at Harry, as if seeing him for the first time since he entered her office.

"You know we just humor that old guy, right? We don't take his theories very seriously around here."

"But he's got clearances up the ass ... I mean ... sorry." *Stupid, Harry, stupid.*

Matos smiled, a thin bitter smile.

"No worries, Harry. You're right. He *is* cleared straight to heaven. He has access to intel so compartmented that even God isn't read in. And we respect him and his career enormously. He was there at the creation. When it all started. Since even before the NSA was founded in 1952. So we're talking a real long time. But like a lot of people his age, and with his background, he sometimes sees things that aren't really there. He wants to remain relevant, Harry, so he might stretch the truth a little, from time to time, just to freak us out."

"So, you're saying ..."

"I'm saying be careful whom you go to with this." She flipped through the photos, one by one, noticing where Harry had circled the tattoo in each.

"I'll be damned. It's the same tattoo. On all these girls. What do you think it is?"

Harry had to be careful because Sylvia often asked questions to which she already had the answers.

"It looks like something medieval."

"Medieval European, medieval Asian ...?"

"Well, European. It looks like some kind of star, but stylized. Not a Star of David, but close. More complex. Maybe even broken."

Sylvia stayed focused on the pictures. "So, what's the connection?"

Harry cleared his throat before answering.

"It's what Monroe was talking about. At the briefing."

Sylvia closed the folder and looked up.

"You mean, about the cults?"

"Cults? Don't you mean terrorist cells?"

Matos shrugged.

"When you deal with Monroe, you deal with a lot of subtext. You know he was involved in the Phoenix program in Vietnam?"

"I heard rumors ..."

"Well, they're true. His specialty was psychological warfare. PSYOP. All very black box stuff. He developed techniques that incorporated a lot of Vietnamese folklore and native religion. Got very involved in all that. Started to half-believe in the stuff himself. For Monroe, there isn't much daylight between a cult and a terrorist cell. Not these days, anyway. Sit down, Harry. It's time you heard something about our Mr. Monroe."

Harry pulled a chair back from Sylvia's desk and sat forward, all ears. He had to wait a few moments while she collected her thoughts, deciding on the best way to approach a delicate subject like Monroe. Unbeknownst to him, Harry had just stepped into a pile of shit, shit that could ruin his career if he screwed it up.

"The way they tell it," she began, making a small pile of folders and documents on the desk in front of her, "He was running an op against a Viet Cong tax collector in II Corps, in a village in Pleiku near the Cambodian border. Middle of the night. Full moon. He had loud speakers set up in the trees, ran the cable to an amp in a hole he dug the night before and covered with leaves.

"There was a tape recorder, reel-to-reel in those days, running off a jeep battery and wired to the amp. He had a Vietnamese musician record some scary music and chanting onto the tape. The plan was for the music to freak out the villagers and for the tax collector to come running out with an AK and an attitude. Then Monroe and his people would waste him on the spot, knives instead of guns. Mutilate the body. The villagers would think it was evil spirits and from then on wouldn't harbor the VC. Stupid plan, in retrospect, but those were the days, I guess.

"It all went as planned at first. The tape started playing, and the chanting grew louder and louder. It wasn't Buddhist or Cao Dai, but some kind of shamanistic thing. The whole effect was pretty eerie, the way they tell it. Full moon, chanting, the rustle of the tall grass and the bamboo along the tree line. In the distance they could hear the bellowing of a water buffalo, probably spooked by the music.

"But no tax collector. In fact, no villagers. Nothing.

"So they cranked up the amp, little by little, until you could have heard the thing in Saigon. Or Hanoi. Still nothing.

"By now Monroe himself was getting pretty spooked. They had

seen the village full of people just hours earlier. They had seen the
VC tax collector. They knew he was there. It didn't make sense.

"So Monroe decides to go look for himself. He takes another
man with him, a Spec 4 assigned to the detail who already had six
months in-country and knew how to handle himself. They creep up
to the village and carefully peer into the first hut they see.

"Bodies. Dead bodies. People who had been alive only hours
before were now on the ground, faces contorted, bodies with limbs
at unnatural angles.

"Figuring this was poison gas, Monroe and the Spec 4 cover
their mouths and noses and crawl over to the next hut. Same thing.
Long story short, the entire village—including the tax collector—
dead. Monroe is starting to think they died of fright. This might
be the reaction of one or two people certainly, but not the whole
village! I mean, everybody? Men, women and children? And the
chickens. The damned chickens were all dead, too."

Sylvia's eyes stared into the middle distance, as if she had been
there, but Harry knew she had not. The Vietnam War had ended
almost forty years ago. She wasn't old enough. But it sounded like
she heard this story from Monroe himself, which made Harry
wonder a little.

"They start to leave the ville when they hear a noise behind
them.

"The Spec 4 turns and is ready to light up whoever it is with his
M-16. But they see nothing. No one. They start to walk away again
when they both hear the same noise. Footsteps. Branches crunching
under foot. Whoever it is isn't trying to hide or disguise himself.

"That's when Monroe looks *up*. And he sees this ... thing ... in
the trees. It's backlit by the moon. It's tall, maybe more than seven
feet. It has what appear to be wings. Ugly, bat-type things. Its eyes are
glowing red and yellow in the dark. And it opens its mouth.

"The same chant that Monroe was playing over the loudspeakers
is coming out of the mouth of this ... thing ... in the trees. Only
it's deeper, more modulated, and the vibration from it is making the
ground tremble.

"Monroe and his man race out of the village, never thinking once to open fire on the thing. The rest of their company is back behind the tree line, confused and frightened, weapons at the ready. When they see Monroe coming towards them, they lay down covering fire, aiming at the village and the ground in front of it. They can't see any VC or anyone else, even with the full moon, but they are not taking chances.

"They fire a flare over the village, just so they can see whatever the hell it is that seems to be chasing Monroe. But nothing. The ville seems to suck in light like a sponge, giving nothing back. They fire tracer rounds into the village at random. Nothing.

"By this time, Monroe and his man are back with the unit, panting and shaking. He tells the men to cease fire. They are not being pursued. As the firing ceases they can hear the creature from the village, singing out the chant they had just played on their speakers. But the tape recorder is off. The speakers are silent. The men look at each other and back at the village. The chant continues for a few more minutes, then goes silent.

"They make it back to base without incident. Monroe has to write up the report, but before he does that he has to find the Vietnamese musician who recorded the chant. He wants to know what it was. He wants to run the story by the musician. Maybe he has an answer. Some jungle creature, something. Some vampire bat that lives in the rice paddies, maybe."

At this point, Sylvia Matos stops her narration and takes a sip of tea from a delicate porcelain teacup that Harry hadn't noticed before. Behind her, on a small table, is an old Chinese-made thermos with a garish red enamel design: legacy of her ten years spent decrypting Chinese telecommunications traffic from a listening post in Singapore.

Harry starts putting it together.

"So he goes to Cholon, the Chinese section of Saigon. The musician has a small shop where he sells handmade instruments. He's done some work for CIA and the Army from time to time, mostly cultural consulting, that sort of thing. Cholon is off-limits to the

Americans, but Monroe is already well-known to the local MPs and they let him have the run of the place. He wore a gold bracelet that used to be a dead give-away at the time. The kind of thing spooks wore so that if you were ever in a tight spot you could buy your way out. That, and a Rolex. All standard CIA issue."

Sylvia was rambling, talking around what happened next, afraid to walk up to it directly. Harry could sense that there was something pretty dark coming, as if that story about the village and its dead inhabitants wasn't dark enough.

"Anyway," she said, pulling herself together with a visible effort, "Monroe gets to the shop and it's closed. Cholon is usually pretty busy, a real Chinatown. But the street where the shop is located is dead quiet. Monroe gets a little nervous. He peers into the window of the shop, but it seems deserted."

Another sip of tea.

"So he looks around, makes sure no one is watching, and he forces the door open. He walks inside the shop and in the front room everything seems normal, as if the owner had just stepped outside for a smoke.

"But when he pushes aside the beaded curtain that separates the rear living area from the front business area he gets the shock of his life.

"The musician is sprawled on the floor, a look of astonishment on his face. His mouth is open, gaping. His eyes seem alight and lively, but they're dead. He's dead. He has one leg broken at the knee and the other twisted behind him. One hand is raised, palm up, and the other is palm down. It looks like a yoga pose, a mudra of some kind. The entire effect is uncanny. Monroe checks for a pulse, finds none, but can't shake the feeling that the corpse is watching him.

"It's just like the bodies from the ville.

"Next to the body is a small notebook. The handwriting inside is tight and cramped. It's the musician's. It's all in French. Monroe can read French. He pockets the notebook and then notices that in a corner of the room a tape recorder—the twin of the one Monroe used in Pleiku—is plugged in and the reels are turning."

Sylvia picks up her teacup, then sets it down again.

"He goes over to the machine and sees that the volume is turned way down. He turns the dial, slightly, knowing what he is going to hear and not wanting to hear it, but not willing to walk away not knowing.

"All he does is touch the dial but the volume suddenly blares out. The same chant as in Pleiku. But this time it's not the musician's voice he hears, but the double bass of that creature in the ville.

"At that moment, the body of the musician jerks upright. His legs move, creaking as if breaking their bones, and his arms move, and he is sitting up. He's in the lotus position, like some kind of satanic yogi, mouth still agape, eyes wide open, one palm up and one down, but he's still dead. The medics will say later that it was a case of cadaveric spasm. Bullshit, of course, but what's the alternative explanation?"

Both were silent a moment.

"And the notebook? The one Monroe found next to the body?"

Sylvia regarded her charge quietly for a minute before answering.

"The notebook had the musician's description of the work he was doing for Monroe. Some of it was pretty mundane stuff. But there was mention of an old *len dong*, or shaman, who had some special abilities where contact with the spirit world was concerned. There was a reference to something called Saub or Shub, a god who lived on the moon or maybe some planet. And there were drawings. Illustrations. Almost childlike, primitive.

"Drawings of a weird bird, a tall black bird with bat wings. This shaman, this *len dong*, was the medium for this 'spirit bird.' And the chant? It was used to call the thing from hell."

Harry swallowed. The tension in the room was palpable, made more so by the strange juxtaposition of the computers, comm devices, and advanced technology all around them.

"From ... hell?"

Sylvia Matos, with advanced degrees in computer science, math and cryptography, merely shrugged.

"Hell, or outer space. Something like that. Not from here, anyway. That's what Monroe said."

"Monroe?"

"Pardon?"

"No, it's just that … I thought you were saying you heard this story from other people."

"Whatever. Anyway, I will look at these tattoos and get back to you when I've had a chance to analyze them. That dark blue or black design is what got to you, right?"

"Uh, yes. It's what I saw during …"

"I know. During Monroe's presentation. No worries. Leave them with me."

Harry nodded.

"Anything else, Harry?"

"No, ma'am."

He got up from his chair to leave. It fell together for him, and he didn't want her to know that he figured it out. That Monroe and Sylvia Matos had, at one time—maybe decades ago—been an item. But Sylvia was only in her, what, fifties? Monroe had to be eighty. He was around for Bluebird, back in 1950. He had been a college graduate then. Shit. That meant he was more like eighty-five now. There were thirty years between Sylvia and Monroe. Damn.

"And Harry?"

"Ma'am?"

"What I just told you stays between us. Got it?"

"Yes, ma'am."

He closed the office door behind him as he left. Sylvia was sitting in the same pose, not moving, her eyes fixed on something in the distance. The distance of time, not of space.

That notebook in French had been included in what Monroe called the "Lovecraft Codex." Educated Vietnamese in those days spoke French, the language of their colonizers. Even when they defeated the French at Dien Bien Phu, the language—and some of the cuisine—remained as a sometimes uncomfortable reminder. The last half of the notebook consisted mostly of the musician's handwritten texts, measurements for an instrument he was working on, and the specifications that Monroe had given him for the PSYOP against the VC. The first half, though, was not in the musician's handwriting. It was still in French, but it was someone else's hand. It would be more than two decades before Monroe figured it out and made the connection to a bizarre mathematician living in obscurity in the French countryside.

Those first few pages of the musician's notebook were the notes for a major work by Alexandre Grothendieck, one he would not begin in earnest for another few decades.

It was called *The Mutants*.

Sylvia Matos was a mathematician. She had to be, in her profession. In fact, it was the manipulation of numbers and formulas, algorithms, that were at the heart of cryptanalysis. The name of Grothendieck was well-known to her and her colleagues. When she first saw the notebook in Monroe's possession, she gasped out loud.

That is when he told her the story of how he came to possess it: Grothendieck had himself visited Hanoi in 1967, out of solidarity with the North Vietnamese. That visit took place only a few months before the Tet Offensive of 1968 would turn the war upside down. And only two years before Grothendieck would himself turn his back on mathematics entirely and become a communard, a spiritual seeker, and eventually a total hermit.

Before then, however, Monroe and his people were keeping tabs on everyone who visited North Vietnam at that time, from Jane Fonda to Alexandre Grothendieck. The mathematician would soon undergo a series of spiritual crises, one of which involved an angel he called "Lucifera."

And now, unknown to her, Aubrey was at that moment sitting in a café in the Pyrenees, thinking over his meeting with the famous mathematician while sipping an aperitif.

Grothendieck is mad, he thought. There was no question about it. But it is a divine kind of madness, the type where the victim is "touched by God." He saw that in other men in the course of his career. Mostly men, it was true. Women did not seem to go quite that mad quite that often.

Monroe was almost that mad, but his was an obsessive kind of madness. Grothendieck ... well, he had seen more deeply into the fundamental structure of reality than most and was unable to communicate what he saw since no one else spoke his arcane sort of language. It was the typical weakness of saints. Experiencing the ineffable meant that you could not tell anyone else what you had seen, no matter how hard you tried. You had to talk around it. And that only made you seem more insane.

Grothendieck had a Kabbalistic language and it was mathematics. And that meant that he could not describe what he saw as the structure of reality using common speech. It was frustrating. Grothendieck rebelled against the idea that only other advanced mathematicians like himself could understand him. So he sought out spiritual gurus, those who had seen what he had seen but had used other media in order to communicate the experience. And during that quest he had come to understand that there existed on the planet—at various times during its history—individuals with uncanny insight into the nature of reality. They included poets, psychologists, philosophers, spiritual leaders, and even anarchists and pacifists. They were so far advanced where their fellow human beings were concerned that it was almost impossible to think of them as the same species. The only possible characterization of them was as *mutants*.

Teilhard de Chardin made the cut, and this caused Aubrey to smile a little to himself.

Pierre Teilhard de Chardin was a famous Jesuit priest and paleontologist who tried, in his writings, to bring together science and religion (specifically Darwinism and Catholicism). De Chardin was the inspiration for William Peter Blatty's fictional character, Father Merrin, in his novel *The Exorcist*.

Aubrey remembered how he stood on line for hours in a freezing cold New York City winter to see the movie version. The opening sequence was shot in Mosul, in Iraq, and depicted Merrin at an archaeological dig coming across a figure of the Sumerian demon Pazuzu. "Evil to fight evil," was the famous line. It was something Monroe believed in passionately. As for Aubrey himself, he was not so sure.

Mosul. How could Blatty or movie director William Friedkin have known that Mosul would become the center of a global pestilence—a real-life Pazuzu—decades later?

They sent a man into Iraq a few months ago. Another religious man. A professor. Gregory Angell. And Angell had confronted evil, and had used evil to fight evil. At least, that is how Aubrey interpreted the event. He had no idea what Angell thought of it, since the professor had disappeared. And it was at Mosul during the American occupation where Angell had lost his faith. The other priest in the story, Father Damien Karras, had lost his somewhere between Washington, D.C. and New York City.

And that whole tale was about demons and possession, and Gregory Angell didn't even believe in any of that anymore. Until he had to confront it.

Aubrey knew that Monroe, his boss, had analyzed and cross-checked the names on Grothendieck's list a hundred times. There was a link there to the Lovecraft story, and Monroe had included a summary of the Grothendieck document in the Lovecraft Codex. Monroe did what Monroe always did: he created timelines, related people and events, drew solid lines and dotted lines between them, and basically just connected the dots. Aubrey could understand some of it. No one could understand all of it. Except, maybe, Monroe himself.

He knew that they did not have the luxury of skeptical disbelief. Atheism was for the rich, thought Aubrey, who could buy safety and health and long vacations and enjoy economic security and didn't need to pray to a merciful God for these amenities. They could buy what the poor prayed for every day. The rest of us need something else to get through the horrors of modern life. Religion, mysticism, astrology, whatever. Religion is the search for meaning, and science tells us there is no meaning. No life after death. No possibility of future happiness. No redemption. Those who practice evil in this life and enrich themselves at the expense of the blood, sweat, and tears of others will die sated, fat, and happy—with a self-satisfied smile on their faces and no expectation of hell or a wrathful God. There is only raw data, cold measurements with fancy instruments, and whatever passes for the scientific definition of reality this week. It's nice to have science to develop tools for improving life or defending the country: satellite intel, drones, nuclear weapons. But at some point, it's just not enough. You don't devote your entire life to the defense of the greatest superpower the world has ever known without attaching meaning to what you do. You don't contemplate exterminating your enemies with weapons of mass destruction without some thought as to the moral or ethical consequences. Maybe you don't think about God or heaven or hell. But you do get pretty damned philosophical.

Aubrey took a last, lingering sip of his drink and sighed. He looked around at the scenery and thought that it would be nice to retire here, in the south of France. There were ghosts, of course. Knights Templar, Cathars, Inquisitors, Crusaders. Otto Rahn had been through here looking for the Holy Grail, before Heinrich Himmler recruited him into the SS. Father Sauniere had lived down at Rennes le-Chateau, now a tourist attraction for anyone who had read *The DaVinci Code* or *Holy Blood, Holy Grail*. Thankfully, there was very little of *that* in Monroe's Codex.

It was interesting, he thought. Of all those eighteen "mutants," from Darwin to Freud to Riemann, Albert Einstein didn't make the list. The man whose theories of relativity revolutionized physics was not one of Grothendieck's mutants. He wondered why.

It was another "mutant," but one not mentioned in Grothendieck's list, that attracted the attention of Monroe. It was a man who called himself Abd-Ru-Shin, or "the Son of Light," the pen-name of one Oskar Bernhardt, a German mystic who died during the War, but not before he penned a number of works claiming to know the secret of the Holy Grail. Why Grothendieck would consider him a "guru," as he told his friends, was anyone's guess. What got Monroe's attention was the decision to adopt a Persian-sounding name and the fact that Bernhardt had come to the attention of the Gestapo. Monroe thought this was a lead worth chasing down.

Aubrey stood up from the zinc-topped table and left a few Euros next to his glass. He would catch a late flight from Blagnac Airport in Toulouse to Orly in Paris. He had a lot of reading to do on the plane, and then in his hotel room overnight. He knew he would not sleep. He rarely slept more than two or three hours a night anymore. Old age, he thought, and a failing prostate. No matter. Tomorrow would begin the next phase of his mission.

The mission to find Gregory Angell.

And that damned Book.

CHAPTER TWO

JAMILA SAT IN THE PEACEFUL GLOOM of the mountain temple. Old thangkas—paintings on silk of gods and goddesses and mystical diagrams, colors faded with the centuries and the encrusted prayers of the faithful and the dried tears of the dead—hung at intervals around the room, a mute congregation of souls. Butter lamps burned on the altar and incense smoke clouded the air with delicate wisps like an angel's wings brushing the skin of her face and weaving into the strands of her hair. The old monk, whose name was Rabten, sat before her and marveled at the young girl's poise and at the way the incense smoke formed a kind of halo around her head in combination with the faint glow from the butter lamps. She was cross-legged in a modified asana, and her breathing was slow and measured, as he had instructed her. If the others knew what he was doing he would be criticized (or worse) for he was not permitted to instruct anyone, much less a woman, much less a woman from Iraq. Much less a Yezidi woman.

Jamila, however, was no ordinary woman. At least, not like any of the Nepalese or Tibetan or Indian women he had known in his long and eventful life, escaping Tibet with the young Dalai Lama so many decades ago. There had been several advanced adepts among the women to be sure. They could perform miracles, see the future, heal the sick. Raise the dead. Some performed as mediums, physical vessels through which spiritual forces entered our world. The State Oracle of Tibet is one of these, but he is a man. Jamila had an ability that rivaled that of the State Oracle, and the spiritual force that spoke through her was something he could not understand, not even with his nearly fifty years of practice in the rites of the Kalachakra Tantra.

Every religion boasts a cosmology, a way of looking at the world that is all-inclusive. Phenomena are interpreted according to its theology and its world-view. But religions can disagree. In the worst-case scenario, the angels of one religion can become the demons of another. Tibetan Buddhism is no different. Its central symbol is the mandala: a graphic representation of all of creation as a set of circles within squares within circles. Every circle contains 360 degrees, just as every square does. The combination of the two symbolizes the union of heaven and earth, of light and darkness, of male and female. The Kalachakra Tantra is a central text and practice of Tibetan Buddhism, the word Kalachakra meaning the "Wheel of Time."

The old monk was an expert in meditation, and in interpreting the text of the Tantra. There were rituals that were largely unknown to the masses of people—many from Western countries—who flocked to the Dalai Lama's initiations. Sometimes Rabten wondered what the Westerners would do if they knew some of the more ... exotic ... information and instructions contained within the revered scripture.

Jamila was beyond considerations of this type. Her spiritual gifts were signs of a deeper comprehension; such powers could not be bought or simply learned. She could communicate with him using only her mind: an ability that normally would require many years of intense study and practice. Yet Jamila was a young woman, and from a distant land that was in imminent danger of being invaded by a hostile army, her people slaughtered, her sacred sites reduced to rubble.

He could relate.

Years earlier there had been a delegation to Dharamsala—the head-quarters in India of the Tibetan Government in Exile—by a group of rabbis. The Dalai Lama wanted their advice on how a people in diaspora could maintain their culture, their language, and their religion after losing their homeland. Who better to advise the Tibetans in this matter than the Jews?

Now, the same circumstances were facing another ancient people, the Yezidis. And now, as he saw it, the time had come to repay the favor the Jews had done for the Tibetans by paying it forward to the Yezidis.

Jamila's abilities were strong but required conscious control. For

most of her young life she had been shaken like a rag doll by the
forces that used her as a channel, forces that left her limp, drained and
unconscious, especially when her "episodes" were violent enough to
suggest grand mal seizures. What the monk offered was a way for her
to regain some measure of autonomy over her own consciousness
and reduce the damage to her body as well as to her psyche.

So for the past few days she had soaked up his teaching, his
methods, the entire arcane technology of what they called a *kuten*:
the material basis for a spiritual force. He fed her a simple diet of
rice and stewed vegetables and she gradually regained her physical
strength even as she became mentally stronger. But it was in odd
moments of her meditations when he felt the overwhelming
sensation of something old and dark prowling around the edges
of her mind that he began to fear for her life. Whatever it was, it
regarded her as its property and was not pleased that she was now
learning to push back.

He tried to warn her, even to ask her what that thing was and
why it had chosen her, but she only would respond with a sad smile.
He was Tibetan; he understood fate and destiny. He knew not to
hold onto emotion, to the illusions of the material world, not even
to life itself. All sorrow comes from attachment to external things
and when those attachments are dissolved it becomes necessary
to separate oneself from internal things as well: one's past, one's
personality, even one's identity. Eventually, one breaks all attachments,
even the attachment to existence. But that is a voluntary decision,
one made at the end of a long process of initiation. What the ... the
thing ... that hunted Jamila desired was to bring that poor woman
to the edge of existence itself, to the abyss separating human beings
from consciousness, and when her mind was stretched to its limit
and her sanity shattered into a thousand useless pieces, to use her
to enter this world. It was trying to ... to modify her, to rearrange
the cells of her body, so that it could birth itself in the stark and
unforgiving daylight of this world. It was as if the thing dwelt in a
realm that was a photographic negative: black where there would

be light, light where there should be darkness. Jamila provided that thing a way to enter the world of human beings and the end result would be to take all the color and beauty of this world and render it a negative—a reverse image, all dark where there should be light, all despair where there should be joy—even as the thing itself would become a positive: a fully-developed image too hideous to contemplate. Jamila, poor Jamila, had the ability to make this nightmare three-dimensional and visible.

The monk knew all the stories about Shambhala and the Kalki Avatar, stories from the same Kalachakra Tantra that was the state religion. Shambhala: the mysterious kingdom that was as real and substantial as any earthly kingdom but nonetheless invisible to humans. The Kalki Avatar: a king who would come roaring out of Shambhala at the Last Days to wreak vengeance on the unbelievers. It was not a story he loved, for its tale of violence and hatred was antithetical to everything the old Buddhist believed in his heart. But it was canon, and even though it had been interpreted in various ways—as if to remove any stain of the apocalyptic theme it seemed to represent—it still awakened the baser emotions in all who heard it.

And now something about Jamila was reminding him of Shambhala, and especially of the Kalki Avatar. No, the thing that hunted—and haunted—Jamila was not the Avatar; but something about the extreme violence and pure evil of the thing—the thing she had called by a name that sounded like the Tibetan *kusulu* but which she pronounced Kutulu—brought to mind the Last Days, the end of human existence, and the penetration of this world by something so alien, so foreign, that merely to contemplate it was to fall under its spell, to summon it to visible appearance.

To invite it *in*.

No, not Shambhala then but what some of the old ones called *Aghartta*: a kind of anti-Shambhala that could be approached only when the stars were right and the physical world aligned with the cosmic, the astral. The beings that dwelt there could assume human form—it had been said—but otherwise were not identifiable as human. Their movements in this world were jerky, uncoordinated, and stiff. Their speech was like what had happened to the cassette tape he had of one of the Dalai Lama's sermons, when the tape got old and damaged and the voice came out as an electronic garble: now fast, now slow. It was impossible to know the reasons for their actions, for these bore no logical connection to anything human or divine.

Yes, Aghartta, maybe. A place that existed between life and death, between the Earth and someplace that was Not Earth. Was that what Jamila meant by "dead, but dreaming"?

It was during their most recent meditation that Rabten began to suspect the true nature of the being she called Kutulu.

Jamila had begun as she had every day for the past week since she arrived. She washed herself in cold water before entering the small wooden temple. She washed her hands and feet, her face and hair, as if she was performing *wudu*: the Islamic purification ritual. Then she crossed the threshold of the temple, stepping barefoot over the wooden beam and into the darkness that was lit only by the lamps and the glow of burning incense.

She took her place on an old cushion in the center of the floor, facing the main altar. Soon, the monk would approach and sit facing her on another cushion. He would begin with a mantra, a kind of invocation in Sanskrit that was a combination of syllables and sounds that held potency and intelligence in their specific arrangement. As before, she seemed to actually understand the sounds as if they were words in her own language, which he knew to be impossible. But she had told him that her people, the Yezidi, were the first people on the planet, remnants of a civilization that modern people knew as Sumer, and that the seemingly meaningless words of his mantras were perfectly comprehensible to her as the Sumerian language.

He had changed the mantra this last time, as a kind of test, and she responded automatically to the new mantra in a lilting, yet almost percussive, chant of her own that seemed to pick out the syllables of his invocation and string them together in a different order of her own choosing. He began to understand that she was having a dialogue: with him, or with the ancient master who had first created the mantra he had selected. He maintained his delivery as long as he could, but he felt the power of the young woman's mantra defeating his as she grew more insistent, as she moved from a chant to a song, and from a song to a shout.

The mantra was an old protective chant, a series of syllables that wove a shield around the practitioner and all those in his or her vicinity and from there to the rest of the world. The syllables were largely unintelligible with the passage of so much time. Yet Jamila kept coming back to one set of three. She repeated these over and over again, overwhelming him with the force of her understanding:

ཡོག་ གསོག་ གོག་

It was usually understood to mean "an unreal thing, which creeps, from below the earth." One of the demonic forms the mantra was designed to restrain. It was pronounced *Yog gsog gog*, in the Tibetan manner, in Rabten's voice.

But it was *Yog Sothoth* in hers.

Her chanting, although perceived only as a whisper to anyone eavesdropping on the unusual couple, was a terrifying scream in his mind as the thin, frail being before him took on the dimensions of something huge and disturbing. Something with wings. Something with limbs that appeared to be writhing snakes. And a head that was in a vile borderland somewhere between insect and reptile.

And underneath the hideous chant in the old language was the still, small voice of Jamila herself, whispering at last—through a rictus of gritted teeth and frozen jaw—that one word: *Kutulu*.

The meditation was over when she collapsed into herself as the chant subsided. He broke from his own asana and moved next to her, feeling her forehead which was dripping perspiration in the freezing temple. She was unconscious, as had happened before. He believed this was the only time when Jamila knew any peace, or any rest: after the internal struggle with the being she called Kutulu.

He knew that *kusulu* was the word the old ones used to mean a dead shaman, a high priest of the old cult, the one that existed before Buddhism came to Tibet. He was certain that this is what she intended by her own word, for she described Kutulu as a high priest of some ancient denomination, moreover one who was both dead and dreaming. But a *kusulu* was a dead shaman that came back to life, and the monk believed that is what she meant by "dead but dreaming." It was a Being in the *Bardo* state, the state between death and life. While Jamila indicated to him that Kutulu—as she called It—was not human, but something non-human or perhaps pre-human (he couldn't understand her completely), he knew that all beings enter the Bardo state after death. It may be for different lengths of time for different beings before they are reborn. But this was getting way too complicated. He would have to search through the ancient texts of the pre-Buddhist religion, the religion of Bön, to gain a clearer understanding of the nature of Kutulu and the threat it seemed to pose to Jamila and to those around her.

He found nothing. The important information was not contained in any of the available Bön texts. Much of that sect's ritual and scripture was written in an arcane language from the old kingdom of Zhang Zhung, and there were not many of those texts extant. He would have to consult a practitioner, and for that he would have to go outside the precincts of Dharamsala, outside the protection of the Kalachakra Tantra, and seek an introduction to one of the old shamans who still practiced the rites of *dchod*.

Tibetan Buddhism is divided into three sects: the Yellow Hat sect which is that represented by the Dalai Lama; the Red Hat sect, led by the Gyalwa Karmapa; and the Black Hat sect, which is closest in nature to the old religion of Bön. He knew a lama of the Black Hat sect, and he hoped that with an introduction from him he would be able to locate an existing shaman and find out all he could about the mysteries of *kusulu*, and maybe lay his fears to rest … or, if not, then to obtain the weapons necessary for the defeat of Jamila's Kutulu.

Jamila came to, alone in the temple and feeling its coldness like an old friend. Physical sensations were acknowledgments that she was still alive. Hunger, pain, and exhaustion had been her constant companions since leaving her ancestral home in northern Iraq months ago. She wondered about Fahim and the rest of the People she had been forced to leave behind when she was abducted from the refugee camp and brought to Nepal.

The monk was gone. She felt his absence like a tangible thing. She reached out with her mind and could sense that he was on a journey of some kind. Not far. She looked around her and found the bowl she normally used for meals. It was porcelain, old and chipped, and held a small amount of cooked rice and what appeared to be a green vegetable. He had provided for her before he left.

Next to the bowl was a covered teacup. It was hot to the touch. She wrapped her palms around it to get the warmth into her blood, and as she did so she thought back to her childhood in Mosul and the way the agent from the dreaded Mukhabarat—the Iraqi secret service under Saddam—had touched her in order to threaten Fahim. The agent wanted the Book, and Fahim would not surrender it until he saw that Jamila—then only a child—was going to be assaulted if he did not comply.

She had been too young to know what it meant to be raped, but the hostility burning off of the agent's soul was so strong that she knew it meant something evil and irreversible. Something inside herself had snapped—the Being, the one that she knew used her as a vehicle, had come to life as it had become aware of the danger to Itself—and the room had exploded and suddenly she and Fahim were free and running for their lives to Sinjar.

Fahim had been like a father to her, her real father having perished at the hands of the secret police. Fahim had brought her to his own home, and she was treated like one of his own children. For awhile she had clean clothes and food and a place to sleep. But then they had to flee, for after the American invasion the situation grew dire for everyone but especially for the Yezidi who were hated by everyone. It was during one night when the sound of small arms fire echoed off the mud and stone buildings that she had another "episode" and that is when the People came to realize that there was something strange and terrifying about Jamila.

As the years went by and she grew from a small child to a teenager and then to the threshold of womanhood the time had come to find her a husband, but none of the People would agree. Even as her friends were all being married off, Jamila had no suitors and there was no one to arrange a marriage for her. She had been touched by some spiritual force, and it slowly dawned on her that she would never have a family of her own.

As the situation grew worse and they found themselves fleeing to a refugee camp on the Syrian border, her episodes grew more and more frequent. The onset of puberty came late to Jamila, but the hormonal changes seemed to make her condition worse. Fahim was forced to keep her away from the others, for her own safety but also for his. Should her condition become well-known to the people in the camp there was no telling what that would bring down upon them. Not everyone in the camp was Yezidi, and those who were came from different clans. The others were Christians, and there were Kurds who were Muslim. So she remained a pariah, sitting alone in the back of the tent with her face covered, wrapped in a threadbare blanket, and looking for all the world like a small pile of discarded clothing should anyone enter their living quarters.

And then the strange Americans came, and she had another episode, and it was impossible to keep her secret any longer.

The man they called "Angell" had seen her, and had spoken with Fahim about the Book that Fahim had been at pains to rescue from the Iraqi secret police. But then the Americans left the camp, and she and Fahim had to face the other families. It was not for long, however, for one night there came the hand over her mouth and the dirty cloth over her nose with its strange but overwhelming odor and the next thing she knew she was in the back of a truck, heading for Nepal, kidnapped by members of something called the Keepers of the Book.

The one thing she remembered was looking into the eyes of the man called Angell. First, at the refugee camp. Then, at the underground temple in Nepal. The force of the Being was rising up within her and around her as the chant from the Book poked and prodded and teased Kutulu from his slumber into the waking world. She looked again in the eyes of Angell, and to her shock she saw horror instead of joy. This was confusing. As Kutulu rose from the grave beneath the earth—beneath the *Earth*—she felt exhilaration. Every nerve in her body was singing, and she thought that this feeling must be what the other women spoke of when they whispered among themselves of their husbands and of nightly things.

Was this God? Was this Melek Taus, of whom the elders speak? Was it Shaitan itself?

Was the experience of God the experience of terror?

Was God good … or was God only power, the power wielded by men in a world of powerless women?

Angell was ready to stop her, to kill her if necessary, so that the High Priest of the Great Old Ones would not rise. What did that mean? If he would kill her, then *who was she?*

And then, suddenly, it was over. And everyone—or almost everyone—was dead. Those who were wounded, Jamila herself assisted with the training of a field nurse gained from a life lived on the run from guns and terror. But Angell was gone, and so was the Book.

She was confused in her heart and soul. As a child she had felt God slipping away, just as Kutulu gained in strength inside her, along her spine, through her limbs, pressing on the back of her neck with a heavy hand, forcing open her jaws and pulling at her tongue. She was being stretched, molded, and re-formed by this unseen force. She even experienced uterine contractions, as if she was giving birth: she a virgin and untouched by any man was now being touched by something that was not man.

She was so alone, even in this realm of smiling monks and silent snows.

She had to get back to the People. She had to make her way back to the refugee camp or, barring that, to Sinjar and the sacred land.

But at the thought of Sinjar, the Holy Mountain that was the ancestral home of the Yezidi, a sickening feeling rose in her throat. She saw a rush of images. Men, women. Children. Blood. Screams. Explosions.

Slaughter.

She turned and vomited, a thin pale vomitus streaked with blood. In its puddle she could see the homes of the People being destroyed. She could see men in black uniforms marching under a black banner.

She had to get back.

"The old ones are still in Tibet," the lama told him. "They derive their strength from their home, for it is there that the old texts—the *terma*—are buried, still to be found. The very earth hums with their wisdom, and they can feel the vibrations through the soles of their feet."

"They are in hiding, then?"

"They can hide even in front of you. Your eyes would not see them if they did not wish to be seen."

Rabten had hitched a ride in the back of a truck to a village somewhat remote from Dharamsala but within a half-day's journey by car. It was a village that he knew about from his time on the run from the Chinese Army. He and His Holiness, the Dalai Lama, had passed by on their way to this section of northern India. The village had no name, and in certain types of weather the village itself seemed to become invisible as the heavy fog that would roll in and cover the hillside where it was located.

The lama lived in a hut festooned with bones and skins. The smell was rank, a combination of poor hygiene, old incense, and the fat the lama used to "season" the bones, to keep them from drying out and developing cracks.

There were femurs and tibia, and skulls. All human. These were the remains of other lamas who had died, and still others of small children who had succumbed to illness or starvation or simple neglect. A few were of those who had been murdered, or who were executed as criminals. These latter were the most prized for their occult power.

The fat used to keep and preserve them was itself of animal origin. Rabten dared not ask too many questions about that.

The bones were used to make ritual implements. The leg bones became trumpets, called *kangling*, and the skulls became cups, *kapala,* or drums, *damaru*. Some of them would be carved with complex diagrams or images of the gods. Others would be inlaid with silver and precious metals. Rabten was familiar with all of these practices, of course, but the lama before him represented a particularly old and particularly strange version of the faith that relied more on the spirit possession of the lamas by frightful demons and gods than the image of the calm meditation and contemplation of scripture that was more familiar to Westerners.

"So," said Rabten, coming back to the reason for his visit, "If they are still in Tibet, how can I discover the secret of the *kusulu?*"

The lama, who was nearly eighty years old but looked about forty, smiled and nodded.

"There is a text, a *terma*, which was hidden for many centuries but which the old ones speak of every now and then. It is written in a language older than that of Zhang Zhung but some of the teachers from Tibet understand the words. There was a translation of certain sections of the text for use by the teachers to protect their people from the *kusulu*."

"It is dangerous, then?"

"The *kusulu*? You remember when the religion of the Buddha came to Tibet? And then it was rejected for awhile, before coming back into favor again?"

The old monk nodded. It was a familiar story to anyone who had studied Tibetan history, and certainly every Tibetan knew all about it.

"That is the same with the *kusulu*. He was a priest of the old cult that existed long before even the teachers of Bön. It was a religion that came from the west, farther even than the kingdom of Zhang Zhung. It is said that they worshiped Death, and annihilation. But that was incorrect."

"In what way?"

"It was not their own death they worshiped."

It was growing dark outside, and the light inside the hut grew dim. Shadows lengthened along the walls, and the bald, round head of the lama began to take on a kind of aura, glowing in the gathering gloom like one of his disembodied skulls.

The wind picked up, and the bones hanging from the beams of the hut began to move with the breeze. As they did so, they knocked into each other producing an unearthly rattle. The wooden pillars holding up the roof began to creak.

"*Kusulu* is what you say: a dead sorcerer adrift in the *bardo*. But he is also a high priest of the Ancient Ones, the ones who were here before us, before human beings walked the Earth. It was the time of the *Srin-Mo*, the primordial goddess who was pinned to the earth to keep her from destroying us. It was the time of the *Mi-ma-yin*, the 'Non-Human Ones.' Our shamans climb to the stars to obtain knowledge and power from the gods. Their shamans came down from the stars to the Earth, using those same channels to transport themselves to our world. If this *kusulu* is awakened in the *bardo*, he will open that channel and bring his gods to us. There will be many, many of them and they will devastate this world."

The lama became quiet, and let the silence wrap around them like a cloak of invisibility. Rabten reflected on what he had just heard. He had listened to stories like this before, as a child in Lhasa. They were usually told of the Bön and their priests, like Buddhist bogeymen. The reference to Srin-Mo in particular worried him, for it indicated that this chthonic goddess—who was nailed to the country of Tibet in thirteen places, each the site of an important temple—was somehow connected to this. He knew that the destruction of some of these temples during the Cultural Revolution was said to have roused Srin-Mo from her prison in the earth. It seemed to resonate with what Jamila had said, about beings that were "dead, but dreaming."

"This may have already happened."

The lama opened his eyes wide, startled.

"What do you mean?"

"There is a woman. A foreigner. Jamila. She carries this … this *kusulu* within her. She calls it Kutulu in her own language, a speech older than Zhang Zhung. But I have seen it. I have seen it testing the boundaries of this world."

The lama hissed, a kind of sharp intake of breath that signaled his dismay.

"There is more. I tried the *m ra ya phad* mantra of the *dgra lha* …"

"The *ngak* of the Great King, to restrain evil and evil doers."

"The same. I used the old syllables, the secret pronunciation, but she knew it."

"That is not possible!"

Ignoring him, lost in his reverie, Rabten went on.

"Yet the most startling thing … she *changed* the syllables, spoke them in a different way …giving them new meaning … as if … as if *I* had been saying them wrong all this time."

The lama leaned forward, the forefinger of his right hand touching the ground as he spoke.

"Listen. The *kusulu* is an enemy of *advaita*, of non-duality. But not in the way we think. Not like ordinary human beings. To the *kusulu* and his race it is not a question of duality but of multiplicity, the endless multiplication of forms. In this way, they devour matter like a plague of locusts. They are enemies of nirvana, which they view as a cancer of the mind, a kind of tumor of consciousness. The endless round of birth, death, and rebirth is to them the rhythm of existence, the machinery they need to travel through space, to leap from star to star. Hope is not known to them, nor remorse. They have no conscience, no introspection. They reduce what we think of as Perfect Mind to flesh, and then they devour the flesh.

"These beings reproduce in ways that would disgust even a follower of the Vama Marg conducting sexual rituals in the charnel grounds along the Ganges. They have multiple genders, and to them the yab-yum position represents but a single being in the act of feasting. They do not *see* what *we* see the *way* we see. They do not come from here. At all."

Rabten, the old monk who had been initiated before the Chinese had come to Tibet and who had seen horrors too numerous to count when they did, shivered to hear the yab-yum described this way, for it was a sacred mudra: a god consorting with his goddess, the two in embrace, she with her legs wrapped around his torso as they gaze into each other's eyes. It was a glyph of the act of Creation and a pathway to *advaita*, to non-duality in which there is no division between one and the other, no separation between an individual mind and the cosmic mind. Total immersion in the ocean of consciousness. But what the lama was saying was hideous, a travesty of Buddhism. Of any religion.

"This is not Bön."

"No, of course not, even though it is sometimes said that the Old Religion performs rituals in mirror-image to that of the Buddhists, as if to negate them."

"Then ... how do the priests of the Old Religion know this much about the *kusulu?*"

The lama looked away, as if into a great distance. In his mind's eye he saw Mount Kailash, the axis mundi of the kingdom once known as Zhang Zhung. The snow was thick, as deep as two men, the one standing on the shoulders of the other. And there were sounds, sounds that no human or animal could make. Sounds that the low drones of the long Tibetan horns tried—but failed—to reproduce.

"In the days of Zhang Zhung, before the coming of Buddhism, before even the coming of humans, there was a race of beings that lived there known as the Ma-sang. These were like demons. They had succeeded several earlier races, such as those known by the Indians as Yaksha, Mara, Rakshasa, Naga, and the bTsan for which even the Indians have no name: a demon that devours flesh and blood.

"There were priests who developed methods for containing these non-human beings, and they became known as the Bonpo, the priests of Bön, as you know. But there were also priests of the Ma-sang and the bTsan, semi-human beings who worshiped these foul creatures. Their origins were non-human, but their demon fathers had mated with human women and given rise to a generation of the priests the foreigners call shamans.

"When such a shaman has died there must be procedures to ensure he does not return from the Bardo to the human world. But such a shaman—deprived of reincarnation—cannot enter nirvana, either. This is a *kusulu*.

"In all of the history of Zhang Zhung, only one such shaman is known to have survived to the present day. This is the one you saw. The woman you mention, she is the vessel, the vehicle for kusulu. If she provides him a way to reincarnate then ..." The lama's voice trailed off.

In the mountain temple, alone in front of a thangka showing a god with many arms each hand holding a different object—a skull, a string of beads, a knife, etc.—Jamila had a sudden thought.

64   PETER LEVENDA

"I am not a vessel," she said to herself, not quite understanding what she was saying. "I am *not* a vehicle."

The memory of the past decade spent on the run, in the back of one pickup truck or van after another, or on the back of a donkey, or in a military convoy ... all those cars and trucks, all that time as a passenger fleeing from one hostile army after another, from men whose languages she did not understand dressed in uniforms she did not recognize, or no uniforms at all. Waiting for water. Waiting for food. Waiting for a toilet. Waiting for a bed. Waiting for the shooting to stop. For the killing and dying to stop. For the sickness to stop. For the fevers that wracked her brain and her mind to stop. Enough. Enough was enough.

The People had tried to mold her, and contain her, from the outside. With texts, and teachings, and the disapproval of the elders and the whispers of the families.

The ... the Thing ... Kutulu ... was trying to mold her from within, from the inside of her brain and her body.

Who am I? she asked herself and the silent idols around her in the gloom of the mountain temple. Who am *I*?

Was she her body? Was she *only* her body, only that which could be seen, or despised, or valued for its parts? Her body was gripped, grasped, handled, clothed, fed, protected, endangered, pushed this way and that, manhandled by unseen forces. Without ... without *permission*. It was a kind of country, a place to be invaded, conquered, made to serve. To serve ... men? If not men, then the thing that tried to use her as a vehicle to enter the world.

She ran her hands over herself, as if knowing herself for the first time. She touched her arms, her torso. She splayed her fingers across her face. She clasped her waist with her arms. She looked up and saw a painted god embracing a goddess and felt the breath in her own body as she saw the rise and fall of the painted chest of the goddess. The blood that ran through her veins was her blood, and for the first time she felt that she owned that blood. That it was hers. It was as if she were beginning to inflate, to fill with air, with prana, with spirit.

The phrase "coming into her own"—a curious expression of those who spoke English—now made sense to her.

If she was more than her body, or other than her body, then only she could know that. That knowledge would come from within, from the same place that the thing—the dead shaman, the Kutulu— arose, which is why she had let it flow into her, through her, out of her. It had made her feel alive, and that was its power and its betrayal.

She had already been alive. Asleep, but alive.

Slowly, she stood up from the floor and stared the painted god in the eyes.

"I am not the car," she said to the painted god, aloud, pointing to it with her finger, getting its attention, as if it could hear her. And see her.

"I am not the car. *I am the driver.*"

CHAPTER THREE

MONROE USUALLY DIDN'T ANSWER THE PHONE or a knock at the door. This was for the simple reason that most of the NSA staff didn't even know he was there, and those who did were of no interest to him. Aubrey was in France at the moment and knew better than to call him on the office line. So when the phone rang on his desk, he ignored it. And when a knock came at the door about fifteen minutes later, he just kept working. He was the only one who could open the door, so he had no fear that he would be interrupted.

Then the knock came again, this time in a pattern. The old familiar one. He doubted many people even remembered it anymore.

Three short knocks, three long ones, and another three short. The Morse Code for S-O-S. Very retro in the bowels of the NSA: the world leader in cryptography and cryptanalysis.

With a heavy sigh, Monroe swiveled in his chair to face the door and got up, his bones or maybe just his nerves creaking, and went through the technical ritual of opening the door.

On the other side, as he suspected, was Sylvia Matos.

He held the door open long enough to allow her to enter, then shut it behind her.

"Sylvia."

"Dwight. How are you?"

"As you see. Older and hardly any wiser, I'm afraid. You, however, remain oddly and persistently beautiful. Is there a painting in your attic that is ageing aggressively?"

"An Oscar Wilde reference? I guess we *are* getting old."

He pointed her to a seat and took his behind the desk.

"That was you on the phone?"

"I thought I would give it a try. See if you've mellowed any."

"Operational security, Sylvia," he said with a self-deprecating smile.

"OpSec was never your strong point, Dwight."

"It is now. More evidence of age, I suppose."

"I had a visitor today." She jumped right in. "One of my staff. He caught a trace and brought it to my attention. In this case, tattoos."

"Tattoos? Seriously?"

"On small girls. Kiddie porn. Or close enough to it."

"Yezidi?" He was thinking of the children turned into sex slaves by the Islamic State.

She shook her head. "Doesn't appear so. Eastern European, Asian …"

"When were the artifacts created?"

"Don't know. It could have been anywhere from a few weeks ago to years ago. It's a large selection, actually. Ranging across continents."

"And the same tattoo?"

"Identical. Across all samples."

Monroe was silent a moment.

"It's a message. They're ramping up," he said, finally. "Going to phase two, I should imagine. Getting more desperate. Seems our boy was successful at that cavern in Nepal."

"But what if the artifacts are years old? Wouldn't that mean they were anticipating failure in Nepal?"

Monroe shook his head.

"It's their backup plan. They always had one. We just didn't know what form it would take. I was betting on drugs, actually. Or bio-weapons. CBW."

Chemical and Biological Weapons. The worst-case scenario.

"It had to be something that could be set off globally, on a tight schedule. If it was a contained detonation of some kind, a localized event—even dozens of localized events—it would not have the desired effect. Pure ritual was the weakest approach, even for a team of gifted remote viewers, but they probably had to humor one of their leaders so they started off that way. They might have succeeded if not for Angell. Pure ritual combined with … well, with what you've been telling me … that's another story."

He looked up.

"Who else knows about this?"

"Only my staffer. No one else."

"Can he be trusted?"

The question was loaded. Everyone at NSA had clearance. It was compartmented, on a need-to-know basis, so that some staffers were cleared for some projects and others for different projects. What Monroe was asking was not if Harry was cleared by NSA—that was a given—but if Sylvia trusted him with information that was outside his purview. A different story entirely.

"I read him in on the basics. He would have figured it out on his own or, worse, come to some wrong conclusions. He already tied you to the tattoos as it was."

Monroe raised his eyebrows as a question.

"That lecture you gave, months ago. Or was it a year ago? On terror cells and their semiotics. The sigil was prominent, and it jumped out at him when he saw the photos of the girls."

"Ha. And I thought no one was really paying attention."

Sylvia smiled benevolently.

"You don't realize what a reputation you enjoy around here. Especially with the younger generation. They see you as some kind of wizard. Mysterious and aloof, maybe, but nonetheless an object of fascination."

"How odd."

She shrugged.

"It's the result of what we do. Everything here is technical, digital, the manipulation of data. It's all numbers and patterns. And then someone like you comes along and challenges some of the basic assumptions we make about what is knowable and what resists logical processes. The patterns you reveal are not based on the same algorithms or numerical systems we employ or decode. And that makes you a wizard in their eyes."

"A wizard without a wand."

"But a wizard with a magic book."

"You mean the Codex."

"For someone who was at the forefront of digital cryptanalysis back in the day, it *is* a little peculiar to see that you still compile a hardcopy text of which there are no digital exemplars, not even a photocopy. But that's not the magic book I mean."

Monroe was silent, considering how much to reveal.

"I don't have that *particular* magic book."

"But you will. We both know that. Unless it has been destroyed in the mean time."

"I don't believe it has been. I am certain that Angell would have put it somewhere safe, to use as leverage."

"Is that why Aubrey is gallivanting all over the globe these days?"

"To find Angell, who went off the reservation after Nepal."

"And the book?"

"Of course. *That* book almost started another conflagration, one that was not restricted to the Middle East. It could still be used that way." He stood up and began pacing in his small office. "Imagine a different kind of Arab Spring, one that is so violently … antinomian … that it challenges every human institution. Governments, religions, armies, human society in general. We don't realize how much of civilization is based on an agreement, a kind of contract among human beings that they will abide by a certain set of norms, of laws. This contract is fragile, but is based on a shared system of beliefs. In God, or in democracy, or an economic idea. Basically, on fantasies. This … book, this text is a challenge to all of that because it claims to be the revelation of a different order of existence, one that would abrogate all such existing contracts."

"How? Why?"

"Think of all those rumors of a US government cover-up of the UFO phenomenon. One of the suspected reasons for this cover-up is that the acknowledgment of an alien race with superior technology would threaten the stability of the entire world. It would throw everything we think we know about our existence into a cocked hat. That is why, say the critics, 'disclosure' will never happen. Governments and religions would fall because people would no longer have faith in their institutions. This book is a form of disclosure, and that is why it is dangerous. Its very existence is a threat to the religious fanatics on one side, and yet is considered a holy book, a revealed scripture, to the cultists on the other. Worse, it reveals a kind of technology for which only a handful of people on the planet are suited."

Sylvia was silent a moment as she let that sink in. For a moment, she didn't know if Monroe was as crazy as they said behind his back, or if he was the only one with genuine vision. His conviction was obvious, but what if he was wrong?

"There are rumors that this … cult … had spread to the United States."

"Long ago, yes, but there are still adherents today."

"Can't we roll them up?"

Monroe shook his head.

"They are members of a secret society that has learned how to communicate under the radar. They had passwords and secret identities before Moses was born. Nothing they do is digitized. They are off-grid. We don't know how they communicate with each other, but they do. We had some remote viewers who were looking into it, but we lost every one. To madness, to terror …"

"And one defector."

"You mean Miller. Yes. And we lost him to a bullet in Nepal."

"So what are you saying? Some kind of telepathy?"

Monroe stopped pacing and shrugged.

"It's in the Codex. They are supposed to communicate via a kind of web of dreams."

Sylvia smiled. "That sounds very poetic."

"Scoff if you wish, but I've been monitoring the channels. There *has* been chatter, mostly among the terror cells, but the confirmation—the actionable intelligence—was obtained from remote viewers."

"Not the kind of evidence you can take to a FISA court."

Monroe shrugged.

"I'm not looking to tap anyone's phones, Sylvia, or read anyone's emails. It wouldn't do me any good if I had the authorization anyway."

Sylvia knew about the history of the remote viewing project. It had been under CIA's aegis, and had involved spying on everyone from Russian diplomats to Iranian revolutionaries and locating missile silos and submarines. A lot of what they had done had been declassified—but not the choice bits—and was available on the internet for anyone to download.

There had been anomalies, however, and that is where Monroe and his project were concerned. When viewers seemed to "log on" to esoteric content or bizarre images and scenarios they came to his attention and were peeled off for targeting of his own. Some of what he got was crap, or it seemed that way anyway, but some of it was gold.

And it had gotten one of his viewers killed.

"What do you think the tattoos indicate?"

Monroe had to think carefully before answering. In the first place, he didn't want Sylvia to be vulnerable to charges of covering-up or of running interference for his little operation. She had a solid career at the "crystal palace" and he didn't want to jeopardize that.

In the second place, he didn't want her to think he had totally lost his mind since Vietnam.

"How much of the Bible do you remember?"

"Seriously?"

"Specifically Genesis. That whole rigmarole about the sons of God and the daughters of men ..."

"The Flood story? Noah?"

"Well, there's more to it than that."

Going into the sheaf of papers, maps, word lists and timelines that comprised what Monroe called the "Lovecraft Codex," he found what he was looking for: a short paper published decades ago by a young Gregory Angell when he was an adjunct professor jockeying for a tenured position. It was entitled 'Fallen Angels and Abandoned Men: the Story of the *Nephilim* in Biblical and Apocryphal Literature.'

He handed it to Sylvia.

"This was written by your boy?"

"When Professor Angell was still a young man, before his posting to Afghanistan."

"And this will shed some light on the tattoos?"

"In a way. It will at least give us some context for the explanation."

Sylvia flipped through the densely-worded, footnoted pages.

"It will take me a little while to get through this."

"No worries. Ordinarily I would say to read it here while I wait, but the paper has been published and is open-source."

"All the same, I wouldn't want to impair the integrity of the Codex. Can I find it online?"

"Most certainly. It's on that website for academic papers, and of course you can access the journal of the American Association of Religion where you will find it archived."

She noted the title. She already knew the author.

Handing the document back to Monroe, she got up from her seat.

"I'll give it a look, Dwight. I'm sure I will be back here soon for the rest of the explanation."

He showed her to the door.

"You're welcome any time, Sylvia. Your usual discretion?"

She smiled at him.

"Of course. Wouldn't have it any other way."

As the door closed behind her, Monroe looked at the paper Angell had written when he was still a brilliant and somewhat naïve young scholar. He started to put it back with the Codex where it belonged, but stopped instead and sat down with it. It had been a while since he last read the paper and just reading it always excited him. It was not so much the theme of the paper but the way Angell wrote it, his use of language and the brilliance of his mental processes. Like Ioan Coulianu before him—the genius Romanian scholar who was murdered in a men's room at the University of Chicago by Ceausescu's secret police—Angell had a command of Classical Greek and Roman as well as Middle Eastern literature and sources in their original tongues and every paragraph radiated confidence in his perspective. To read Angell's writing from that period was to see the ancient world through the eyes of someone who seemed to have witnessed the cuneiform inscriptions being incised, the deerskin parchments being stretched, and the heated but learned discussions among the Sanhedrin taking place all around him—and at the same time was able to make them all seem very modern, very contemporary. Religion had been a living thing for Gregory Angell until that massacre in Mosul strangled it in its prime and left it for dead.

Monroe checked to ensure that his door was locked, and then sat back down and started to read.

Back in her office, Sylvia opened a secure Internet connection to the JSTOR website—knowing her search would be recorded by the NSA computers since all government employees searches were thus archived—and found Angell's paper easily.

Rather than read every word she scanned it quickly. Her day was usually quite busy and she worked anywhere from two to four hours overtime every night, more if there was "something on." She anticipated another interruption like the one with Harry so she raced through the paper, noting that Angell's conclusion was summed up quite easily at the very end of the document. She read it, and then read it again.

"So this is what Dwight wanted me to see," she said to herself. She leaned back from her terminal and picked up her teacup, noticing that its contents had already gone quite cold. She sipped it anyway, appreciating the way the tea had developed another, sharper, character as it had cooled. There was a lesson in there somewhere, she thought.

Angell was suggesting that the entire mythology of good versus evil, of angels versus demons, had begun with the simple association of two or three sentences in the Book of Genesis, the ones immediately preceding the story of Noah and the Flood.

The passage—from Genesis 6:1-4—was controversial and one

that had perplexed Biblical scholars for millennia. The passage—in various translations over the years—reads simply but ambiguously:

> When human beings began to increase in number on the earth and daughters were born to them, the sons of God saw that the daughters of humans were beautiful, and they married any of them they chose. Then the Lord said, "My Spirit will not contend with humans forever, for they are mortal; their days will be a hundred and twenty years."
>
> The Nephilim were on the earth in those days—and also afterward—when the sons of God went to the daughters of humans and had children by them. They were the heroes of old, men of renown.

Who were the "sons of God," the *bene elohim* as they were called in Hebrew? And how was it that they were not identified with human beings but instead "went to the daughters of humans and had children by them"? These "sons of God" are specifically identified as being non-human. And who, then, were the Nephilim?

Angell's theory was that the sexual relationship between humans and non-humans—the "daughters of humans" or "daughters of men" and the "sons of God"—was the beginning of a general understanding among the Jews that sexuality had to be tightly controlled. This was the first instance in the Bible of a sexual relationship that led to disastrous consequences, for the story of the Flood follows this passage immediately:

> The LORD saw how great the wickedness of the human race had become on the earth, and that every inclination of the thoughts of the human heart was only evil all the time. The LORD regretted that he had made human beings on the earth, and his heart was deeply troubled. So the LORD said, "I will wipe from the face of the earth the human race I have created—and with them the animals, the birds and the creatures that move along the ground—

for I regret that I have made them." But Noah found favor in the eyes of the LORD.

The implication is that the episode concerning the sons of God and the daughters of men is what convinced God to destroy the human race altogether. In other words, this physical relationship between the two species is what doomed humanity to destruction.

Generations of scholars, faced with these passages, came to the conclusion that the "sons of God" were in reality what the Second Temple Jews had called "watchers" and who by their very nature were more *fallen* angel than angel. This point of view received traction when it was discovered that the term *Nephilim* could be translated as "giants" and that it was assumed they were the offspring of the sexual intercourse between the daughters of men and the sons of God, i.e., human women and fallen angels. The first *Book of Enoch* contains a section entitled "the Book of the Watchers" and there is also a *Book of Giants*. These texts seem to confirm the idea that the *Nephilim* were the offspring of the illicit unions and that they were of gigantic stature, i.e., were genetic abnormalities. They were also "heroes of old" and "men of renown" and some of them managed to survive the Flood. Obviously, this entire passage is deeply problematic but only if we interpret "heroes" and "men of renown" as moral judgments. Heroes can be flawed personalities, praised for their strength but not necessarily for their virtue. As Pappy Boyington once said, "Show me a hero and I'll show you a bum."

Or, as F. Scott Fitzgerald wrote, "Show me a hero and I'll write you a tragedy."

As Sylvia read more deeply in Angell's paper, it became obvious that he thought that this was a pivotal moment in the history of the Western world. There was some kind of contact between humans and non-humans in the antediluvian era before the Great Flood was said to have wiped out entire civilizations. It was this contact, in fact, that somehow resulted in the Flood. Angell had interpreted this to mean there was some kind of incubus or succubus myth current in the Middle East at the time, a kind of *jinn* idea of ghostly sexual predators, and that sexuality was understood to be so powerful a force that, unchecked, it could lead to hideous consequences. Angell ended his paper by suggesting that the restrictive laws in the Bible concerning sexuality and the severe punishments meted out for transgressions—representing ideas that would be reprised in both Christianity and Islam, the two religions that share the Abrahamic origins of Judaism—owed their existence to this ancient event.

Adam and Eve were believed to have discovered sex, and for this were driven out of Eden. But when humans began mating with non-humans, this was too much for even God to endure and he planned on destroying the entire human race, "heroes" or no heroes.

Sylvia poured herself another cup of tea with hot water from her thermos. This time it was piping hot and the aroma of the steam rising from her cup sent her back for a moment to her native Melaka. She thought how her parents had been of Portuguese Catholic descent, living in a town that was largely Malay and Muslim or Chinese and Buddhist. There were always outsiders in every society, and outsiders were considered at once sexually desirable and spiritually taboo.

"Wait a minute," she said aloud. "Why only the *daughters* of men and not the sons of men?"

There were no "daughters of God" in that Biblical passage. Whoever these "sons of God" were, they were obviously only male. How was that possible?

She re-read the passage and it came to her.

Well, she thought, what other large group of beings would there be in those days, in that region, that would be composed of men only?

Armies. Armies of conquest and invasion.

And, according to the Bible, they weren't even human.

CHAPTER FOUR

THE BUSINESS OFFICES OF CHROMO-TEST, INC. were located on two floors of a new office building in downtown San Diego, not far from the naval base. The offices were all chrome, glass and steel in design with large flat-screen computer monitors on every desk. The actual labs were in another building, under tight security. The labs did the genetic analysis on samples that were sent to them from interested persons all over the country. Chromo-Test advertised heavily on television and on Internet sites, showing people who thought they were one ethnicity and then finding out they were another, all credit due to the latest state-of-the-art technology.

The business offices were used to accept the samples and match them with the online payments. The samples came in small tubes into which the interested party would spit, the saliva containing microscopic cells of genetic material that would then be sent to the labs for processing. Normally the personnel of the two separate units did not interact very much but today there was a little commotion in the conference room as men in lab coats stood around in strained communication with their CEO. It all started that morning when the test results on two kids from Providence, Rhode Island had come in and were flagged by the lab coat guys.

They ran the analysis again. And then again. Something wasn't right. Had the sample been contaminated? No, that didn't make sense. They had two samples, one from each child, and they were both returning the same results.

They ran a separate Y-DNA test on each sample, because that seemed to be where the problem originated. The mitochondrial analysis was within normal limits. The X-Chromosome of the mother and the whole maternal line were relatively consistent with a number of Western European haplogroups. It was the test of the Y-chromosome of the paternal line that was getting them nowhere.

Even though she hadn't paid for more than the basic "family tree" option, which would have returned some ethnicity information, they decided to run a whole battery of analytical tools on these three samples: the mother and her two children. The anomalies were only present in the children, with the mtDNA (the mother's mitochondrial DNA) as a base line for comparison purposes.

The fact that both children—both boys—had the same Y-chromosome anomaly would seem to argue in favor of them having the same father. Their mitochondrial results showed that the woman who claimed to be their mother was, indeed, their mother.

So what was the problem?

The father's line did not represent a single known haplogroup. There was no line of descent from Europe, Asia, or even Africa. There were no connections to known haplogroups in Australia, the South Pacific, or the Americas. None. The Y-chromosome data was unique, which was … well … impossible.

Except that it had happened before, and they had the tests to prove it.

They were going to have to dumb it down a little for Nathan Dowling, the CEO of Chromo-Test who had a pretty good general understanding of genetic science but who was not a scientist himself. All the talk of biallelic markers, A to C transversions, and nucleotide positions, as well as Y-specific microsatellites—topics that had dominated the discussion for the last two hours—would have to give way to genes, chromosomes, and haplogroups.

"Neanderthal?" was the first question Nathan Dowling had asked when everyone gathered in the conference room. Neanderthal DNA was all the rage these days.

"No, not Neanderthal," replied one of the men in lab coats, a middle-aged man named Frye. "This group does not seem to have descended from a common human ancestor."

"Meaning?"

"Well, you know how they say we are all descended from apes? That's not true. The other primates—the apes—and we humans share a common ancestor. We split off from each other at some point in dim prehistory. They're always pushing those dates backwards and forwards, by the way, so we don't know exactly when that happened. Anyway, that's not the point. Look here," the analyst commanded, pointing to a computer screen that showed the double helix of the DNA molecule slowly revolving horizontally.

"In the first place there is a weird incomplete duplication here, of SRGAP2A."

"Shit." The implication of this was suddenly very clear, even to the CEO.

After all, Chromo-Test was his baby and he had millions invested personally in the company. He knew the basics when it came to genetics, and SRGAP2 was one of those fancy terms he had come to recognize over the past few years.

"Right. The last known incomplete duplication of this gene was 2.5 million years ago. It's believed to have signaled the rise of brain development in humans, the development of the neocortex."

"And this duplication is found in both samples?"

"Affirmative. In fact, in all of the anomalous samples which we've tested and re-tested. Which, as you know, makes no damned sense at all."

"Wasn't there another duplication less than a million years ago?"

The analysts looked at each other with surprised glances. The CEO must be up late every night reading the literature.

"Yes, but that duplication, SRGAP2D, is not believed to be functional. At least not in humans."

Dowling nodded to himself, mesmerized by what he was seeing on the large computer screen he had set up in the conference room. He turned to another one of the analysts, a young geeky-looking kid whose name he forgot.

"I take it the mothers don't have it?"

"No, sir. It has to come from the father. And that leads us to the next problem. I don't even know how to address it without sounding … well, crazy."

"Look," smiled the businessman. "A documented new duplication of SRGAP2 is already the stuff on which Nobel Prizes are awarded. What else could possibly be of interest after that?" He looked around the room, but no one else was smiling.

"As we all know," started the geeky analyst, "There are 23 chromosomes. The 23rd chromosome determines gender. In a female, that's just another X chromosome but in a male that 23rd chromosome is a Y. There are complications at times when a male may have an extra Y chromosome for instance, but that isn't the case here.

"The Y chromosome is itself a kind of anomaly. The X-chromosome is the standard chromosome, you might say. If nothing else happens during fertilization the fertilized egg would be expected to develop into a female. The Y chromosome changes all that, throws a monkey wrench into the works so to speak and a male offspring is created."

"Okay, so?"

"In this case," interrupted Frye, "The Y-chromosome is considerably smaller than a normal human Y-chromosome—which is already pretty small—about one percent of the male's total DNA. In this case, though, it has been 'stripped down,' you might say. A lot of what we used to call 'junk DNA' is not present here. The SRY gene *is* present, otherwise these children would not be male. And there are less than seventy of the genes that code for proteins. It's not what we found on the Y that concerns us, but what we didn't find. The chromosome has been stripped, and we don't know why. The MSY or "male specific region" of the Y-chromosome should be palindromic. In other words, there is a certain level of redundancy in the Y-chromosome which is to be expected. We don't know for certain why it's there—maybe something to do with recombination, for the repair of genetic mutations. That's theory. Anyway, in this case, there is no redundancy; no palindromic characteristic. The genes are there to insure that males are created, we know that much. But … well, much of the rest of the boys' DNA has been altered as well, cleaned up you might say. Streamlined maybe? I don't know …"

"CRISPR? Somebody thinking overtime and splicing ..."

"No, sir. CRISPR wasn't in use at the time these kids were born. You couldn't use it to snip genes like they do today. And it hasn't been used on human genes in this country. The Chinese are doing it, we understand, but these kids ... well, short answer, we haven't seen this before."

"So? It's a chromosomal abnormality. The kind that can contribute to mental deficits of some kind. Psychosis, schizophrenia ..."

"Ordinarily, I would agree with you. And this condition may very well result in some kind of mental disorder if it was simply a case of an abnormality, a mutation in a gene. But in this case, we are not talking about chromosomal abnormality, but of a genetic contribution from an unidentified ... ah ... from an unknown source."

"Are you saying the father is an ... ape, or something like that? An animal? That would be impossible. We know that different species cannot interbreed ..."

"No, sir. Not an animal. As you say, it's impossible but just to be sure we ran some tests of our own. The tests were negative for mammals. *All* mammals." The analyst raised an eyebrow as if to communicate the only possible conclusion without actually having to say it out loud.

"So ... the father *must* be ... what? Some kind of test tube accident? Something at an IVF lab?" In vitro fertilization had its vulnerabilities, and some labs around the world were known to ... tinker ... with ova and sperm.

"Again no, sir."

"Excuse me?"

"Look at this," he once again pointed to the screen. This time he used his mouse and bracketed a section of the Y chromosome.

"The mother's mtDNA can be traced to a few haplogroups in Western Europe. Haplogroups U5A1 and H1B, for instance. Pretty normal stuff, about what you'd expect."

"Okay."

"But when we look at the Y-chromosome contribution we see this."

He pointed to the screen which now showed a breakdown of the father's Y-chromosome composition. The sequences were unusual, compared to their rather large database of exemplars.

"We typed some Y-specific microsatellites to construct haplotypes for analysis." There followed some virtually incomprehensible discussion of variability analysis, fluorescent labeling, and PCR amplification. But in the end, the result was the same.

"We're talking maybe a Haplogroup Z."

"There isn't any such group on the paternal line," objected the CEO. "They run only to R. The Eurasian group. Or the S and T groups. Australia, right?"

"Precisely. What we are looking at would represent another haplogroup entirely. A new one. One that hasn't been discovered yet. In fact, I can't determine if my proposed Haplogroup Z *is any kind of descendant* of A."

The A haplogroup is referred to as the macrohaplogroup. It represents the African genes from which all humans descend. There is a Haplogroup X in the mtDNA family, mostly associated with the Druze of Lebanon, but there is nothing controversial about that and certainly no Haplogroup Z.

In other words, whoever was the father of the two boys in Rhode Island was not a descendant of the original "Adam." His genetic endowment did not reflect the "out of Africa" heritage of all modern humans.

"Sir," clarified the geeky guy. "This doesn't come from any known animal on the planet. Not mammal, not insect, not even plant. In fact, it's neither animal nor human. It's … something else."

He blinked behind his glasses, gulped, and sat down. Everyone else in the room just stared at him as the full import of his statement landed like a rock in the middle of the conference table. This was the Holy Grail.

Alien DNA.

CHAPTER FIVE

Detective Cuneo covered his mouth and nose with his handkerchief. He was old-fashioned enough to still carry a handkerchief, and it came in handy at crime scenes. He stood there, staring down at the corpse, and wondered (not for the first time) if it had been a good idea to leave his old precinct in Lower Manhattan—the Nine—and move to the Big Sleazy, New Orleans, in the aftermath of Hurricane Katrina. He had wanted a change. He already had put in his papers at NYPD and had his pension and a nice send off in a cop bar in Bay Ridge. But here he was, at another crime scene, populated by another corpse.

From the Ninth Precinct to the Ninth Ward, it seemed like he hadn't moved very far at all.

The body was of an older woman. White. Gray-haired, and dressed formally in what appeared to be some kind of evening gown. Cause of death was most likely due to the fact that her face was leering at him over her narrow shoulder blades. Her neck had been broken and her head turned completely around. Her eyes were robin's egg blue, and wide open. Her mouth was a sneer.

"Who called it in?" he asked the room in general.

A patrolman who was studying a bookcase turned and replied, "We don't have a name. Someone called 911 and said there was a DB at this address." DB was code for "dead body."

"We got a phone number?"

"Maybe the emergency operator has it."

"Yeah," Cuneo muttered, more or less to himself. "Maybe."

There were uniformed patrolmen setting up a perimeter outside with the usual crime scene tape, and a photographer taking shots of everything and anything, including several shots of the bookcase.

The medical examiner was bent over the body with his kit of vials and thermometers, and was just getting up from a cursory examination. He stood on creaking knees and looked at Cuneo with absolutely no interest at all.

"Whadda we got?"

"Time of death, probably somewhere around midnight last night based on liver temp and rigor. It's a little iffy, because of her age and the ambient temperature. I'll know more when I get her on the table. Rigor set in quickly, also due to her age probably."

"Cause?"

"Well, there are no wounds that I can see. No petechial hemorrhaging in the eyes, or bruises around her neck, so there's no immediate indication she was strangled or suffocated. I'll do a tox screen to rule out any of the more popular poisons, but if I had to guess I'd say someone snapped her neck, just the way it looks."

"Somebody strong, maybe."

The ME shrugged.

"She was an old lady, probably somewhat frail. Bones are brittle at that age, muscle tone deteriorated. She might have put up a fight, but I don't see any defensive wounds."

He wanted to ask if there were any signs of a sexual assault, but figured that could wait until the ME had examined her more completely at the morgue.

"Lividity shows that she died here, right where we found her. No signs the body was moved."

Cuneo nodded, and looked around. He already knew that there were no signs of forced entry. In fact, he knew the house well from a previous visit.

The body was in the living room, the same room where he first had met the old lady—a Mrs. Galvez—a few months ago. It was during another murder inquiry, a double homicide that took place in a strange underground room in the Ninth Ward that had been uncovered by some earth-moving equipment during the course of an excavation. The room had been used for some kind of ritual purpose and contained what appeared to be a Faraday Cage.

And, you know, two dead bodies.

That crime was still basically unsolved. A series of real estate transactions concerning the property had led him to this elderly woman in her home in the posh Belle Chasse neighborhood and an interview with her that left him with the hairs standing up on his neck. The woman had spun him a weird story about a cult and someone she called "the Chinaman." He still had his notes from that meeting, and no matter how often he re-read them, they still didn't make much sense.

And now here she was. Dead as a doornail on her own Persian carpet, leaking fluids.

"If she's only been dead about fifteen hours, in air-conditioning, why all the decomp?"

The stench crept up on you, at first just under the radar but then becoming more horrendous, as if she had been dead for days in a hot trailer rather than her air-conditioned home in a somewhat luxurious section of New Orleans.

"Oh, the smell isn't from her."

Cuneo's eyes widened and he almost dropped his handkerchief. "It isn't?"

"No. *That* smell is from the basement. Pretty nasty, huh?"

The medical examiner had wiped a huge dab of Vapo-Rub beneath his nostrils to fend off the odor.

"The *basement*? We got another DB down there?"

"Not that we could find."

"So ... what?"

For the first time the ME looked at Cuneo with some interest, and amusement.

"I think they call it *ichor*," he said. And laughed.

That nice clean smell you get after it has rained is called petrichor. It's caused by the release of spores from the earth. These spores contain geosmin, an organic compound whose name means "earth smell." The smell itself is caused by a type of bacteria called actinobacteria. All in all, quite pleasant to the human nose.

The ichor referred to by the medical examiner, however, was distinctly unpleasant. A dead body's organs begin to break down within 24-48 hours after death, releasing a plethora of noxious-smelling gases into the air. The smell has been called a combination of sulphur and rotting fruit, depending on how long the body has been dead. Cuneo supposed you could call it thanatosmin, the "death smell," but his Greek was rusty.

He made his way down into the basement as directed by the pathologist. Basements are not common in a part of the world where the water table is so high that burials have to be above ground in vaults and mausoleums. Like the underground chamber in the Lower Ninth that Cuneo investigated months ago, this one was built of concrete and steel. It was much larger and lacked a Faraday Cage, but it did boast the obligatory strange symbols painted on the walls. Symbols, and stench.

Cuneo couldn't figure it out. There were no bodies, dead or otherwise, in the basement. There seemed to be no organic matter at all. In fact, it looked impeccably clean and well-organized, not like the usual basements and cellars of his experience. So what would account for the smell? It was getting worse the lower he descended down the wooden steps.

The walls around him were damp. They glistened in the light from the overhead fluorescent bulbs, one of which was flickering and making the detective even more uncomfortable.

A voice from behind him said, "It's a bad transformer."

He whirled to face the intruder. It was a uniformed cop.

"What?"

"The light." He pointed at it. "It's a bad transformer. Sorry, Detective. Didn't mean to startle you. I was told to wait down here and see if I could find the source of the smell."

"And did you?"

"Not exactly." He started to wander off in the direction of a large oil burner.

"What do you mean, 'not exactly'?"

The uni talked to him from over his shoulder and kept walking.

"The smell comes from everywhere. There seems to be no

point of origin. There are no bodies down here, if that's what you're thinking. The place is clean, organized. Hardly any piles of ... well, anything. See for yourself."

As Cuneo followed the uniform at a slower pace he allowed himself to stare at the symbols painted on the walls.

They were executed perfectly. This was not the work of an amateur, or of a deranged mind. The symbols were precise, almost as if etched into what appeared to be concrete walls. Whoever had done this had taken his or her time, worked from a plan, was meticulous in his habits. There were no drips of paint on the floor, no smudges anywhere. But the smell ... that was something else.

He stepped closer to one wall with its strange glyph that suggested something broken, or diseased. The smell became stronger, overwhelming.

Oddly, however, the nature of the smell seemed to change slightly. It became less noxious. Cuneo imagined that he was just getting used to it, but there was a nagging sense at the back of his throat that he was smelling something familiar. Not just the smell of decomp, but there were hints of something having to do with embalming or burial.

Whatever it was, it was making him dizzy. He held out a hand to balance himself, pulling away from the wall at once because he wasn't wearing gloves. And, anyway, he didn't want to touch whatever it was that was making the walls damp.

He stood there, in the middle of the floor, and swayed slightly. His eyes closed and he inhaled another whiff of the strange, unyielding odor.

"Detective?"

He opened his eyes.

"This way. I've found something."

Almost reluctantly, Cuneo began to walk after the uniformed officer but then stopped himself. Something was wrong.

"Officer?"

The uniform kept on walking.

Something made Cuneo reach under his jacket for his weapon.
Then it hit him. The smell.
It was myrrh.
And then he lost consciousness.

The odors of decomposing human bodies are composed of esters
and other chemical compounds. Indeed, even the scent of pineapple
has been associated with the smell of decomp. The specific chem-
istry depends on the stage of decomposition. In ancient times, the
resin known as myrrh was used to mask the smell of decomp and
was used in burial rites. When the three Wise Men brought myrrh
to the baby Jesus, it was a prediction of the violent end of the Christ.

Cuneo came to on the floor of the basement. His hand held his
service pistol, but it had not been fired. Standing over him was the
pathologist from the crime scene upstairs.

"What happened?"

"I was about to ask you the same question. When you didn't
come back upstairs I decided to come down here and look for you.
Figured you got lost somewhere."

Cuneo looked around and tried to get up, but a wave of nausea
hit him and he had to stop.

"Where's the uniform?" he managed to croak.

"What uniform?"

"The officer who was down here. The one you sent down to
find the source of the smell."

The pathologist shrugged.

"I didn't send anyone down here. Everybody's upstairs and
accounted for. Once we secured the scene, that is. We looked down
here but didn't find anything."

So who the hell was Cuneo talking to before? He rubbed his
eyes. He remembered that there was something strange about the
guy, or the circumstances, which is why he pulled his gun. What was
it?

"What about the smell?" he asked the pathologist.

"It seems to be coming off the walls. That strange shiny stuff. My guess is that something's buried behind them. We won't know until we get a sledgehammer in here, though."

Cuneo finally managed to stand upright, helped by the other man who grabbed his arm, but he swayed a little on his feet.

"You've got a nasty bump on the back of your head," offered the pathologist. "Who hit you?"

Cuneo felt the back of his head, gingerly, and winced when he touched the bruise.

"Damned if I know," he said.

"Damned if you don't," was the cynical reply.

A short time later a small squad of crime scene techs and uniforms were in the basement, tearing apart the walls where the strange stench originated. They first photographed every inch of the walls taking care to ensure that they had the strange symbols recorded digitally in case the damage done to the walls obscured or erased the evidence. They struck the cinder block façade with sledgehammers careful, in the relatively narrow confine, not to do more damage to the structure or themselves in the process. High-powered electric lights were brought in to make the job easier and cables snaked around the floor and back up the stairs to the ground level.

There were no electric outlets of any kind in the basement. The light came from the flickering fluorescent lamps overhead and they were hard-wired into the house's main electrical supply.

"Can anybody do something about that?" he asked, pointing up at the lights. The constant flickering was getting on his nerves.

The officers looked back at him and shrugged. They were too preoccupied with their work to bother about the lights. And, anyway, the work lamps they brought in washed out the flickering a little.

With a heavy sigh, Cuneo walked back to where the uniformed officer had been going before he was knocked out. He saw a small vestibule, no larger than a prison cell, and a narrow window to the outside world that was up too high to reach without a stepladder. Conveniently, there was just such a stepladder right below it.

"So this is how he got out," Cuneo said to himself.

There was dirt on the steps, presumably from the uniform's boots. But there was something else, as well.

As he strained to look up at the window—not wanting to use the stepladder for fear of contaminating evidence—he could see a symbol drawn in the dust of the glass. He stepped back a little for a better look, and then snorted.

It was a smiley face.

"Detective?"

It was one of the crime scene techs.

"Yeah? Whaddaya got?"

"You better come and see this for yourself."

The techs stepped back from the huge hole they had made in the basement wall. They shone one of their heavy-duty lights into the opening, and what he saw almost made Cuneo draw his revolver again.

There was a face staring out at him.

"Relax," said the medical examiner. "It's a statue of some kind. But have you ever seen that degree of detail in a statue before?"

"What ... what the fuck ... is it?"

It was the face of something, something not human but not animal either as far as he could tell. It looked vaguely familiar, but seeing it this close disoriented his memory. It had eyes, but that was it. The rest of its face was a mass of what appeared to be ... well, entrails. Tentacles, like an octopus or a squid, except that there was a kind of symmetry to an octopus and a squid, something that told you Nature had been trying for a certain effect, like how to walk under water if you have no legs. These ... tentacles ... did not seem to serve a purpose at all, unless that purpose was to excrete something which is what made Cuneo think of entrails. Well, that and the unholy stench.

"That's not the worse part. Notice how the smell gets more intense the closer you get to the hole?"

Cuneo could only nod. If he opened his mouth he would gag.

"That's because of the ... the freezer?"

The ME shone the light down, below the gaping, staring face of the statue, to reveal a kind of pedestal. It was about the size of a regular freezer, the kind you would have in a basement or garage for storing frozen food. But it was painted in an array of colors in such a way that just looking at it made his head hurt.

"Evidently, the unit was shut down a little while ago. Freezers hum or vibrate or something, especially one this old, but it seems to be dead. And it's warm to the touch. We're looking at the fuse box now to see if maybe it was just a blown fuse or if someone deliberately shut it off. Which, as you know, doesn't make a whole lot of sense. Why is the power on in the rest of the house? Why just cut off the freezer?"

Cuneo nodded at the uni.

"Can you open it?"

"We'd have to get that ... that thing off of it first. It looks damned heavy."

Cuneo took a picture of it with his cell phone, and then another of the freezer. In the flickering fluorescent light he now saw that the strange color scheme on the freezer was composed of various symbols—like those painted on the walls—superimposed over each other.

It suddenly hit him. The weird signs he had been seeing were discrete elements of a larger symbol. One had to arrange them on or around each other in order to get a glimpse of the whole symbol.

He flipped through the other photos on his phone, looking for the ones he took earlier at that doomed house in the Lower Ninth. The symbols were there. He could make out some similarities between the ones on the sunken cellar room in the first house and the ones on the walls here. You had to merely rotate the photos and you started to see that they were identical.

"Get that thing off the freezer!" he shouted to the crew who were standing around, staring at the strange statue and ignoring the horrible stench coming out of the hole.

He jumped in and started throwing pieces of sheetrock and lathing into the corridor, digging like a madman.

Organic material moves. Not just people, but animals, birds, fish. Microbes. Even plants move, albeit imperceptibly. They grow, reach for the sun, open and close. If something organic stops moving, one can assume it has died.

Non-organic material doesn't move. Rocks, stones. The earth. If it does move, look out. Earthquakes. Avalanches. Volcanoes. When non-organic material starts to move, then this is not life but death.

The ancients understood this relationship between organic and non-organic materials. They crafted statues—some of them huge—out of non-organic material. Clay. Stone. They gave them human features, or animal, or divine. Then they anointed them with oil, or blood, or saliva to make them conscious, to animate these corpses, these dead bodies. To make them live. To make the stones walk.

They tried to make the non-organic, organic. To make it think. To make it hear their prayers and petitions. To make it move. They understood there was a point—a supernatural point—at which the organic became the non-organic, and at which the non-organic became sentient. This was, after all, how God created the First Man, Adam, out of non-organic materials, breathing life into a lump of clay.

And it is how Rabbi Loew of Prague created the Golem: an artificial being of enormous size, to defend the Jewish ghetto from the Christian soldiers. Rabbi Loew used the letters of the Divine Name to animate his creature.

The Cult of Dagon used their own alphabet, a language forged in the stars, a chthonic babbling of vocal chords more accustomed to burbling under water as they, the first amphibians, crawled sightless and unblinking onto the shores of Hell.

"What ... what are we looking for?" The ME shouted at Cuneo, pitching in and removing blocks of broken wall from around the base of the freezer.

Cuneo shouted back over his shoulder.

"Help me lift this thing!"

He got his hands in a crevice between the statue and the freezer and tried to move the statue, but it wouldn't budge.

The ME squeezed in next to Cuneo and put his back into pushing the statue from the top, trying to give the detective leverage to rock the statue back and forth, off the freezer. The smell was by now almost overpowering, that obscene combination of rotting fruit, expired hamburger, and incense, and it seemed to radiate from somewhere between the freezer and the statue.

The other uniforms searched around looking for something to help leverage the statue off the freezer. The opening was too small for the others to get in and help the other two men.

One of the cops came up with a length of rebar. It might not be strong enough to lift the statue but it would help shift it off its base on the freezer.

Two of the officers shoved the rebar into the crevice made by Cuneo and the ME and they began to jiggle it into position.

They were all moved to frantic action by the excitement of their strange, New York-born detective, but they had no idea why there was any degree of urgency at all. The sight of Cuneo on his hands and knees, scrabbling away at the arcane construction in the wall was enough. He obviously knew something they didn't, and time was of the essence.

As more chunks of lathing were tossed out of the hole, it could be seen that Cuneo's fingers were bleeding. He seemed to be unaware of the fact, and moved with increasing speed and determination.

The other cops looked at each other with bewildered glances, as if to say:

There couldn't be ... there couldn't be anything alive in that freezer? Could there be? It was entombed behind a solid wall, who knows for how long? Nothing could remain alive under those circumstances.

Could it?

The statue with its freakish tendrils and bulging eyes moved an inch and then another. There was a groan as it scraped across the top of the freezer, and then stopped.

"It's stuck," said the ME.

Cuneo shook his head, taking a breath, his hands on the legs of the statue which seemed to be in a kind of squat ending in feet with webbed toes. He was getting used to the smell. Decomp mixed with myrrh. The smell of Biblical burials.

"No, it's not stuck. It's attached."

"Shit."

"I've got to get around to the other side."

Cuneo stepped over the debris in the hole and gingerly made his way around to the back of the statue, dodging wires and pipes as he did so.

"Hand me a flashlight, will you?"

The medical examiner passed a flashlight over to the detective who played the light around the interior, first into the rest of the space they were in and then to the rear of the statue.

They were running out of time, but they couldn't open the box until they separated it from the statue. And for that they would need an instrument that he didn't think they would find outside of a museum.

Or a zoo.

There. He found it. The way the statue connected to the freezer. He would need a chainsaw. Or maybe Excalibur.

"Crap."

"Whaddaya got, detective?"

Cuneo shouted back from behind the statue. "What do you have in your black box? Stryker saw?"

"Here? No, detective. I don't carry one of those with me."

A Stryker saw is used in the post-mortem, for cutting through bones if necessary, such as the skull to get at the brain matter. The coroner didn't keep one of those in the van. Cuneo knew that, but he was grasping at straws.

The other cops kept positioning and re-positioning the rebar between the statue and the freezer, trying to get an angle that was good for leverage. Cuneo kept himself behind the statue, giving them more room to work, as he grasped one edge of it and tried pulling it towards him. Just touching the statue made him physically ill, and he now knew why.

The seals or symbols or sigils or whatever they called it had told the story. You didn't have to have a degree in western esotericism to know what they meant. You just had to have been present when your wife gave birth.

There was a sudden loud, metallic groan as the statue shifted a few inches off the top of the freezer. To Cuneo, that purely mechanical noise sounded like a scream of agony from the statue. If you could call it a statue. A pagan idol was more like it. Something from a sick adolescent's fevered nightmare.

Cuneo grabbed his end of the object and pulled down with all his strength. The other cops continued to push from their end, the gap growing between the statue and the box until they could see that the two objects were connected by a tube or flexible pipe of some kind. The best they could hope for was toppling the statue so that they would have a better chance of opening the freezer box. The two components were separate, just attached by the tube, but the tube looked indestructible.

That was when the medical examiner noticed that one end of the freezer had another tube connected to it, one that ran into the plumbing system of the house. It was low on the box and until now hidden under the debris from the shattered wall. The electrical connection, however, was nowhere to be seen just yet.

"Detective! Whatever this thing is, it's part of the plumbing system of the house. If we rip this thing apart, there is no telling what might happen. We might find ourselves in a sea of sewage!"

The ME was not telling Cuneo anything he hadn't already figured out. The statue fed into the freezer, which fed into—or out of—the pipe that ran along the floor and into another wall. There were no valves he could see. The whole thing had been installed behind the wall, and then the wall covered up and plastered over, and covered with weird signs.

But he knew that if they did not pull the statue off the freezer—and do it within the next few minutes—whatever was in the freezer would die.

Outside the house a small crowd had gathered, attracted by the squad cars and the yellow crime scene tape. Most were neighbors from the surrounding homes, but there was one woman who stood a little apart from the rest, across the street from the house. She stood perfectly still, her arms at her sides, and just stared.

She was about forty-five or fifty years old. At first glance she seemed to be Caucasian, but that was because of her short white hair and the large sunglasses that covered half of her face. On closer look, she appeared to be Asian. Chinese, perhaps. She was slender, dressed in a pastel-colored dress in a floral pattern that had a belt around the waist. She would have gone unnoticed had it not been for her strange stance across from the crime scene. It looked as if she was trying to stare it down.

She opened her mouth, wide, wider, and began to scream.

CHAPTER SIX

GREGORY ANGELL ENTERED THE ANCIENT CITY of Beijing in the back of a pickup truck. He was covered in dust from the road and held his backpack in a tight embrace. He wore an old blue Mao cap to cover his head, enabling him to blend in. No one would give him a second glance on the street, which is what he wanted. There were a lot of foreigners in China these days, and one more would probably go unnoticed, but he couldn't take the chance that Aubrey or Monroe had not alerted the Chinese Public Security Bureau under some pretense or another.

He could have remained in Mongolia, blended in, stayed underground, but the life of a fugitive was getting old. He had been having terrible dreams, sickening nightmares, and frequently awoke screaming. His companions on the road were getting nervous, and he knew it was only a matter of time before someone pulled a knife and left him to bake in the shifting sands of the Gobi. He had to leave, but he had nowhere to go. He had a point of origin, but no destination. His life had become a scribble instead of a straight line between two points.

There was a smell of cooking fires and an aroma of broiled meat and hoisin sauce coming from a tiny café at the corner, and it made him realize how hungry he was. He was still a few miles from the center of town and the area close to Wangfujing and Tiananmen Square. He could walk down the broad avenue in front of the Forbidden City, mingle with the crowds, and manage to get to the train station in an hour or so, but he was exhausted and hadn't eaten in almost a day. He had some yuan in his pocket after selling his watch to a Mongolian cell phone salesman in Hohhot but he had to be careful with spending. He could not buy a ticket and get out of China by train or air. He had to find another way. They would be watching transportation and one couldn't buy any kind of ticket without a passport, something he didn't have. His documents were all with Aubrey. He was a man without a country at the moment, and if he was stopped by anyone he was screwed.

More importantly, he had possession of the Book. Wrapped in its black silk shroud and covered again in a piece of oilcloth, it took up most of the space in his backpack. If he was apprehended for any reason, the Book would be discovered and the whole nightmare he had just endured would begin all over again.

A few months earlier he had been safe if not particularly sound in his apartment in the Red Hook section of Brooklyn, lecturing on religion at Columbia a few times a week—and spending the rest of his time with a nine millimeter handgun under his pillow as he slept, dreaming fitful dreams of lost landscapes populated by the souls of the murdered and the cries of the desperate. It was a vast underground land, this geography of his dreams, devoid of hope, and with a howling emptiness at its core: the absence of God.

In the weeks since then he had traveled through Turkey, Iraq, Iran, Afghanistan and Pakistan only to wind up in Nepal at another underground landscape, a real one, to witness a ritual that was older than humanity itself, the remnant of some kind of religion of apes and aliens. He had been sent on a mission by an American intelligence agency to find a Book that was at the center of a massive revolt spreading from North Africa to the Middle East, Central Asia, and beyond, involving a cult that had remained silent and secret for more than a thousand years.

He had believed that there was no God, that God had been taken from him on a side street in Mosul years earlier, as twenty-three Yezidis lay dying after being mowed down by automatic weapons in retaliation for another killing in that counter-spinning spiral of hate and revenge that was all most people ever knew of the Middle East.

But then … in that cavern beneath the groaning mountains of Nepal, he had witnessed something that only belief could explain. A supernatural occurrence, a shuddering manifestation of something that was not human, not animal. A spiritual force. The eruption of a hideous Being, clothed in shredded robes made of the callously unanswered prayers of millions—*billions*—of believers, clouded by the incense of the blood shed by religious maniacs and pious, psychopathic prophets. The very fact of this Being meant that Angell's faith in faithlessness had been shaken to its foundation. He realized that it wasn't that he did not believe in God; instead, he simply did not *want* to believe. There were those who loved God. Angell had hated God. Belief was not the issue.

And then that night in the underground cavern at the frozen border between Nepal and Tibet. Whatever had happened there had whiplashed Angell's entire worldview. Whatever that thing had been—from whatever hell that Being had escaped, if only briefly—it had to be fought and destroyed and torn into a thousand pieces.

And if Gregory Angell had to believe in God, or invent a God who could do that, then so be it.

As he trudged along a narrow *hutong* (or alley, one of the few left in Beijing) on his way to the main avenue he saw a poster that had been plastered to a wall. It announced a seminar in Daoist medicine to be held at Peking University, and the main speaker was to be a colleague from Columbia: Dr. Stephen Hine.

Angell stood and stared at the poster. This was unbelievable luck. He knew Hine from a few joint conferences that were held between the faculties of the Religious Studies department and the Asian Studies department. Hine had a background in Chinese religion but also in Chinese medicine. His dissertation on the Chinese origins of Zen Buddhism had earned him his Ph.D. as well as the accolades of Sinologists on both sides of the Pacific Ocean. It was possible—just possible—that Hine could hide him for a few days while he examined his options.

Peking University was not far from where Angell was standing. It was in the Haidian District, to the west of Tiananmen Square, near the old Summer Palace buildings. The seminar was scheduled for the next day, but Angell knew that Hine was probably already in residence at the university. All he had to do was get to the campus and find out where the "foreign experts" were housed. He knew that Hine would see him right away if he could recognize him after all Angell had been through.

His stomach growling with hunger, Angell resolutely set off in the general direction of the Summer Palace. There were large signs on the main thoroughfare in Chinese and English pointing the direction. It might take him hours to get there on foot, and every moment he spent on the street made him feel vulnerable and exposed but there was no choice.

Dr. Stephen Hine was falling asleep.

It was the middle of the afternoon, but he was jet-lagged from arriving in Beijing from New York City only hours before. He just wanted to take a nap, but was prevented from doing so by the three gentlemen from Peking University who sat before him. They were all drinking jasmine tea from porcelain cups with lids, and sitting on overstuffed sofas boasting a plethora of embroidered antimacassars. Hine could not remember the last time he saw an antimacassar outside of China.

The three men were professors from the university, one of whom was an old friend and the other two were more like political appointees than academics. They had invited him to participate in the seminar and were paying for his room and board at the university so there wasn't much Hine could do except to smile and nod and try to be polite.

Hine's specialty was Daoist alchemical practices and their relation to ancient Chinese medicine. It was well-known that Chinese alchemy consisted of a great many herbal and chemical compounds that were used to treat various illnesses, but that the main focus was longevity. Chinese documents were replete with references to "pills of immortality" and other creations that could eliminate disease and increase one's lifespan dramatically. Hine had published English translations of some key Daoist texts, including his own interpretation of the classic *Dao De Jing*. His interest was in the idea that the human being could not simply take a drug to heal an illness, but that the body had to be prepared first to accept the medicine in order for it to function properly. That was at the heart of his understanding of the role that meditation played in the healing process; and that in turn led him to Ch'an Buddhism, which was the forerunner of Japanese Zen Buddhism.

This was the substance of the conversation he was having with the three men from the university and even though he was always energized by this type of discussion he felt himself crashing.

Thus it was with gratitude that he realized the meeting was coming to an end. He would be expected for the "welcome dinner" in the evening—early, around 6 pm—but that was okay. That meant he had about two hours for a nap, which was probably all he would need.

Everyone stood up, shook hands, and then Dr. Hine was left to his own devices.

As he opened the door to his room, the weariness he felt hit him like a Mack truck. He saw the bed in front of him and stumbled toward it like a zombie.

That was when he heard a voice coming from the doorway to the private bath.

"Doctor Hine?"

He whirled around to face the intruder, half-suspecting that he was hallucinating the whole episode.

"*Whaaa* …?"

"Doctor Stephen Hine?"

The academic nodded, stupefied. The man standing there was an American, young, dressed impeccably in a dark blue suit, pastel blue shirt and power tie.

"Forgive the intrusion. My name is Maxwell Prime. I'm with the FBI."

Hine swallowed, and managed to croak: "What does the FBI want with me?"

"Do you know a man by the name of Gregory Angell? I believe you worked together at Columbia?"

"Yes, of course. Dr. Angell and I are old friends. Why? Is he in some sort of trouble?"

"He may try to contact you, Dr. Hine."

"He's here? In Beijing?"

"We have reason to believe he is in China. He was spotted in Hohhot a little while ago and we feel he is on his way here. To Beijing. To see you."

"To see … me? Why?"

"We really don't know, Dr. Hine, but it is of vital importance that we make contact with him. We would like your cooperation."

It didn't sound like a request.

"Wait a second. You said 'worked.'"

"Excuse me?"

"You said we 'worked' together at Columbia. Past tense. Has he left the university?"

The agent thought for a second before answering.

"He has been out of the country for months. He may be in some sort of trouble. He will need funds, most likely, and possibly documents. Passport, identification papers, that sort of thing. If he approaches you, I want you to call me at this number." He handed Hine his business card. Embossed on it was the FBI seal, his name, and his contact info in Beijing. "I work out of the US Embassy in Beijing," he clarified.

"This card says you are with the anti-terrorism task force."

The agent nodded.

"So … is Angell a terrorist?"

"Just let me know if he tries to contact you, Dr Hine. We'll take it from there."

Special Agent Prime let himself out. Hine still couldn't figure out how he had gotten into his room, but chalked it up to his Chinese hosts being somewhat lax where security was concerned. After all, he was only an academic. The security he assumed was present in his room was there to spy on him, not protect him from other Americans.

He had been ready to collapse, but now he found himself a little wired after the visit from the FBI. He looked again at the business card the agent had given him. Something about it … he had spoken with FBI agents before in his career, since his travels had taken him all over Asia and sometimes during times of political unrest. They were usually very nice people, considering what they did for a living. And he had his share of Bureau business cards and none of them had ever listed a specialty.

This one said "Counter-Terrorism Task Force," and he wondered at that. It was off. Those guys didn't advertise, and when they did the correct nomenclature was "Counterterrorism Division" or CTD, except when they were referring to the Joint Terrorism Task Force, or JTTF, which was a cooperative body that included the FBI but also members of the other intelligence and law enforcement agencies in the United States.

But there sure as shit was no "CTTF" or "Counter-Terrorism Task Force."

Hine sat on his bed and rubbed his face. He was getting too old for the cloak and dagger stuff. It was different when he was younger, when the world was a different place. These days there were more than a dozen intel agencies in the United States under the Homeland Security umbrella, and they competed with each other just as often as they cooperated. There was SIGINT and ELINT, and damned little HUMINT. It was all about cyberwarfare, and enemies you couldn't see or identify except maybe from their URLs. Signals Intelligence and Electronic Intelligence was all well and good as tools or adjuncts to the real thing: HUMINT or Human Intelligence. Actually meeting people, in-country, making friends and identifying enemies. But everybody was putting all their resources into bigger and better server farms, scooping up every phone call and text message and email in the expectation that newer and better algorithms would be found to sift through all that noise and extract a useable signal. How different was any of this from astrology when you got right down to it? Astrology, or reading entrails, or Tarot cards? It was a kind of modern Kabbalah, this manipulation of numbers and words and symbols. And when the enemy was invisible, pure smoke, it was like conjuring spirits or rising on the astral plane.

It made his head hurt.

And then there was the question of Gregory Angell.

"What the fuck has Angell gotten himself into now?" he asked himself, aloud.

"Whatever it is," came the voice from behind him, "It sure as hell doesn't look good."

Gregory Angell was standing in the same spot where SA Maxwell Prime had been standing only minutes before.

"Jesus, Greg, you look like shit." The two men embraced a little awkwardly, and then Hine held the younger man at arm's length to get a better look.

"You could use a shower, and maybe some food."

"You're right on both counts," he replied, in a voice hoarse with exhaustion. "But right now I have to know what that guy wanted."

"He says he's FBI. Based out of the embassy."

"But ... you don't believe him?"

Hine shrugged. "I don't know. There was just something about him, about all of it, which seemed a little ... off. Anyway, right now, we have to get you somewhere safe. You're on the run from someone, right?"

"You could say that. The problem is, I don't exactly know who."

"Seriously?"

"Could be a lot of people, actually."

And Angell collapsed.

When he came to on a couch in Hine's room about an hour later, Hine was standing over him with a cold washcloth and a cup of hot tea.

"What happened?"

Angell moved up to a sitting position, holding his head in his hands.

"You just dropped out. When was the last time you had anything to eat?"

"What day is it?"

"That's what I figured. Look, you can stay here for now. I have a meeting I can't get out of, one of those obligatory dinners with my hosts, but I will be back as soon as I can. I'll use jet lag as an excuse, which isn't far from the truth. In the meantime, here's some tea." He handed Angell the porcelain cup with its lid. "There's more hot water in that thermos next to the desk. On top you'll find a bunch of snacks I brought with me on the plane. Sorry it can't be a hot meal, but I can arrange that when I get back. The bathroom is right through there, and you'll find towels and anything else you might need. Don't answer the door, and don't go near the windows. You can catch me up on everything when I return. Right now, though, I have to get to that dinner or people will get suspicious."

Angell simply nodded. He was enormously grateful to his old friend, but could hardly put two words together. The events of the past few weeks were taking their toll. He needed to sleep in a real bed, and eat something hot and nourishing.

By the time he looked up to thank Hine, the other man had already left the room.

Hine walked quickly down the hall and one flight of stairs to the main lobby. His hosts were waiting for him, standing around and speaking softly. When they saw him they smiled and walked towards him.

He shook their hands and nodded, and they nodded, and smiled, and he smiled, and they eventually made their way to the university's dining area. They waited for him to go through the door first. He waited for them to go first. They insisted. He insisted. They took him by the arm to force him through. He took their leader by the arm to force him through. They laughed. He laughed. They eventually got through the door with no one losing face, and to the rear of the dining area where a private room had been set aside for their welcome banquet.

Back in the guest room, Angell took a look at himself in the bathroom mirror for the first time in at least a week. Maybe longer. He was astonished to see how pathetic he looked. Filthy, hair matted, clothes torn and ill-fitting, a stubborn growth of beard that he had been keeping at bay with a dull plastic razor he found at an abandoned campsite in the Kumtag Desert outside of Dunhuang.

But it was his eyes that startled him most of all. They were hollow, shrunken into their sockets, with the thousand-yard stare normally reserved for soldiers in active war zones or Syrian refugees seeking asylum. He dared not stare into his own eyes for too long, as he began to see his face changing in the mirror into something alien and threatening.

What the hell had happened to him?

Gingerly, he took off his clothes and put them in a pile on the bathroom floor. He reached for the shower and was grateful to notice that the water was hot. Quite a change from the last time he was in China, more than two decades ago, for a conference with Hine, when the water came in a tepid trickle from a hose attached to the wall with a clip.

Putting aside feelings of vulnerability as he stood naked under the shower head he allowed himself to enjoy the rush of water as it removed layers of desert and road dust and God knew what else.

God. That was the start of this whole adventure, wasn't it? God, and the lack of God and the anger at God or at the absence of one.

And then that ... that thing that oozed up from the bowels of the earth under a mountain in Nepal. A thing that was not supposed to exist. And all the death that followed.

How could he remain an atheist in the face of supernatural horror?

The answer was simple. He was not an atheist. An atheist doesn't believe in God. He, on the other hand, was angry at God. He hated God. He wanted God to be accountable for human suffering.

And then … this.

As the water rushed over his body like a purification ceremony he stood motionless, eyes closed, and was transported back to that night in the *beyul*, in the unknown country that had been hidden for millennia in the Himalayas, and watched as the Keepers of the Book—high priests of the Cult of Dagon—chanted the impossible into existence. He saw the slight figure of Jamila, the Yezidi woman with the strange ability—or disability—of channeling arcane forces, her eyes alight with the fire of creation as if she was giving birth in that chthonic chamber. The walls and ground of that enormous room shook with her efforts and the seals and sigils carved into the walls began to take on a glow and a throbbing luminescence that Angell knew was impossible but which he also knew he could see and feel.

There was a gun in his hand.

And a Book.

And then there was death.

He found himself outside the mountain cavern as the heavens erupted with rocket fire, walking east amid the flames and the smoke. Hours later he was picked up by a flatbed truck full of workers going to a construction site and from there managed another ride to the Chinese border. He wound up in Gansu province, an area that had once belonged to Tibet and which was still populated by people of Tibetan descent. Buddhists who helped him get the rest of the way to Mongolia. For some reason, they all wanted to help him. They risked their lives and their livelihood to get him from once place to another without being spotted by the authorities … or by the other people who were looking for him: strange foreigners who spoke their languages with the slight trace of accent one might expect from those who lived with reliable sources of food and water.

Angell himself understood a little Mandarin, and that was enough to enable him to move from one remote village to the next, always heading east, until finally in Mongolia he knew he had to get to Beijing and from there to the coast. He felt the draw of the sea. It was not a pleasant attraction; more like the vertigo one feels standing at the top of a very high building and looking down. But he had to go. Something about the sea, and the Book in his knapsack, made it imperative.

The water began to run cold. Angell welcomed that, as well, for it woke him out of his reverie. He stood under the shower for another minute, then stepped out and toweled off. He would have to put his old, filthy clothes back on again, but he felt better now.

He walked into the room and saw the pile of energy bars and chips that Hine had laid out for him.

He was suddenly very hungry.

At the banquet, Hine was sitting next to the leader of the group that had invited him to the conference. There were three glasses in front of each diner. One was small, like a shot glass but with a stem, and that was for *mao tai*: the over-proof liquor that was inevitable at these things. The next was a wine glass, usually for the kind of sweet sherry that the Chinese liked. The last glass was a large tumbler for beer. He had been toasted, and was toasting, in all three drinks which meant that—with his jet lag—he was becoming increasingly drunk, especially when each toast had to end in an empty glass. "*Gan bei!*" they would shout, "empty glass," and no matter what it was they were toasting with it all had to go down in one swallow. Thank God they were eating, thought Hine, otherwise this would not be possible.

The food was delicious, as always. Cold chicken with a sesame sauce; jellied octopus; lobster sashimi with the lobster still alive and trying to escape the table; pickled meats of various kinds. And that was just the first course.

Finally, the fish was brought out which signified the end of the meal. He had eaten as much sea cucumber, roasted duck, and various unidentifiable dishes as he could manage. The fish was largely symbolic, a large sea bass flavored with ginger and scallions, and then platters of *jiao zi*—steamed or boiled dumplings—also appeared.

The banquet was officially coming to an end, and Hine desperately wanted to see what time it was, but he dared not look at his watch for that would be interpreted as rudeness. Instead, he wondered what his "guest" was doing, and hoped Angell was fast asleep. He would ask him about the FBI agent's visit when he was fully rested.

Angell thought he would crash completely after the shower, but somehow he was still awake. He ate two energy bars and drank more tea, and then sat on the edge of the bed. He was exhausted, but wired. He was afraid the FBI agent would be back, or that the Public Security Bureau had been alerted to his presence. He didn't want to get his old friend in trouble, but he seriously needed a few hours' sleep or he might as well surrender to the authorities himself.

He looked over at his backpack, and wondered again at the provenance of the book that was hidden there, wrapped in silk.

With a sign of resignation that he would not be able to fall asleep any time soon, he hefted the backpack, opened it, and withdrew the book. He had not looked at it very much since his escape from Nepal. He had to worry too much just to stay alive, and never really had the leisure to study the text. He didn't now, either, but he was stuck in that room for the time being so he might as well open the book and look at it, and maybe then he would be able to sleep.

Something about it—the smell of the brittle pages, the feel of the leatherish cover—brought back all the memories of Nepal in a rush, nearly overwhelming him. He set it down on the desk, and opened it randomly to a page somewhere in the middle.

When Hine finally returned to the room, cautiously locking the door behind him and securing the chain, he saw Angell fast asleep on his bed. He had evidently showered and shaved, so he looked a little better than he had only hours earlier. The empty energy bar wrappers told the rest of the story.

That was when he noticed the open book on the desk, and decided to take a closer look.

It was old, obviously, and written in what appeared to be Greek letters. Hine had studied Biblical Greek when he was working on his undergraduate degree in religious studies, but that had been a long time ago. He was a specialist in Asian languages and culture, but still remembered enough of his college Greek to stumble through some of the words.

He dared not touch the pages. They looked like they would crumble to dust if he so much as breathed on them. So he stood over the desk, hands at his sides, and sounded out what he could.

The book was not printed, but hand-written, which made reading it all the more difficult. The cursive Greek script seemed to stab the pages rather than flow across them. He could not tell how old the physical book was by this cursory examination, but judged it to be older than five hundred years, at least, if not much older. The Greek itself was problematic, as he could not recognize some of the words at all as they did not seem to be Greek in origin but were perhaps a kind of transliteration from some other language.

All of this was made even more compelling by a diagram that was drawn in the center of one of the pages. It was a kind of triangle with hooks at each point and more writing inside of it. It dawned on Hine that was he was looking at was a magical workbook of some kind, something Gnostic perhaps. The type of Greek seemed later than the Biblical Greek he studied, maybe an early form of demotic. Later than the Nag Hammadi texts, which were in Coptic anyway, and dated primarily to the second century C.E., if his memory served. Later than the Dead Sea Scrolls. Fifth century ... sixth century C.E.? Perhaps a little later, but not by much. But if it was a magical text, that would explain the nonsense Greek that he couldn't make out. Some kind of abracadabra, probably. *Voces magicae.* That sort of thing.

He tried sounding out one of the lines.

"*Me ... períerges aionia akómi kai ... o thánatos boreí na pethánei ...*"

No, that didn't make any sense. Maybe he read it wrong. He tried again.

"*Me períerges ...aioniés ... akómi kai o thánatos boreí na pethánei ...*"

With strange aeons even death may die? That didn't sound magical. It sounded more ... poetic ... than anything else.

He tried another line, but this one was even more obscure and the letters seemed jumbled together, senseless.

"*Phi 'Eng loo im eglo 'en aph 'e Kootooloo Oor'illieh oe ga 'en ag ph ta gen ...*". No. No sense at all.

"What ... what are you doing?"

Hine turned.

"Ah, you're awake. How did you ..."

"Are you reading from the ... that book?" Angell was suddenly standing up next to the bed as if he had been shot from a gun.

"What *is* this?" Hine asked, pointing to the pages.

Angell slammed the book closed.

"Were you reading aloud? Just now?"

"Well, not really. Greek is not my language. Just sounding out the ..."

"Don't do that. Ever."

"Gregory ..."

"I mean it, Steven. Not ever."

Angell rewrapped the book and shoved it into the bottom of his backpack.

"Is that why you're on the run, Greg? You've stolen antiquities, or something? If so, you know I can't be part of that."

Angell was silent for a moment, and sat back down on the edge of the bed. The short nap he had gave him a little extra energy now, but he knew he would crash again if he couldn't get eight hours.

"Listen, I wouldn't get you involved in any of this if I wasn't desperate. I've been on the run for ... I don't know ... weeks now? But I wasn't stealing antiquities. I was working for our government."

"The government?"

"Well, part of it, anyway. Some guy in DC that was running an operation in Iraq."

"Shit, Greg. Iraq? I thought you never wanted to go back there."

"You're right. I didn't. Still don't. But they pressured me. Made me an offer I couldn't refuse and, no, it wasn't money. They said I had the necessary expertise and qualifications. Long story. Anyway, they sent me to Turkey, and then Iraq, dropped me into Iran …"

"Jesus!"

"And from there to Afghanistan, Pakistan, and eventually Nepal."

"You're shitting me."

"And I made it from Nepal to Gansu Province on my own, and from Gansu to Mongolia. And now I'm here."

"So what's the problem, then? If you were working for us, you can just go home, right?"

"It's not that simple. I have something they want, but I don't want them to have it."

Hine pointed at the backpack. "The book, right?"

Angell only nodded.

"Look, Gregory. We've known each other a long time. I know about your two tours in Iraq and Afghanistan, courtesy of our government, and of how you came home from the last one. I can't imagine what you've gone through, so I won't even try to put myself in your shoes. But I got a visit today from a Fed who says you have no passport, no money, and that you're on the run, wanted by the Counter-Terrorism people. Or so he claimed. I have my doubts. But anyway … I want to help, but I don't know how. As far as we know, this place could be watched. In fact, it probably is being watched, and not just by our people. So whatever that book represents, is it worth it to keep it out of the hands of the people who sent you here?"

Angell was quiet for a moment, then he looked up with that thousand-yard stare.

"I saw people gunned down for this book. In a refugee camp in Turkey. In a public square in Iraq. In Yazd, in Iran. In Afghanistan. And in Nepal. Especially in Nepal."

"Jesus."

"A lot of people. Some Americans, too, and Europeans, but mostly Iraqis, Iranians, and there was a … a Yezidi woman. Hardly more than a girl. If you could have seen her face when all the shooting started... and there was an agent they sent with me into Nepal. He got shot in a cave somewhere in the Himalayas. I watched him die. And it all has to do with that damned book. A book! Everyone has gone absolutely batshit over a book. I have to know why, but I haven't had time. I've been running from the guys back in DC. Some guy named Aubrey, who recruited me off the street in Brooklyn. And all his friends."

"Why you? Because of Iraq? And Mosul?"

Hine was speaking gently, as if to a child who had just lost his parents. He had the feeling that Angell could explode at any moment.

"Yes. But ... that, and other things. My past, for one."

"Your past? What past?"

"My family. My ancestors. My fucking family tree."

"You're kidding."

"I wish I was. I can't seem to get out from under it. No matter what I do, or did, as a human being, it's always going to be seen in that context. Gregory Angell, scion of the Angell clan. You know, the ones who were involved with that murder case back a hundred years ago. The one on the Providence docks. And that xenophobic asshole, Lovecraft."

Angell's back story was whispered about in the department offices and hallways at Columbia, where he taught, but no one had ever heard him speak about it before. Everyone knew the story, or thought they knew it. The horror writer, H. P. Lovecraft, had mentioned the Angell family in his most famous short story, "The Call of Cthulhu," and linked it to his twisted idea about a cult of devil worshippers, or something. The fact that Angell's ancestor—George Gammel Angell, Professor Emeritus at Brown—had died on the Providence docks one holiday season back in the 1920s was seen as some kind of evidence that the cult actually existed. But the Angells were a well-known and well-respected dynasty in New England.

Thomas Angell came to Rhode Island with Roger Williams in

1636. From then on he gave rise to a family tree with an enviable pedigree. His grandson opened the Angell Tavern in Scituate, Rhode Island where George Washington once stayed. A later descendant, James Burrill Angell, was a professor of modern languages at Brown University—when Francis Wayland was president there—and had been an ambassador to China and to Turkey in the late nineteenth century; he also held posts as president of the University of Vermont as well as president of the University of Michigan, and had been an editor of the *Providence Journal*. James Angell's nephew, Frank Angell, founded an experimental psychology laboratory at Cornell in 1891 and the following year at Stanford University.

Thus, Gregory Angell came from a long and distinguished line of educators and Ph.D.s at a time when such advanced learning was much rarer than it is today. Gregory represented a legacy, and Hine was well aware of it. To see him now in such straits was inconsistent with what he knew of the man and his eminent background, regardless of the scurrilous tales told about the other Angell—George Gammel Angell—who was a respected academic and an authority on Middle Eastern languages himself. It wasn't George Angell's fault that a young Rhode Island writer of fantasy stories had stalked him and pestered the old man about rumors he had heard concerning a death cult somewhere in Louisiana or someplace. These days the H. P. Lovecraft field was undergoing a kind of renaissance, with renewed interest both at home and abroad in this strange recluse and his spooky yarns about octopus gods or some such thing. Hine had never been a fan, finding Lovecraft's style too ornate and purple for his tastes. Even as an adolescent, he had preferred the stories of Lord Dunsany or Arthur Machen to those of Lovecraft, and would rather choose a Marvel comic over a Lovecraft paperback any day. He had never taken seriously the story put out by Lovecraft that Gregory's ancestor—the aforementioned George Angell—had been murdered on the Providence docks and that it had to do with something called the cult of Cthulhu. He figured it was just because a relative nobody, a creep like Lovecraft, had used the name of a famous family to make a reputation for himself. What are they calling it these days? Fake news? Lovecraft had to be its godfather.

Now here was the result of all that nonsense. His good friend and colleague was on the run from government agents and some other bad guys. He was probably on the verge of getting himself kicked out of Columbia for whatever it was they claimed he had done. And all because some guy in an office somewhere in DC thought someone with Angell's ancestry would be a good choice for a dangerous overseas assignment in the most perilous place in the world.

He didn't think Angell ever had any kind of therapy for what must have been a severe case of PTSD after that Mosul event. All he knew was that Gregory started to withdraw from the academic world in so far as he was able to do so and still keep tenure. He stopped going to conferences. He stopped publishing. He kept up the bare minimum of classes, and Hine had the suspicion that Angell walked around strapped. If it ever came to light that he was carrying a concealed weapon onto the campus, he would have been arrested, probably convicted, and certainly would have lost his tenure and been kicked out of the university. Columbia is in New York City, which has some of the strictest gun control laws in the country.

"The whole Lovecraft episode came back to bite me on the ass, Steven. And I wasn't even born when that happened. Sins of the father, and all that." He looked up at his old friend, his eyes hollow and haunted, and said, "I killed a man, Steve. I shot him."

Angell started to talk about what happened in Nepal, hesitantly at first and then couldn't stop. He talked about the visit to the refugee camp in Turkey on the Syrian border, where they were attacked; the trip to Iraq and the firefight at the ancient site of Cutha, the Sumerian "Gate to the Underworld"; the insertion into Iran and the battle in Yazd at the Towers of Silence, the Zoroastrian burial site; the overland drive to the Afghan border, and his capture by the Nuristanis

in the area that used to be known as Kafiristan. He spoke of his
subsequent rescue and the ultimate confrontation with a sect or cult
that was conducting a weird ritual in the bowels of some mountain
in the Himalayas. It was there, amid the chanting and the incense
and the strange throng of devotees, that violence erupted once again
and someone—a spook who worked for one of the intelligence
agencies—was actually working with the cult, reading aloud from
the book that Angell was sent to retrieve. The agent seemed to be
working with the young woman he had seen at the refugee camp in
Turkey when this all began, and she was becoming possessed—"like
a priestess of *vodun*," Angell said, using the Haitian pronunciation,
but what would a voodoo priestess be doing in Nepal?—and over-
powered by whatever it was that the cult was summoning.

"It was some kind of priest. A high priest. Of that ... cult. He
was doing something ... I don't know ... something. He was raising
some kind of force. A spirit or ... or... or a ghost ... a monster.
Something. I didn't hesitate. I shot him. He was just some fruitcake.
A fanatic. But there were all those followers, chanting with him.
Armed to the teeth. We were down in the tunnels, in the caves.
And she was there. The Yezidi woman. I ... I hit her. In the head.
Knocked her down. I had to stop her, stop what she was doing. And
then I got out of there. Made my way to the Chinese border," he
said, skipping the most important part, the part that stopped the
entire process dead in its tracks. The part where he took part in the
ritual, chanting the invocation that would put the monster back in
its cage. At least for now.

Hine suspected Angell was keeping something back, but he
didn't press him.

"We have to get you out of here."

Zou Yin or "Traveling to the Underground"

They waited until the sun was down and the city crept into a sooth-
ing darkness. Hine brought in some food from the local restaurant,

one specializing in Szechuan fare, and the chilies restored Angell somewhat and brought some color back into his cheeks. He borrowed a few articles of clothing from Hine—they were roughly the same height but Hine was bigger around the waist—and since he had taken a shower and shaved he felt like a new man.

Hine went out first, to make sure the coast was clear, and Angell followed a minute later. They made it to the broad thoroughfare outside the university and mingled with the crowds.

Beijing had changed a great deal in the past thirty years, from a dark and paranoid city where locals were afraid to talk to foreigners and where everyone rode bicycles everywhere, to a brightly-lit, busy metropolis with traffic jams and stores bursting with goods both foreign and domestic. It would have been impossible for Hine and Angell—two Caucasian foreigners—to walk unnoticed in the Beijing of 1984; in 2014 it was almost too easy.

"Do you know where you're going?" he asked his friend.

"Greg, you know that I come here a few times every year. After a while, you get to know people. Especially in our field. When was the last time you visited the Lama Temple?"

The place Hine was talking about was a popular tourist attraction northeast of the Forbidden City. It was a Tibetan Buddhist institution, a former palace of the Ming Dynasty, replete with statues and thangkas.

"Not in a long time. Decades, maybe."

"Right. Well, that's where we're going. It's too far to walk so we'll get a taxi. There are always a few in front of the hotels. What we'll do is take one to another hotel I know and then switch cabs there. Just in case. If we're stopped and anyone asks for your passport or visa, just tell them you left all that back at my place. When they realize we're at the university they'll probably let us off without an argument."

"Does that happen a lot here?"

"Getting stopped by the Public Security Bureau? Not really. We'd have to be doing something to attract attention. This isn't like the old days when *waiguoren* stuck out like a sore thumb. There's a large expat population here now. No, we'll be okay. Just keep your head down and try not to act nervous."

Hine was as good as his word. They got a taxi in front of a busy hotel that catered to western tourists and took it as far as the International Hotel to the east of Tiananmen Square. There, they got out, walked into the hotel lobby, stood around briefly and then left again and got into another taxi that had just let out an American couple who were obviously on their first trip to China. They waited patiently as the couple's luggage was removed from the trunk and the husband spoke in very loud English to the driver as if volume could accomplish what a week with a Rosetta Stone course in Mandarin could not.

Hine bit his lip and stopped himself from helping the couple out. He did not want anyone to remember that he was there. Eventually the couple and the driver got sorted out and the two men got into the cab and headed for the Lama Temple.

In the northeast district of Dongcheng, the Lama Temple—or Yonghe Temple, as it is known locally—is a temple and monastery complex that was a center of the type of Tibetan Buddhism known as the Gelugpa—or Yellow Hat—sect, the version that is represented by the Dalai Lama. It houses some magnificent religious artworks. It is located within what used to be the walls of the old city, walls which were taken down after Mao's revolution liberated the country from both the Nationalist Chinese under Chiang Kai Shek and the foreigners who had effectively carved China up among themselves for centuries, starting with the infamous Opium Wars and extending through the bloody suppression of the Boxer Rebellion.

A look at maps of the old city of Beijing show that the layout of the metropolis was designed according to Chinese mystical principles. In the north of the city—not far from the Lama Temple—is the Temple of Earth. Directly opposite, in the south, is the famous Temple of Heaven. On the eastern side of the city is the Temple of the Sun, while the Temple of the Moon is directly opposite in the west. Roughly in the center of this layout is the Forbidden City: the residence of the emperors in pre-revolutionary times, and now a vast museum complex that is visited by millions of tourists every year. Directly opposite the Forbidden City is Tiananmen Square: the site of the student rebellion of 1989 that was brutally suppressed by military units from outside of Beijing under orders of Chinese Premier Deng Xiao Ping.

Earth and Heaven, Sun and Moon: these four temples form a kind of axis of spiritual power according to both Daoist and Confucian philosophy. The emperors would perform sacrifices in the appropriate temple according to the Chinese calendar, which itself was divided into "stems" and "branches" which divided up the hours of the day and the months of the year into occult segments, a practice that is still in use today in the geomancer's compass and the art of *feng shui*. The emperor himself stood at the very nexus between Heaven and Earth, and maintaining a solid and balanced relationship with Heaven meant that his kingdom on Earth would prosper. China is called the "Middle Kingdom" or *Zhong Guo*: which indicates the belief that China itself is midway between both Heaven and Earth, as well as being in the very center of the World.

Their taxi turned right onto Yonghegong Street, which would lead them directly to the Lama Temple itself. Angell had been there once, years ago, as part of an obligatory tour of the city while doing his post-doc. Although his specialty was Middle Eastern and Central Asian religions, China was important for several reasons not least of which was the Dunhuang Caves—a repository of thousands of ancient texts in various languages and scripts—and the discovery of a survival of an old and nearly forgotten Jewish community in Kaifeng. So even though his field was the religions and cultures of the ancient Middle East, there was considerable crossover with those of China and the cities along the Silk Road across the Gobi Desert and into Beijing itself. When he fled the underground cavern in

Nepal he had no particular direction in mind and simply followed roads and streams to the Tibetan border, evading capture by Chinese soldiers and relying on the kindness of random villagers. At last, freezing and starving, he hitched a ride on the back of a truck driven by some congenial smugglers that led away from the Himalayas and skirted the borders of Sikkim, Bhutan and Bangladesh. As they traveled, they distributed small bundles of what Angell could only assume was some kind of narcotic, probably opium, in exchange for gold, some greasy bills in a currency he did not recognize, and what appeared to be pieces of jade. He spoke some Mandarin and was able to communicate in brief phrases with his hosts whose native language seemed to be a Burmese dialect. Angell stayed quiet and sat in the back of the truck as a kind of good luck charm for the first few hundred miles. He was dirty, his clothing reduced to rags, so no one paid too much attention to him as the smugglers paid off border patrols and local gendarmes in a kind of hit-and-run all the way to the Chinese border.

That would not last, however, as the truck and its criminal passengers ventured across another border and into Assam State in India. There was one particularly dangerous moment outside Dibrugarh, their ultimate destination, as his companions considered robbing him and leaving him for dead by the side of a desolate stretch of road. They grabbed him by the arms. Angell was too physically weak to resist very much. Then they opened his backpack in search of valuables and saw the Book. The sight of it seemed to exert a strange influence over them and they released him, abandoning their original plan, and taking it upon themselves to assist the stranger in any way they could. They could not read the text of the Book, but they saw the diagrams and recognized them for what they represented. They knew that killing the man who had the Book would not terminate the Book's existential threat to themselves. Better to keep him alive so he could remain in possession of the Book. Better to keep him responsible for whatever happened.

Once in Dibrugarh, a city on the banks of the Brahmaputra

River, famous for its tea and for its scientific establishment—the India Space Research Organization held a symposium on space science in Dibrugarh earlier that year —the smugglers introduced Angell to one of their "associates" who helped escaping fugitives cross over from Assam into Yunnan Province in China. To do that they would have to enter Kachin State in northern Burma: an area notorious as a center of the global opium trade.

"We're here."

Angell jolted awake, unaware that he had dozed off in the taxi on the way to the Lama Temple. For a second, he thought he was back in Kachin State and not in Beijing. This was happening more and more frequently, and he would have to get a handle on it. He could not afford to drop off at every opportunity.

He looked outside the window at the building's entrance. It was typical of the Ming style you saw everywhere in China, all dark red walls and tan sloping roof with a giant black door.

"It looks like it's closed for the evening."

Hine smiled. "Not a problem. I've got a friend 'inside'."

He paid the driver and they got out, gawking like two tourists in front of one of China's most famous Buddhist temples. Angell was still exhausted, but felt better after his rest and shower in Hine's room plus the quick meal. He realized that Hine was the first congenial person with whom he had spoken ever since that day Aubrey accosted him on the Brooklyn Heights Promenade and convinced him to go to that refugee camp on the Turkish-Syrian border. That was probably what prompted his heartfelt confession to Hine about all that had happened since then: merely the presence of an old friend who knew him from "before" and with whom he could speak English instead of Farsi, Urdu, Arabic or his broken Mandarin. Seeing the professor had reminded him of who he was, and of what he had left behind when all of this began, and even caused him to doubt some of the things he witnessed in the underground cavern in Nepal. He vaguely wondered what had happened to his apartment in Red Hook in the meantime. Was the US government paying his rent? And what had Aubrey done with his Glock?

He hitched his backpack with its sinister contents onto his back and followed Hine through a side door he had not noticed before.

As it shut behind them, a man standing across the street watched them enter. Academics were some of the easiest marks to follow, he mused. They were too smart for their own good and knew it. Hubris made them sloppy. He appreciated the little tango with the two taxis and the hotels, like something out of a 1950s spy novel, but tradecraft was not their strong suit.

Special Agent Maxwell Prime—formerly of the FBI but now with an obscure agency whose roots were buried within the war room of the White House—shrugged and opened his encrypted smartphone, sending a message to a man he knew only as "Aubrey." The message was brief.

"Chatter confirmed."

BOOK TWO

To succeed in this operation, it is needful that whosoever makes the experiment shall do in all things as hereinafter enjoined. Let him choose a small chamber or cabinet which has not been frequented by impure women for at least nine days. Let such place be well cleansed and consecrated by aspersions and fumigations. In the middle of said chamber let there be a table covered with a white cloth; set as follows thereon—to wit, a new glass phial filled with spring water, drawn shortly before the operation; three small tapers of virgin wax mixed with human fat; a sheet of virgin parchment six inches square; a raven's quill cut ready for writing; a china ink-well filled with fresh ink; a small pan furnished with the materials for a fire. *Let there also be a young boy of nine or ten years, cleanly and modestly dressed and of good behaviour, who must be placed near the table.*

> — "The Invocation of Uriel," from the *Grimorium Verum*, as printed in *The Book of Ceremonial Magic*, Arthur Edward Waite

CHAPTER SEVEN

AUBREY STARED AT THE DECRYPTED communication he had received from his agent, Maxwell Prime, in Beijing. "Chatter confirmed," was all it said, but it spoke volumes. Their frantic search for Gregory Angell was nearing an end. How the hell did that middle-aged college professor make it all the way to China from Nepal on his own? And not just China, but across the whole damned country, west to east, without being discovered or apprehended by border patrols, internal security, or tribal chieftains? Hell, James Bond had gadgets, weapons, and an entire British intelligence service backing him up. All Gregory Angell had was himself, and whatever inner resources he could muster. Hollywood had glamorized secret agents and that was the problem. There is no glamour in what they do, only a constant baseline of anxiety bordering on sheer terror, with equal amounts of boredom.

He admired Professor Angell. A man so consumed with self-doubt that he could hardly get out of bed in the morning back in Brooklyn, who then rose to the occasion (albeit reluctantly) and surprised them all. But there was another aspect to Gregory Angell, and it haunted him.

Aubrey was nothing if not a company man. He had been in service for longer than many had been alive. But something about the Angell episode tore at his insides. What they had done to him was unfair. Angell previously had served his country faithfully, twice: once in Afghanistan and again in Iraq. He served honorably, embedded with the troops, translating, interpreting, trying to save lives in the middle of a battlefield environment.

And then we did this to him. Pulled him out of his comfortable berth in Brooklyn, a scholar's apartment of books and antiques and solitude, and sent him into a veritable Hell. And he succeeded in his mission, averting a catastrophe. In fact, he did everything they had asked him to do and more.

And now Monroe was willing to set him up for murder if he didn't come in from the cold and bring the Book with him. Aubrey had a mind to ignore the communication from Beijing and let Angell have his lead. Let him go to ground. Disappear and become someone else. Hide from his memories. Drown his sorrows. Whatever. Just … *run.*

But he couldn't do that. Aubrey was a company man. He served Monroe, and Monroe served the nation and, truth be told, much of the world as well.

Aubrey was already on his way on another segment of his itinerary, as per Monroe's instructions. He knew he would not be pulled off and sent to China. They had other agents for that, less senior but younger and faster and more capable in the field. This was no longer a recruitment operation, or running agents in hostile territory. Not any more. This was "search and apprehend" or, failing that, destroy.

Aubrey forwarded the message to Monroe, and then broke the encrypted connection. The die was cast. They would send the hounds of hell after him.

"God help you," he said to Gregory Angell in a whisper that was more prayer than suggestion. "God help you."

CHAPTER EIGHT

THE INTERIOR OF THE LAMA TEMPLE was dark, and redolent with the aroma of incense and old wood. As Angell's eyes got accustomed to the gloom, he saw a man standing in front of them. He was bald, about forty-five, and dressed in deep, burgundy-colored robes. About five-nine, he wore glasses with round, wire-frame lenses, like John Lennon. Or Janis Joplin.

He and Hine seemed to know each other well, for the two men embraced and exchanged pleasantries in a mixture of Mandarin and some other language that Angell took to be Tibetan.

Hine switched to English, for Angell's benefit.

"This is my colleague and friend, Doctor Gregory Angell, of Columbia University in New York."

The monk bowed.

"You are welcome here, as is your friend, Doctor Hine," the monk replied. He spoke English with a faint British accent.

"I understand your visit here tonight is something of an emergency." It was said as a statement and not a question.

"That is correct, Rinpoche. We are being followed by agents of our government."

The monk nodded, turned, and signaled for them to follow him.

"They will not enter here, not at this time. They have no jurisdiction in China. It's the Public Security Bureau that worries me. They enjoy unfettered access."

He led the two men down a corridor. On the right, Angell could see a large courtyard with an enormous brazier in the center. There were lit coals still in the brazier, which was probably the source of the incense smell.

On the left were doors leading to small rooms. Some of these appeared to be offices for the organization and maintenance of the temple. Farther down, there were individual cells for the monks who lived on-site. There were no depictions of the Dalai Lama, no evidence at all. A mere photograph of the Dalai Lama would be grounds for arrest and imprisonment.

The monk opened a door about two-thirds of the way down, and inside there was a small wooden table, a few chairs, and a lamp that was burning with a warm, inviting glow. On the wall facing the door was a thangka—an icon painted on silk. Angell could see at once that it was of the Green Tara, a goddess whose veneration is believed to have begun not in Tibet or India, but in Indonesia. The significance of that was lost on him at the time, but would come back to haunt him later.

The three men entered and the monk waved the two foreigners to the seats facing the low table. In a moment, another monk entered with a tray carrying three tea cups and a clay pot of tea. He set the tray down, bowed, and left without a word, closing the door behind him.

The monk proceeded to pour the tea, and everyone was silent for a moment.

It was only after he had handed the cups to the two Americans that he asked the first question.

"Steven, what kind of trouble are you in?"

"Well, it's not really me, Rinpoche, but Doctor Angell here. My government thinks he's some kind of terrorist or something. I know that's not true. But I don't think we can trust them to come to the same conclusion."

The monk turned to Angell, who was sipping his cup of tea.

"This is delicious."

"It's called Guan Yin tea, the real one. It was a gift from a local businessman who does not wish to be identified. I am gratified by the pleasure you take in it."

Angell nodded, and set the cup down.

"Rinpoche, thank you for your hospitality," he said, addressing the monk directly for the first time. "I have been wandering through Asia for some time now, spending a great deal of time among Buddhists in Nepal and in Gansu Province, before going to

Mongolia and then to Beijing. I have always been received warmly and without hesitation. But I am fearful that my presence here may endanger you or your community."

The monk nodded, thoughtfully, before answering.

"You need not worry on that score, Doctor Angell. If I may speak freely, and among friends?" He glanced at Hine, who nodded in encouragement. "We are accustomed to interference from the authorities, but this temple is an important propaganda tool for the regime. It draws tourists from all over the world, which is important, but it also implies a greater degree of religious tolerance than actually exists.

"So, perhaps you can tell me what the problem is, and how we can help you?"

Angell was silent for a moment, not knowing where to begin or even how this Buddhist monk and scholar could possibly help him. That was when his friend came to his rescue.

"Doctor Angell was involved in a sensitive mission for an agency of our government," Hine began. "Something went wrong with that mission, and Doctor Angell had to escape in order to survive. We need to get him to a safe haven somewhere so that he can clear his name."

The monk nodded, and was silent a moment.

Then he looked up and stared directly into Angell's eyes. "Did this have anything to do with the events that transpired in Khembalung?"

The mention of the name of the cavern where Angell was forced to kill a man only months earlier had the effect of a right hook to his jaw. Angell sat back, eyes wide, shocked that this man in a monastery in the middle of Beijing would have any idea about what had taken place thousands of miles away in another country, in secret, among members of some kind of cult that even Angell could not identify.

Steven Hine looked similarly startled, and his eyes went from the monk back to Angell and back to the monk again.

"You knew?" was all Angell could croak.

"Our country was invaded, Doctor Angell, but our communications networks are quite reliable. Tibetan people have remained in contact with each other since the invasion, using primitive forms of correspondence supplemented by more—shall we say—arcane methods? When something happens in one of the *beyul*—the hidden cities—it is transmitted almost immediately through the network of monasteries and temples that range from Nepal and Ladakh all the way through Tibet, Gansu Province, Szechuan … well, many places. You get the idea. And that means that our people learn of it even in the West. For instance, in your Tibet Houses. The ones funded by your famous actor, Richard Gere, I believe?"

Steven Hine could only smile and shake his head, but Angell was considerably more agitated.

"That means that what happened there, in Khembalung, is common knowledge?"

"No need to worry," the monk replied, with a calming gesture that Hine recognized immediately for what it was: a *mudra*. "In the first place, the Tibetan people—well, most of them, anyway—are on your side. They will not endanger you and, in fact, I believe you are aware that they protected you along the way? Even the Mongolians you met were Buddhists. Word had spread. You were among friends. Always, in fact."

"But … but I … I had to …"

"You killed a man. Yes. We know."

"But, you're Buddhists. You believe killing is wrong. That I have defiled myself, maybe even this temple by being here!"

"Do not agitate yourself, Doctor. Let me tell you something you may not know. Even His Holiness, who must not be named within these walls or even in this country, raised an army to fight his invaders. An army that was trained and funded by your CIA."

"It's true," offered Hine. "I wrote a paper about this myself. The Tibetans were trained in our American northwest, and then sent back to wage guerrilla war."

It was intended to soothe Angell and to relieve him of his burden of violence and death, but somehow knowing that even the Dalai Lama could authorize killing made a rock sink deep within his heart. He was grateful for the support he was getting, both from his old colleague and now this venerable monk, but he was still uncomfortable with the thought that the Dalai Lama—whom some considered the highest spiritual authority in the world—had sanctioned warfare.

This meant that the massacre he had witnessed in Mosul all those years ago was not the exception, but the rule. The name of the religion didn't matter. Muslim or Christian, Jew or Buddhist, everyone killed. Everyone slaughtered. Everyone died.

He suddenly was exhausted. He was a stranger in a strange land, and in peril of his life, but all he really wanted to do was sleep. Sleep, and maybe, if he was lucky, never wake up again.

"People don't see us," explained the monk to Angell. "They see Tibetans as spiritual refugees. As exotic individuals who do nothing but pray and smile and suffer. The Chinese are more observant, of course, because we represent a political threat to them as well as a spiritual one, but the propaganda value in providing some resources for Tibetan Buddhists—especially among the foreign tourists— outweighs the negatives.

"But we are as human as anyone else, Doctor Angell, and perhaps even more so."

"Please. Call me Gregory."

"As you wish. You see, Gregory, Tibetans represent a nation in diaspora, like the Jews for thousands of years. We are new at it, but are working hard to perfect our mechanisms for survival. The intense opposition of China is one issue, but the casual opposition of a western world consumed by materialism is another. Ironically, both Marxism and capitalism are manifestations of materialism. Marxism bans religion; capitalism merely tolerates it, like a cultural artifact. We Tibetans intend to preserve not only our own national culture and our religion, like anyone else, but also a way of looking at the world.

This way is not unique to us but nevertheless it is under assault from every corner of the globe.

"You witnessed this first-hand, in Khembalung. Neither Marxism nor capitalism could have prepared you for what you saw in that mountain cavern. You are a scholar of religion, and yet when confronted with the terror of the Divine, you were shocked. Traumatized, I think?"

"The terror of ... the ... *Divine?*"

"You know the history of religions, Gregory. You know that the Divine has always been experienced with terror."

"Yes, but not all experiences of terror are divine. What I experienced in that cavern ... the chanting devotees, the trembling of the very ground itself, the growing realization that something ... something truly terrible was coming ..."

"It was all exactly as you would have reacted had God appeared to you on a mountaintop in Sinai."

Angell shook his head. "I thought Buddhists don't believe in God?"

"We don't. We understand 'god' to be an illusion, or a delusion if you wish. The opiate of the people?" he added, mischievously.

"I'm sorry. I guess I'm exhausted, or maybe just dense, but I'm not following you."

"What I am trying, inexpertly, to say is that what you experienced is what we monks experience every day. It is contact, contact with the Other. Another mode or manifestation of existence. As one gets closer to the experience of *advaita*, of non-duality, one will be beset on all sides by fearsome entities tearing at the moorings of the mind. It is difficult to tell a god from a demon, Gregory, and at a certain point there really is no difference. No difference at all. That book you guard with your life should tell you that."

"The book. How did you know ...?"

"The same network that told me of your difficulty in Khembalung also informed me of the reason for it. The book you protect contains the Tantras for making contact with primordial powers, does it not?"

Angell looked over at his backpack with its explosive contents.

"To tell you the truth, Rinpoche, I have no clue what that book contains. I have had it now for months, and I have tried to understand it, but its meaning is elusive. You called it a Tantra?"

The monk nodded. "Like some of the Tantras of Buddhism and of the worshippers of Shiva and Shakti in India, your book is on the surface a text of black magic, of pacts with demonic forces, of the summoning of dark powers."

"On the surface?"

"But if you look deeper into the structure of the text and weigh the commentary carefully you will understand that it is—like our Tantras—a book about the creation of the experienced world. A creation that took place long before there were human beings on this planet yet when the Earth still harbored sentient life, and a sentient race of beings as different from us as whales are different from mosquitoes."

Hine, who had been silent during the exchange, chose this moment to intervene. He saw Angell's discomfort with the whole discussion as it did not seem to address his concerns directly.

"Your tradition speaks of underground cities and ancient races, does it not?" he asked.

The learned monk nodded soberly, his eyes trained on Angell. "You have heard of Shambhala? And of the Kalki Avatar?"

Angell shrugged. "Asian religion is not my field, but I had a crash course recently."

The monk smiled in acknowledgement.

"It is said that the Kalki Avatar will ride out from Shambhala at some point in the future, when the stars are right. Some of the western experts believe this may refer to your Kutulu."

That name again. How was it that everybody seemed to know about Kutulu except him?

"Excuse me. When the 'stars are right,' what does that mean? Some kind of astrology? An occult calendar?"

"Not exactly. The western calendars and the Asian calendars are not identical, as you know. The division of time into segments has some similarity between cultures, but what the phrase means in this case is something more astronomical than astrological. It refers to the actual positions of certain stars as seen against the backdrop of the sky from the vantage point of a specific location on Earth."

"Which location?"

The monk shrugged apologetically.

"That, we don't know. We have a guess, but it is pure speculation."

Angell and Hine looked at him expectantly.

"Well, we believe it is at the Eurasian continental pole of inaccessibility."

Angell and Hine looked at each other, clueless.

"This point is the furthest inland one can be without access to any of the oceans. The center of the landmass, in other words. That point is said to be here, in China, but far to the west near the border with Kazakhstan."

"Why there? I mean, why would anyone derive astronomical calculations from that point? Is there a city there, a shrine of some importance, something like that?"

"There are several schools of belief, but the most relevant one pertains to a tomb that is said to have been constructed there, below the earth."

"Is there such a tomb?"

"Only in legends, and even then the legends disagree with each other. There is no verifiable historical source for this information, and in truth there is nothing there. It's a restricted area. The roads have no names, and there are no official cities or towns. It is at the edge of the desert. One cannot imagine a more lonely or isolated spot. Well, there is one other …"

"And that would be?"

"Point Nemo. It is a point in the middle of the Pacific Ocean, thousands of kilometers from the nearest islands. Another pole of inaccessibility."

"So, you have two poles of inaccessibility, one on the earth and the other beneath the waves. Which one is the cult using?"

"We don't know, of course. They may be using both."

"Both? Why?"

"The legends concerning their High Priest, the Being they refer to as Kutulu, state that he is buried in this sunken city. But there are conflicting statements. In some cases, this city is believed to be beneath the waves, that is, in the ocean somewhere. In other cases, his city is below the earth. Some even say it is somewhere in Saudi Arabia, in the Empty Quarter. Again, just legends."

It was Hine's turn to interrupt.

"Rinpoche, we are not so much concerned as to which of these places is the *real* location of the *mythical* tomb, but which one the cult *believes* is real. That is the one they will be using for their calculations."

"Just so. In that case, it could be the one in China. All the earlier legends have Chinese references. A place called the Plateau of Leng, for instance, or Kadath. These all reflect an Asian locale, most likely near the western desert in the same general region as the pole of inaccessibility, a whole day's drive out of Urumqi. There was also a 'Chinaman,' I believe, in the story told by your famous American author, the story dealing specifically with Kutulu?"

"You have heard of Lovecraft here in China? In a Tibetan Buddhist temple in Beijing?" Angell was, if anything, more depressed at this thought than anything else he had heard so far.

"Lovecraft is well-known world-wide, but you knew that Gregory, did you not?"

"So people keep reminding me."

"The geographical location of the tomb, however, may not be as important as its position in time. To the people of the legends, the position of the stars at a certain time will reveal the location of the site on Earth. Like your New Testament, with the magicians following the Star of Bethlehem to the birthplace of the Christ child."

"So ... this Cthulhu is as real in some sense as, say, the Judeo-Christian God?"

"His Cthulhu is our Kutulu, or more properly Kusulu. It means a dead shaman, but one who is still somehow alive. A dead shaman coming back from the dead. When we of the Vajrayana tradition read this story, we recognize the references immediately. Lovecraft's Cthulhu is a high priest of an ancient race of gods, is he not? Who lies 'dead but dreaming'? To us, this means he is in the *bardo* state, the state between incarnations, after death and before birth. The people with whom you are struggling, and from whom you are fleeing, are devotees of this high priest, this Kusulu, and are attempting to awaken him, to force him to incarnate in this world, to leave the bardo state.

"That, Doctor Angell, would be a disaster."

Angell was getting sick and tired of being told that the world was coming to an end and only he could do anything about it. It would be understandable if there was somebody standing there with a finger on the nuclear button and all Angell had to do was stop him somehow. But this ... this was all smoke and mirrors, gods and demons. How was he supposed to do anything about this ... this chimera? It was like asking someone to save the world but without telling them how or why or where or when. You might as well hand him a pineapple and a three-hole punch and tell him to make blueberry tacos.

Of course, he could not deny what he had been through the past few months. He could not deny what he had experienced in the caves of Khembalung. But that was when he was surrounded by a dangerous cult, with weapons all over the place, and people dying. That was over now. Whatever that cult had been up to had failed. So why couldn't Angell go home? Why were people still hunting him?

"Greg?"

He started. Evidently he had been daydreaming. Or dozing. He looked around and saw that the light was coming up. It was a new day.

"How long have I been asleep?"

"Only a few hours," replied Hine. They were alone in the room where the monk had been talking to them. "We decided to let you crash. But we're going to have to get out of here soon. We can't stay. And, anyway, we need to get you out of China."

Angell stretched his arms and legs, trying to get some feeling back into them. He had fallen asleep half-sitting and was a little stiff.

"How do you propose we do that? I don't have any identification. I'm in the country illegally."

Hine smiled.

"We've got it covered."

CHAPTER NINE

THE FLOOR AROUND GREGORY ANGELL was covered in hair. His own hair.

Steven Hine stepped back with the scissors and razor and examined his handiwork.

"You look like an ascetic. You're so malnourished that the bald head looks good on you."

"I'm sure this was necessary."

"It's for your own safety, Greg."

"So everyone keeps telling me. Remind me again how this is supposed to work?"

"Like we told you. It's simple. We monkify you as best we can. Shaved head, no beard. Some maroon colored robes. Maybe a pair of horn rims if we can find them. You're already pretty tanned after a month wandering around Mongolia, so your white skin won't stand out. Then we throw you in with a group of monks traveling south, to Shanghai. From there, we can get you out, at least as far as Hong Kong."

"What'll I do for papers?"

"Rinpoche is working on that. There are some foreign visitors who are here for the same conference I am. They're Buddhist scholars from the West. We're going to make an arrangement with one of them. We'll know better in an hour or so, depending on Rinpoche's powers of persuasion."

"And if that doesn't work?"

"We'll figure something out before you reach Shanghai. There's another temple there, and Rinpoche has a good relationship with the abbot. At any rate, you will be met at the station when the tour group arrives. You'll be separated from the rest and taken to a safe house."

Angell got up from his rickety chair and examined himself in an old hand mirror.

"Jesus."

Hine grinned. "Not quite, unless you mean the day *after* the crucifixion, in which case you would be right."

"Thanks."

"Don't feel bad. Hair grows back in, whether you're in prison or a free man."

Angell put down the mirror and looked his friend in the eye.

"Do you trust this man?"

"You mean the Rinpoche? Sure. I've known him since they opened China to religious studies scholars. Before that, we had a written correspondence for about two years. He's had to put up with a lot, just to maintain this temple. He was in prison himself, during the Cultural Revolution, as a young Buddhist."

"That means he has a lot to protect. Why would he risk all that for someone he never met, a foreigner and an atheist besides?"

Hine shook his head, the smile not leaving his face.

"You're not an atheist, Gregory."

"I don't know what I am. Not after Nepal. Not after that … that thing I saw rising up from the ground like a horror-movie monster. That thing existed. Maybe still exists. That's the closest I've ever come to God, and it wasn't pretty. Maybe until I have an answer for what that is, I'll have to say I'm … I don't know. An agnostic, or something. But I'm not a believer."

"You're a jilted lover, that's all. A lover may lose faith in his love. Maybe the spark isn't there anymore. Maybe she cheated on him. Maybe he just stopped caring. But he doesn't deny she *exists*."

"I'm sorry, Steve. Whether God exists or not is not the issue. Not for me, anyway. I reject a God who allows horrible things to happen to innocent people. If God is an evil megalomaniac, then we should do all we can to defeat him, or at least undermine his plans. But if God is the God of Love, where the hell is he today?"

Hine shrugged. "Helping you to escape?"

At that moment, before Angell could voice his objection, the lama walked into the room and admired Hine's handiwork.

"You will pass for one of us, Doctor Angell."

Angell wasn't sure if that was intended as a comment on his appearance, or on his philosophy.

"There may be an inspection of your papers on the train. Keep them close. Guard them with your life. You will only have one opportunity to make it to Shanghai. After that, it will be too hot in China for you."

They were walking out of the Lama Temple and to a waiting bus. A row of monks was waiting to board for the short ride to the main railway terminal. Angell was self-conscious in his new bald-headed state and monk's robes, but he held onto his backpack with the infamous Book and tried to look pious. Or, at least, casual.

The owner of the passport and train ticket was a foreigner, a devotee from Boston named Stuart Weinberg. The photo of Weinberg was a good match for Angell, especially since both were bald and roughly the same age. Weinberg had been initiated at the Tibetan temple on Staten Island: a place Angell knew well from his graduate student days. The real Weinberg was staying in seclusion at the Lama Temple in his street clothes. He would wait a few days before reporting his passport stolen.

Steven Hine had stayed behind. He did not want to be seen on the street with Angell in case the temple was being watched, because that would give the game away. Instead, they had made their goodbyes in front of a statue of the Buddha before the tourists were let in.

"I hope to see you again, Greg."

"I hope it'll be with more hair."

"Take it easy, man. I'll do the best I can to cover your escape with the authorities, especially with that guy from the embassy. Whoever the hell he was."

"I appreciate everything you've done. I mean it."

"Don't worry about it. And be careful with that Book. If I were you, I would use whatever time you have during this trip out of China to find out as much as you can about it. Maybe there's something in there that will make sense to you. Something you can use."

"I've been avoiding reading it. I carry it around like a bag of karma, after what happened. But, you're right. I have to man up and see what it's all about."

"Do you need anything done back in the States? Any messages you want me to bring? Phone calls, rent checks, that sort of thing?"

Angell shook his head. He looked over to the street entrance, and saw that the monks were forming up to board the tour bus.

"I can't think of anything. My rent is paid with direct deposit, but I have no idea how much cash is left in the bank. Probably enough for the next few months, especially since I'm not spending anything these days."

"That reminds me," said Hine. "Weinberg had some cash on him, but we let him keep it. He's gonna need all he can get once he tells the embassy he's out a passport. Here." He held out a small roll of bills. Some American dollars and some *renminbi*. "You'll need both."

"I can't …"

He pressed the wad into Angell's hand.

"Don't be *meshuggah*. You'll need cash. You can pay me back when you return Stateside. And if you don't, mail it to me. I'll look forward to receiving a bunch of strange-looking bills in an envelope with an exotic postmark."

Angell accepted the cash. He knew he needed it, regardless of how obligated it made him feel.

"Now I'm a real fugitive, I guess. Fake identification, bumming cash from friends."

"And I'm aiding and abetting. So what? What are friends for?"

"Not for this."

"Damned straight! Take it easy, Greg. Be careful. And find a way to let me know you're okay."

They shook hands and Angell turned at the sound of the bus starting up.

"That's my ride."

"See ya."

Angell walked away from the man who had just saved his life and through the door to the waiting queue of monks, not knowing what the next few minutes—much less the next few days—would bring.

Steven Hine watched him go for awhile. This had to be the strangest few days in his own life in a long time. He hoped he would not regret it.

He turned around and went into the small room where Weinberg was waiting, drinking tea and flipping through an old copy of *China Daily*.

"So, what's a nice Jewish boy like you doing in a place like this?"

CHAPTER TEN

CUNEO WRENCHED HIS BACK but the effort was worth it.

The thing they were calling the "freezer" had surrendered to their feverish attempts to crack it open. The statue or idol that formed its lid had bent over sufficiently so that it lifted the freezer's lid partway. A hideous stench roiled out of the compartment like the fog of death, but cleared away almost at once to reveal precisely what Cuneo had feared he would find.

"Back away!" he shouted to the assembled cops. "Make a hole!" The uniforms and detectives pressed back against the walls as Cuneo motioned to the medical examiner.

"We need a gurney," he whispered. "And a bus."

The CSI could only glance inside the box and suppress a gasp.

"You gotta be shitting me, detective."

"I shit you not. It's still alive."

"How the fuck can you tell?"

Across the street, the Asian woman who had screamed had disappeared into the crowd. Two uniformed patrolmen who were assigned to watch the perimeter ran after her, but it was a half-hearted attempt. Just some crazy bitch, they told each other. They walked back to the yellow tape and just shook their heads at their sergeant.

After a few minutes an ambulance arrived at the scene which made the assembled crowd curious. They had heard that the old lady had died, sure enough, but she lived alone. Who was the ambulance for? And why were so many cops still milling around?

Two EMTs raced out of the ambulance with a gurney and entered the fine old home. Within minutes, they were fast-walking the gurney out and into the ambulance. On top of the gurney, secured by straps, was a small body of some kind, covered in a hospital issue blanket and hooked up to an oxygen mask.

Something had been alive in there, and it wasn't an adult.

When Cuneo finally made his report later that evening he had to explain why and how he knew that there was something alive in the freezer.

In the first place, it wasn't really a freezer, he explained. It had the same dimensions and a metal shell of some kind, encasing a construction made of stone which was why it was so damned heavy, but in reality it was now a kind of incubator. He realized this when he analyzed the arcane symbols that had been painted on it. There was a line of what appeared to be Egyptian hieroglyphics across the bottom of one side of the box and prominent among them—repeated several times, standing alone and not part of a word group—was the symbol of a circle bisected by several horizontal lines, like a sieve or a grate. Below that some figures were crudely drawn, what appeared to be men in loincloths carrying poles or standards in a procession, single-file. On top of these poles were birdlike creatures—half-bird, half-man?—and banners of some kind, and in one instance a representation of what Cuneo recognized as … a placenta.

In ancient Egypt, the pharaoh's placenta was referred to as the "king's twin." It was believed to contain a spiritual double of the pharaoh. It was depicted on the Narmer Palette, for instance, as having two lobes and a descending umbilicus: a remarkably precise anatomical rendering amid all the other more abstract iconography. Other ancient cultures had similar beliefs, and in some cases the placenta was buried with great ceremony.

A quick look at the other symbols on the box—some crude, some intricately and artistically drawn and painted—confirmed his suspicion. They were all representations of conception and birth, and in some cases of the vaginal opening and the birth canal. But these were not clinical depictions, or even very accurate. What they were—Cuneo realized, due to the research in ancient religions he had performed after that bizarre case in the Ninth Ward—were occult symbols, pagan semiotics, sorcerer spells. He didn't recognize all of them, or even half of them, but the ones he did remember—coupled with the fact that the box was connected to a tube or pipe and the idol was, too—all came together to suggest that what he was looking at was a giant, artificial placenta.

And therefore the only object it possibly could contain would have to be some kind of fetus.

But what kind?

The crime scene techs had photographed everything before it was moved, and Cuneo now examined the printouts. He hated looking at evidence on a computer screen. He always thought he missed important data that way. Holding a hard copy in his hand meant that he could pass a number of sheets back and forth and look at everything from different angles. He never got the knack of doing that with a PC or a tablet.

When they had opened the box at last, Cuneo could see a tiny chest rising and falling at a tremendous rate. It seemed it was gasping for breath. He could not make out its gender from the accumulated fluids that covered its body, nor could he identify its race or anything else about it except for the fact that it was about eighteen inches long and seemed to have four limbs and a head. When the med techs got there, they balked at reaching in and removing the thing from the box, insisting that whatever it was, it wasn't remotely human and may not even be mammalian. But Cuneo insisted, and they pulled on thick rubber gloves and gingerly reached into the box, feeling around the body for anything connecting it to the box—as Cuneo instructed—and, finding none, carefully lifted it out of the box and set it down carefully on the gurney. That's when Cuneo insisted that they attach an oxygen mask.

There was resistance to that, since they could not identify a nose or mouth. The CSI tech shone a halogen light at the small body and what stared back at them was enough to cause one of the med techs to lurch out of the basement and up the stairs, finding a toilet just in the nick of time.

It was a face, of sorts. It had two expressive eyes and a nasal opening that seemed to be flush with the rest of its face. That is, there was no nose to speak of. A slit below that "nose" seemed to serve as a mouth. There was no umbilicus that they could find, and Cuneo suspected that the large tube that ran into the bottom of the box served as a connection to whatever was sending nutrients into it. They would have to trace the line to discover the source, but it would be tricky as the tube ran into the retaining wall where it met the concrete floor.

As long as you thought of the being in the box as human, you would have nightmares. As a human it would be considered horribly freakish. Cuneo thought back on the day forty years earlier when he was on detail in Brooklyn Heights. He was a rookie then, and they were making a movie called *The Sentinel* in the apartment buildings facing the Promenade. There were buses arriving with passengers who were congenitally and hideously deformed, being used as extras in the film and representing demons. Cuneo thought it was the most exploitative and callous thing he had ever seen at that point in his young career. The fetus reminded him of that day long ago, and it wasn't a pleasant memory.

But if you thought of it as some kind of hairless animal creature, you could get through the day. The problem was, he didn't know what it was and he was waiting for the hospital to get back to him. The emergency room docs didn't have a clue, but they were fascinated nonetheless (which Cuneo found a trifle weird). They were measuring and weighing and prodding and probing when he left and returned to the station house. But Cuneo knew that someone had gone to great length to build and maintain that bizarre contraption in the basement—and to brick it up behind a wall, like some modern-day Montresor from Poe's story "The Cask of Amontillado"—and murdered the old lady who lived there, to boot. The case had a lot in common with the other murders in the Ninth Ward, and when he put the photos from both crime scenes together on his desk it was like the storyboard for some low budget horror-flick.

Some of the signs were duplicated in both scenes. The *vesica piscis* for instance, and the lingam and yoni glyphs, but there were disturbing distortions of these standard religious icons, as if representing sexual organs that had been altered in some way, through surgery or maybe radiation. Or something. He wasn't sure.

But if you had gone to all the trouble to build and conceal a crazy-ass incubator in the basement of a house in a wealthy New Orleans neighborhood, why would you call attention to it by killing the old lady who lived there? And why would you leave that elaborate device unplugged and powering down with a live specimen of ... something ... abandoned within it? It didn't make sense.

In the midst of these ruminations two uniformed patrolmen walked into the station at the end of their shift. He recognized them as part of the detail at the crime scene earlier.

"That was some crazy bitch, right?"

"Screamin' like that, in the middle of the street."

"But how did she just disappear like that? Right in front of our eyes?"

"She didn't disappear, man. We're just too fuckin' fat to chase anything faster than a cheeseburger."

Cuneo turned around in his swivel chair and regarded the two men thoughtfully.

"Excuse me?"

The two cops turned, the smiles fading from their faces when they realized it was the weird detective from New York who was talking to them.

"Detective?"

"Just now. You were at the crime scene, right? The DB in Belle Chasse?"

"Yes, sir."

"You said you saw something strange when you were there?"

"Sir?"

"Crazy bitch, right? Screaming?"

The two cops exchanged glances. Then one of them replied,

"Yes. That's right. An Oriental .. I mean, Asian ... woman. Just stood across the street from the scene."

"And she was screaming? Was she saying anything? I mean, words and not just a scream?"

"Well, yeah," said the other cop. "But we couldn't make it out. It wasn't, like, in English or anything."

"I see. Was it Spanish?"

"Don't think so. Not French, either. My daddy spoke French to my mother, so I would have recognized it."

"Was it Chinese, maybe?"

"Could have been, I guess. She looked Chinese. Or Asian, anyway. Is it okay to say 'Chinese'?"

Cuneo ignored him, and asked instead:

"Was anyone out there filming the scene?"

"You mean, like TV?"

"Yeah. TV, or maybe somebody with their cell phone? Or camera?"

"No, no TV that I remember. I dunno about cell phones."

There had been something like four thousand homicides in New Orleans parish the previous year. It was the third most-dangerous city in the United States. TV crews did not show up for all of them, but a murder in Belle Chasse should have attracted some attention, Cuneo thought. Just as well. If TV had been there, they would have been all over the weird infant in the box, and the psychos really would be coming out of their closets then.

"You say she disappeared?"

"Well ... she screamed, and we thought that maybe she saw another body, or maybe she was in some kinda distress. We ran towards her, but she up and left. Turned a corner and was gone."

"We looked for her some," added the other uniform, "but we were there to secure the scene so we didn't go far. Just came back to the tape and stayed there."

That would have been enough time for someone to duck under the tape, Cuneo thought, either going in or coming out. The screaming woman might have been a planned diversion. Not likely, but possible.

"Who's at the hospital with the … the infant?"

"That would be DeVille and Landry."

Two solid, if unimaginative, cops. They were detailed to stand guard over the infant and to call in if there were any developments. Or if the doctors could figure out what it was.

"Okay. Thanks, guys."

Cuneo went back to his crime scene photos. Something else was nagging at him, and he couldn't put his finger on it. Wasn't it an Asian man who bought that property out at the Ninth Ward? The one with the Faraday Cage? Probably didn't mean anything. What if it was a white guy who bought the property and a white woman who was screaming at his scene? No one would link the two on the basis of race, right?

But the Asian woman and the Asian man suggested a link anyway, at least to his cop's brain. And didn't the woman in Belle Chasse tell him something about a "Chinaman," as she put it?

He shuffled through his notes on the previous case, and his interview with the old lady with the occult books and the arcane references to some kind of cult. He knew that she was linked to the first crime scene; that's why he interviewed her in the first place.

And now the Asian angle. Something was starting to come together, and he was damned if he could figure it out.

CHAPTER ELEVEN

Rabten, the old Tibetan monk who had befriended Jamila, the strange woman from another race, another culture, and a religion older than even his own, trudged back to the temple where he had left her. He was weighted down with his new knowledge, of Jamila as the *kuten*—the material basis—for a demon so similar to the banned Dorje Shugden that it pained him to think he had make provisions for her spiritual growth when it could mean an internal attack on the community. Her particular demon—known to her as Kutulu and to him as *kusulu*, the dead shaman awaiting rebirth from the *bardo*—was powerful, angry, and ancient. This was not a *tulku*: a being that decided its own time and place of rebirth. The Dalai Lama was one such, who would determine where and when he would return after death so that the sacred lineage would be maintained. Kutulu was waiting to be drawn back into the world by his followers, by those who worshipped him, at a time when "the stars were right."

He looked up and saw that the temple was at peace. Peace was such a valuable commodity to one who had been on the run from violence, bloodshed and war for all of his life … and all of her life, too.

One thing his contact told him, though, had disturbed him. The meaning of the phrase *Yog gsog gog*, or as she spoke it, *Yog-Sothoth*. The Bön priest had said that Yog-Sothoth was even more powerful and more ancient than Kutulu. That Kutulu was the High Priest, but that Yog-Sothoth was the god he served. Thus, he speculated, Jamila was serving as the medium for Kutulu; and when Kutulu was manifest on the planet then Yog-Sothoth would be summoned. Kutulu was the point of connection between this world and that Other.

Yog-Sothoth, he said, was "the key to the gate, whereby the spheres meet." And with that, he drew a mandala on the ground. It consisted of two concentric circles with a square in the middle and four gates: one in each cardinal direction. That was familiar enough, but then he drew another mandala, exactly the same, touching the first. The sight of these two in such proximity actually made Rabten feel ill. A mandala is a unity, a symbol of wholeness. There cannot be two such, next to each other, jostling for position like two boys in a schoolyard.

And then the priest pointed to the place where the two mandalas met, their point of tangence, at the space between two gates in the first and between two different gates in the second, like two gears out of synch, and said, "Yog-Sothoth *is* the gate. Yog-Sothoth is the key and guardian of the gate."

That image haunted him the entire way from the Bön priest's village back to his own. There was nothing like it in the Tantras. It seemed somehow blasphemous, and powerful at the same time. Buddhists were brought up to transcend petty desires, confident that their pursuit of nirvana would enable them to proceed along the spiritual path to a place of pure *oneness* and bliss. They understood the world was not a safe place (Tibetans more than most) and that they could not expect the rest of humanity to accept them or to adhere to their principles, but they did witness progress. This, though, was something else entirely. The bravest among them could interpret it as a delusion, a chimera, something to do with ghosts and demons, but Rabten knew this was something quite different. This … this Kutulu and his Yog gsog gog / Yog-Sothoth represented an existential threat to the entire planet in ways that the holiest of them could only imagine. They could deal with duality and non-duality, with different religions and forms of spirituality. They may not be able to deal with a reframing of the entire argument from the ground up: an outside agency that existed, that was powerful, and that could cause widespread destruction without firing a shot: simply by *being*.

The lamas and the rinpoches were not prepared for this assault on everything they knew, everything they held dear.

There were no exorcisms for these forces, for they didn't come from *here*.

As he stepped over the threshold into the temple, Rabten noticed a sensation of overwhelming peace. It stopped him right at the entrance. It was so rare, so excruciatingly real that his breath caught in his throat. And that was when he realized that Jamila was gone.

It was as if she had left him that moment of peace like a goodbye note. Or perhaps it had a more mundane reason. Perhaps it meant that the evil that she brought with her, the lurking fear that infected her aura like ink spilled into a glass of milk, left with her.

He went back outside after searching briefly through the temple, and began to walk over to one of the public buildings that formed part of the complex where the Dalai Lama conducted affairs of church and state. His idea was to ask around and find out where she had gone, if anyone had seen her. That is when he noticed a crowd of people at the entrance to the Dalai Lama Temple, almost a mile away.

In that crowd, unseen by Rabten, Jamila made her way among the tourists and official visitors. The Dalai Lama was having an audience today, meeting some foreign politicians and greeting a few lucky tourists who had made the long trip to Dharamsala to see him. Jamila was not sure what she was doing or where she was going. She let the mood of the moment guide her footsteps. All she knew was she had to get back to her people. She had to take the initiative. Rabten had been teaching her how to control her mind to protect herself from the possession of Kutulu, and those lessons had empowered her in other ways. She had to take advantage of what she was feeling and get back to Sinjar before it was too late.

The day had been cloudy and overcast, but suddenly a ray of sunlight pierced the gloom and shone directly on the main entrance like a spotlight. There was a gasp from the assembled crowd as the Dalai Lama himself appeared at the top of the stairs. Tall, bald, wearing his trademark glasses, big-boned and smiling, he waved good-naturedly as a sigh went up from the audience. Jamila stood and stared at him for a long moment, trying to see what they saw, and in that instant her path was suddenly open to her.

A woman standing in front of her was transfixed by this opportunity to see the Dalai Lama in person. Oblivious to everything else she stood with her back to Jamila and her purse on a strap around her left shoulder. The purse was open, its clasp broken, and its contents open to the world and plain to see.

Jamila simply reached in and removed the woman's wallet.

Rabten made his way down the small street that separated his tiny temple from the grander complex. Perhaps someone there had seen Jamila. It would take him a few minutes to walk there. He was already tired from his trip to see the Bön priest, so he wasn't moving as quickly as he might have.

That was when he noticed a commotion in front of the red and gold building and saw a whole group of people backing away from the main staircase.

Jamila had stolen the woman's wallet, but at the moment no one was aware of the theft. The wallet was tucked into her waistband, out of sight, but everyone was staring at her anyway.

She was rock-solid in the middle of the space before the grand staircase that led to the temple itself. Her mouth was open, making strange sounds that were nonetheless quite loud and forceful. The sounds of an older man with a deep, bass voice. Or a demon with a head cold.

Standing before her was the 14th Dalai Lama, Tenzin Gyatso himself, wide-eyed.

Jamila was talking to him in the language reserved for the State Oracle of Tibet, a language that very few other people understood.

And she was a woman. *And* a Yezidi.

This was clearly impossible.

Rabten made it to the staircase in just enough time to see Jamila finish what evidently was a meaningful speech to the Dalai Lama in a language no one but him could understand. The Tibetan leader had conferred with the State Oracle on many occasions when the latter was possessed by the divining spirit and speaking in a secret language. Now here was this thin, undernourished young woman from a strange land with a strange religion using the same language *to warn him that a catastrophe was coming and that many innocent people would die.*

And there was nothing he could do about it.

There was the sound of laughter, as of an old man, a deranged old man, a psychotic serial killing machine vomiting forth from the young woman's throat like a stream of acid bile, of gross invective. The sound came from everywhere at once, as if broadcast through giant speakers. Rabten had just enough time to hear the word he dreaded the most, coming from that gentle refugee woman to whom he had been teaching meditation and mindfulness:

Yog-Sothoth!

Monks in their yellow and maroon robes rushed out to form a phalanx around the Dalai Lama, as if to shield him from a terrorist attack or perhaps a deranged fan. When they saw the source of the threat, they were confused. It was a small woman, and her hands held no weapons.

Just as Rabten reached her, she collapsed onto the ground.

CHAPTER TWELVE

RABTEN CARRIED THE UNCONSCIOUS BODY of Jamila into a room in the temple complex, surrounded by monks who watched him warily. Rabten was not connected to the complex and was a member of the Red Hat sect—as opposed to the Dalai Lama's own Yellow Hat sect. The Red, Yellow and Black sects were all Tibetan Buddhist but there were differences in practice and in some Buddhist theory as well. Rabten was well-known as one of those who came with the Dalai Lama from Tibet decades ago, so he was treated with respect if not a little suspicion. This was exacerbated by the fact that the Gyalwa Karmapa—the leader of the Red Sect—had died. There was the inevitable struggle over his successor, which made the tension among some of the Karmapa's followers rather intense.

And the way he was carrying a woman—and a woman who was not Tibetan or Buddhist—made them uncomfortable. There had been a lot of stories about some lamas who abused their authority by seducing young foreign women with promises of advanced initiations and old age didn't seem to be a problem; but no one would voice such a suspicion of a man who fled Tibet in His Holiness's entourage. And, anyway, didn't the woman become possessed by the Oracle and speak directly to His Holiness?

He set Jamila down gently on a rug and held his finger near her nose.

"She still breathes," he told no one in particular. "She will survive, as before."

"As before?"

The voice behind him was of the Dalai Lama's personal secretary, a monk of about fifty, who stood staring down at this spectacle in the sacred precincts of His Holiness's quarters.

Rabten looked up, and nodded. "Yes, as before. This woman is known to me. She is a refugee from Iraq."

The secretary was shocked. "Iraq? Are you *insane*? Do you wish to call the wrath of the Muslims down upon us? Do you realize how close we are to the border with Pakistan?"

"Yes, Rinpoche. But she is not a Muslim."

"A Christian, then?" he replied, somewhat relieved.

"No, Rinpoche. A Yezidi."

"What is a Yezidi?"

"A minority group. Much persecuted. She came to us for help."

The Dalai Lama himself had been escorted to a secure room deeper within the structure, surrounded by a phalanx of monks, like the Secret Service guarding the President of the United States. The threat from which they were protecting him in this case was less mortal than it was, well, immortal. They were protecting him from a spirit.

The secretary shrugged. "Well, I suppose we should help if we must. If we can. Where are her people? Her family?"

Rabten got up heavily from the floor and dusted his knees.

"Being massacred, as we speak."

That shut the secretary up. He took advantage of the shocking statement to take his leave of the unsightly scene and run to His Holiness's side.

Another, much younger, monk approached gingerly, carrying a carafe of clean water and a white towel. Rabten was grateful for the consideration, and accepted the water and moistened the towel with it. He bent down to dab at Jamila's forehead and cheeks. He was rewarded by a flutter of the woman's eyelids in response.

She looked up at him, frightened at first, and then relieved. It was Rabten, the monk who had befriended her. That meant she was alright. She had had another of her "spasms," she knew, but didn't remember very much of it. But where was she? And why was she surrounded by so many monks?

That was when her hand went to her waist, to the place under her shirt where she had hidden the wallet that she stole only moments earlier. Rabten noticed the movement, but said nothing, only looked at her quizzically.

There was a commotion outside the complex, down by the foot of the large open-air staircase. A small crowd was gathering.

A woman's voice could be heard, complaining, in English.

"I don't know who took it. It happened when that … that young woman started hallucinating, or whatever. Maybe she was part of a group, you know, a bunch of pickpockets or something. Where is she, anyway?"

Another commotion had begun almost simultaneously. The secretary ran down the hall to tell Rabten that the woman—the refugee from Iraq—was wanted by His Holiness. At once. For an important audience.

Jamila stood up on shakey knees. She didn't understand the words people were saying, but she knew she had to get out of there as fast as possible. Rabten sensed her discomfort and her urgency. He nodded to her and gestured that she should follow him.

"I will just get her cleaned up," he told the secretary. "She can't be brought before His Holiness in this state." At that, he lifted up one edge of her shirt, exposing maybe an inch of her naked flesh.

The secretary and all the monks present backed away in horror.

"Of course! Of course! But come right away. His Holiness is most eager to speak with her." He ignored the fact that the Dalai Lama did not speak any Kurdish dialects, and Jamila did not speak Tibetan, or very much English.

Rabten only nodded and gestured to Jamila in the general direction of the washrooms. As the two walked quickly down the hall, more voices could be heard from outside.

"I don't know how much money. A few hundred dollars, that's all. And my plane ticket! Oh, my God. And my passport! My passport! How will I get back to Toronto!"

Just before they reached the washrooms, Rabten pulled Jamila aside and showed her a side door.

He grasped her by the shoulders and looked straight into her eyes. Then he spoke a mantra, softly, over her head. He knew he would never see her again.

He took a deep breath.

And pushed her through the door.

"Now run!" he said, in English and then again in Tibetan, but most especially with his mind, the only language they had in common.

"Run!"

CHAPTER THIRTEEN

CUNEO STOOD IN THE MAKESHIFT MORGUE while he waited for the medical examiner to offer his final word on the cause of death of the old lady from Belle Chasse.

New Orleans used funeral homes as morgues, owing to a lack of funding for a real morgue and the kind of fancy medical examiner equipment you saw on television shows. In this one, the morgue was in the basement but you could still hear weird organ music from upstairs on some kind of tape loop. It was driving him nuts.

"COD is what we thought back at the scene," he told the detective after his examination had confirmed the cause of death. "She had her neck broken."

"Any sign she was messed with?"

"No evidence of any kind of sexual trauma. I mean, not exactly."

"What the hell does that mean?"

Hesitating, the medical examiner queried Cuneo, "How old you figure she was, detective? Seventy-five? Eighty?"

"Not a day under."

"Well, we have her birth certificate and passport. They found them in the house along with a lot of other personal papers."

"And?"

"She was one hundred-and-two..."

"What?"

"... and sexually active. We found evidence of fluids. She had had sex shortly before she died."

"So she was raped."

"Uh, no. There is no evidence of vaginal tearing or anything like that. What sex she had was consensual."

Cuneo wiped his forehead with his handkerchief. It was stifling hot in a room that should have been ice cold.

"You have fluids. Semen?"

"Affirmative."

"Can we get a sample of that for genetic testing? We need to identify whoever saw her last, and I assume that would be whoever was schtupping this crone."

"Pardon?"

"Oh. 'Schtupping.' It's a term of art, at least in New York. It means 'screwing.'"

"Ah. I see. Thanks for the language lesson, detective."

"With any luck, lover boy will be in the database and we can wrap this up. At least, this part of the case. I have no clue what to do with the … the whatever we have at the hospital."

"I heard. Some pretty weird shit going around, even for New Orleans."

"You're a poet. Seriously."

With that, Cuneo left the medical examiner to his work and went upstairs, happy to be out of earshot of that awful organ music and out on the street. He got into his car and pulled out into traffic, heading for the hospital. He wanted to see for himself what the doctors had been able to discover about the baby in the box.

"It's a boy," they told him. "Well, it's male, anyway. Got all the right equipment. But we still don't exactly know what it is."

Cuneo sighed. "I've been hearing that a lot lately. Why don't you just give it to me straight. Is it human, animal, or …?"

The one who seemed to be in charge, a Doctor Hussain, took Cuneo by the arm and moved him out of the way of the rush of medical staff that were responding to a three-car pileup.

"It's this way, Detective. It appears to be human, but it's badly deformed. That's why it took us so long to come to any kind of conclusion about its chances for survival. From the waist up it has human characteristics. It appears it may have Elephant Man's disease. You know what I'm talking about, right?"

"Jesus. Yeah. All those growths. Poor kid."

"That's not all, though. From the waist down it appears that the infant is uncommonly hairy. I mean, his thighs and calves are covered in hair. This is just one unfortunate child. You say you found it in a box, in a cellar?"

Cuneo swallowed. "In a box, yeah. It was hooked up to some kind of plumbing. The box was covered in these weird letters and symbols. I thought ... well, it looked like someone was trying to say it was a ... a placenta. Like the baby had not been born yet, but was gestating there. In a box. In the cellar."

"No parents? No nurse or midwife or anyone like that around?"

"No. No one. Just this old lady, but she had been killed. That's how we found out about the boy in the box. It was at a crime scene."

The doctor just shook his head. "Detective, I've seen a lot of crazy shit in this town. Voodoo murders, religious cults, serial killers. Fucking Katrina. But this is ..."

"Yeah, I know. Hey, are you able to do any kind of DNA testing on the ... the boy?"

"Oh, we will. Matter of course. With this many birth defects and the fact that he was born premature ..."

"Wait. What did you say?"

"Oh, right. You didn't know. The baby is about two, three months early. Hard to say with this many problems, but lung and cranial development ... yeah, about three months premature. It's still a little touch and go. We have him in neonatal ICU, but he seems strong and will probably survive. The poor kid."

Cuneo walked back to his car after checking with the two uniforms he left in charge of security over the baby. If the baby was premature, it implied that the murder of the old lady was intended to interfere with the boy's birth. In other words, the perp wanted to kill both the woman and the child. If the baby didn't survive, he would have a double homicide on his hands.

Was the baby the motive? Did someone want to make sure the baby died?

Why?

He reached his car in the parking lot, and was about to get in when he noticed that someone had drawn a figure in the dust on his windshield.

It was a smiley face.

CHAPTER FOURTEEN

AT THE CRIME SCENE IN BELLE CHASSE, the police were finished with their inspection of the house. They had photographed every inch and made an inventory of the old lady's library of esoteric works which ran to several pages of text. These were not pop books on horoscopes or love spells, but heavy tomes on ceremonial magic, alchemy, Egyptology, and the like. There was an old copy of the *Zohar* in Aramaic, all twelve volumes of it. There were first editions of Budge, Waddell, Scholem, Idel, Couliano, Guenon, Evola, the complete *Golden Bough*, a full set of the *Equinox* (white and blue), the works of Jung ... and these were just the ones whose authors or titles they could understand. The volumes in foreign languages were harder to identify.

There was a complete set of the *Kangyur*, the Tibetan Buddhist canon. Studies in the *Kalachakra Tantra*. The *Shiva Samhita*. The *Hevajra Tantra*. Works on Daoist alchemy, many in Chinese. An entire section on Santeria, Palo Mayombe, and Candomble. Scholarly works on the Yoruban divination system known as *Ifa*.

And then there were the grimoires, the magicians' workbooks. The *Clavicle* of Solomon, *Goetia*, *Le dragon rouge*, *Le petit Albert*, Agrippa, *Abramelin*, *Picatrix*, works by Crowley, Grant, Levi, Papus, Idries Shah, Waite, Mathers, translations by Joseph Peterson, Stratton-Kent, Daniel Matt ... the breadth and depth of the collection would have been astounding to the investigators had they the first clue of what they were looking at. How could they be expected to recognize any of these titles, however? It required a very specialized knowledge and a background in a discipline that was professional suicide for most academics. So they photographed the collection and created an inventory list, title by title, that they would attach to the case file and which could be used to settle the estate if they did not uncover a will.

In a desk in the woman's bedroom—and old roll top affair that looked out of place amid the fine furnishings—they uncovered a large piece of paper that had been folded several times to fit. When they unfolded it, they saw it was an old blueprint of the house they were in. It was dated 1877, and had been developed by an architectural firm in Providence, Rhode Island.

The crime scene tech who found the blueprint was about to include it with the other personal effects of the deceased when she noticed something unusual, something that caught her attention. She rushed out of the bedroom and down the hall to the basement door.

The phone rang in Cuneo's pocket as he was driving back to the station. He had forgotten what pocket he put it in, and almost caused an accident trying to find it. When he did locate it, he pulled over to the curb to see who was calling. The call had gone into voicemail waiting for him to pick up.

"Detective Cuneo," he heard a woman's voice say. She identified herself as a crime scene technician. "There's something you should see. If you can come back to Belle Chasse, or I can meet you at the station, the old lady left behind a blueprint to the house. It has … uh … inconsistencies … I guess you could say. Let me know where you want to meet."

The call and the request were unusual. He never experienced close cooperation with the crime scene units who tended to do their own thing and then file reports. They were hopelessly understaffed, like the entire department, and simply didn't have the time for chatting with detectives.

He called her back and said he was on his way to the station and would meet her there in fifteen.

He drove the rest of the way in a fog of confusion and anxiety. First, that weird scene in the Lower Ninth a month ago, with the dead bodies in the Faraday cage under the earth. Then the old lady. Then her murder, and the boy in the box. Then the smiley faces he'd been getting lately. This case was getting stranger by the minute and he knew it would not end well. He knew it in the pit of his stomach.

When he got to the station, the tech was waiting for him. She was small, but then everybody was small next to Cuneo. She was about thirty and looked vaguely Latin, with an olive complexion and short-cropped black hair, but he knew better than to jump to assumptions in the Big Easy.

"Detective Cuneo? I'm Lisa. I'm the one who called you." She thrust out her hand.

He took it and they shook professionally. "Lisa, what've you got for me?"

She opened a large purse that hung from a strap on her shoulder. She pulled out a plastic evidence bag, and in it he could see the unmistakable tint of a blueprint. She handed it to him, and he pulled on a pair of the latex gloves he kept in his jacket pockets.

He went over to his desk and gingerly opened the bag and withdrew the blueprint.

"It's folded in a few places and kinda fragile," she offered.

He spread it out carefully on his desk, moving a stack of reports and a stapler out of the way as he did so to give the print a perfectly flat surface. The paper was completely blue, with white ink, showing the dimensions of a building. The house in Belle Chasse.

It wasn't very large, but it did show the floor plan of the house on one side and the elevation perspective on another side. It was old, and Cuneo wondered if they did blueprints like this that long ago. The box at the lower right-hand corner bore the date, 1877 and the name of an architectural firm in Rhode Island.

"What was it about this that made you call me?" he asked over his shoulder, peering at the lines and dimensions of the plan.

"It's this," she said, pointing to a section of the floor plan. "See, this is the cellar. This section here is where you found the ... found the box. See? It was accommodated in the plan from the beginning."

"Okay, that's good. That's helpful, but I still don't see ..."

"Now look here," she interrupted, a little self-consciously. "This is another section of the same cellar, the side opposite. And what do you see?"

Cuneo bent down to look at the plan more closely, following where the tech was pointing. His eyes went back and forth, from the wall that he battered down to get at the boy in the box to the wall on the other side of the hallway.

That's when the realization dawned on him.

"This section is identical to the first. It even shows the strange plumbing feature as the first one. Ah, Christ…"

Lisa just nodded as if in sympathy, but secretly excited.

He looked at her, an expression of utter horror on his face.

"There's another box."

CHAPTER FIFTEEN

CUNEO SQUEALED TO A STOP in front of the house in Belle Chasses. The yellow crime scene tape was still up, and there was a uniform standing at the front door with a sledgehammer. He had phoned ahead to make sure he had some assistance in case it came to that. With him in the car was the crime scene tech, just to be on the safe side.

He jumped out and ran up the steps, the tech struggling to keep up. The uniform opened the door and stepped aside.

The scene was pretty much how he left it. There was black fingerprint ink everywhere, but Cuneo had asked the tech to bring luminol and an ultra violet light. He didn't know if he should expect fluids, but based on the last time he was in this house …

He and the tech raced down the stairs into the basement.

They had a photocopy of the old blueprint with them. The original had been logged in as evidence and was back at the station. Cuneo roughly unfolded the print and oriented it to the layout of the basement. The place where the boy in the box had been found was identified on the print, and then all they had to do was look across the hallway to the other wall. The other box—if there was one—had to be there, somewhere. Behind the wall.

Before he would tell the uniform to start to work with the sledgehammer Cuneo decided he would take a breath and look carefully at the site. The ceiling did not give up any clues or anything that looked out of place. The wall on the left he had broken through was pretty much how he left it, a total mess. The box was still there, too heavy to move at once, although the fluids had been cleaned out of it and placed in evidence bags. They would send a team in there later to disconnect whatever electronics or piping was still attached and then remove the unit as evidence. Maybe they could get an anthropologist or an archaeologist to take a look at it.

The crime scene tech followed him, wondering why they had stopped. They had been in such a hurry to get here she thought he would be ripping out the wall with his bare hands. Now he seemed stuck, lost in thought. It was weird.

Cuneo walked up and down the hall, staring at the wall. There was another box in there, he was sure of it. If anyone or anything had been alive in there once, it was a good chance that it was already dead. The wall was sealed just as tight as the first one. The strange drawings or glyphs or whatever they were seemed identical to those on the first wall. All the evidence pointed to there being another box with another … being, creature, baby … inside. He knew he should get to work at once, breaking through the wall to see whatever was waiting for him, to rescue whatever was in there, but he couldn't get past the feeling that maybe it was the wrong thing to do.

There was a sensation creeping up his spine the longer he stayed down there. He remembered the stories his African-American mother had told him about the "night doctors" and of how black people would wind up missing from their beds in the morning, seized by the night doctors for some hideous experimentation. His mother, the daughter of Haitian immigrants, had come from the South and wound up in New York City, in Harlem, where she met his father, an Italian-American cop: the first in his family of immigrant warehousemen and movers. She brought her folklore with her; at least, that is what Cuneo thought at the time she told him those stories. Folklore. Old wives' tales. Cautionary tales, perhaps, told by people who had a legitimate reason to be paranoid. Now, he was not so sure. The television cable channels were full of stories of alien abductions, which sounded a lot like the night doctors. And here he was in the basement of a house where some kind of old witch or spirit medium had been murdered and where they kept fetuses alive in boxes in the basement. Maybe he had stumbled upon a lair of "night doctors."

Wonderful.

He walked back around to the storage area where the uniform had clocked him before. He stood and looked at the basement window with the smiley face still drawn in the dust. Everything was immaculately clean, except for the dusty window.

He walked up and down the wall across from the window, knocking on it as he did so, trying to see if it was hollow at some point. But it seemed solid. Cinder block, maybe. With sheetrock over it. Expensive.

"Detective?"

It was the tech.

"Yeah?"

"Should we get started?"

"Yeah, sure. Sorry. Right. Officer?"

"Sir?"

"Start right about here," he said to the man with the hammer, pointing to a spot on the wall. "That's directly across from the first hole we made."

"You got it."

He pulled back with the hammer over his shoulder, standing with feet apart as if addressing a golf ball, and then swung with all his might at the very center of the basement wall.

The wall shuddered with the blow from the policeman's hammer. You could hear chunks of lathing spilling inside the wall, but not much damage was done to the outside. Cuneo nodded, and the officer swung again. And again. With each stroke it seemed as if the whole building was shaking to its foundations.

Eventually, a crack began to appear and with a few more whacks a hole was opened large enough for Cuneo to shine a flashlight inside and look for another boy in another box. Outside he could hear the arrival of the ambulance he had summoned on the way in, just in case what they found was still alive. In another few seconds there would be the sound of the footsteps of the EMTs pounding down the stairs to the basement.

Cuneo shone his flashlight into the hole, peering in after it.

There.

Another box. He breathed a sigh of relief that his instincts were correct, and another sigh that represented the fear he felt that whatever was inside the box was either dead, or some sort of monstrosity still alive.

He could make out the silhouette of another idol affixed to the top of the box, and what seemed to be plumbing or tubing similar to the first box snaking out the front. The whole setup looked identical.

Twins, thought Cuneo to himself. *Jesus.*

He backed out of the opening and nodded to the uniform.

"Let's open it up, officer. We have to get in there."

The cop nodded, and hefted the hammer for another strike.

Cuneo stepped back to let him work, and wondered why the EMTs had not shown up in the basement. In fact, it seemed strangely quiet upstairs.

He turned to the crime scene tech—what was her name? Lina? Lois? Lisa!—and asked her to go and check on the ambulance. She nodded and ran up the stairs just as the hammer smashed through the basement wall.

Lisa stood at the top of the stairs, frozen in place. From the doorway to the basement she could look across to the living room where the murder had occurred, and there were the EMTs, standing like statues and staring at a woman.

She appeared to be Asian, dressed simply in a nondescript sort of way, flat shoes, vinyl purse, as if she was going to church. Or the mall. She was standing in the middle of the living room floor, directly over the outline of the murder victim, and urinating on it. She was staring at the EMTs who were staring back at her, open-mouthed. It was a weird tableau, and no one was moving or speaking. There was no sound, save for the splash of urine on the old lady's carpet.

Before Lisa could utter a word, a thunderous crash from the basement told her that the wall had been breached.

In the hospital's neonatal ICU the small, monstrous child-thing from the first box opened its mouth and screamed.

CHAPTER SIXTEEN

LISA STOOD AS STILL AS THE REST OF THE TABLEAU, but for different reasons. She saw the urinating woman standing over the outline
of what had been a murdered lady as a challenge and not as a des-
ecration. She knew that the EMTs saw the same thing she did but
could not process it. Two men in uniforms carrying equipment: it
was almost an icon of power, the power of the state. Before them was
a woman, maybe forty, Asian, of no apparent means, and the urine
flowing down onto the site where only hours ago another woman's
body had been left as so much refuse on the floor of her own house
… the sheer physicality of it, the emphasis on gross bodily function,
elimination, the desexualization of her own body transferred to the
corpse … and Lisa herself as the third woman in the tableau.

And downstairs, in the basement. It suddenly became clear to
her. She, who had no children of her own but who suffered the lewd
comments of coworkers and potential lovers because of her looks,
her profession, her own uniform … she knew what was going on.
Those two boxes, with their two babies … mechanical reproduction
of reproduction. The usurpation of motherhood. The denial of
humanity. Planned obsolescence.

Who was Viktor Frankenstein after all but a man who wanted
the power of procreation: of conception, gestation and bringing to
term? All those women she knew who joked about not needing
men, women who understood science like she did, who had been
to medical school, who knew about in vitro fertilization and all
the other technologies that would make the presence of a man in
their lives superfluous, they joked. They didn't see it. Men had been
fantasizing about the same thing for centuries. The old lady—the
dead one, the murdered one—had found a way to do this, had found
a way to procreate even in old age, even when it was biologically
impossible due to menopause—which for her must have happened

171

decades ago. Men could procreate their entire lives; women had an expiration date programmed into their genes.

Frankenstein had created a monster because no woman was involved. It was a man creating a man. It was pure Y chromosome fantasy become reality. And that is what you get, what is created from a wet dream when there is no ovum in sight: when the succubus now heavy with semen lifts itself off the sleeping man's groin, and carries the load away to one of the "night doctors" to perform the procedure: you get a monster.

And the monster that was created in the old lady's basement, even now struggling for life in the hospital while another one may be gestating in the basement ... A woman's wet dream? An expulsion of fluids containing ... *what*? A woman creating ... *what*? What was it? Was the baby—the monster baby, the teratoma baby—male or female? She didn't know, and suddenly she had to know. Which would have been the greater victory?

All of this went through Lisa's mind in a heartbeat. She reached out a hand to touch the woman before her but to her shock the Asian lady turned to face her with a smile of acknowledgment. *You understand*, she seemed to say by a look. *You know why I'm here.*

You know why this was done.

Downstairs the two men cleared the rubble from the large opening they had made in the wall. Another freezer-style box presented the same set of obstacles as the first: the heavy idol affixed to its lid; the weird plumbing apparatus that snaked out from one end. The painted glyphs and symbols all over it.

Like last time there seemed to be no power or other services actually working, supplying whatever was in the box with air or fluids. Cuneo didn't have time to figure out how the elaborate system worked, but he needed to get into the box as quickly as possible. Last time he had the benefit of several other cops to help him push the idol off the lid and open the box. This time he thought he could accomplish the same task more quickly with just himself and the other officer. Last time they were falling all over each other, getting in each other's way in the small opening. This time they had opened a larger hole and the two of them could get into the opening on either side of the box and shift it.

Cuneo had forgotten all about the EMTs and his crime scene tech, Lisa.

Upstairs, the EMTs finally came to their senses. They dropped their equipment onto the floor and rushed to the Asian woman, as if believing that she was ill and in need of their services. After all, they really didn't have a clue as to why they were supposed to come to that address in the first place. Maybe this was the patient? And what was the emergency then? Incontinence?

But as they moved to take her, to strap her down and wheel her out to the ambulance, Lisa stopped them.

"No," she said. "Not her. Downstairs." She pointed to the basement door, and the EMTs looked at each other in confusion. The woman in front of them was obviously in need of some kind of medical attention. But they obeyed and began clattering down the basement steps.

When Lisa turned back to the Asian woman, she was gone.

CHAPTER SEVENTEEN

CUNEO COULD UNDERSTAND BLACK PEOPLE and voodoo. The Bible says "for rebellion is as the sin of witchcraft," and black people have been in rebellion all over the Americas for a long time. His mother used to have a little bag of juju in her purse, even though her husband was Catholic. She didn't see a problem with that, since her ancestors practiced Catholicism and voodoo side by side for generations, using the one as a mask or disguise for the other. And it was real Haitian voodoo, too. Her mother's people two or three generations earlier were from Leogane. So Cuneo understood New Orleans and voodoo.

It was crazy-ass white people practicing voodoo he couldn't get his head around. What was the point? They had the state, the culture, and the economy in the bag. They should line up at church on Sunday and thank God for all that. They have no need to be messing around with animal sacrifice and blood rituals and weird boxes in their basements.

All of that went through his mind as the last blow from the sledgehammer permitted him to get inside the wall and step gingerly over the broken lathing and scraps of concrete to see the box from the other side. As he did so, he heard the EMTs coming down the stairs to the basement.

"In here!" he shouted, unnecessarily. They set up a stretcher next to the hole and waited, expectantly. The officer with the hammer just looked at them, and shrugged.

The idol was the same as the first box, and positioned exactly the same on top of the box. There was a large pipe or tube extended outward from the same end as in the first. Everything looked identical, except that this one looked as if it had been tampered with recently. Cuneo was confused. How was that possible when the entire apparatus had been sealed up behind a wall?

The edges of the cover looked as if someone already had taken a crowbar to it. The metal was bent out of shape all along the far side, the side away from the hole. The scratches were recent, shiny, and sharp. There were indentations on the cover, near the base of the idol that looked as if something had tried to punch out from inside the box.

Cuneo moved to push the idol—and with it, the cover—off the box as he had the last time, and as he pushed with all his strength he almost fell over on top of it. The entire upper part of the apparatus simply fell over, as if it had been loosened by an earlier attempt. The idol toppled and fell out of the hole and the EMTs and the police officer jumped back to avoid being crushed by what looked like a really large hunk of iron in the shape of some kind of octopus. Or a thing with an octopus head.

"Shit! What the hell …"

Lisa, who had been standing far enough away out of fear or loathing or some other, unfamiliar sensation, just stared at the fallen idol in disbelief. She had never seen anything like that before today and now there were two of them. She had suspected as much, once she discovered that there was another box in the basement, but this was getting too close to home. There was something very familiar about all of this, and that strange Asian woman from upstairs was part of it. It was déjà vu. But how could she have experienced anything even remotely like this in her life as a student of forensic science and now a crime scene tech? You have déjà vu about real things, not about weird shit like this.

The EMTs tried to help, pulling at the idol and looking into the hole to see what Cuneo needed. They were there for a living body, not some damned pagan statue, and were getting a little antsy. First the urinating woman from upstairs and now this.

Cuneo was leaning over the open box. There was the same mass of fluids, the same horrible stench.

But otherwise the box was empty. And on the inside of the cover was a symbol that had not been on the first one.

A smiley face.

CHAPTER EIGHTEEN

THE PENULTIMATE PAYMENT had been made to the agent of Daesh, the group otherwise known as the Islamic State. Their contact was urbane, bearded, about fifty and dressed like a European businessman, not in the melodramatic black uniform of the terror organization's executioners. He had a Belgian passport, a German accent and an Italian name. Nothing about him was real, except for the shipment.

They were in a warehouse at the edge of the Istanbul airport. There was a crate with antiquities which had just been examined by Dagon's archaeological expert. These were items stolen from various museums in Iraq where IS now had jurisdiction. They were looting what they could for cash, and their buyer had deep pockets.

The prize artifact was a Sumerian copper dagger with a lapis lazuli handle. It was in excellent condition, and was necessary for some special purpose that the Dagon people would not divulge. No matter. The price was good, and Daesh was in need of a lot of money, very quickly.

"Where is the rest of it?" asked the archaeologist.

The agent smiled to cover his distaste and motioned to a twenty-foot container in the rear of the warehouse.

It was the middle of the afternoon, and dust was swirling in the sun beams coming in from the upper level windows. It was like some dystopian movie, with the ashes of the dead settling on the horrified faces of the living.

As they walked, their footsteps resounding hollowly on the wooden floors, the agent signaled to two men who were standing by and they opened the container's doors.

The archaeologist peered in and recoiled—angry and sickened.

"This is not what we agreed to! A container full of corpses is useless to us!"

"Relax, sir. They are not dead, only dreaming."

"What do you mean?"

"They have been drugged. It was the only way we could transport them securely."

"They have not been damaged? They have not been ... touched?"

"Not at all. We have followed your instructions carefully. We did not use needles, only made them drink some water with a sedative. And they have not been touched, as you say. They are all virgins, every single one. There has been no sexual contact of *any kind*. And we have access to more, all from the captured territories. But I would need an order soon, before the soldiers ... well, you know. Some are set aside as brides for the men. Others are merely concubines. It is not natural for them to isolate some of the girls without first ... touching them—but for money they would be sure to ..."

"We will determine that," he interrupted. "If they all pass the medical examination, then you will receive the balance of the money as we discussed. If any of them do not, the transfer will be reduced by that much. Understood?"

"Of course."

"When will the sedative wear off?"

"Not for a few hours. I have supplied an extra two doses for each girl, should you need to re-sedate them during the trip." He handed over a manila envelope full of drugs. "The price of the drugs is included."

He signaled once again to his two assistants, and they immediately closed and locked the container. One of the men walked over to the group and handed his boss the key, who then handed it to the archaeologist.

"With my compliments, sir."

The archaeologist had assistants of his own. He nodded to them and they walked back to the container while a third started up the truck that would haul the container to the section of the airfield that was restricted to military use. The archaeologist was tempted to waste the oily agent right there in the warehouse, him and his steroid-enhanced assistants. But they might need his services later. Dagon had an unquenchable thirst for antiquities. And for human flesh.

So he let it go. By the time they were driving to the airport the man from Daesh had already gone.

The first leg of the flight would take them to Lisbon. There, they would dose the children again with sedatives, this time for the long transatlantic flight to Miami. The Customs agent at MIA was one of their own. The container would wait in the restricted area, but the Dagon people would empty it of its cargo that same night, which is when the second sedative would be administered. Another container would be waiting and they would set off for their final destination:

The Rites of Dagon. The Opening of the Gate.

CHAPTER NINETEEN

AUBREY WAITED IN LINE PATIENTLY at the airport for his flight
to board. He had spent the last two days in Paris, reviewing the
Grothendieck material as well as keeping Monroe up to date on his
progress, and getting more detail from Monroe as it came in. There
had been rumors that Angell was in Dubai, but that was ruled out
once it was discovered that the man in question was an Italian from
Sardinia. Another rumor had Angell in the Australian outback, and
still another sighting was in Hokkaido. All of these were eventually
discounted as either mistaken identity or overzealous field agents
looking to make a name for themselves.

They earlier had pretty good intel that he had made it as far as
the Chinese border, but after that the trail ran cold. They knew that
the Book had not surfaced—that would have been impossible to
keep secret—and if the Book was still in play, so was Gregory Angell.
When Aubrey got the communication from Prime it ratcheted up
the search considerably. Prime was reasonably reliable, if something
of an arrogant little prick, so if he said the chatter about Angell being
in Beijing was confirmed, it was confirmed.

At the same time, that was when Aubrey got word from Monroe
about the human trafficking angle, and his mission took a sharp turn
into territory that was, if anything, even darker than it already had
been.

He checked his watch and saw that the flight would board on
time. At this point, everything was commercial. Should they get
actionable intel on Angell or the Book, then military transport
could be utilized, if necessary. As it was, Aubrey was now due to sit
down with one person they suspected might be able to shed some
light on the Order of Dagon, the dread "Keepers of the Book," and
their connection with the dangerous and sickening world of child
trafficking. The meeting would prove uncomfortable for a variety

of reasons, and when it was over the otherwise unflappable Aubrey would feel the need of a hot shower and a stiff drink.

Aubrey had heard of the existence of the Order on and off the entire time he knew and worked for Monroe, but it had never come fully into focus for him. Aubrey's background was in counter-intelligence and special operations. While his pedigree was nowhere near as extensive as Monroe's, he had been around in his career: Haiti, Panama, Nicaragua, and black insertions into Cuba, among other places in the western hemisphere. And then there was Singapore, where he was stationed for a few years in his role as interrogator of Chinese defectors under Robert Mullen cover, the same firm that provided cover for Watergate Plumber E. Howard Hunt back in the day. Aubrey's languages were Spanish, French, Haitian Creole, Brazilian Portuguese and Mandarin. He was fun to be around in his native Jackson Heights, Queens, particularly as his patrician air—born of generations of Americans who traced their lineage directly to the Mayflower—seemed so totally incongruous with his vulgar street Spanish and a Mandarin littered with obscure profanities.

In Europe, Aubrey seemed especially at home. While he suspected his French was not elevated enough to charm waiters in expensive Parisian restaurants, it was sufficient to get by for most applications. He had a good workmanlike command of some Eastern European languages from his days working this side of the Iron Curtain out of Vienna. His Spanish was perfectly fluent, if a little snooty, having learned it from a beautiful but somewhat reserved Colombian spy in Bogota. His Portuguese, however, frequently had the locals in Lisbon or the Algarve in fits of giggles, tainted as it was by his Brazilian postings.

Today, after mulling over his conversation with the mathematician Grothendieck, Aubrey was relieved that he would be able to talk to someone to put all of this in some kind of context and perspective. It was all getting a little too theoretical and other-worldly. Gregory Angell was out there somewhere and the Book was most likely with him. Monroe had assets all over the world looking for him, and now they would be focused on China. But sometimes their methods were a little clumsy: honed as they were on Cold War operations against the Soviets or, later, the mostly unsuccessful infiltration ops against Al-Qaeda or the other terror groups in the Middle East, Africa, and South Asia. The remote viewer, Jason Miller, was confirmed dead in Nepal and he had been their best resource—ironically enough, since Miller was not only a kind of psychic but was also a renegade intelligence operative who had been hunted as aggressively as Angell. So he and Monroe were thrown back onto their own devices, and were calling in favors from all over the globe.

Although it was Grothendieck's mathematics that had attracted the attention of Monroe in the first place—his unique perspective on how algebra and geometry (left brain and right brain) could be combined to understand the peculiar dynamics and non-Euclidean structures of Dagon's ritual schedules—Grothendieck's fixation on the idea of mutants deserved some closer scrutiny. After all, the man was the most important mathematician of his generation. Somehow, his calculations had resulted in a kind of political and spiritual *satori*: a moment of intense vision, of enlightenment, that derived meaning from—or gave meaning to—the geometric algebra of his dreams. If his mathematics could be used to help define and identify the "spaces between" spaces and angles, then the same approach might be applied to his idea of mutants: people "between" people.

Grothendieck's mutants were all advanced souls, individuals of great scientific and philosophical achievement. But what if there was another category of mutant, one that Grothendieck either did not recognize or did not wish to acknowledge? What if the benign mutants of his philosophy were not the only ones?

Aubrey knew that Monroe had developed his own ideas about the nature of Evil. Monroe had spent his entire life in the trenches of wars both hot and cold. Korea, Vietnam, Eastern Europe, the Middle East, Africa. Monroe felt that Evil was a tangible thing, a living Being, that stalked the Earth unopposed and forever hungry. He sometimes thought that human beings had been sent to the planet specifically to counter Evil on its home turf. It was a wild idea, but no stranger than a lot of Monroe's speculations: some of which had turned out to be right over the years. The Earth, according to Monroe one winter night about twenty years earlier (after sharing a bottle of Laphroaig with Aubrey), was the material basis for Evil. Like a magic circle drawn by sorcerers to evoke demons, the Earth was a magic globe that had been put to the same purpose. Humans were the only beings in the created world who could combat this Evil, and hence were seeded onto the planet to grow, evolve, and develop the moral and spiritual tools—and the political will—necessary to confront the Being that had possessed—as in *demoniacal* possession—the planet.

But there were humans who had lost the faith, who had abandoned their original purpose, and who had sided with the unbelievable strength and power of this Evil. Unaware of their danger they were like desperate gamblers who had borrowed money from a loan shark, paying the vig every week but never quite able to touch the principle, and who would eventually have their legs broken by the Mob.

It was this class of human being—the dark side of Grothendieck's "mutant" coin—that Aubrey was sent to identify and locate. These "mutants" were probably disorganized and scattered around the globe, but they had some point of contact with the Evil they worshipped. Some gate, some portal … either a physical location, or a human being, or a confluence of ley lines, star charts, and battlegrounds that existed in some dimension parallel to, or conterminous with, our own. If they were going to find Angell, they would almost certainly find the Order of Dagon, the most likely point of contact for the Evil that Monroe and others long before him had referred to as *Cthulhu*.

And in order to find an evil cult, one could do no worse than trace the actions of evil enterprises to find their source. The problem was: there were all sorts of evil in the world. Where does one begin?

It was Monroe who provided the answer to that question.

Something had happened back in the States, some new evidence or clue had surfaced and it connected some dots for the old spymaster. Monroe told Aubrey that the most fruitful line of enquiry at the moment would be the world-wide trafficking of children, specifically those children selected for ritualistic purposes. To that end, he sent Aubrey an encrypted file full of artwork.

On the flight from Paris to London Aubrey scanned the file. The first few images were familiar ones to Aubrey: the Goya paintings of "The Sabbath" and "Saturn Devouring his Children." The first hung in the Museo Lázaro Galdiano, and the latter in the Prado, both in Madrid. The painting known as "The Sabbath" depicts a goat with garlands of leaves in its horns accepting the sacrifice of a child. There were those who claimed that the Goat—a familiar representation of the Devil—was initiating the child into its satanic service, but the skeleton of one child in the painting and the offering of a child's corpse by an old woman seemed to favor the original interpretation.

The painting of Saturn eating a child required no further explanation.

There were then some reproductions of old woodcuts. The notation accompanying them said that they were from something called the *Compendium Maleficarum*, by the seventeenth century monk Francesco Maria Guazzo. They depicted demons in various scenes, including one in which human children were brought before them. A caption read, "The demons took prompt advantage of this opportunity by coupling them in incestuous unions." Brother and sister; mother and son; father and daughter. This was a theme that would arise again.

Picture after picture, painting after painting, all from an earlier time and all depicting the ritual abuse or even murder of children. Aubrey was fortunate that the seat next to him on the plane was unoccupied, so that he could examine the artwork without fear that a seatmate might consider him some form of reprobate, or worse. He flipped through the screens, one after the other, getting the message

Monroe wanted to convey. It was not just about child abuse, and it was not just about some gaggle of cultists. It was both.

These disturbing images were followed by a number of photographs of young girls. Aubrey viewed these with trepidation, fearful that even worse images would follow. The girls were clothed, but they were posed suggestively. It nearly made him ill to be confronted with this material, and to think how these photos might have been arranged, lighted, and shot, and by whom.

In each photo there was a tattoo prominently displayed.

Aubrey recognized the symbol, and then understood why Monroe had sent him the file. The last page contained a name and an address, somewhere in Wales. Another file—undated and unmarked—contained some background information on the person he was requested to see. It was an intelligence file, probably NSA, with the identities of the targets unmasked.

Aubrey scanned this second file. It was disconcerting, to say the least. The file had information on an obscure author of occult texts which, if the information was ever disseminated, would destroy the author and all of his friends and family for a generation or more. It was the type of information that only the NSA could obtain with its worldwide access to private internet accounts.

He closed the files on the approach to Heathrow, and looked out the window at the clouds and the sky. His counterparts in the intelligence community were doing much the same type of work he was: accessing forbidden files, drawing connections and conclusions, identifying private individuals with links to terror cells or intelligence operations. He had begun his career in just that way, but when he was selected by Monroe to work on a project whose security classification was so restricted that it could choke you if you took a deep breath, his training and experience were suddenly kicked up a notch or two and his targets changed from fanatic ideologues with bombs and swords to cultists, UFO freaks, and dangerous books. Just as lethal, he realized after decades with Monroe, but, well, still weird.

They told him it was career suicide, working for Monroe, but Aubrey figured that it was career suicide for a congressman to become president. Presidents had term limits. A congressman could be reelected forever. That was how Aubrey looked at his own career. He was right where he wanted to be, working for a man he respected in a war that was already old when Moses was a toddler. He didn't need to rise up the ranks in the intelligence community just to wind up with an administrative post at Langley or Fort Meade, running the managers who ran the officers who ran the agents half a world away. With Monroe, he got involved in every conceivable kind of operation, and now it was a satanic cult trafficking in children, a cult trying to bring about the end of the world as we know it. Beats chasing your garden variety smugglers, terrorists, and lowlifes any day of the week.

The plane landed and taxied to the gate. Aubrey lifted his carry-on and headed for immigration control, and then the car rental area. He was in a gloomy mood, and the weather didn't help. It had just begun to rain.

The one known as Calvin George, his target, was a man now in his eighties, living in an isolated farmhouse in Wales. He had been a life-long occultist, and had been reviled for almost as long due to some rituals he had published in the 1970s concerning the ritual initiation of children. This was in a pop occult paperback that purported to reveal the secrets of modern "witchcraft." While most of the book was what one might expect of such an endeavor—magical calendars, magic circles, priests and priestesses, horned gods and woodland goddesses—the rituals with regard to pubescent children were precise to the point of obsession, even extending to the deliberate piercing of the hymen by either a parent or one of the members of the coven prior to the actual initiation itself, a rite that included sexual intercourse of both girls and boys by adult men and women. Monroe believed that George did not come by this system on his own, but had received it from another source. It was a long shot, but since Aubrey was already in Europe it was decided a visit was worth the time and effort.

After securing his rental car he drove down the M4 to Cardiff. It was faster than taking another plane or the train, and he would need the car in any event as the cottage where Calvin George and his wife Hywen lived was off the beaten path. Also, he could use the two hours or so to think of what he would ask, and of how he would get the information he needed. He had no illusions about the way he would be received, and would have to convince the old man to give up the names he required. He knew that this was a tricky mission, since if the old man was a pedophile he would do whatever he could to deflect Aubrey's questioning and deny everything.

He found the cottage, several miles west of Cardiff, along the coast, with little trouble. It stood by itself against a gunmetal grey sky, its lone chimney squeezing out a thin stream of dirty smoke. It was spring, but with the cold drizzle in this part of the Welsh coast it felt like a late winter. He got out of the car and jogged to the front door and knocked.

He was received by the man's wife, Hywen—a woman of a certain age about whom it could be charitably said she looked the part of a medieval witch. After he flashed his identification and gave his cover story for why he was there, he was led into a kind of sitting room. She was obviously worried, startled by Aubrey's sudden appearance at her doorstep and the possible bad news it would bring. She bent over her husband's head and whispered into his ear.

Calvin was enthroned on a reclining chair, surrounded by pillows, and enveloped in a cloud of what Aubrey guessed was some kind of incense or perhaps a lotion, something vaguely medicinal. He had the physique of a man who had once been heavy but who was now reduced considerably in girth. His face was covered in a whitish beard and topped off with heavy, bushy eyebrows. He was wrapped in a frayed, light blue dressing gown and there were the remains of an afternoon tea set before him on a small wooden tray.

The room was filled with pagan knickknacks: statues of various European deities, satyrs, dryads, nymphs, a Green Man or two. Candlesticks with stubs of white and black candles. A vaguely Asian-looking incense burner. And, of course, shelves of books on suitably esoteric topics with the obligatory *White Goddess* by Robert Graves taking pride of place alongside Calvin's own published work, which even included a book on Tantra.

When he spoke, his voice was cracked with age but nonetheless clear. Something about him made Aubrey think of a petulant child who had just been smacked and who is bracing for the next one.

"I understand you have come to me for a consultation?"

Aubrey nodded. He had introduced himself as someone working for the US government, which was not exactly a lie. He had waved his NSA identification card—one of several IDs he possessed—on his way in. Before Calvin became a spokesperson for the allegedly ancient religion of witchcraft, he had worked in the defense establishment for decades and Aubrey knew that the NSA identification would be the ticket in, rather than FBI or CIA. Calvin was a geek in that respect, and the NSA was the Oz of Geekery.

"Yes. I was told you had the expertise needed in a specific area of interest to us."

Calvin eyed him suspiciously. "And what specific area would that be, then? Specifically?"

"I was told you were the person to ask about certain practices that might seem objectionable if taken out of context."

The old man was slimy but not stupid.

"You've read my books, I take it? Especially the one that gave me so much trouble?"

Aubrey hadn't, but let the old man think he had.

"In that case, there is nothing left for me to say to you." He gestured to his wife to lead Aubrey to the door.

Aubrey, however, remained seated and pointedly ignored Hywen.

"I didn't want it to go this way, but if it must, it must. We know all about you, you and your wife. We have a file on you that goes back to your days working aerospace and missiles. And before. All it will take is one phone call from me and you will be facing a variety of felony charges, both here and in the States, so I suggest you answer my questions. Truthfully, mind." He held up his cell phone. "I have an excellent provider plan with unlimited calls," he smirked. "It won't cost me anything—not even the proverbial dime—to uproot your entire life, such as it is."

"Just … just what are you suggesting … what felonies?" But it was a lost cause, and Calvin knew it. Aubrey had the file on his host and would not reveal its contents, but he knew human nature well enough that the mere suggestion of government interest in one's affairs was sufficient to turn the most law-abiding citizen into jelly. In Calvin George's case, as a promoter of neo-paganism and witchcraft, and possibly pedophilia or at the very least hebephilia, he would be particularly susceptible to threats. Guilty or innocent, everyone's reputation suffers irreparable damage with the merest hint of scandal.

All Aubrey had to do was remain silent and return the man's aggrieved stare with a quiet one of his own.

A furtive sound behind him caused Aubrey to break his silence, but not his stare.

"I wouldn't do that, Hywen. Put it down."

The old lady had grabbed an *athame*—a ritual dagger—from off their personal altar and was advancing towards Aubrey with murderous intent. *These people are crazy*, he thought. Aubrey was less concerned about getting stabbed with the relatively blunt device than he was of getting sepsis from God only knew what blood and bodily fluids had stained its blade over the years.

The witch froze in place, the dagger held forward in a right hand that trembled with the effort. This was, after all, an elderly couple regardless of their reputation and Aubrey felt sympathy for them. Their beliefs had attracted ridicule and opprobrium throughout their long lives, and Aubrey knew that the ridicule hurt them far more and cut more deeply than the fear and loathing they inspired. Witches, indeed.

Calvin looked over at his wife and, momentarily beaten, simply nodded. Fuming, she turned and replaced the knife on the altar and fled the room.

"What do you want to know? Get it over with, then leave."

Aubrey finally broke the stare, nodded briefly as if to accept his host's surrender, and settled back into the threadbare upholstery with a sigh.

"The rituals. The ones involving children. Of all the rituals in your book, these were the most explicit, the most detailed. Great care had been taken to present the material in a specific—almost elaborate—way. The rest of the rites and recipes in your text were relatively common, consistent with what had been published before in other popular formulations of the witchcraft movement. But not these. Not the rituals involving the sexual ... education of underage children." He had almost said "abuse" of children, but there was no sense in alienating the man even further.

"I've been over all of this with the authorities, many times, not to mention all the shite I had to take from the pagan community. What more is there that I can tell you?"

"Where did it come from? Where did those rituals come from? Either you were—and presumably still are—a raging pedophile who used neo-paganism and witchcraft as a cover, or an excuse, for your depravity or ...?"

"I am not a pedophile!" he shouted, struggling to stand amid the pillows and the woven comforter that covered his knees.

His wife, Hywen, at the sound of the shout began to rush into the room but Aubrey held up his hand to stop her.

"I am not saying you are, Calvin," he responded, gently. "But in that case, I need answers. Where did you get those rituals? Who fed them to you? I realize it was long ago, and the person or persons may already be dead but you can give me a name anyway. In fact, what do you have to lose? Whoever was behind this is probably long gone. They can do nothing to you any more."

The old witch fell back into his easy chair. The effort of trying to stand winded him, and Aubrey realized that he was sicker than he had previously understood. The man was dying. Would he die with this knowledge on his conscience? Aubrey had to pick at that particular scab.

"When you go to the Summerland, you will be greeted by the souls you had most affected, both during your life and after. That means that those who read your books—even decades from now—will be among those who judge you. We can do a great deal to ameliorate any suffering that these rituals may cause. You can demonstrate your honorable intentions by revealing the source of the stain and exposing it if need be."

That was when color came into Calvin's cheeks and fire burned in his eyes. Aubrey then knew he had miscalculated.

"I'm not going to any damned Summerland!" he shouted. "I don't believe in any of that rubbish! It was a business, that's all! Look at Gerald Gardner, Ray Buckland, Alex Sanders. At the Farrars. I had a seat at that table. I should have been the leader of the pack. Instead, because of that one ... that one *problem* ... I was ostracized. The only ones who came to me after that were the freaks and the perverts."

Aubrey remained silent and watchful. The old man was in a dangerous place, dangerous mostly to himself but lethal nonetheless.

"Yes, we had orgies. Why the hell not? We were pagans, see? We were overthrowing the old, Judeo-Christian morality, the repressive superstructure of our pathetic lives. Yes, our rituals had sex. What was the point of calling yourselves witches if there was no sex? Gardner had introduced naked rites, back in the 1950s. He called it 'sky clad' then, after a term he picked up in Asia. Then the witch covens in New York, following his lead, with the wife-swapping and the swinging. How could you have a bunch of grown men and women standing around naked in candlelight, drinking wine, and there not be sex? You see? And all that about the Great Rite. The Great Rite was sexual intercourse, and it was the logical conclusion of all that dancing about naked. We were open about it, mate. We were in your face. Unapologetic. That was the idea back then."

Aubrey, still silent, nodded. He wanted to encourage him to go on until he ran out of steam.

"And then ... the thing about the kids. No one else had spoken of this. No one else had brought kids into the picture. But we were dealing with a lot of middle-class couples in their thirties and forties who had kids. The upper class snobs were not into witchcraft. They had their secret societies, their underground cults. Their Golden Dawns. Their rituals required so many gadgets and instruments and robes you needed a bloody fortune to participate. Witchcraft needed none of that. A place to meet, some candles, maybe a bit of incense, and Bob's your uncle. The middle class could relate to that. But what to do about the kids? Well, bring them in. Make them part of the rituals. But ... won't there be naked men and women about? How to deal with that?"

He fell silent for a moment. Aubrey knew he was on the verge of getting the information he needed. All he had to do was wait him out.

"How to deal with that?" Calvin repeated, almost in a whisper. "Well, my idea was to create a kind of kids' ritual, just for them, that would happen in a separate place or at a different time. It was all quite logical, all above board. I started writing up the lessons. We were to have a correspondence course, all legal and incorporated. And then ... and then *he* showed up. The man in black. The summoner. And it all went to shite."

Aubrey leaned a little forward in his chair to see and hear Calvin more clearly. His host seemed to be receding a little with every word he uttered, as if he would disappear if he finished his story, like a deranged Cheshire cat leaving not a smile but a grimace of despair. That is when he noticed the vial of pills on his tray, next to the tea cozy, and prayed Calvin had not taken a sedative or a pain-killer.

"The man in black?" he prompted.

Calvin roused himself from his reverie.

"That's what we called him. The man in black. Not like those flying saucer blokes, but a proper man in black. In witchcraft circles we call him the summoner. He's the one shows up just before the sabbat is to start, to summon you to the ritual. He was like that. A mysterious person, reserved, but sinister. And he even dressed all in black. He just shows up one day when we lived in Missouri, me and the wife, and tells us he is going to give us the missing piece of our program. He says we are on the verge of learning the secret, the essential mystery at the heart of all occultism, all witchcraft, and he needs us to hear it first hand so that there are no mistakes."

"And you believed him?"

Calvin shrugged his shoulders.

"It was the Sixties, mate. There was no Internet. No personal computers. No smart phones. There was no way to check up on people, find out who they were, where they came from. Not for regular people, anyway. Your lot would have found a way, I'm sure, but we didn't have that luxury. When a stranger walks into your home and seems to know all about you already, and offers you the crown jewels … Well, it happened to Crowley, didn't it? That German bloke walks up to him one day and says he's just revealed the secret behind the Order, the Ordo Templi Orientis, and that Crowley had to be initiated in order to keep it secret. Right? Same thing. And, basically, the same secret."

At this, Aubrey's eyes widened slightly.

"The same secret?"

"Well, damn, man, just look at the ritual. *The Star Sapphire.* The one that caused Jerry to have a fit."

"Jerry?"

"The Hun, man. The Germans!"

"Ah."

"He said that the key phrase was something in there about a mystic rose, which is bullshit of course. The key was the *Star Sapphire* itself, with all its Latin mumbo jumbo about the father and the daughter, the mother and the son, and the like. What do you suppose *that* was all about?"

Aubrey thought back to one of his conversations with Monroe on the subject of Crowley, who was of tangential importance to the Lovecraft Codex: that enormous hardcopy file Monroe kept locked away in his safe. Aubrey remembered that the sexual interpretation of religion and occultism was the reason Crowley was best known. He also knew that Crowley's famous maxim "A male child of perfect innocence and high intelligence is the most satisfactory and suitable victim" was meant metaphorically, as he himself clarified on the same page of his *Magick: In Theory and Practice*. But Calvin was suggesting something else.

"You know the passage? It's in Latin—probably for good reason, yeah?—but translated it says 'Father and Mother, one God; Mother and Son, one God, Son and Daughter one God; Daughter and Father, one God.' Or words to that effect. You see what I mean? You add all that about a mystic rose and a magick rood, and the implication is clear."

Aubrey merely raised an eyebrow. He knew what Calvin was getting at, but he needed him to say it himself.

"Are you simple, mate? It's everyone shagging everyone else! Fathers and daughters, mothers and sons, even sons and daughters. *Incest.* And now Crowley is, like, academically respectable, even with all that shagging and buggering going on. And they call *me* a pervert and a pedophile!"

"So, what did the man in black want you to do?"

"Well, it's obvious, right? He wanted me to expand on the theme, so to speak. He wanted me to develop the idea, to get it out there. He said that it wasn't just sex that was the secret of occultism and occult power but the *kind* of sex. *Transgressive* sex, he called it. And with the sexual revolution of the Sixties going on, there wasn't much left that was transgressive anymore."

"Except sex with children."

"Aye. Sex with children. He said I would be on the cutting

edge. A Crowley in my own time, he said. That I would put the likes of Gardner and Buckland in the shade. And all that. Well, the rest is history, as they say. I published my book, and reaped the whirlwind. I got banned from a lot of pagan events. Was pilloried in the underground press."

"So the other witches weren't too keen on the incest angle? The child abuse … initiations?" Aubrey said, a little maliciously.

Calvin turned to face him directly. Up to now, he had been staring into space as he recounted the injustices of his past.

"You know what, mate? Fuck you, and the unicorn you rode in on."

"Not so fast, *mate*. I need a name."

"Jesus, I don't remember his name. Not after all these years."

"On the contrary, I am certain you remember his name as well as you remember your own. He initiated you, didn't he? Into his group? Otherwise what you just told me doesn't make sense. He initiated you, and we both know you know the name of the group and can identify the ones who brought you in."

Calvin swallowed, and looked away. Aubrey heard Hywen come into the room behind him and stand in the doorway, as if unsure if she should enter. He noticed that Calvin and Hywen exchanged a glance, and then Calvin appeared to deflate before his eyes.

"If I tell you … if I identify these … these individuals, then I stand to lose my own life, don't I? I'm a goner, and that's for sure. And you have no idea what they will do to Hywen here. It could be even worse for her."

Aubrey thought he saw the trickle of a tear in Calvin's left eye, but that could have been a trick of the light.

"These people are monsters," Hywen offered, and her voice was stronger and firmer than her husband's. Aubrey turned to look at her.

She was shorter than her husband, and an American. Her hair was white, and cut close around her skull. She wore a black wool dress with some red and green embroidery and clunky shoes. Her hands were empty of weapons, Aubrey noted with some relief.

"They are monsters, and they will do anything to achieve their ends."

"What are their ends?"

"Damned if we know," chimed in Calvin. "We're just pawns to them, or were. We don't hear much from them anymore."

"Not until last month anyway," Hywen added.

"Damn it, woman!"

"What's the point? He's going to find out soon enough. The stars ... the stars are right."

"What happened last month?"

Hywen took a deep breath, and then raised her eyes to his.

"They made contact. We hadn't heard from them in years. Once we published that damned book, we were abandoned. The only time they made contact in the past was to threaten us. To keep us quiet. They thought the pressure against us was too great, and that we would crack. They didn't understand us, though. We didn't much care about the negative publicity. We were *initiates, true* initiates of a *real* coven. Or magical lodge, or order, or whatever you call it."

"What did they call it?"

"Hywen ..." Calvin tried to warn her, but there was no stopping the witch woman.

"Hush, you old fool. It's time we got this off our chest."

She turned to Aubrey. "They called it Dagon. The Order of Dagon. Their symbol was a kind of fish-man, like Oannes of the Sumerians. But it had wings, too."

As Hywen ran on, Aubrey almost stopped listening. So, it was true. It was Dagon, the same cult or group or terror cell or intelligence agency that had targeted Angell. That wanted—that needed, that *required*—the Book. Dagon had been operating in the States since at least the late Sixties, early Seventies. That's when they made contact with Calvin and Hywen and set the program in motion. Before that—long before that—it was New Orleans. They surfaced there in 1907, at that weird orgy in the bayou. And before that ... well, Monroe had the timeline. But according to scholars of religion the cult was ancient. It predated the Freemasons, the Cathars, the Gnostics, the Mandaeans ...

But what was the connection between Dagon and the whole pedophilia angle? Was it just an attempt to discredit the two people in front of him, and by extension the entire neo-pagan movement? It certainly did do a lot of damage. The conspiracy types were still talking about secret international cabals of child molesters involving high-ranking politicians in satanic cults. Or something.

"Anyway, the man who contacted us and who brought us in was the one they called the Magister Templi, the 'Master of the Temple.' It's a Golden Dawn reference, I guess. But these types were not Golden Dawn by any stretch."

"He was the leader?"

She shook her head. "No, there were others above him in the hierarchy. And they were stretched around the globe. There were centers in Prague, in Turin, in Vienna, plus the ones in the Middle East and America. Others, too, most likely. We were never allowed into the deeper layers."

"And what of the children, then? What does all this have to do with children?"

It was Calvin's turn to speak, and he spoke in a monotone, as if giving testimony at his interrogation. Or his trial.

"The children are critical, see. They are the batteries, the energy source, for the rituals. Children have special abilities. Teenaged children are always present during poltergeist activity, for instance. And they were used as scryers and diviners by the medieval magicians. Their spiritual sight is quite pure. And they are easily possessed..."

"Possessed? What do you mean? By devils?"

"By demons, yes. Well ... *like* demons. They can be used as channels, as the material basis for magical evocation. And sometimes ... sometimes they develop multiple personalities and these can be manipulated by the sorcerers."

Aubrey was attentive now. Some of this was known to him, but some of it was new. He had to get as much as he could out of this shell of a man and back to Monroe. Something about this conversation was nagging at him, some detail he was overlooking. What was it?

"How can you develop multiple personalities at will? This sounds improbable ..."

"Trauma, you see. Trauma. If the child does not prove to be a good subject for seeing in the mirror, or as a vessel for the ... the Old Ones, then he or ... or she ... can be splintered, broken down into pieces, and his mind ... her ... soul ... rearranged ... into several different ... entities. They become like familiars to the sorcerers. Like witch's familiars. They can be told to do things, and they just ... do them."

"Trauma? What kind of trauma?"

It was Hywen's turn to become nervous at the line of questioning.

"Trauma, that's all. Just trauma. Haven't you learned enough? Isn't this what you came for?"

"*What kind of trauma?*"

Calvin seemed to have become comatose. Drool was dripping from his lips and his stare became fixed. Hywen ignored him, and instead directed all her attention to Aubrey. He could feel waves of hatred and fear emanating from her. She spoke, but she sounded like a woman standing at the edge of a tall building, wondering if she should just jump.

"You *know* what kind. You work for the government. You know all about this. It's your people that perfected this back ... back in the day. Bluebird. Artichoke. *MK-ULTRA.*" The last she spit out, like a curse or imprecation. "Our people had the Black Mass. Your people have the Black Ops."

"What kind of trauma, Hywen? Tell me, and then I'm gone."

"Physical trauma. Psychological trauma ..."

"What *kind?*"

She glared at the intruder, this impeccably-dressed and sophisticated elderly gentleman who probably came from old money and privilege. Calvin could have been like him, had he stayed working for the defense industry instead of dropping everything for this chimera of witchcraft and paganism, creating a tradition out of whole cloth and piecemeal fantasies. They could have had money and position in the world. Instead they had a two bedroom cottage in the middle of Wales that leaked when it rained and froze when it snowed, crammed with tea cozies, old books and regret.

She gestured to him.

"You want to know what kind of trauma. This should tell you all you need to know."

She turned on her heel and walked out of the room, pausing only briefly in the doorway to ensure that Aubrey was following her.

He got up, leaving the barely conscious Calvin drooling in his easy chair. He followed Hywen through a beaded curtain and into another room. She stood at the doorway and waited for him to pass her and enter.

"I'll stand out here, if you don't mind," she told him.

Aubrey looked at the closed door and wondered what lay on the other side. These old people seemed harmless if the only weapon they had was an old ceremonial dagger, but he decided to keep playing as long as he had a hand.

"Before I go in, I need to know about that last contact. Who contacted you? What did they want?"

She stood with her arms folded across her chest, head bowed as if in thought, as if trying to come to a decision.

"He said his name was Vanek. We hadn't met him before. Sounded American. Younger than us, but maybe fifty-five, sixty? He called us on the telephone, so we didn't see his face." She shrugged.

"What did he want?"

"He told us what we've been waiting for, all this time. He said … he said 'the stars are right.'"

"What did that mean to you?"

"It meant that it was going to happen. That everything we had worked for, sacrificed for, all these years … these *decades* … was finally coming to pass. He said the *stars* were *right*, and that the

Dark Lord had been in contact with the Order, and the Priest was awakening. Then he hung up."

"I thought the man who contacted you was in the Order?"

"Oh. No. Vanek is with some other group, but one that takes its authority from the Dark Lord, and the Dark Lord is empowered by the Order. You only know the one above you, and that one knows the next one up the hierarchy. It's for operational security, you see."

"This … Dark Lord. It's some kind of god?"

She gave a bitter laugh. "No, that's just his initiate name. He's flesh and blood. We met him once, in Turin, but he wore a mask during the ritual and we didn't actually see what he looked like."

"And the Priest? Who is he?"

At that point, Hywen shivered and drew her arms more tightly across her chest, shaking her head as she did so.

"Not a he. Not the way we think, anyway. The Priest has been asleep for thousands of years. Under the sea. But the stars are right, the time is near for him to rouse himself from his slumber of aeons and take what is rightfully his."

She said all of that as if she was reading from a cue card. It was something from memory, probably something she was taught during her training. She presented it in a monotone, and for a moment she reminded him of her husband in the next room. These were damaged people, and they had elected to live out here in a rural backwater—the back of beyond—to escape their own history.

Aubrey nodded to himself. He figured he had about as much as he was going to get. With more time they would start to spin stories, just to keep him interested. They were lonely, and felt misunderstood. Aubrey called it Scheherazade Syndrome; a lot of confidential informants do the same thing. They make up stories just to stay relevant, or to keep their captors from killing them.

After a long look at Hywen, gauging her intentions, he opened the door and made his way into what appeared to be a bedroom that had been turned into a kind of shrine. Not a pagan one, not something from a witch's bible, but a deeply personal one.

The wall in front of him was covered in photographs that had been pasted up in what appeared to be random order. They were all of the same person, a young man who bore a striking resemblance to Calvin from one angle, but to something unearthly from another.

"Is this …?"

"Our son. Yes. That's young Lucius. At various times. That one, the one you're looking at, was taken his first day of school. The other one, next to it, was taken at Yule shortly before … before it happened."

"I don't understand. What happened? Where is he now?"

For once, an almost human smile graced the old witch's lips.

"There is a single answer to your two questions. Where is he now? He's in a facility. A mental facility. I won't tell you which one, because I don't want you bothering him. It wouldn't do you much good, anyway. You'll never be sure which one of him you'll be talking to."

Photo after photo showed a happy, intelligent-looking young boy until the photos turned somewhat darker. The boy's expression went from carefree and almost joyful to withdrawn, depressed, and … eventually, in the later shots … sinister. There was a vagueness in his expression, deadness in his eyes, a mouth that seemed to want to chew itself out of existence. Even his hair seemed darker, and his skin more sallow. The later photos looked like they had been taken covertly, from a hiding place, and showed Lucius in a kind of stagger on a dark city street. He had turned to face the general direction of the camera, and one could see he was snarling.

"That one, that was taken only a few days before his thirteenth birthday." He looked at least twenty. More to the point, Aubrey had seen photographs of victims in various stages of demonic possession: in Italy, in Africa, and in Sumatra. The later photos of Lucius were eerily similar. A soul in torment, or more likely a body robbed of its own soul and replaced with another. But with *what*? Merely looking at Lucius's photos was enough to bring the Thing into greater focus, as if It had possessed even the paper and the ink. Possession was believed to be the result of demonic activity or, in the case of voluntary possession such as in the trances of Haitian *voudon*, the *loa* or the gods. This seemed to be neither the one nor the other. Neither god nor devil. Then ... what?

Aubrey turned to face her.

"He has MPD? Or what they now call dissociative identity disorder?"

"Yes. That was the diagnosis. It's rare. Not as common as the books and movies would have you think. Some psychiatrists even think there is no such thing. But I know my son, and I know the personalities he has are not his own. He won't be getting out. That's another thing I know."

"Your file says you have another son. A twin, as I recall? Where is he?"

Hywen's eyes opened wide at this. "You know that? You knew that when you came here?"

"I told you, Mrs. George. We know everything about you and your husband going back decades."

"So then you must know what happened to ... to the other one."

"I want to hear it from you."

She shook her head. "You won't hear it from me. You won't hear anything about him from me. He's gone, and that's all there is to it. He was never part of this. He left when he was quite young, before what happened to Lucius."

He pointed to the latest photo of Lucius, in which the boy is hunched over in what seemed to be an examination room. Screaming at the camera.

"They did this to him?"

"*They*? Yes. *They* did this to him. But *they* had help."

To clarify, she nodded her head in the direction of the sitting room.

"Your *husband*?"

She nodded, watching Aubrey's expression, trying to gauge his reaction.

"Not just him. *Me, too.*"

That's when Aubrey felt something inside of him drop to the floor. He was face to face with evil, but the kind of evil that is mixed liberally with despair. And guilt. He wished the woman in front of him was pure evil, pure and unadulterated. Then he could hate her. Then he even could kill her.

She saw it, saw the rage flicker across Aubrey's features before it was suppressed. She started speaking quickly, trying to get it all in, trying to make him comprehend her role in the destruction of her own son.

"They promised us so much, you understand? They promised us unbelievable achievements. All we had to do was offer our son. No, not a human sacrifice! No blood-letting! No killing! They assured us. We just had to bring him into the ritual, and they would do the rest." Her voice went down to a whisper. "I mean, it was only sex, after all. That's all it was. He would have found out about sex eventually. A year, maybe two, later. But they needed him *virgin*. You understand this, right? You know what I'm talking about? They needed him 'untouched' is how they put it. So that he could *see*. So that he could see in the mirror. They strapped him on a table, an altar, in the box. The box … it was all wires, a cage. Something to do with energy, with electricity. But it wasn't working. The ritual lasted for hours. They tried everything. Incantations in Arabic and Greek. In Enochian, where the words vibrate the very air! Even drugs. Drugs I had never heard of, and I'm from California." She tried for a smile, but she had a tough audience.

"When that didn't work, they went to the next degree. The next initiation. And that worked. Not at once. Not right away. But it worked. They were on top of him. *In* him. You understand? They dragged the blood of the Lion out of him, drop by drop. It took hours, but the voice broke through. The voice! It strummed his vocal chords like guitar strings. It was the most awful sound I have ever heard, as if three people were speaking through him at once but all saying the same words. I can't really explain it, you see. Unless you hear it yourself, it doesn't make sense. The room was shaking.

The *whole room*. And Lucius? Our *son*? He was not seeing, he was being. *Being.* But by that time, he was already gone. Our son, I mean. He was gone. Down ... down the Tunnels. The ritual was a success. They told us. They were pleased. It worked. But they used my son like ... like an old radio set, twisting the dials and moving the antenna until they got the signal they wanted. That poor little naked boy. Covered in his own ... I can't say it. *He* was on top of him. Doing terrible, awful things to our son. He screamed then, the first time I ever heard him scream. Ever in his life. But it worked. The transgression, you know. Powerful. Powerful. The psychic shock. The ... the neurophysiology was beyond me. The explanations were dense with references to glands, to hormones, to the *chakras* and the rise of the Serpent. The pineal gland. The *kalas* of a child who has not had ... who was a virgin. Clean. Pure. And then the voice and we heard. We heard the Priest! It blinded our ... our third eyes. It tore the light from our darkness and splintered the darkness into a thousand slivers of ... He was shivering, he was so cold, and I wanted to cover him, but they wouldn't let me near him. I wasn't advanced enough, they said. And then there was much talk about the Lion and the Eagle. The Menstruum. And the Moon. My very touch could be dangerous to him when he was exposed like that, they said, trembling with the forces ramming into him like tidal waves on a tiny ... *tiny* beach. He was lost then, wandering alone and terrified in the Tunnels of Set ... that's where he is now, you know. The doctors don't know it, but ... the Tunnels. They lead to the City of R'lyeh, the sarcophagus of the High Priest of the Great Old Ones. But Calvin ... Calvin ..."

"He couldn't do anything to stop it?"

Her eyes shot up to stare into his. He saw a madwoman's eyes, a woman in the grip of insanity. How much longer could she sustain this within her before she went mad?

"Stop it? *Stop* it? This was Calvin's initiation into the Order! He couldn't *stop* it. He was an essential *part* of it. Don't you understand? Don't you get it?"

In the car, driving back to Heathrow, Aubrey thought of what he had almost done. He wanted to kill her. He almost had. And her husband. And then burn down their little house and all the sickness it contained. He wanted to rid the world of their evil, to cleanse at least that little corner of Wales and send them both straight to hell. But he realized that is precisely where they already were. So he left them there. The old man drooling in his chair. The old woman with the crazed eyes and the rictus of a smile. But the sound of her voice followed him out of the house and down to the car and all the way to Heathrow and his next flight.

Her last words had chilled him to the bone, and had made him seriously consider blowing her head off. And he was not, never had been, a violent man:

"*Stop it? Why would he stop it? Those screams. The terror and the pain. That man on top of him? It was Calvin!*"

CHAPTER TWENTY

HIS NAME WAS JEAN-PAUL BECKETT JONES. His parents had named him after Jean-Paul Sartre and Samuel Beckett. They were psychology and lit majors in the community college where they met. It should have been a fruitful relationship, full of deep psychological insights into literature, and literary depictions of deep psychological states, but that didn't happen. It was a lot of *Nausea* and a little *Malone Dies*. The only fruit of the union was Jean-Paul, who was born three months after his parents split up.

He lived with his mother in a wood frame house on the outskirts of Whately, Massachusetts which was itself an outskirt of an outskirt in the middle of nowhere, north of Springfield and south of Brattleboro, Vermont. Route 91 went straight through the town in a hurry as if it had somewhere else to be.

The University of Massachusetts at Amherst was close enough to be a tease but far enough away to be unapproachable for Jean-Paul. He and his mother hugged the poverty line like a flotation device, but he got the course catalogues anyway—they were free—and drooled over the humanities offerings. Linguistics, now there was a field. A few linguistics courses might help him understand the language of his rituals and the messages in his dreams.

The catalogues were stacked up in his room in the basement of the house. Some of them were old and faded with time, the occasional plumbing leak, and mold, and had the patina of ancient texts full of indecipherable mysteries. He had those, too.

One shelf was groaning with the weight of big books on occultism and ceremonial magic, like Arthur Edward Waite's *Book of Black Magic and of Pacts*, and Lewis Spence's *Encyclopedia of Occultism*, and Grillot de Givry's *Picture Museum of Sorcery, Magic and Alchemy*. He had Idries Shah's book on ceremonial magic, and Francis Barrett's *The Magus*. For someone who had very little discretionary income, Jean-Paul had a good basic library of books representing all the broken promises of the western world. These were course catalogues, too, in a way. They described in tantalizing detail what would happen if you followed all the lessons to the end. They promised a graduation replete with robes, speeches, and singing angels.

To his credit, Jean-Paul knew that he could not attain the state of enlightenment and spiritual power he sought unless he had some kind of instruction from someone who had already done all of this and who could guide him in the right way of summoning demons and invoking the celestial powers. He had already tried magic on his own. The results were frightening but in the end did nothing to improve his personal status in life. He still lived with his mother, who was growing increasingly insane from a steady diet of unfiltered cigarettes and Krispy Kremes. He stole books from libraries when he was able to do so, because he could not possibly afford to buy them like a normal person, and was always in danger of being caught. If the authorities ever found his stash of over one hundred stolen volumes he figured he would wind up in prison for sure. He didn't steal from bookstores, though. They had better security and no sense of humor.

But it was while he was in a bookstore, browsing in the section that mixed up astrology with tarot with secret societies, wicca and magic, that Jean-Paul found a card stuck into a copy of *The Book of Lies* that advertised meetings of something called the Ordo Templi Septentrionalis, or OTS. One had to write to a post office box in order to be advised of the meeting location and to receive approval to attend same. Oddly, there was no email address, nothing electronic at all.

He went home and did a web search for the name of the group, and found nothing. That in itself was strange. You would have thought that someone, somewhere would have at least registered the name as a URL, but there was no indication that it had been. He looked up "septentrionalis" and discovered that it was Latin for "north." That meant that Ordo Templi Septentrionalis was the Latin form of "Order of the Temple of the North." What did that mean, though? Was it in Canada?

He pondered the problem for awhile, but then decided to take the plunge. He wrote to the address on the card, giving them his particulars: including sun sign, rising sign, favorite color, books read, and omitting anything having to do with his economic condition or the fact that he was still living with his mother.

He sat back and waited for a reply.

To while away the time, he searched the classified sections of various internet sites for a job. He had virtually no qualifications, other than he had summoned Belial to visible appearance two years earlier and scared the shit out of himself. Belial did not appear as he was supposed to, but as a particularly sinister wisp of incense smoke. No matter. Jean-Paul knew a demon when he (almost) saw one but how was he going to put that on a resume? He had started a LinkedIn profile, but when they asked him for "education" and "experience" he had to leave those sections blank. When it came to filling in his personal preferences, he had enough common sense to realize that "ceremonial magic" and "Tarot cards—intermediate" would be contra-indicated. Needless to say, his job searches were largely fruitless. Thank God for food stamps.

Jean-Paul was twenty-seven years old. And a virgin.

But he was also a Magus of the Dark Realms, a Master Magician of the Order of the Demonic Forces of the Third Veil, and a Sorcerer-in-Waiting of the Archduke of the Ninth Circle. He had mystical attainments up the yin-yang! The diplomas covering the wall in his basement proved it. He was a fourth degree in one secret society and a seventy-second degree in another. (Sometimes all that was required was a Paypal account and a balance of at least ten dollars, which Jean-Paul could usually swing one way or another.) He made his own robes from swatches left over from when his mother toyed with the idea of becoming a seamstress, and he had an old Masonic sword from a garage sale in Springfield, bought one year when they were feeling flush. There was some satisfaction in knowing that, even though he lived in his mother's basement, he was a fully-qualified Mage with enormous powers on the astral plane, if not the earthly one.

Let thy servants be few and secret, the great English magician Aleister Crowley had written (or the Spirit that had inspired him), *they shall rule the many and the known*. Jean-Paul Beckett Jones was nothing if not "few and secret" and in his most intense private fantasy he knew he ruled (or should rule) the "many and the known."

When the response from the OTS arrived, Jean-Paul felt his luck was beginning to change. It came in a plain white envelope with no return address, but the letter it contained was cordial and welcoming. It was written on fancy letterhead, replete with the seal of the OTS: a bird-man figure in an oval, around which was inscribed something obscure and most likely profound in a language he didn't recognize but which seemed strangely familiar.

The bird-man was shown head on, facing Jean-Paul as if looking right at him. Its wings were arrayed behind it and it had what appeared to be claw-like feet and scaly skin. It was hovering over a cup or chalice with the word "graal" inscribed along its rim. That was the one word he did recognize, for it was the old form of the word "grail." The bird-man, though, was a mystery. It wasn't quite an angel—not with those claws and the beak-like nose—and it didn't seem demonic, for since when do demons appear in the same image as grails? These people obviously had access to some deep layer stuff, something from the Tunnels of Set maybe, or the realm of the Shells. And they were acknowledging *him* as one of their own!

"*Cara Frater*," the letter began. "Dear Brother." That was already a rush. They were calling him "brother" even though he hadn't sent any cash.

"Cara Frater, we are pleased to learn of your interest. You will be gratified to know that our Order maintains an Oratory in your town. Our brothers pass through on a regular basis, to make contact on the inner planes through the Portal that is open there. But you may already know this, as it is obvious you are an Advanced Adept on the Path."

Finally, he thought. *The recognition I deserve.*

The letter went on to give particulars about the time and place of the next Oratorical Ambulatory, or OA. Evidently, that was when members of the Order—who called themselves Templars of the North—passed from the worldly plane to the more rarified atmosphere of the Upper Levels. There was some Kabbalistic jargon and an occasional reference to another Frater, someone called Perdurabo, but by then Jean-Paul's eyes were glazing over. The most important detail was the fact that he would actually meet these Adepts, including maybe the Master of the Inner Order who enclosed a flyer for his latest book: *The Archon and the Abbess*. The blurb said it was a "rousing tale of antiquated occult intrigue, accidental comedy, philosophical pratfalls, and pious pronouncements on religion and sex, penned by an Adept of Obfuscation and Animadversion. Sure to delight those of any age, from eight to eighteen!" The story seemed to focus on an ancient spiritual Being, one of the Archons of Gnostic lore, a kind of angel, and its attempted seduction of a famous Mesopotamian prostitute who converted to Catholicism and joined a convent in order to escape the Archon's Manichaean clutches, hence the "Abbess" of the title. It was promoted as a thinly-veiled exposé ... but of what, Jean-Paul could not fathom.

No matter. The die had been cast. *Ovum ruptum est*, and all that. The date of the meeting would be advised. The Oratory was evidently located in an old tobacco field. Jean-Paul knew the place, but there were no buildings anywhere near it. The Oratory, he concluded, must be an astral temple of some kind. Invisible to the eyes of the profane.

How cool was *that*?

To prepare, he figured he would have to go on a three-day fast, which meant no junk food between the hours of 11 am and 2 pm, and devote himself to prayer and invocation in the evenings during the hours when his TV programs were not on. He would burn incense at the prescribed times determined by recourse to the schedule set down in his copy of *The Magus*, once he figured it out.

To set it all off right, he performed the Lesser Banishing Ritual of the Pentagram as per the instructions in Israel Regardie. He wasn't sure how to pronounce all the words, but he had it on good authority that precision in foreign languages was an elitist, globalist obsession and he need not worry at all about how well or poorly he accomplished this task.

"*Atoh*," he intoned as he began, solemnly mispronouncing the Hebrew word as "A toe!"

In the aether all around him, the demons gathered for their feast.

At the headquarters of the Ordo Templi Septentrionalis—a fifth-floor walkup studio apartment in New Bedford, Massachusetts—the Magister smiled grimly. He, Frater Vanek, had found a way in. The Dark Lord would be pleased. He took his orders from the Dark Lord—the Master of the Inner Order—who was his only connection to the *real* organization: the Order of Dagon. The OTS functioned as a kind of "outer court" for Dagon, weeding out the sane and the accomplished in favor of the crazies and the destitute, the druggies and those suffering from any one of a number of pre-approved psychological disorders. (They had a list, updated annually.) In point of fact, there was no OTS. Not any longer. Not really.

Years ago, in the 1920s, there had been such an Order, formed in good faith by a triad of German occultists who suspected (or hoped) there was something about sex under all the fancy trappings of religion and ritual. These were Freemasons, and they began to interpret the Masonic degree system in terms of sexuality and were amazed at what they found, incorporating their findings into newly-minted rituals. The binding and hoodwinking of the First Degree initiation were reinterpreted as a sado-masochistic allusion, something out of *The Story of O*. By the time you got to the Third Degree ritual, there was gang rape, spiritualized orgasms, and *le petit mort.* These were *German* occultists, though, so the sex was replete with stout women, chunky men, large breasts in both, and copious gruntings and messing about with fluids. One of their early members would go on to produce the first ever German pornographic film and thereby create the standard against which all subsequent German porn is judged.

However, as more and more individuals were initiated into their group they were infiltrated by members of a genuinely ancient secret society who were not amused by the Order's discoveries and teachings. This was the Order of Dagon. When they learned through the occult grapevine that one of the initiates was talking about the "rediscovery of the Sumerian tradition" they shook their heads. *No,* they said. *Oh, no. Uh-uh. Not in* our *house.*

What happened next is familiar to all students of western esotericism. Schisms abounded. Shouts and accusations. Theft of property. Claims of invalid succession. Unwanted pregnancies. Dire predictions. Restraining orders. Overdoses. Deportations. Publications. Elevations. Implosion.

Now all that was left of the OTS was a post office box in New Bedford and the Magister himself, nursing a shot of Jack Daniels before the flicker of his computer screen. Why it would flicker, when no one else's seemed to, was beyond him. He wasn't very technical.

No matter. Vanek sent a flash email to the Dark Lord. They finally found a patsy in Whately. And just in time, too.

In another week, the stars would be right.

CHAPTER TWENTY-ONE

THE MAN THEY CALLED THE DARK LORD glanced at the email account he shared with Vanek and saw that he had received a communication from that idiot in the States. The email wasn't actually sent: it was kept as a draft in their joint account. Since he had the same password as Vanek he could open the email without actually having "received" it, or Vanek having sent it. It was one way to stay a half-step ahead of the NSA.

How that greedy cretin Vanek had been elevated to the head of the OTS was anyone's guess. In another year or so, Vanek would have to leave the country and find asylum somewhere in Europe maybe, or Latin America, once his financial (and other) crimes caught up with him. But that was fine by the Dark Lord. Setting him up for the fall was part of the plan.

The email told him that they had found a willing participant in Whately. That had been an important—though not essential—part of the project. They had been forced to find other alternatives now that their Soror had been murdered in New Orleans, an event that threatened to expose the Opening should any cop be wise enough to see the signs and sniff out the Mysteries. Not likely, but you never knew.

Few people knew the Dark Lord's real name, and that was the way he liked it. His real patronymic was an old German word meaning "warrior," and his most famous ancestor was a fifth century King of Burgundy, which made the Dark Lord smile for he was indeed particular about that grape and had a case of it in his wine cellar. Not for nothing was he the head of another secret society, this one called the *Argon Archon*, or A.A. The resonance with that other A.A.—the one of the twelve steps or initiatory degrees—was amusing. At least, to him.

But, OTS or AA, the real power lurked behind the thrones of both. This was the Order of Dagon and it held sway over all the western esoteric lodges and orders, and had done so for centuries. Some say, millennia. These were some scary guys, and the women were even scarier. The Dark Lord was a kind of middleman between the OTS and the Order of Dagon. He had a single official contact in the Order, although from time to time he met some of the other members in Prague, Berlin, and Turin during the bi-annual Rites of the Equinox. He shuddered at the memory of the last such Rite, and wondered if he would be able to absent himself from the next.

His own order, the Argon Archon, served to manage the occult poseurs. The OTS was the waste bin where the psychos were consigned. Sometimes they would prove useful for some menial task, but otherwise they were the flotsam and jetsam of the esoteric world. The Argon Archon, on the other hand, was a magnet for those who had intellectual pretensions and romantic notions of exclusivity. The OTS was AM talk radio; the AA was NPR.

The Order of Dagon was where the true initiates worked. They ran things. Quietly. And they considered groups like the OTS and the AA useful for handling the wet work. It gave them plausible deniability. After all, if a perp starting talking about secret lodges of reptilian masters it pretty much guaranteed a guilty verdict … or a lengthy stay in an institution devoted to the warehousing of the criminally insane. The Dark Lord assumed that he was valuable to them, a cut above the rest, and they let him think that and keep that ridiculous sobriquet. He would meet the *real* Dark Lord soon enough, and pay dearly—pay *sweetly*—for his presumption.

Unaware of the opprobrium in which he was held by the people he considered his spiritual mentors, the Dark Lord forwarded the notification from the States to his point of contact in the Order. It took the form of a text message to a burner phone, and he had no idea where in the world the phone was physically located. It was none of his business, of course, but still he was curious. Time was running out, and schedules had to be maintained. Ritual timings were tricky things. They depended on accurate astronomical data— easy enough to come by these days—but also on the interpretation of that data by experienced ritual specialists and that was an art requiring a lengthy apprenticeship to a Master. Some things could not be learned from books or, horror of horrors, the Internet. The Order stayed off-grid, like a terror organization, and indeed was set up in individual cells around the world that communicated with each other through burner phones and one-time use email accounts. They did not use Internet search engines or anything else, but they did have a tech crew that monitored Internet activity. They were the only ones permitted use of the Net, and they were fluttered every year. Not with a polygraph, though. The Order didn't trust machines. Torture, however, while not particularly reliable, was much more satisfying.

All things considered.

CHAPTER TWENTY-TWO

CUNEO, BACK AT THE STATION, LOGGED ONTO his computer and did a search for crimes involving a smiley face. Lisa sat in a swivel chair and … swiveled.

The EMTs had been sent home, or to wherever it was EMTs went when they didn't have a patient to transport. He had Lisa take samples of the slime from the box for analysis, and she walked it over to the crime lab. When she got back, she found Cuneo lost in thought.

He knew there had been a controversy years ago about a presumed gang of killers operating in the Midwest who were drowning young men and drawing smiley faces near the crime scenes. That theory had been debunked by the FBI since smiley faces are pretty ubiquitous as graffiti and they had not all been found at the crime scenes but often at some distance away.

But there had been a real serial killer, one who was doing life, for mailing letters about his kills using the smiley face as a kind of signature. That was Keith Hunter Jesperson, known as the "Happy Face Killer." He had at least eight murders on his ticket, all of them women and mostly prostitutes. Cuneo found the file and read through it quickly.

He had a corpse—the old lady in Belle Chasses—as well as the two other murders in the Ninth Ward that had so far resisted investigation. The empty box at the crime scene with the smiley face—together with the smiley face that had been drawn on the window in the basement and on his windshield—indicated either a warped sense of humor by the killer or some kind of link to Jesperson, which didn't seem logical at all. The victims in this case were not prostitutes, and the old lady wasn't strangled, which was Jesperson's m.o.

"No," he shook his head. "No relation to Jesperson. Anyway he's in prison forever. And this isn't a copycat, either. The victimology is all

215

wrong. Plus the fact that the occult aspect of all this is the domi-
nating theme, it seems to me. These were cultists, both at the Lower
Ninth and here. Too entirely different neighborhoods, economically
and culturally, but linked by the old lady and her weird set of friends
and relatives. Plus, how did the guy who clocked me manage to get
into the box that I had to break a wall down to get to?"

Lisa sat and listened to Cuneo talk to himself, but a million other
thoughts were going through her head.

"Don't cults usually have an identifiable purpose … a theme,
like worshipping the Devil, or some weird interpretation of the
Bible, or something?"

Cuneo looked up at her. "Yeah. So?"

"So what's the theme here? This all seems so … mechanical.
Like a science experiment."

"With idols?"

"Okay, granted, there's this religious or spiritual or whatever
you want to call it aspect to it, but there doesn't seem to be a … a
devotional nature to any of this. Even Devil worshippers have altars
and … well, they're a travesty of organized religion, right? This smells
different. Like all those books in her library. They were all 'how-to'
books, if you look at them the right way. They weren't devotional or
ideological or theological or anything like that."

"Yeah, I get all that. I got it when the first case showed up, the
one in the Ninth. And now the boys in the boxes. It's all about some
kind of … I don't know what to call it."

"Exactly. We don't know. What *do* we know?"

Amazed at her tenacity, he folded his hands on his lap and looked
at her questioningly.

"Two boxes," she began. "Each outfitted with some kind of
support apparatus. The tubes or pipes. Each with a large idol on top
of it. And both behind solid walls as if the boxes were put there first
and then the walls built around them."

"Except we know that can't be true, since we have the old
blueprints and they show both walls in place."

"Right. The boxes had to have been installed there before the house was built. The piping had to have been installed at that time, as well. They knew what they were doing from the outset. Like, *a hundred years ago*. And whatever happened inside those boxes … whatever was put there … began when the house was built and before the walls went up."

Cuneo nodded, thoughtfully. "Sure. That much we know. The problem is: it can't be true. There's an infant in the hospital right now that argues against it. It wasn't conceived a hundred years ago. In fact, the docs seem to think it's premature by a few months." Cuneo still referred to the infant as an 'it'; he couldn't bring himself to humanize it any further. He was surprised at his own lack of sympathy as a child of mixed parentage of which the African-American component was the most obvious to his colleagues, but there was nothing he could do about it.

"Have they found out where the piping leads?"

Cuneo had asked an architectural specialist to trace the pipes and tubes from the boxes to their origin somewhere else in the house. It should have been an easy task, but the tubing disappeared into the walls and since they did not show up on non-invasive scans they would have to try other methods. His captain was already balking at how much this investigation was costing his grossly under-funded department.

"Not yet. They're working on it."

"What does that tell you?"

"What do you mean?"

"The service tubes or whatever they are do not trace back into the house at all. Look, if you try to trace them on the blueprint, they disappear. They are simply not there. But they had to have been there at the very beginning of construction, just like the boxes. We're just not looking at this right. It must be right in front of us, but we don't see it."

Cuneo picked up a cardboard cup of cold coffee from his desk and absently sipped at it.

"That's disgusting." Lisa made a face. "That must have been there since Katrina."

"Hey, coffee's coffee." He thought for a minute while Lisa went in search of something a little fresher. "Yeah, of course."

Lisa turned from the small table where they kept the coffee machine and filters, but couldn't find any coffee.

"What? What of course?"

"The boxes. They were part of the original house, right?"

"So far as we know, yeah."

"We're assuming that ... well, we've got the timeline all wrong." She put down the empty coffee pot and went back to his desk. "What do you mean?"

"The boxes, the tubing ... what did you call them? 'Service tubes.' Right. Those. They were there since the beginning but maybe were never put into use until now. We're thinking that somehow they got those boxes in there recently, or ran the service tubes recently, but that's not the case, is it? This whole thing was created by design almost a century ago. It just wasn't actually used until now."

"That means that whoever built the house ..."

"Not only installed the boxes and the tubes, but the idols as well. The whole place was created for one purpose and that was the two boxes in the basement. The house was built around them. Where is that blueprint again?"

They shuffled papers on his desk and found the plastic evidence bag with the blueprint. Lisa pulled it out after putting on latex gloves and smoothed it out.

"Look at the architectural firm. They were based in Rhode Island, right? They had to have known all about this from the beginning. They were in on it. We have to trace the firm, find as much about it as we can, assuming it is already out of business. Trace the owners, the architects, and their clients. Something this intense, with a leadtime of a century, had to have left some trace behind."

Lisa agreed and began searching through computer databases, but in her heart she almost hoped they would find nothing.

Nothing at all.

CHAPTER TWENTY-THREE

THE REPORT CAME IN as a hard-copy from Chromo-Test, the genetic testing company, as per prior arrangement. Monroe didn't want any of this material to go through digital channels. He knew that meant longer lead-times, but at this point he couldn't afford some other agency finding out what he was up to and doing an end-run around him. Even worse, digital channels were vulnerable to hackers, and they could come from anywhere. While hacking into NSA computers was seemingly unthinkable due to multiple layers of security, there was always the off-chance that someone, somewhere had found a way in.

Monroe had feelers out to a number of commercial enterprises who were likely to have access to the type of information he needed in cases where government agencies would not. Gene testing labs were one such avenue, as the government did not have its own clearing house for that kind of data collection (for obvious reasons; eugenics had been under a cloud since the Nazi era). He also had standing invitations to astronomical observatories, meteorological institutes, NASA, and other scientific establishments to send him anything of interest: which meant anomalies, strange inexplicable phenomena, and the like. It was all done on a voluntary basis, but most companies—except social media operations—were usually happy to oblige.

In this case the sender's address was a blind, a mailbox service in San Diego, but he knew at once where it came from. He slit open the thin cardboard envelope and withdrew the report.

It was about ten pages, single-spaced, and contained an analysis of six different genetic tests the agency had done within the last three months. They were all anomalous, all with the same weird Y chromosome, stripped down and with no identifiable source of origin. In other words, all of these tested individuals were related on the paternal side, but they came from widely-different geographic, racial, and economic backgrounds. They were scattered from coast to coast, and these were only those individuals—children—who had been signed up and tested through Chromo-Test. Who knew how many others there were, with parents who had not yet had any genetic testing done?

Monroe briefly considered whether the "father" was really nothing more than a deposit from a sperm bank somewhere. That would account for the fact that none of these tests represented people who knew each other or were from the same area. He rejected the idea almost at once, though, when he realized that different races were involved. Unless there had been some kind of tragic error—which, of course, was possible—it was doubtful whether a black parent would want sperm from a white donor.

He examined the report more thoroughly after his initial quick scan. That is when he noticed another anomaly.

They were mostly twins, in much higher proportions than the general population.

For a moment, he flashed on Josef Mengele. The famous Nazi doctor—the "Angel of Death" at Auschwitz—had an obsession with twins and experimented on them in the death camp. Mengele would escape justice and die peacefully in Brazil in the 1970s, but it was rumored that he continued his experiments in Latin America even while he was on the run from Mossad.

Briefly, he considered whether there could be a Nazi angle to all of this. Nazi scientists at work in some secret laboratory, using modern genetic techniques such as CRISPR to edit DNA … but that didn't make sense. They would work on individuals to which they had access in the first place, and that most likely would not be in locations so geographically diverse. If they had a secret lab, it would be in a developing country somewhere, in an area where they could abduct young men and women—teenagers, probably—and tinker with their DNA in relative security, being present at the birth of the children so that more testing could be done.

Anyway, what was he thinking? The last of the Nazi doctors had died decades ago. This would have to be some kind of new iteration of eugenics theory. However, gene editing equipment was getting cheaper and cheaper. Even CRISPR technology would soon be within the reach of high school science departments with minimum dollar investment.

But he couldn't get Mengele out of his mind. There was that novel by Ira Levin, *The Boys From Brazil*, that imagined a world where Mengele continued his genetic experiments but this time with Hitler's DNA: impregnating women with the Nazi leader's genes so that they would give birth to baby Adolf's. There was talk even now of extracting DNA from the mummies of Egyptian pharaohs, actually cloning them.

Every new technology provided challenges to the social order—religion, culture, politics—as well as to the world of intelligence-gathering and the military. Monroe knew this; he had been keeping step with every new development since the hydrogen bomb as part of his professional brief. But now it seemed that technology was becoming more mystical, and mysticism was becoming more technological. This was the "convergence" he was most concerned about.

Of course, the report from Chromo-Test was not proof of anything. It could simply be an anomaly that had not been discovered until now, maybe something affecting a significant percentage of the human population. A result of chemicals in the air or water, or some dietary issue. But the reason he had asked—discretely—for this type of information was due to some misgivings he had when analyzing other data.

It was the old French genius mathematician Grothendieck who started him along this particular path. All that talk about "mutants" mixed in with digressions on the higher mathematics: a field about which Monroe knew mercifully little. But what the old mathematician had suggested was that there was a change taking place on the planet that was producing savants, people of extraordinary mental and spiritual capabilities. Naturally, there would have to be a genetic component which is why Grothendieck called them "mutants." He meant it in a positive way, but Monroe—

as an old intel officer—had to see the other side of that particular coin as well. What if there was a change taking place on the planet, a change across all demographics, another step in evolution? What if one demographic was favored more than another? What if Russia or China had a greater proportional share of these "mutants" and what if that would pose a threat to national security in the States?

Conversely, what if this new form of "mutant" represented a deeper change taking place in the human genome, one that would provoke a reactive process, a kind of "devolution" in another demographic? What if there were negative mutants of a type Grothendieck had not mentioned, a mutant of great powers but of low empathy, a kind of super-narcissist?

Even more unsettling was the idea that a foreign power or a criminal organization could employ gene-splicing and gene-editing techniques—like CRISPR—to create just such a genetic anomaly. A programmable human being, with great intellectual capabilities.

He would have to re-read the Grothendieck material, supplemented by what Aubrey had learned in France. The answer was there somewhere. Too many dots were swirling around and it was only a matter of time before they all started connecting. If the Chromo-Test report reflected a more general trend in the human population then DHS had to be informed. If, on the other hand, this was the result of specific and willful tampering with genetic material by a bad actor somewhere, then there was no point in going off half-cocked to the Director with this scant bit of intel. He would have to know more before bringing anyone else in on this. Especially if, as he now suspected, he was dealing with something a little off the beaten intelligence track.

Something to do with why he sent Angell to Iraq.

Something to do with tattooed children and the Cult of Dagon.

He went back into his safe, where he kept the Lovecraft Codex, and pulled out the Grothendieck file.

CHAPTER TWENTY-FOUR

GLORIA GOT OFF THE PHONE with customer service at Chromo-Test. She sent in her samples weeks ago, and had not heard anything back from them. She really wanted to know her boys' genetic inheritance, and the money for the tests had not been easy to come by. But hanging up from the call she was more confused than ever.

She heard words like "anomaly" and "haplogroup" and a lot of scientific stuff that was way over her head. But the gist of the conversation from their end was that they wanted to meet her and the boys, and were willing to pay their airfare to see them. That got her attention.

At first she was a little excited by the prospect of a few days off for a plane trip with her children, like a mini-vacation. It was like her husband had been good for something after all; he had some weird genes that made all those pocket-protector types stand up and take notice. They assured her that there was nothing wrong or even different about *her* genes (thanks a lot) but that whoever was the father had some "anomaly" in his genes, and could she bring him along, too.

Well, that wasn't going to happen, and she told them so. She had been separated for a long time, the father of her kids had been abusive, and that was that. They understood, they said, understood perfectly in fact, but didn't withdraw their offer. They really wanted to see the boys.

So she started making preparations. They were going to send her the air tickets by FedEx; she would get them in a day or so. She had to pack for all three of them, and found a suitcase that would accommodate all their clothes for the short trip, and had to let her boss know that she would be out for maybe, like, three days or so. She knew that would be a problem, but it wasn't insurmountable. She could get Claire to cover for her at the cash register; she'd be grateful for the extra money. And, anyway, she hadn't taken a sick day or a vacation day all year.

As she fussed with clothes for herself and the kids, in the back of her mind was another problem. This whole "anomaly" thing had her thinking. What if this had something to do with her ... episodes? That missing time? What if ... well, she didn't want to think about that. *That* could not have anything to do with *this*, could it?

"I mean, my kids are normal. They're beautiful, and bright, and full of life. There's nothing wrong with *them*, no matter what some test tube geeks might say," she said to herself, aloud. She started shoving clothes into the suitcase like she was punishing them.

"This is just some computer glitch or something. And what if it isn't? What if ... what if my episodes are related to this ... this anomaly? Could they somehow find out?"

She stopped moving suddenly as a thought occurred to her.

"Shit. What if that's why they want to see me?"

Then she started to laugh at her own paranoia.

"Come on! Get real. What goes on in your head has nothing to do with DNA. Nature and nurture, right? I read that somewhere. You're born with certain traits, and ... and characteristics but then as you grow older you acquire other ... behaviors. Those you learn, the ones you pick up. And, anyway, it's not my DNA they're freaked out about, it's the boys.' Calm down, Gloria. Chill." But as she kept packing the suitcase, collecting spare toothbrushes and finishing up the laundry she kept thinking back to the unavoidable connection between the boys' weird DNA and her own nocturnal experiences. She wasn't stupid. She had heard of alien abductions on TV. She always felt uncomfortable whenever the subject was brought up or when one of those shows appeared on cable insisting that there were multiple alien races and that they subjected humans to bizarre experiments.

But she also heard experts talk about night terrors and sleep disorders that could account for what she experienced, and she usually accepted those explanations with a sense of relief. She had done some drugs in her youth—not when she was pregnant, of course—and had a glass of wine now and then, so maybe there was some kind of residual tripping taking place, maybe brought about by stress.

These efforts at self-diagnosis—usually with the aid of the Internet or the supermarket tabloids—made her feel better, more in control of the situation, until the next time she awoke in her bedroom, soaking wet with perspiration and the terrifying sensations in her body that felt just like she had been raped. Night terrors, she told herself. That's all they were.

She had been standing still and silent in the boys' room for about fifteen minutes without being aware of the passage of time. Her mind was elsewhere. A train of thought had started and it was going so fast she couldn't get off.

As a woman, she was used to being objectified. The care she took with her appearance had the unintended consequence of attracting strange men; but was it unintended? She didn't know anymore. She had been brought up to think a certain way, behave a certain way. The end result of all this thinking and behaving was to attract a man, get married, and have kids. She was a commodity, something to be valued by others. But she had a bad marriage, and wound up wondering what her value really was.

She liked sex. Craved it from time to time. But did that mean she was a tramp if she wanted it and wasn't married? The whole value system started to fall apart as soon as things went wrong in a marriage. Then lawyers got involved, and your value was translated into alimony payments and half the possessions and joint custody. Her love, her passion, her intelligence, her beauty, her pregnancies (excruciatingly painful, and resulting in c-sections both times) ... all converted into cash. Nothing else. No other form of acknowledgment. She was ... not quite human.

Something was wrong somewhere.

And then her ... episodes. Talk about objectification. She was kidnapped while still asleep and her body used for whatever they

wanted, things done to her by strangers … but wasn't that some kind
of delusion? If it was, didn't every woman share the same delusion?
"Weren't we all being kidnapped, abducted, all the time, used for
our bodies and what our bodies could do?" she asked herself, aloud.
Were other women, her neighbors, her relatives, being abducted the
same way, for the same reasons?

A human body becomes a laboratory, a petrie dish, in the hands
of this strange government of the sky. These little grey officials with
their retorts and alembics and time schedules …

"Jesus!" she said, aloud again. "They were *grey*! They were little
and *grey*!" The splinter of memory came back, landing on her like a
log.

But there was something slimy about them, too. Something
briny. Even scaly. Little fish-men. She struggled to remember more,
but found her thoughts separate out, alone and distant from each
other. Nothing connected between them, so they dissipated like
smoke.

Abductions, slimy grey officials, her body being probed,
manipulated, penetrated. Like what she read about slave markets in
the South, before the Civil War. Humans as commodities, as objects.
Men putting their fingers in mouths, up skirts, cupping breasts,
laughing, measuring, bargaining.

She learned that in the United States there was separation
between church and state. It was there, in the Constitution. It was
the law. But there was no separation between body and state. The
state owned your body, just like it owned your money, or your land.
Eminent domain. It let you keep it until they needed it, or wanted
it, and then look out.

And now these people in California. Chromo-Test. They wanted
her and the boys to fly out there and talk to them. This wasn't
normal. It wasn't … this wasn't what she expected when she sent
in her hundred dollars and the swabs from the boys. There was no
separation between body and state, and now there was no separation
between your DNA and the state.

God, she hadn't been this paranoid since those months she was doing coke and had to mellow it out with 'ludes. She roused herself from her reverie and saw that she had packed the suitcase, locked it, and was ready to go even though their flight would not be for three days.

The government of the sky. *What did that mean?*

She looked toward the door. A little voice in her head said, "Run!"

CHAPTER TWENTY-FIVE

JAMILA RAN.

Dharamsala is a center for the exiled Tibetan community in India. As such it attracts its share of westerners, mostly young people in search of yoga, Tantra and dope. There are areas of the town that look like throwbacks to the 1960s "flower power" era, replete with jeans, beads, incense sticks and flutes. Jamila, in her refugee status and few words of English, fit right in.

The police took down the statement of the Canadian woman whose passport and airline ticket Jamila now had in her possession. The airport at Dharamsala is small and regional, with flights to Indian cities. From there, one connects to the international routes and that is what Jamila had to do.

She broke into a run from the Tibetan center and fled down the side streets that she knew from when she turned up a few weeks earlier. She knew she would never see Rabten again. This was the life of a refugee, a person with no home to go back to, no roots she could rely on, no forwarding address. In a year, she could be speaking another language, dressed in unfamiliar clothes, and eating strange food in a country she had never heard of before in her life.

Except Jamila knew exactly where she had to go and what she would do when she got there.

The money in the woman's wallet would get her a taxi to the airport. The ticket would get her on a plane for Delhi. She would connect for Istanbul. She would take it from there.

Rabten, meanwhile, had a lot of explaining to do. The Dalai Lama's secretary had him in a small room at the Center, surrounded by several other lamas of various ages and disciplines. They all wanted to know how a foreign woman could become the medium for Shugden Dorje. Was this some kind of witchcraft? Black magic? Something from the shamanistic period before the arrival of Buddhism? The Dalai Lama himself was shaken, for Shugen Dorje had shown up unannounced, with no ritual preparations and besides the girl was not the State Oracle and had no business channeling this demonic being.

But she spoke in the true voice of the Spirit, using language only Rabten and the Dalai Lama could understand. And he scolded the Dalai Lama for banning the rites due to him. And warned that a conflagration was coming that would make the Chinese invasion of his country look like spring break in Daytona Beach.

All Rabten could do was punt. He had to give Jamila enough time to get out of town. So he smiled, and shrugged, and began chanting over his beads.

CHAPTER TWENTY-SIX

GREGORY ANGELL WAS MET at the train station in Shanghai by a man dressed as he was, wearing a Tibetan Buddhist monk's outfit. He approached Angell and bowed, and spoke to him in English with a British accent that Angell couldn't quite place.

"I was sent to fetch you," the man said. "I have organized a taxi for us. We will go to the monastery in case you are being followed. We will rest there for awhile, and when the situation is favorable I will take you to the harbor."

He made this entire speech as they walked through the crowds and to a waiting taxi.

Angell had been to Shanghai before, but the city was changing so rapidly it was difficult to recognize it anymore. The Bund was still there, of course, and Angell had fond memories of the Long Bar at the Peace Hotel, and the orchestra composed of elderly gentlemen who had survived the Cultural Revolution. But there would be no visits down Memory Lane today. Angell was a wanted man, and he wasn't quite sure who was doing the wanting.

They got in the car and the man-dressed-as-monk spoke to the driver in the Shanghai dialect and they set off for the monastery.

"You do not have any luggage except that bag, which is good. We may need to move fast."

"There is a ship?"

"Yes. Well, a kind of ship. It will do. But let us not discuss this at the moment." He rolled his eyes towards the driver in the front seat. "Let us instead discuss the Hundred Thousand Songs of Milarepa. You know them?"

Angell wanted to say, "No, but if you hum a few bars ..." Instead he bit his lip and shook his head. "I know of Milarepa, of course, and his songs are famous, but I could not enter into a learned discussion on the subject."

The man nodded and smiled.

"No one can, good sir."

The taxi stopped in a section of Shanghai that was unknown to Angell. There was the temple—an imposing wooden structure of reds and blues—and the two men exited the vehicle and made their way to the gate. Another monk beckoned them inside and the three of them walked down an outdoor corridor to a room on the left side of the building where tea had been set out.

They were left alone, and before Angell could start asking questions the monk introduced himself.

"You may call me Drakpa. I am not really a monk, but I work for the Tibetan Government in Exile. I am a kind of spy, I think you can say. I am partially Tibetan, and partially German. My father was a German soldier who came to Tibet in the 1930s. My mother was a noblewoman."

"Your English is excellent."

"I learned it the way we all did, from the BBC. Do you know the program 'Follow Me'? No? Pity."

Drakpa poured the tea and changed the subject.

"Milarepa was said to have perfected the art of *lung-gompa*. Do you know it? It is a way of running very, very fast. As if in a trance. He was also quite a con-man, I think you say? Very nasty in his youth. A practitioner of the dark arts, of sorcery. But he repented and became a famous teacher. He said that knowing the dark and knowing the light, he attained enlightenment. In other words, he did not disavow his earlier evil ways but used them to balance an excessive ... ah ... *fetishization* of the good. Do you *follow me*?" He then laughed at his little joke, but Angell didn't get it.

"This is all by way of saying that we will need Milarepa's cunning, his sense of balance, and his ability to travel very, very fast if we are to get you to safety."

The tea was bitter and strong. Angell tried to appreciate its aroma and flavor, but he was exhausted. He had not been able to sleep much on the train ride down as he was nervous about being identified or challenged. Now, what he needed was a nap and some food, and maybe even a shower. But he couldn't rest until he knew what was in store for him.

"Drakpa, what is the plan for today?"

The monk set down his tea cup and thought for a moment, losing his monkish attitude and becoming all business.

"We will wait for a signal. When it is convenient to leave here, we shall do so and make our way to the harbor. The ship's passage has been arranged."

"Where am I going?"

"The ultimate goal is to get you to Singapore. From there, our people can arrange travel and papers to other parts of the world. You are being sought by American intelligence, it seems, and they are very good at what they do. We have to be better. Eventually, they will figure out that you escaped Beijing with a tour group of monks. There are not that many monks in China. They will trace you. We have to stay one step ahead of them. That means, no cellphones, no internet, nothing. You have to stay off the grid for as long as possible.

"But there's another problem, one for which we are making other arrangements."

Angell shuddered.

"*Another* problem? Really? Look, I am very appreciative ... I mean, *very* appreciative of everything you and the monks have been doing on my behalf. But I don't think I should take any further advantage of you. You are putting yourselves in danger by helping me."

Drakpa nodded in agreement.

"Yes. This is true. But ... we have no choice, really. We have to help you."

"But ... why?"

"Because if we don't, then we are in even greater danger."

Angell was getting tired of tea. He longed for a tall latte or a double espresso. He hadn't had coffee of any kind since ... since Nepal? Earlier? He knew tea was healthier in some respects, especially the green variety he seemed to be offered at every stage of this impossible journey, but he would risk his life for a cup of joe.

Nevertheless, he paid careful attention to everything the strange Tibetan spy was telling him.

"If it was only the governments of the world who were interested in you, our work would be cut out for us but we would know what to do. We have survived for so long with so many enemies—and so many friends who sometimes are worse than enemies—that we have learned all sorts of shortcuts for escape and survival. But you have attracted the attention of another sort of group, and these individuals do not play by the rules. Their actions are difficult to anticipate, their motives obscure."

"You mean Dagon? The Keepers of the Book?"

"Those are some of the names they go by, yes. But it seems that right now you are the Keeper of the Book. Yes?"

"It seems to be my default position, yes. I saved it from being destroyed because I don't believe books—no matter how offensive or dangerous—should be destroyed. But I am not especially a defender of this particular book."

"Have you read it? Do you know what's in it?"

Angell was becoming uncomfortable with this line of questioning. Here he was, a well-known scholar of the ancient Middle East, and he had in his possession a text that cults and terror groups around the world have been clamoring to obtain, at the cost of much bloodshed, and he had barely opened the book itself to try to understand its hold over so many disparate cultures. True, he had been running for his life and he was still running, but it did seem strange—even to him—that he had not really tried to delve into the text and its proclamations.

"There has been so much blood and terror surrounding it, I

have been hesitant even to open it. I am holding onto it until I can get it somewhere safe, somewhere it can be studied and evaluated in peace."

"Ah. And where would that be? Washington, DC perhaps?"

"Well, no. Probably not."

"New York City? Los Angeles? Perhaps Moscow? Or maybe leave it here in China?"

"I get your point."

"Do you? There will always be a sectarian or partisan attitude towards the Book. One side will always try to exploit it for their own ends, or bury it so deeply that no one else can exploit it. You remember the controversy over the Dead Sea Scrolls? For decades no one was allowed to publish translations of them. The public was deprived of knowing what secrets they contain. The Catholic Church in particular was worried that they would contain information that would challenge their spiritual authority, or the validity of the Gospels. You remember."

"Yes, of course. It was my field, part of it anyway."

"And now you are in the same position, aren't you? You have in your hands a text that could change the course of history. No, not like the Dead Sea Scrolls or even the Bible itself, but in a covert way. The course of history is not always visible from the ground, am I right? Sometimes, it flows in subterranean caverns, surfacing only once in awhile, once every hundred or thousand years. The Qur'an was one such text. Look at how much history has been changed because of that book."

"And you're saying that …"

"No, no. I am not saying that your Book is the equivalent of the Qur'an. Not in that way. Your Book contains information and prescriptions that no sane political or spiritual leader would want disseminated to the public at large. There are already instructions available to anyone for making bombs, chemical weapons, and even nuclear devices. Your Book, Doctor Angell, would ignite a massive campaign to develop all those weapons of war in an effort either to destroy the planet, or to save it. In any case, wholesale destruction would be inevitable. That is why we need the wisdom of Milarepa to walk between sorcery and religion and refuse to accept either one."

Angell got his wish. He had a few hours to nap before he would be summoned to the ship. He was also able to bathe, albeit from a bucket and a cracked porcelain sink and with cold water. But he wasn't complaining. They provided him a threadbare towel that was the size of a handkerchief, but he still wasn't complaining. The reason? Drakpa had "organized" a paper cup full of rich, black coffee with the familiar Starbucks logo printed on it. Angell could not believe his good fortune.

He dressed again in his monk's robes since no one had thought to provide him with anything else, and hefted his knapsack with the infamous Book and met Drakpa at the entrance to the temple.

"I will not accompany you to the ship. It is too dangerous for me to do so. Instead, I will leave you with one of our comrades. He knows nothing about your mission, only that you are to be boarded safely. As for me, I will return to Gansu Province where I am needed at once.

"I pray you find what you are looking for, Doctor Angell, and I pray that your enemies do not!"

They bowed to each other, remembering that they were supposed to be monks, and Angell expressed his gratitude to him and to the others of the network who were helping him get out of China.

Before he knew it, Drakpa was gone and he was standing in the street with a young Chinese man in a new suit.

"Come with me, Rinpoche," he said to Angell in heavily accented English. Angell wanted to object that he was no 'Rinpoche' but decided against it.

A car pulled up from a parking area near the temple. It was an old green Toyota, a model made specifically for the Chinese market by the Japanese manufacturer, which meant it had a projected lifespan if anything even shorter than Angell's. It was a miracle it had lasted this long, with no availability of spare parts anywhere in the country.

Angell was guided to the back seat, and his new friend took the seat up front, next to the driver.

Not far away, at Shanghai International Airport, the man who called himself Prime had just arrived on a flight from Beijing. He had good intel that Angell had made his way to Shanghai and may be in the disguise of a Buddhist monk. They had lost him at the Lama Temple, but Prime had a good feeling that the noose around Angell's neck was about to be tightened.

CHAPTER TWENTY-SEVEN

THE CAR STOPPED AT THE EDGE of a vast container port, the largest in the world. Angell had no idea how they would find his particular vessel in all the confusion, but he was assured that the port was a marvel of organization and efficiency.

There is nothing quite like a container port, and the larger they are the more they appear like giant cities made of building blocks. Ships were stacked up in the harbor with an average wait time of over 15 hours in some cases depending on congestion and weather before they could dock and offload their cargo, or load it on. Or usually both. They sat out in the water, the convoy of an invading navy, stretched out to the horizon as far as one could see like something out of the Trojan War, or Dunkirk.

Until recently, Singapore had the busiest port in the world; now it has been overtaken by Shanghai. China's dominance of the sea trade was emblematic of its dominance in other areas as well, and their investment in military ships was monitored carefully by the world's defense establishments. Gone are the days when the British could sail unimpeded up the Yangzi River and force the Chinese to buy opium at gunpoint.

The days of the tramp steamer are also gone. The steam engines have been replaced by diesel and the tramps—ships that contract for one specific load at a time, usually coal or oil or some other commodity, for a limited transport between two or more ports—are now few and far between. Leave it to his hosts to find one, however.

The *Silver Star* was a vessel with a Panamanian registry that probably never saw the coastline of Central America in its entire career. It plodded the route between Shanghai, Hong Kong, Kaohsiung, Jakarta and Singapore like an old street walker claiming her turf. It was berthed down at the end of one large dock, and had just finished taking on a load of frozen seafood, destined for the kitchens along Temple Street in Hong Kong and Trengganu Street

in Singapore. Scallops, shrimp, prawns, squid, and octopus were
packed in ice in cardboard boxes, with more ice dumped all over
the shipment. The days were not summertime warm so there was
a chance that at least some of the seafood would make it without
spoiling along the way. There were live crabs and frogs in another
section of the ship, and boxes of dried sea cucumbers looking like
John Bobbitt's worst nightmare. All of this was being stowed in the
bowels of the cargo ship, the crates disappearing from view as the
cranes lowered them into the holds.

Angell, awkward in his monastic attire, walked up the narrow
gangway behind his new friend. There did not seem to be any
customs or immigration officials in sight, which he thought strange.
He had no papers, but he was boarding a ship in China's most
famous port. Even his appearance did not cause so much as a second
glance from any of the crew working the cranes and the loading
of the crates. They walked down another gangway to the stern
of the ship and up to the bridge where their contact was waiting
for them.

This was a man of Southeast Asian appearance, dressed in a
white uniform with a visored cap. He gave Angell a quick once
over, and then concentrated on the papers he was being given by
the Chinese man in the new suit. He nodded, briefly, and the two
men exchanged words. They whispered, and Angell could not make
out what they were saying but it seemed to satisfy the crew member.
That, and the sheaf of bills he was handed surreptitiously, which
were quickly pocketed without being counted. Angell figured if
there was a discrepancy in payment he would be asked to leave the
ship while they were still in port. Hopefully.

The Chinese man turned and gave Angell a huge smile.

"Our business is concluded. I hope you will have a wonderful
voyage!" He made to leave the ship but Angell stopped him.

"Wait. Where am I going? What do I do when I get there?"

"Ah, no problem, Rinpoche. You are going to Singapore. You
will be met. No problem! No problem!"

And with that, his guide abruptly left the ship, almost running down the gangway without a backwards glance.

Angell was suddenly very nervous. He trusted Hine in Beijing to make the best and safest arrangements, and the certainly the monk in Beijing and the spy in Shanghai seemed competent and supportive. But this …

The crew member—a Filipino whose name Angell would learn was Benny—interrupted his paranoia party.

"Mister Rinpoche," he asked, in perfect English, "Would you like some tea?"

The ship left the port at 6 in the evening and headed out to sea. In two days it would be in Hong Kong, and from there it would go straight to Singapore. After dropping off most of the rest of the shipment—and Angell—in Singapore, the *Silver Star* would then proceed to Jakarta. Benny showed Angell to his berth, a small but clean and comfortable room below and to the rear of the bridge. The captain's quarters were next door to his. Benny was not the captain, he informed Angell solemnly, but the executive officer. The captain was an Indonesian with a short temper and a long memory who had plied this route for most of the past twenty years. He would meet him at meals. Until then, it was better to stay away from him.

Angell had accepted Benny's offer of tea with some reluctance. He had had enough of tea to last his lifetime … or at least the next few weeks. But this was Asia, and tea was ubiquitous. Benny, however, noticed Angell's lack of enthusiasm for the beverage and offered something stronger.

In his own cabin, on the same level as the captain's and Angells,' Benny had a stock of San Miguel beer in a small refrigerator, the type one sees in hotel rooms. He pulled one of them out and offered it to Angell.

"Aren't you having any?"

"Ah, no. Sorry. Not at this time. I am on duty. But perhaps at dinner I can join you. Or tomorrow. *Laging may bukas*, you know."

"Sorry?"

"There is always tomorrow!"

The cheerful man left Angell in his cabin holding a can of cold beer. Well, at least it wasn't tea.

Angell sat on his bed and tried to collect his thoughts. He finally removed the knapsack from his shoulder and set it down next to him. There wasn't much in there beyond the Book. Hine had stuffed a few granola bars in there, but Angell had eaten one at the temple in Shanghai and was saving the others in case he found himself without food for any length of time.

He had shaving equipment—a plastic razor and a small can of shaving cream—as well as a toothbrush, toothpaste, and a new stick of deodorant. There was also a set of clean underwear. That was about it. He would have to make it last.

The cargo ship was stable enough, but you knew you were at sea. The waves were not so bad this close to the coastline, but they would get worse as they traveled south. The weather was holding up, at least. No rain was forecast for the next few days. Angell had never spent this much time aboard ship, and he couldn't exactly count the number of times he rode the Staten Island ferry. Benny had told him to spend as much time as possible in his cabin. This was because they didn't want the other crew members asking too many questions, and anyway the captain was a prick. That was okay by Angell. He was safe—or at least as safe as could be expected under the circumstances—and he could use the time alone to finally tackle the problem of the Book.

But ... not right now. Right now he would take a long swallow of the San Mig and rest his eyes. Benny would come back and fetch him when it was time for dinner.

The beer tasted good. It had been a long time since he had beer, and it soothed his throat going down. The dust and the sand of traveling the last few weeks through deserts and steppes seemed to dissolve in the bite of hops, malt and barley. He leaned back onto the pillow and took another swig.

The solitude, the quiet, the nearly imperceptible roll of the ship, and the beer all was conspiring to put him to sleep. Before that happened, though, he decided he needed to find a place to stow the Book. He took it out of his knapsack and stuck it under the mattress, at the same level as the pillow. This way he would be sleeping on top of it should anyone try to steal it. The knapsack itself he placed behind a chair so that it would look like he was concealing it. If they wanted to steal the knapsack, they could do so. He just took the precaution of removing his clean underwear first.

He looked around at the relatively spacious cabin. He had a narrow bed, a kind of chest of drawers that was small but serviceable, and a small desk and chair. The desk had an electric light, and there was another one over his bed, presumably so he could read.

He checked the door and found that he could lock it with a simple sliding bolt, which he did.

After a last look around, he removed the outer monk's robe and folded it, placing it on the chair. He then got back into bed and finished the rest of his beer.

After a few more minutes, he felt himself dropping off. He knew that Benny was going to collect him for dinner in the officers' mess but he didn't think he could stay awake that long.

That was when he felt, rather than heard, a tapping sound at his door.

He thought he had fallen asleep, or was in that twilight period between waking and sleeping when all sorts of strange phenomena seem to take place, but he moved his arm and then the other one, and realized he was awake. The tapping sound continued, almost as a subliminal vibration, a suggestion of sound rather than an actual hum of sound waves.

He stood up from the bed and hesitated, listening, all his senses alert.

"Hello?" he ventured. Maybe there was a steward or someone like that, sent to rouse him for dinner.

Or maybe it was a crazed assassin, bent on acquiring the Book and killing him in the process.

He had no weapons, and nothing much that could be used as one. He thought of the chair, but had a sudden flash of all those movies where someone picks up a chair to defend themselves and it splinters on impact with a determined adversary.

The tapping continued, and now he could sense a pattern or rhythm to it that he had not noticed at once.

It seemed to be a four-count, with the third beat emphasized more than the others:

1—2—3—4. 1—2—3—4.

At first he wondered if it was Morse Code, the old three dots, three dashes, three dots for "S O S." But it definitely was not an SOS. Unfortunately, that was all the Morse Code he (and most people nowadays) knew. Plus, the four beats were evenly spaced, isolated by a brief pause from the next four beats, etc. A dance beat?

An animal, perhaps? An insect of some kind?

A woodpecker?

Aboard ship in the middle of the ocean?

Angell thought briefly of Coleridge and the albatross.

Then, the incredible happened.

The tapping now seemed to come from *two* places at once. A strange stereophonic phenomenon of the sound bouncing around the walls, surrounding him. Then three places. The sound gradually increased in volume, almost imperceptibly at first. It was as if the noise was advancing on him, as absurd as that seemed. Angell thought his ears were playing a trick on him, that it was only one source of the sound that was somehow echoing in the small room through some freak of maritime architecture.

Then the cabin was filled with the sound of the tapping. Getting louder. More insistent.

1—2—3—4. 1—2—3—4.

It was getting on his nerves. The sound increased so much that it was less like tapping and more like pounding. He held his hands over his ears and raced around the small cabin trying to find its source. But there were so few places that could harbor an animal or an insect, or even a bird. That was when he noticed that the Book was open on the floor next to the chair where he left it, and the pages were turning as if in a strong wind, flipping through the text: some invisible madman looking for a forgotten phrase. The problem was, he had left the Book carefully wrapped in its black silk scarf.

He went to the Book to close it and re-wrap it when the door to his cabin—the one he had locked carefully—burst open.

Benny stuck his head in with a grin. That is when Angell noticed that the tapping had stopped completely.

"Hungry?"

CHAPTER TWENTY-EIGHT

THE POLICE IN DHARAMSALA were used to foreigners losing their money, credit cards, and passports. Sometimes it was other foreigners to blame, people they picked up in the cafes or restaurants or yoga studios, people they trusted in this spiritual place who then robbed them blind. In other cases it was pickpockets, the scourge of any busy town. Regardless, the authorities took each case seriously ... and then filed it. There would be no dragnet of the sari shops or wood carving booths in McLeod Ganj, but they would send an alert to the other stations and wait to see what would happen. The problem with foreigners is that they needed documents in order to leave the country, but there were no consulates in Dharamsala. So the police helped the tourists to contact their embassies or nearest consulates and arrange for temporary passports and the like. When that happened, their embassies would put out an alert on the stolen passports so that the border patrol could keep an eye out for them.

Jamila knew none of this, of course, but had the refugee's innate sense that everything could come crashing down on her at any moment. She wasted no time getting to the airport, and discovered that "her" flight was due to leave in two hours. Nervous that she would be apprehended before then, she hid in the ladies' bathroom and tried to rest. Her broken English might not be enough to maintain her "cover" as a Canadian, but she would brass it out anyway.

She was just afraid that her "spirit" would choose an inopportune moment to manifest itself and if that happened it would be all over for her.

So she went back in her mind to the lessons taught to her by Rabten. She began to meditate by controlling her breathing.

"Everyone breathes without thinking," he told her. "So if you can think about your breathing and control it with your mind, you are on your way to controlling other parts of yourself that you never think about. This control of breath is known in India as *pranayama*. It is the first step to controlling your whole life, even those parts of your life you did not know existed."

Well, he didn't use so many words since they had few words in common, but she understood what he meant with his gestures and his example, and the rest she gleaned directly from his mind. That is when she heard the word *pranayama* for the first time. It sounded like such a soft and silky word. Restful.

She repeated it aloud in her stall. "*Pranayama.*"

And a voice responded, "*Pranayama.* Are you meditating in there? How cool!"

Jamila had no idea what the voice said but her impression was that the voice was pleasant and non-threatening. And she said the word *pranayama*.

She peeked between the door to the stall and its hinges and saw a young woman, around her age. A foreigner. White. With a floppy sort of hat and a colorful outfit that Jamila could not quite relate to anything she knew.

She was terrified of being discovered before her flight, but it might be good to befriend this woman with the nice voice. Two women walking together would not attract as much attention as a single woman walking alone.

Slowly, she opened the door to her stall.

"Hi!" said the woman, stretching out her hand. "My name is Stacey. What's yours?"

Jamila looked a little startled and didn't know how to respond.

"Oops! I should probably let you wash your hands first. Sorry!" She stepped aside and Jamila saw the sinks and guessed that she was expected to wash her hands. So she did that, trying to muster a smile at the same time, while Stacey kept talking.

"My name is Stacey. Oh, I told you that already! I'm from the States. I guess you could sorta tell, right? I mean, who else would start jabbering with a stranger in the ladies? It's just that I heard you say *pranayama* and that is why I came here. I don't mean *here* here, not to the ladies room, but to Dharamsala. I study yoga. I'm a yoga instructor back in Dallas. That's where I'm from? Dallas? In Texas?"

Jamila finished washing her hands, several times, and then reached for a paper towel but there wasn't one. Stacey jumped immediately to the rescue with a packet of tissues she kept in her purse.

"You can keep those. I have more. You never know when you're going to need one in India. You know what I mean? Is this your first time here? It is mine. I just love Dharamsala. Delhi can be a bit much, though, at least for a single gal like myself. I didn't catch your name?"

That much Jamila did understand.

"Jamila," she said. And then regretted it instantly. It didn't match the name on her stolen passport or her airline ticket.

"Jamila … Jamila Isabella," she corrected, remembering the name on the Canadian woman's documents. She could not for the life of her remember the woman's family name.

"Why, that's a beautiful name. What do your friends call you?"

Jamila did not understand the question, so she repeated her name. "Isabella."

Stacey smiled and said, "Then that's what I'll call you. Isabella. Or do you prefer Bella? Or Izzy?"

"Isabella."

Stacey laughed at the look of confusion on Jamila's face. "Okay, then. Isabella it is! Where are you going from here?"

That question she understood. She had been asked that question, in one language or another, for most of her life.

"Ah, Istanbul. *Turkiye*," she clarified, except that her pronunciation of "Turkey" was a dead giveaway.

Stacey noted her friend's accent and realized that they may have a communication problem, but Stacey was an optimist and a people-person and would not let the lack of a common language get in the way of friendship or, at least, temporary companionship. They were in a small regional airport in an exotic corner of the world. Two single women traveling abroad. Practicing pranayama, no less. They had to stick together, and Jamila looked harmless enough.

So she took Jamila's arm—much to the latter's surprise and shock—and they sauntered out of the ladies' room to the airport lounge. Stacey checked the schedule and saw that their plane was leaving on time. If she noticed Jamila's nervousness she said nothing about it.

And when two uniformed police officers entered the airport with the name of Isabella la Giuffria written on a slip of paper they were already airborne and making their way to Delhi from where Jamila would fly on to Istanbul where she intended to join the Peshmerga and fight for her people, and Stacey would continue her journey on her long and privileged voyage of self-discovery.

CHAPTER TWENTY-NINE

Angell had spent an uncomfortable hour in the officers' mess. While the food was great, he was preoccupied with the strange experience in his cabin. He wanted to ask Benny if there were weird sounds aboard the ship—maybe some kind of machinery, or something—but couldn't think of a way to bring it up without sounding weird himself.

He wanted to ditch the monk's robe so Benny said he would find some uniform pants and a shirt that would fit him, but with his shaved head and emaciated appearance he wasn't going to fool anyone into thinking he was a regular passenger. In fact, there were no other passengers aboard ship that he could see. Everyone at the mess was a crew member.

The others were polite enough towards him, but averted their eyes for the most part and let Benny act as the host. The captain sat at the head of the table and drank water from a glass. The food was all *halal*, but the crew didn't mind. Beef and mutton instead of pork was no big deal, not even for the Filipinos whose fascination with *lechon* was famous throughout Asia. It was the absence of alcohol that irritated the crew, but the captain would not allow it onboard. In any case, they spent a lot of time in port and ran a relatively short itinerary with only days at sea at a time, so the crew often smuggled beer, wine and various stronger spirits on board; hence Benny's small stash of San Miguel. Everyone had a bottle of mouthwash as well; Benny made sure Angell took advantage of it before he appeared at the mess otherwise if the captain smelled beer the jig was up.

Benny kept up a patter of conversation on sundry topics, carefully avoiding any mention of Angell's abrupt appearance on board and naturally not referring to the money he was paid to ensure his cooperation. Angell was sure that most of that had been kicked back to the captain, but it was none of his business. He knew that travel on tramp steamers was much more expensive now than it was in the old days, and a trip like his could cost anywhere from eight hundred to a thousand dollars. A flight to Singapore from Beijing or Shanghai would have cost much less. But this method was more secure and so far he had not had to show any papers. He was sure that Benny—or the captain—had asked for a considerable percentage above the asking rate, just for the fact that Angell had no passport. He wondered how his friend Stephen Hine had managed all of that. No one got rich on a professor's salary, regardless of university and tenure.

All of these thoughts ran through Angell's mind as he ate the thinly-sliced stir fried beef and green beans, delicately flavored with soy sauce and a few drops of sesame oil, and listened to Benny's chatter but in the background was the uncomfortable feeling that he had left the Book alone in the cabin and after the unsettling experience with the tapping sound he was eager to get back and ensure that the Book was undisturbed. He would really have to examine that text now and figure out what the hell was going on.

After dinner, Benny walked him back to his cabin. He asked if he wanted another beer, but Angell declined, saying he was just tired and would go to sleep directly. Benny said goodnight, and told him he would organize some clothes for him for the next day and bring them by in the morning.

Angell closed and locked the cabin door and looked immediately for the Book. With a sigh of relief, he saw it was just where he had left it, wrapped in its black silk scarf.

He stood in the middle of the cabin for a minute and listened. There was no sound at all.

He picked up the Book and settled onto the bed, turning on the overhead lamp. He carefully unwrapped it from its scarf and held it in his hands for a few moments before opening it.

A wave of memories rose up from his touch of the antique leather cover. He remembered his recruitment by the man known as Aubrey who worked for some branch of the government that seemed to have no name. He remembered the trip to the refugee camp on the

Turkish-Syrian border, the camp full of Yezidis who were fleeing the violence in Iraq. He thought of his trip to Iraq, then, to Tell Ibrahim south of Baghdad, the site of the ancient city of Kutha: entrance to the Babylonian Underworld. Of the firefight that took place there between different factions seeking to raise demons from the Underworld into this one, basing their efforts on the ancient Sumerian text in which Inanna—a goddess—descends to the Underworld and then ascends back to the Earth, the demons of Hell preceding her.

Then there was Iran, and another firefight: this time at the Towers of Silence in Yazd, a Zoroastrian stronghold, and the death of a Zoroastrian priest by bullets fired from the Revolutionary Guard.

Then the exhausting trip to the Afghan border; meeting the remnants of the once great Kafiri clans—pagans at heart, descendants of the army of Alexander the Great, and the last people in Afghanistan to be converted to Islam by fire and sword in the nineteenth century—and being captured by a terror group only to be rescued on the Pakistan border.

And then, Nepal. And the "hidden city," the *beyul* known as Khembalung, below the Himalayas. The ritual of raising the ancient high priest of the Old Ones, Kutulu, from his crypt beneath the Earth. The death of his friend. The murder of a remote viewer.

And from the beginning at the refugee camp to the final confrontation at Khembalung, the young Yezidi woman: Jamila. A woman who channeled not ghosts but demons. Not spirits of the dead, but spirits of the dreaming. He saw it happen. He felt the ground shake, saw the light stretch like crooked fingers along the walls and heard the awful roaring of something in the pit of his stomach and the back of his head. He felt ... he *knew* that something— Something—hideous was about to erupt from someplace other than Here. A gate, they said. A gate was being opened and something would fly in. Not fly, though. Slither, maybe. Crawl.

Jamila. He had left her behind in his escape from the underground cavern. He didn't know if she was alive or dead. He knew that the place was attacked by forces loyal to Aubrey, or to his master, Monroe. There were explosions, bullets, heavy armor everywhere. Helicopters. Tracer rounds lighting up the Himalayan night.

It was Mosul, all over again, the massacre of religious sectarians and even the possible murder of a Yezidi woman. Only this time he had been the cause, not merely the witness.

He held the Book in his hands, the one everyone had been fighting over. The one that was going to be used by fanatics, murderers, and conmen to further their own agendas. The Book that these fanatics believed contained the technology for opening the Gate: something he didn't want to believe in, but was forced to accept even though he didn't understand it. The Book that Aubrey said must never fall into the hands of the wrong people.

Who the hell *were* the wrong people?

He opened the Book at random. Hell, the whole Book was random as far as he could make out. It seemed to have a beginning, but no real ending. It began in Arabic, a classical style that hinted at its early Islamic origins. But it became a jumble of Greek and Arabic, and eventually Greek won out for most of it. Even then it contained long passages that seemed to be *voces magicae*: a kind of abracadabra of words and phrases that didn't seem to mean anything in any language. This was what stopped him from examining the Book earlier. It just seemed to be a catalogue of nonsense.

The illustrations were compelling, however. He had seen similar drawings and symbols in his research in religious studies over the years and even noticed that one in particular was almost identical to the painted seal on his spirit bowl, the one from Syria that he kept in his Brooklyn apartment. By going back and forth between the symbols and the text, he began to make some sense of it all.

There was a lot in there about a Gate, though. Mostly warnings about keeping the Gate closed. And there were references to gods that seemed borrowed from Mesopotamian religion. That would appear to date the text to somewhat early in the Islamic period, when a lot of the esoteric lore and information about the pre-Islamic religions were suppressed.

Kutha, after all—the Babylonian Gate to the Underworld where he witnessed the weird firefight at Tel Ibrahim—was the home city of the Qureish tribe, the same tribe that was the caretaker of the Ka'aba in Mecca before the rise of Islam. Idol worshippers, according to legend they had 360 idols in the Ka'aba before the Prophet came and threw them all out, making the Ka'aba the centerpiece of his new religion. In fact, the Qureish were the Prophet Muhammad's own tribe.

"Is this what they are afraid of?" Angell asked in a whisper, as if someone could hear him talk to himself. "A link between the Prophet and the Babylonian Gate to the Underworld?" Angell had had numerous contacts with the Islamic communities in the Middle East and the States during his career, and knew that a lot of the Islamophobia one encountered these days was misinformed (or "disinformed" as he liked to say). It was really the result of confusion and paranoia, triggered by hateful fanatics who quoted the Qur'an the way the Devil quotes Scripture and by non-Muslims who were ignorant of the religion but felt qualified to cherry-pick Islamic texts looking for proof that Islam was a religion of hate. Ironically, their behavior justifyied the propaganda put out by the renegade mullahs. Still, there was no denying that there were scholarly imams who preached in favor of jihad. Had some kind of evidence surfaced that the roots of Islam were to be found in a Mesopotamian Underworld … well, that would turn the entire Middle East—and by extension the entire Islamic world—into a massive firestorm. Such evidence would be considered the product of an American intelligence campaign (or "crusade") against Islam; conversely, the Evangelical Christians would consider it proof enough that Islam came from the Devil (or whoever it was who ruled in Kutha).

If the Book could be shown to represent the point of view of an Arab author who lived at the time of the Islamic conquest of

Mesopotamia—that is, if it could be shown that it was an authentic text of the seventh century C.E.—then the information it held could be priceless.

And make it the most dangerous book in the world.

"This could be interesting after all," Angell mused to himself, aloud, all thoughts of the strange tapping sound from earlier in the evening having receded in the presence of a new academic puzzle to be solved.

He took a deep breath, went back to the very first page, and began to read.

"This is the testimony of all that I have seen, and all that I have learned ..."

CHAPTER THIRTY

GLORIA THREW THE SUITCASE IN THE BACK of her car, praying to God it would hold up and not crap out on them along the way. The way where? She wasn't sure. And that was a good thing. That meant that whoever would be looking for them wouldn't know, either.

Her kids arrived on time—another blessing—from school. Without explanation she shoved them into the back seat, made sure they put on their seat belts, and started the engine.

It didn't turn over.

She took a deep breath, said a mental prayer, and turned the ignition key again. This time it took. The engine roared to life—well, didn't exactly roar, more like it belched—and she pulled out of her parking spot in front of her house in Providence, Rhode Island and headed west.

She had a full tank of gas, a few hundred dollars in her purse and another hundred or so in the bank. She would stop at an ATM once she was sure she was out of Rhode Island ... no, wait. Not a good idea. Better to get the money now so they would not have an idea of which way she was headed.

She saw a branch of her bank and pulled into the ATM lane so she wouldn't have to leave the car. There was only one car in front of her.

She drummed her fingers on the steering wheel, impatient to be going. Behind her, the boys were strangely silent. Not like them at all.

She turned to look at them, and they were fine. They smiled back at her. She still couldn't get used to them. They didn't look much like her at all. They looked a lot like each other, though. Weird, because they weren't twins. They were born at different times, conceived years apart. But they were so similar in appearance ...

A horn honking behind her brought her back to the present. She pulled up to the ATM and withdrew her remaining balance quickly. She then peeled out of the ATM lane and back onto the street.

The boys never once asked her where they were going.

She decided to take Route 6 due west. That would take her in the general direction of Hartford, Connecticut. From there, she could take 91 North through Massachusetts and into Vermont. She could make it as far as the Canadian border on the gas in her tank plus the money in her purse and figure out what to do from there. There were a lot of side roads up around the border, and small towns where she could disappear for awhile if she had to.

She had no clue what she was doing. All she knew was she had to get as far away from Chromo-Test as possible. She didn't know why, exactly, but everything was just adding up in a real bad way. In a day or two they would realize that she had not taken the flight and they would start to look for her. By that time she could be out of the country. She didn't need a passport to get into Canada, thank God, just her driver's license and her credit cards (which were all maxed out, but they didn't need to know that). She hoped they wouldn't need more than that for her kids, but just in case she had their birth certificates. She had a girlfriend in Sherbrooke, outside of Montreal, but she wouldn't call her until she was in Canada. She thought that maybe it was safer that way, that they wouldn't trace her call until it was too late to stop her.

Rhode Island is the smallest state in the Union. In much less than an hour of driving she was in Connecticut.

She passed the turnoff for 395, which would have taken her to Worcester if she had gone north but that direction would lead her back to Boston. She stayed on 6.

The sign said she was entering the town of Brooklyn. Population 8,200.

Back in San Diego, there was no concern as yet for Gloria's itinerary. As far as they were aware she would take advantage of the free tickets and bring herself and her two children to the West Coast where they could be examined at leisure. They had no reason to suspect that she would scarper off to the wilderness. Instead, they were working on a formal presentation that they hoped would impress her enough that she would assent to the additional testing they had in mind. They were in California, so they were at least somewhat sensitive, cognizant of gender issues, and wanted to be seen as fully supportive of her needs. But, at heart, her only value to them was her body, her genes, her biology. They knew they would prod her, poke her, and take whatever samples they could. And those of her children especially.

As soon as she arrived, they would send an email to Monroe, who had expressed special interest in the case. They were always happy to be of service to the NSA or DHS or whoever the hell he represented. Couldn't hurt.

Gloria pulled into a parking space. The kids hadn't had anything to eat since lunch, and she was a little hungry herself. They found a diner and ordered some basic fare while Gloria busied herself with a town brochure.

Seems General Putnam was buried here: the guy who said "Don't fire until you see the whites of their eyes" at Bunker Hill.

"Isn't that cool, guys?" she asked her sons, but they were busy dealing with their cheeseburgers.

She kept reading, and found that the town of Brooklyn once had been called Mortlake, and was created by Puritans who objected to the restoration of the Stuart monarchy. She had no reason to know that Mortlake was also the name of the estate of Dr. John Dee, the famous Elizabethan magician who received the Enochian Language and the complex system of communicating with angels. It would become the foundation of the Golden Dawn and, later, other occult lodges such as those created by Aleister Crowley; or that Sir Richard Burton was buried in the cemetery at Mortlake in England. She had crossed over from one frame of reality to another, and all she knew was that the cheeseburgers were good and the Coke was reassuringly the same as any other she had ever tasted: a kind of lifeline of normalcy through the unknown territory of Connecticut.

She paid the check and herded her two boys back into the car. She looked around, as if seeking to spot a tail—which was absurd—and then got in and drove back onto Route 6 West, following the signs for Hartford and for Interstate 91 North. She didn't realize that by stopping in Mortlake/Brooklyn she had changed the course of her destiny.

Jean-Paul Beckett Jones was a bundle of nerves, which was unseemly for an advanced adept. He had not received a single communication from the OTS since that first cryptic letter, and wasn't sure if he should continue his program of fasting between meals and performing the LBR. The Lesser Banishing Ritual was the old-fashioned one, the Golden Dawn version, and not the Crowleyan iteration. He didn't know which one the OTS would have preferred, and if he did the wrong one he could be subject to all sorts of astral flagellations. Or something.

In his basement he began pulling out volume after volume of rack-sized forbidden lore in an attempt to find the answer. Maybe he was supposed to be in telepathic contact with the Order? Maybe they were sending him urgent messages that he wasn't receiving?

He scoured Waite and Shah, and then Francis Barrett and Cornelius Agrippa—all rack or trade paperbacks, and each edition about thirty years old. There was something weird about mass market secret tomes, but he couldn't afford to be choosey. He thought that these powerful texts should be huge, heavy hardcovers hundreds of years old. But then his magical robe should probably not have been sourced at a Party Plus.

He burned more incense and tried to meditate, but every time he did that his thoughts turned to sex, and 'meditate' became 'masturbate,' and he lost his magical edge. He knew there were sexual secrets to magic, but he couldn't figure out what they were.

Still a virgin, he had an idea as to what they would involve but really couldn't be sure. What if being a virgin would be a problem? What if they expected him, an advanced adept after all, to be a man of the world, proficient in all the erotic arts?

He knew he was not living up to what was expected of him, but he didn't know where to go from square one. Initiation: what did that really mean? Getting off square one, he supposed. Going in some direction. Moving. Changing it up. How could he convince other people that he had what it takes, that he was worthy of their attention?

But he unfolded the letter for maybe the hundredth time and re-read it. They seemed to think he was magic material. If they were adepts, wouldn't they know more about him than he knew about himself? Shouldn't he trust their opinion of him more than he trusted his own?

That made him feel a little better. Putting his faith in an authority figure and abdicating personal responsibility: that calmed him down. He had to learn to stop worrying, to stop challenging himself, to stop working so hard. He had to "be in the Now" like that German guy said, the one in all the DVDs. Tollhouse or Tobler or something.

But how can you be "in the Now" if all you do is think about tomorrow?

The time for meeting the other adepts had to be fast approaching. He had already scoped out the old tobacco field. It was kind of desolate, even during the afternoon. At night it would be spooky. That was cool, right?

He unfolded the letter again.

Before arriving in Hartford, Gloria took the exit for 91 North. They would go around the city rather than driving through it. Gloria was nervous driving in city traffic. Well, in any city larger than Providence. Or maybe Central Falls.

She would stop again to eat and get gas before they left Connecticut. So far, so good. But she couldn't shake the feeling that they had not left the worst behind them. She looked in the rearview mirror at her kids. They were unnaturally quiet, but smiling. Thank God for small favors. She had a few granola bars in her purse, in case they didn't find a good place to stop. Maybe she would hand them out in back, just to keep them occupied and distracted.

She looked in the mirror again. Weird. They were looking right at her.

CHAPTER THIRTY-ONE

It was tough going at first.

Angell was an expert on Biblical era languages of the Middle East and was pretty handy with Central Asian scripts and dialects as well. This was especially true of religious texts, everything from Aramaic, Hebrew and Arabic scriptures to the more arcane writings in Kurmanji and those from Persia and Afghanistan. He had the Bible scholar's grasp of ancient Greek and Latin which were his first languages after English. But this ... this was something else.

The Book began with the promise that the author would reveal forbidden knowledge. This was a trope familiar to Angell from other texts. But the context was way off. He was expecting something vaguely neo-Platonic, something with some Gnostic roots maybe, or allusions to Egyptian religion. He was not expecting references to lost civilizations, Mesopotamian deities, and Sumerian demons.

Sumer was known to the authors of the books of the Bible as Shinar. But not much more was known about it than that. By the time the prophet Ezekiel was in Babylon, Sumer was already a distant memory. The Sumerian civilization was not really discovered until the nineteenth century. Its unique language—written in cuneiform—would have to wait even longer to be decoded. Then the arduous task begun of translating thousands upon thousands of the clay tablets Sumerian was written upon, many of which languish today in the cellars of the world's museums, still untranslated.

The author of the *Necronomicon*, however, was writing as if Sumer had disappeared only yesterday. Fragments of Sumerian incantations and evocations were preserved in its pages in transliterated form: the alphabet used was Greek, but the words were a mishmash of Sumerian and Akkadian, and some Babylonian. This was a little like mixing German and Spanish in the same text. While Sumerian and Akkadian both used cuneiform, there was no similarity in the languages. And all of this was preserved in a Greek text supposedly written by an Arab! Angell was perplexed.

Yet, there was an undeniably haunting quality to the text. Its style reminded him of the Qur'an, which has to be heard in the original Arabic in order to gain an appreciation of its poetic power. The *Necronomicon* verged on poetry at times; at others, it was filled with dire warnings that bordered on the deranged. Whoever had written it had been touched by the gods, Angell mused. It was an inspired text, but one that was unnerving nonetheless. And it was taking him a long time to translate, a painstaking process.

The system it presented bore little or no relation to the type of magical or kabbalistic texts one would expect. He couldn't quite make out the system from a quick run-through. He would need more time to figure it out. But essentially one had to progress through a series of seven "gates" which he took to mean seven initiatory degrees (in the western context). He couldn't understand how this related to the opening and closing of a different "gate": the one the author was terrified of opening for it would permit hideous beings to enter our world from wherever they came.

As he read through, however, he came upon the passage he had been forced to read in that satanic cavern in Nepal, at the site of ancient Khembalung, in order to short-circuit the ritual that was taking place all around him—and which threatened the safety of the entire world ... or so he had been told by those beltway types, Aubrey and his boss, the enigmatic Monroe.

It was the Sumerian epic of the *Descent of Inanna to the Underworld* but altered, written in Greek letters. Coming upon it now, in the silence of his shipboard cabin, brought the memory rushing back. It was like Proust's madeleine, except unlike the madeleine it wasn't sweet but bitter. He had killed a man in that cavern, and had seen another—a man he considered a friend, a brave intelligence officer—cut down.

But as he read the context of the ritual—instead of rushing

through the part concerning the closing of the Gate so that the rite would come to an end—he understood what it was trying to achieve, at least from a medieval Arab perspective. But how could merely speaking words achieve anything in the world? The whole presumption underlying the idea of a spell or chant or invocation was absurd from a modern point of view. Yet, it had happened. He had made it happen. And if he could do that then others could too. After all, he was a scholar, an atheist, a man with no religion and no faith, cynical and misanthropic. He couldn't bring some kind of blind trust to the problem. So how could such a man, reciting words in a dead language, cause anything to happen?

He was not a scientist or a geneticist. He didn't know if there was some mechanism by which reciting an ancient prayer could activate long dormant capabilities buried along some string of DNA that had the effect of altering reality. It didn't sound possible or even logical, by modern standards. Sound? Using speech to affect reality? Some weird kind of linguistic-genetic-neurological interface? He could understand this on a psychological level, some kind of self-brainwashing or something, so that he maybe convinced himself that something real was taking place when it was all in his head.

But he knew what he had experienced. He hadn't been dreaming or delusional. People were shooting at him. He shot someone else. Those events were real. People died. He read a chant and whatever was about to happen, didn't.

He closed the Book. He was losing his mind. Once one started along a pathway that was clearly marked "dead end," but insisted on doing so anyway, one risked running into a brick wall. Or pretending the brick wall wasn't really there in the first place, which was worse.

Then he thought back to Mosul, and the event that changed his life. He had witnessed the massacre of twenty-three Yezidis, people taken off a bus and shot, because of a religious conflict with a Muslim man who had married a Yezidi woman. Two different religions—one demonized by the other, literally—and based on different *texts*. The Muslims, of course, had the Qur'an. The Yezidis, the *Mishefa Res* or

"Black Book" and the *Kitab al-Jilwa*, the "Book of Revelation." In the end, people died because of words on a page.

Then he thought of Hitler at the Nuremberg rallies, the power of speech—no matter how illogical, fantastic, or evil—to create reality.

Was that all that had happened? Was it simple utterance that had raised a demon from the pit of hell—or wherever it was that Kutulu had come from—and nothing else? But if someone else had used Hitler's speeches to talk to the crowds at Nuremberg, Angell doubted that they would have had nearly the same effect. There had to be more than the words themselves. There had to be something else, some innate power ...

It was like love, he guessed. If the wrong person tells you she loves you, it's depressing and uncomfortable. It doesn't work. If the right person tells you, it's glorious and liberating. The same words, but different speakers.

"Love"? Where did that come from? Angell had not loved, or been loved by, anyone in decades. When he lost his faith he lost that, too.

Angell nearly had been married once long ago, when he had just won tenure and felt that he had the financial stability to provide for a family. That was shortly before September 11, 2001 and the drunken lurch of his country to a 24/7 war footing. He lost family members in that attack, on board the flight that had left from Boston on its way to LA, a famous television producer and his wife. Suddenly, financial stability—any kind of stability—seemed like a bad joke. And there he was, a professor of religion in a world torn apart by religion.

He broke up with his fiancée shortly after that. Or she broke up with him. He didn't really remember how it happened. He was obsessed and she was depressed, that much he recalled. He volunteered to go to Afghanistan and then to Iraq as an embedded academic to help with language and cultural issues on the ground. It seemed so long ago and so far away. A different country, something

you read about in history books, or historical novels. He tried to
remember what she looked like, but her face was a blur. It was more
than ten years ago now; Angell was a ghost to himself, and to the
faculty back at Columbia, and to his neighbors, and what was left
of his friends. The memories of ghosts are finite things, focused on
a single event, a single person, a single house to haunt. His haunted
house was his own past, the tunnels in his own mind. He was no
good to anyone, not anymore. It would have been callous of him
to get involved with women when he knew how it would end and
the damage he would do. He had lost his own faith; he couldn't be
responsible for someone else losing theirs, even if that faith was only
in him. The world doesn't need any more ghosts.

Angell was no stranger to feeling sorry for himself, but this
degree of pathos was, well, pathetic. He shook himself out of it and
tried to refocus on the Book.

The thing that puzzled him, though, was why it had to be him.
"Why me?" he asked the walls of his cabin. "Why me in particular?"
He didn't believe for a second Aubrey's explanation that it had to do
with his family and his ancestor: the one mentioned in Lovecraft's
story, "The Call of Cthulhu." It didn't make sense. He wasn't a
commando, he despised Lovecraft for the damage the psycho had
done to his family's reputation, and he never wanted to see Iraq
again. Surely they had agents—professionals—much more qualified
than he was.

Yet, there was something about the Book, the physicality of it,
which seemed to hum under his fingers like a musical instrument
that actually *wanted* to be played. It was a feeling that was a mixture of
revulsion and … and desire. Yes, that was it. A sick kind of attraction,
a connection with something that you knew was no good for you,
which actually repelled you.

It was thick, completely handwritten rather than printed, and
the Greek was hard enough to read—but when it slipped into
incantations in other tongues, it became almost impossible to make

out without a lot of patience and even trial-and-error. The diagrams did not help much in that regard, but by providing natural breaks between sections it helped him to understand the structure of the Book as well as the structure of the technology it represented.

For it *was* a technology. A spiritual technology, granted, but a technology nevertheless. It was a tool, a device, for penetrating a world or dimension or universe—Angell wasn't sure which—that touched our own. And it was full of dangers, and dire warnings. Sacrifices were required. That alone didn't faze Angell, for he was used to the fact that at least half the world's religious population were accustomed to animal sacrifice, and that included Islam, of course, as well as the African and Afro-Caribbean religions, and certain sects in India that worshipped the goddesses Durga and Kali. It offended western sensibilities to think about blood sacrifice, but it was routinely practiced in Jerusalem at the time of the First and Second Temples. In this sense, then, the *Necronomicon* was consistent with all of these which made it seem more … authentic, somehow.

All of this was Angell's academic training taking over, but deep within his heart something else was at work. He had avoided opening the Book for weeks, but now that he had he was fascinated by it. He wanted to figure out its secrets. He thought it would make a great subject for a learned paper in some academic journal, perhaps the one published by the American Academy of Religion. Even better, a complete textual analysis, book length, for Brill in the Netherlands. One of those hugely over-priced books that no one could afford but which would establish his reputation forever.

If he had any reputation left after this.

He began to chuckle to himself. "Delusions of grandeur," he said to the empty room. "Here I am, incognito on a tramp steamer, dressed as a Tibetan monk, fleeing for my life across the South China Sea, a murderer no less, dreaming of the day I stand before a group of colleagues in Leiden or New York or Freiburg, expostulating on … on the *Necronomicon*!"

Carefully, and a little regretfully, he closed the Book and wrapped it once again in the black silk scarf. He stowed it beneath his pillow and turned off the overhead lamp.

Delusions of grandeur. Daydreams in the nighttime.

His life, as he knew it, was over. He was no longer a religious studies scholar. He was a wanted felon, on the run from an American intelligence agency and probably from Interpol as well. Just for doing what they wanted him to do. If he surrendered, they would shut him up in some basement room somewhere for a couple of years and debrief him until he lost his mind and was no use to anyone anymore.

Or, they would kill him.

He had to stay alive long enough to know why.

CHAPTER THIRTY-TWO

MONROE WAS GROWING INCREASINGLY FRUSTRATED with the Grothendieck material. A lot of it was couched in abstract philosophical jargon mixed with allusions to mathematical theories that Grothendieck considered self-explanatory. To make matters worse, the bulk of the text was devoted to rambling, almost stream-of-consciousness prose in which Monroe felt himself drowning. The Unabomber's manifesto was easier to understand, if considerably less devotional.

What kept him reading, though, were the occasional flashes of clarity that seemed focused on some easily-recognizable themes from medieval spiritual literature such as the Holy Grail, or the Knights Templar. This would make sense, considering where Grothendieck had spent so much of his time: in the Languedoc region where the Templars were legend, and where rumors of the hiding place of the Grail kept tourists coming back year after year. He had been interested in the works of Oskar Ernst Bernhardt, a spiritual leader who fashioned himself Abd-ru-shin, the promoter of a Grail message who eventually was exiled from Austria by the Gestapo during the war, and who died in Germany on December 6, 1941: a day before the attack on Pearl Harbor.

Monroe decided he would scan the rest of the pages of what he was reading, a long text entitled *La clef des songes* ("The key of dreams") written by Grothendieck sometime around 1987 and never published. He also had a copy—long believed lost—of one of his earlier works, "In praise of incest" (circa 1979), his only work of fiction, which he kept under lock and key. The title alone telegraphed Grothendieck's uncommon approach to philosophy. But it was "The key of dreams" that held the most immediate interest for Monroe, for he discovered within its pages an impassioned and relatively clear defense of Eros as well as the relation of Eros to creativity and to dreams.

Grothendieck's understanding and appreciation of Eros was closer to Crowley's than to Christianity's. For the mathematician, Eros was the power of creation, a divine power, and not something to be repressed or denied. (His position concerning sexuality in general was well-known among his peers.) At the same time, he was just as passionately interested in spirituality, studying Nichiren Shoshu Buddhism as well as Grail lore and Theosophy. He was a child of the Second World War, and as such carried with him the memories of that conflict: death, destruction, starvation, the uncertainty of surviving from day to day, every day, for weeks and then months. He wound up opposing the Vietnam War and promoting ecological causes.

But something happened to him in the year 1970 that he called his "great turning." He abandoned the profession of mathematics, became increasingly involved in pacifism and the ecology movement, and gradually turned towards purely spiritual pursuits. No one has ever offered a convincing argument for why this occurred. They cite academic politics (which are poisonous, granted) as well as the general political situation in the world at the time, and Grothendieck's distaste for the fact that the Institute des Hautes Etudes Scientifiques (IHES) where he worked was being partially funded by grants from France's Defense Ministry. None of these reasons, however, were sufficient to account for Grothendieck's withdrawal from mathematics and his submersion into social and spiritual movements and pursuits.

"All dreams," he wrote in *The Key to Dreams*, "come from the Dreamer." A little later on in the same section he writes that each dream "without exception is a *living word* of the Dreamer." God, for Grothendieck, could be identified this way, as the Dreamer that is the source of our dreams.

This is what caused Monroe to go back and re-read Grothendieck and his notes on the mathematician. Where had he heard a similar sentiment before? The events of the past month had reminded him with full force of that famous tale by Lovecraft, "The Call of

Cthulhu," and the characterization of Cthulhu as a high priest who communicates with his followers through dreams.

The military and intelligence communities long ago had become aware of the threat posed by religious extremism: a phenomenon that was based largely on texts, on the written word, and on spiritual revelation. Apocalyptic groups who preached an oncoming Doomsday were usually basing that belief on an interpretation of scriptures; in some cases, on the interpretation of cultural artifacts, such as pop songs. Charles Manson famously desired to cause a race war in the United States, and based some of his "revelations" on idiosyncratic interpretations of Beatles lyrics. Jim Jones, the leader of another apocalyptic cult, mixed Biblical passages with quotations from revolutionary leaders.

Regardless of what one's personal belief was in the truth or falsehood of religious scriptures, however, they were generally classed as "non-fiction" in the world's libraries and bookstores. Taking a longer view, though, Monroe thought to class religious texts in the same category as science fiction, fantasy and horror: not because he had a low opinion of the former, but because he had a high opinion and grudging respect for the latter. Lovecraft predicted more than he realized; and he understood more than he revealed. Monroe was not sure from where Lovecraft derived his information, but he knew that the cranky old writer had instinctively understood the role the unconscious mind plays in the interpretation and manipulation of reality. Both Lovecraft and Grothendieck suspected that their dreams came from a common source: the Dreamer. For Grothendieck, this was God. For Lovecraft, it was Cthulhu. In both cases, it was an immensely powerful but invisible entity that communicated with people all over the globe, inspiring them to take action. For Grothendieck, the Dreamer produced mutants: savants who were intellectual and moral giants. For Lovecraft, the Dreamer produced another kind of mutant: alien-human hybrids, genetic nightmares, crazed sorcerers at hilltop shrines in the middle of the night.

Grothendieck had been in Vietnam when Monroe was there, when Monroe had seen his own "mutant": the bird-man who flew at tree-top height out beyond the wire, an experience that haunted him still. Grothendieck must have known, must have sensed something in the warm Vietnamese night lit with flares and tracer rounds that caused him to become so intensely pacifist.

And Lovecraft? What had he seen in his relatively short life of only 47 years? What had he experienced that caused him to write obsessively about unseen forces that walked the Earth in other dimensions, waiting only for the right moment and the right place to be invited into our own?

Could fantasy fiction be used the same way as spiritual literature, to rouse a population from its quotidian slumber and inspire it to take decisive, even violent, action? Could memetics be employed in some way that would energize a population, stir them to political or military adventurism? He knew that observers such as Susan Blackmore and others had described religion in terms of memes, which makes the crossover from fantasy to spiritual experience theoretically acceptable as a working hypothesis. Religion, from this perspective, is a kind of social virus that spreads from person to person, mutating all the while, becoming stronger and resistant to external attempts to eradicate it, or amend it in some way. It's a mechanistic viewpoint, of course, but what if there was truth to the idea? What if, at the heart of the meme, there was a kind of universal truth—the "living word" to use Grothendieck's phrase—that gave the meme its energy, without which it would remain a dead image, a tired slogan, and die of extinction?

Was this magical thinking, or does believing in something really make it so?

He thought of the Dalai Lama, a man who had been both the political leader of his country as well as its spiritual leader. Although he had recently resigned from his political post, he was still viewed as the elder statesman of the Tibetan Government in Exile. How do you do that? How do you maintain a pragmatic, political sensibility on the one hand and remain your faith's predominant spiritual authority on the other hand, and both at the same time? Monroe felt that was only possible if you saw one as the outcome or extension of the other. Wasn't that making the fantasy "meme" of religion the bedrock of what in any other society would be the cynical, hard-nosed organization of people and resources, even for the purposes of national defense? The Dalai Lama seemed anything but cynical. Did his dream come from the same Dreamer as Grothendieck and Lovecraft? Was there an esoteric analogue to politics?

And wasn't he, Monroe, living in that analogue even now?

Just as Monroe was becoming more engrossed in this section of the Codex, he received the call from Aubrey over the secure line he was waiting for, the one about Calvin and Hywen George, and everything started to fall into place.

CHAPTER THIRTY-THREE

MONROE HUNG UP THE PHONE after speaking with Aubrey for more than twenty minutes, an unusually long time for a secure call between the two old intelligence officers. Aubrey promised to send along the data he had collected, using the same channel that Monroe had used to send him the background on the Georges, but Monroe already knew all he had to know about Aubrey's contact.

Monroe remembered the old days, back when he was monitoring the progress SRI was making with the remote viewing program. All those thick reports that went flying around between SRI and the military, SRI and CIA. They were teasing at the edges of the weaponization of the paranormal back then, back when Puharich was dragging in the psychics he had found in Europe and Israel. Back when astronaut Edgar Mitchell was a frequent visitor, passionately interested in the subject.

Now, they were interviewing witches and warlocks it seemed. Taking notes on specifics about ritual magic. Monroe was comfortable with all this, of course, since he had been spending decades of his professional and personal life in pursuit of a dark chimera: the insights represented by the Lovecraft Codex. He had been vindicated recently, with the penetration of the ritual in Nepal by his hastily-recruited agent, Gregory Angell. But the war was not over yet.

His instinct had been right. The Georges knew more than they had ever published. Some of what Aubrey had learned was essential in making sense out of the bits and pieces he had put together on his own. The Georges presented him with the technology of the ritual as well as a workable timeline.

Aubrey's report emphasized the ritual initiation of both an adult male and a male child. That there was a sexual component did not, unfortunately, surprise him. He had been aware of the use of children in rituals all over the world, and even in the persistence of forms of child sacrifice in cultures ranging from Asian and African to American and European. It seemed that in times of stress—political, military, economic, or ecological—people turned to extreme forms of religion and ritual.

There was something about the information that nagged at the back of his memory, though. Something about the idea of twins. It was entirely possible that what was missing from all his planning and analysis was something as simple as that: twins. There were the twins with the anomalous DNA in the Chromo-Test report, and now he learned that the same phenomenon had turned up in the interview—interrogation was more like it—of the Georges. The boy known as Lucius had a twin brother, about whom virtually nothing was known. Yet it was Lucius who had to bear the brunt of the torture and rape of the rituals of Dagon, a rape seemingly carried out by several individuals including his own father. Setting aside his emotional response to that data, he focused instead on the dynamics of such a rite. What was it really for? How did it work? What could he glean from any of the statements Aubrey had faithfully recorded and transmitted to him?

He glanced over at the open pages of the Grothendieck manuscript. Then it hit him.

"Ah, wait. That was it. Twins. A ritual. Perverse sexuality. One of the twins goes missing, the other remains grotesque and insane." He was talking to himself, aloud, as the excitement began to build. He was at the threshold of understanding, but it was a threshold that looked out over an Abyss.

"It has to be … It must be … 'The Dunwich Horror.'"

There was nothing about twins in the Lovecraft story "The Call of Cthulhu" that had started this mess, but there was a lot about twins in "The Dunwich Horror." Monroe went back to his Codex and retrieved a typescript copy of the story and glanced swiftly through its pages.

In the story, an albino woman—Lavinia Whateley—gives

birth to a boy named Wilbur. She has no husband, and there is no identifiable male in her household other than her own father. When she becomes pregnant, the townspeople assume that her own father was responsible. Themes of incest abound in the Lovecraft story, and there are repeated references to "orgies." Further, as in "The Call of Cthulhu," Lovecraft is very specific as to dates and places. This, to Monroe, was always a "tell." It meant that Lovecraft wanted the story to be taken as literally as one could, under the circumstances. Monroe had read between the lines in the first story, and years ago he had made copious notes on the second. It was time to refresh his memory.

The basic elements of the story consist of depictions of the area around the fictional town of Dunwich as inhabited by people who had been isolated and inbred over many generations. Primary among them was old Wizard Whateley: a man who had an unhealthy devotion to ancient texts dealing with the evocation of demonic forces. His wife was dead, but his daughter—Lavinia—was alive and unwed. At the age of 35 she becomes pregnant and gives birth to her son, Wilbur. We learn that the night on which Wilbur was conceived—April 30, 1912—was the occasion of a hideous ritual in the woods near the Whateley property conducted by Wizard Whateley himself. Somehow, because of this ritual, Lavinia became pregnant. Either her father impregnated her, or she was the victim of a kind of supernatural rape, similar perhaps to the type alluded to in Ira Levin's novel (and subsequent film) *Rosemary's Baby*.

("Ha," thought Monroe to himself. "Ira Levin, again. Another author who has touched on something relevant to the case at hand in more than one instance.")

Lavinia is described as a pink-eyed albino and as generally homely and unattractive. Her son, Wilbur, grows quickly, learns to speak and to read when still a toddler, and is also uncommonly ugly, even "goatish." Eventually, Lavinia's father—Wizard Whateley—dies, leaving some cryptic instructions for Wilbur. Lavinia herself later dies mysteriously, or simply disappears.

Wilbur, however, continues in Wizard Whateley's mission and constructs a huge building to house an invisible creature of some kind, feeding it blood from vast quantities of cattle, and constantly performing ritual magic in an attempt to have the invisible Beast break through some kind of dimensional gate and enter the human world. Wilbur dies in the process, and the Beast is let loose to rampage through the countryside.

The Beast is Wilbur's twin.

Monroe now knew exactly what those tattooed young girls indicated.

He couldn't talk about this with Sylvia or with any of the other members of the NSA staff.

Intelligence agencies were a lot like secret societies. On one level, there was only the hair's breadth of a difference between the culture of the CIA—for instance—and that of the old Hermetic Order of the Golden Dawn. Both were secret organizations. Agents used code names in the Agency, and Golden Dawn initiates had secret names and mottos in Latin or other languages. Both groups believed they had access to specialized information and secret sources of power. And both had hierarchies to serve and to ascend.

Hell, even the powers-that-be at NSA had a sense of what they were doing that went beyond the purely intellectual. Their spying tools had codenames like MYSTIC (that was being used to capture all the telephone calls in Afghanistan, for instance) and IRATEMONK. They had a group called Tailored Access Operations or TAO that was at the forefront of developing hacking tools. All of these codenames employing religious or esoteric terms were like Satan winking at Monroe. What was computer code anyway but actual code? A game with numbers, with logic; a manipulation of tiny bursts of electrons dancing through microscopic gaps in tiny pieces of silicon. A slight error in any one place, any single line of code, and the whole project falls apart. This is exactly what the medieval grimoires—the workbooks of the magicians and the sorcerers—cautioned you against. All those warnings that every symbol be copied precisely; every incantation uttered with perfect pronunciation, not a letter or a diacritical mark to be changed or altered in any way. Abbot Trithemius, the magician who was the father of modern cryptography (of "code"), would be proud. And even a little jealous.

Monroe was very aware of this, and knew that some types of information could not be trusted with the ordinary "initiate" of the spy agencies. He knew that, as one became more and more experienced within CIA or DIA or any of the other sixteen or so organizations that existed under the umbrella of the Department of Homeland Security, that one's understanding of the nature of reality was correspondingly altered. One knew the story behind the news, could anticipate the news even, and realized that what they read in the papers or saw on television was not necessarily what was really happening. Cause and effect were not always as clear-cut or obvious as the media would make it seem.

Yet, there was an even deeper level of realization that went beyond what the DCI or the flavor-of-the-week director at DHS thought was real or true. Monroe understood that there was significant difference between the political appointees who ran the agencies and those who were career intelligence officers. One simply could not trust the former, and as for the latter ...who knew? They were overworked and underpaid, seducible by money, sex, or mere approval by a foreign power. Men and women who could, like Faust, sell their souls to the Devil for a little recognition, a few extra dollars, or a night of passion. So Monroe kept the biggest secrets to himself.

And this was one of them.

God help us all, he thought to himself, *if a true initiate, an adept of one of the Dark Lodges, also managed to achieve sufficiently high status and security clearance within one of our intelligence agencies.* With what Monroe already knew of both worlds, he was himself in such a position and he knew it. The secret he possessed—the key to understanding the tattooed children—was enough to shatter the Republic if it was understood. The only consolation he felt was due to the fact that none of his colleagues would or could understand it. Not without years of training in both tradecraft and ... well ... witchcraft.

He restrained himself from poring through the Lovecraft Codex again. He had been wearing out the pages with his constant perusal of the timeline and the associated file on the darkest secret Lovecraft had kept to himself, the one that was inadvertently revealed in his short story, "The Dunwich Horror." Lovecraft, the sexually-ambiguous author of scary stories, had put his finger on why he was so revolted by the sex act, and it had everything to do with his sexual awakening as a young teenager.

The story of Dunwich is the key to understanding Lovecraft's own personal horror. It centers on a tale of "miscegenation": of a single woman, Lavinia, and her pregnancy due to the involvement of an alien Being that had been conjured or otherwise contacted by her father. Lavinia was characterized as a "deformed, unattractive albino woman of thirty-five," living alone with her "aged and half-insane father" whose wife had died twenty-three years earlier. While Lovecraft did not come out and explicitly state that Lavinia was the victim of incest, the implication was plain: only to be refuted when it became clear that Lavinia's seducer was someone, or something, not of this world.

The parallel with the Christian tale of the Virgin Mother and the conception and birth of Jesus was obvious to Monroe, but there was another aspect to the story that caught his attention, and that was Lovecraft's own conception and birth. Was he trying to tell us something?

In the Lovecraft story, Lavinia had actually given birth to twins. To a Kabbalist, this is a critique of the Christ story, for Jesus was born to a woman who conceived him without benefit of normal sexual intercourse. To Christians, Jesus is the Son of God. In the Lovecraft recension, Lavinia gives birth to a hideous pair of twins, as if in affirmation of a duality, of "two thrones in Heaven," which would be blasphemous. Thus, Lavinia's offspring are the anti-Jesus. Whereas

Mary conceived Jesus with the assistance of an angel—at the time of
the Annunciation—Lavinia's conception was at the hands of either
her crazy father or a supernatural or alien being (which might well
be a screen memory for an act of incest).

Lovecraft's own mother was a neurotic mess. Her husband
—Lovecraft's father—died of syphilis when Lovecraft was only a
toddler. Lovecraft was thus conceived under a medical cloud—with
a syphilitic father and a neurotic mother? Did he himself wonder at
his own actual paternity? His mother was known to dress her son in
her dead husband's clothes. The possibility of psychological and even
sexual dysfunction has to be contemplated.

But what of the story of the twins that one encounters in "The
Dunwich Horror"? What was Lovecraft trying to tell us?

Actually, Monroe had the answer to that, too.

In ancient times, and to this day in cultures around the world, the
placenta was thought to be an infant's "twin." It was also believed to
have magical properties. In Egypt, during the time of the pharaohs,
the king's placenta was considered sacred and his "double." Was
Lovecraft aware of this, or was he unconsciously referring to this
atavistic belief in his writing?

The other possibility, of course, is that Lovecraft was born with
a twin: one that died, or perhaps took the form of a teratoma, a
monstrous being with his genetics that lay—half-formed—in the
body of his mother until her untimely death in the same hospital
where his father had died.

Monroe suspected he knew the truth. He had had Lovecraft's
DNA analyzed himself, under a code name. The details of how he
obtained the sample would remain buried in secrecy, just as the
unorthodox and illegal method he had used to obtain a sample of
Hitler's DNA (in case he ever needed it). Lovecraft's DNA bore
the same anomaly as the reports coming in from the more recent
samples. At first, he thought it was due to a degraded sample. Now
he knew better.

He knew why the young girls had the tattoos of the Cult of Dagon.

Thus he knew what the report he had just received from the genetic testing laboratory in San Diego signified.

He knew how all of this tied together: the girls, the tattoos, the genetic anomalies.

And that is why it had been so important to him to have Gregory Angell, himself, involved in the search for the *Necronomicon*.

Book Three

An ordinary man would not have touched the Thing. It was on a different plane, and would no more have interfered with him than sound interferes with light. A young magician, one who had opened a gate on to that plane, but had not yet become master of that plane, might have been overcome. The Thing might even have dispossessed his ego, and used his body as his own. That is the beginner's danger in magick.

— Aleister Crowley, *Moonchild*

The Old Ones were, the Old Ones are, and the Old Ones shall be. Not in the spaces we know, but *between* them, They walk serene and primal, undimensioned and to us unseen. *Yog-Sothoth* knows the gate. *Yog-Sothoth* is the gate. *Yog-Sothoth* is the key and guardian of the gate. ... By Their smell can men sometimes know Them near, but of Their semblance can no man know, *saving only in the features of those They have begotten on mankind...*

—H. P. Lovecraft, "The Dunwich Horror"

CHAPTER THIRTY-FOUR

MAXWELL PRIME HAD THE INFORMATION Aubrey wanted. Angell had definitely arrived in Shanghai from Beijing. He was being passed from safe house to safe house: all Tibetan Buddhist monasteries. That was pretty outrageous when you thought about it. China was a Communist country that pretty much only tolerated the religious communities. Yet, Angell had managed to find the one underground network that used monasteries. Good one.

He sent the information to Aubrey and sat back and waited to see what would happen. He couldn't cover the airports and train stations and seaports by himself, especially not in a city the size of Shanghai. He would need a team of covert operators, people who would not come to the attention of the local authorities. And he would need 24/7 coverage, which meant he had to double up on personnel.

The only alternative would be to bring the Chinese cops in on this thing, but Prime didn't know if there was any way they could do that without making them think that the US government was running ops on Chinese soil.

Otherwise, they would just all have to wait until Angell popped up somewhere else, somewhere it would be easier to catch him without causing an international incident.

On a hunch, though, he decided to call on all the Tibetan Buddhist temples in Shanghai to see if anyone answering Angell's description was in residence or had just left. There couldn't be that many temples, right? And he would be bound to discover if an American had been passing through.

He opened his tourist map and headed off to the first one on the list.

CHAPTER THIRTY-FIVE

THE SHIP MADE A SCHEDULED STOP in Hong Kong to offload some of the frozen seafood.

Coming into Hong Kong Harbor was quite an experience, and Angell watched from the officers' mess until Benny found him and told him to make himself scarce in case someone from Customs and Immigration decided to inspect the ship. Angell complied and headed back to his cabin but, thinking that would be the first place they'd look, he went looking for a less likely spot.

He wanted to stay on the starboard side of the ship, figuring that any officials would come up the gangway on the port side. He found a set of stairs that seemed to lead into a dark interior below. He heard voices coming from topside so he decided to take his chances and descend into what would be a cargo hold.

The ship had four such holds, and the one he was entering had a flush hatch that was open. He peered down and it looked oddly clean and squared away. As he descended into the gloom he noticed that there were wooden crates stacked high with a narrow passageway between them. The crates bore legends that were indecipherable to him. He found an electric lamp hanging from a hook, took it down, and switched it on to see where he was and where he could possibly hide if he had to.

The light did not exactly "pierce the darkness" like the novels would have it, as the light seemed to wash out only a few feet from where he was standing, casting more shadows than illumination. He walked a few more steps and discovered that all the crates bore the exact same markings and seemed to be destined for a medical supply company in Singapore.

He was starting to get a bad feeling.

"Probably just syringes, or blood pressure monitors, or something," he told himself. He walked down one small passageway and found his progress blocked by another stack of crates.

That's when he heard what sounded like footsteps coming from the same hold he was in, perhaps only ten or twenty feet away.

He turned and backed out of the passage he was in and faced another set. He chose one and turned down the passage, shielding the light from the lamp so he would not be discovered. That is when he saw that there were two people standing with their backs to him, inspecting one of the crates.

He squeezed himself into a space between two stacks of crates and peered out, trying to see who was down there with him and what they were looking at.

They were speaking a language he did not recognize, but it sounded South Asian. Tamil, maybe, or Malayalam. They had their own lamp and adjusted its light so they could see better. When they did, Angell saw what they were looking at.

It was a crate full of human skulls.

Angell realized he was standing in what was, for all practical intents and purposes, a floating ossuary. The other crates contained femurs, tibia, skeletal material of hands, feet, and spines. Some crates had full skeletons. He didn't know if this trade was legal or not, but he didn't want to wait around to find out. He figured he would take his chances with the Border Patrol.

When the two other men were fully occupied with opening random crates and making considerable noise doing so, Angell crept out of his hiding place and made his way back to the ladder that would lead him up and out of the cargo hold. As he did so, he replaced the electric lamp where he had found it and saw to his relief that there was no one in the vicinity who could see where he had just come from.

He made his way back to his cabin, shaking like a leaf in a strong gale. This was a ship of death, and he was its only passenger.

As night fell, the ship became quiet. Some of the crew had shore leave in Hong Kong, and they went out into the South China night. Benny was not among them, for he knocked on Angell's door around 7 pm.

Angell put away the Book, tucking it under his pillow. He was making headway on the section that had a lot of the rituals for something called "Opening the Gate." This was, he was certain, the ritual they had been using in Nepal for he recognized some of its features, but the translation was slow-going.

He opened the door to admit Benny, who seemed excited about something.

"What's up, Benny?"

"Has anyone been to bother you?" he asked. "Customs?"

"No. Not at all. It's been very quiet."

"Good, good." He seemed agitated and started pacing up and down the small cabin.

"What is it, Benny? What's wrong?"

"Nothing. Nothing is wrong. Do you have any beer?"

When Angell looked at him, confused, he said, "No, no. Of course not. You don't have any beer. I don't have any beer. No one has beer."

"Benny? You're not making sense."

He stopped pacing and turned to face Angell, eyes wide.

"A man ... a man was here. On the ship. A little while ago. I saw him. They say he disappeared years ago. But I saw him."

"A man? What sort of man?" It was like talking to a crazy person.

"A man, that's all. A bad man. Yes, a bad man. A very bad man."

"Does it have anything to do with what's in cargo hold one?"

"You *know*?"

Angell nodded. "I went down there, looking for a place to hide. I heard some men talking, in Tamil I think, or some other Indian language. I saw the crates. And the skulls."

Benny blessed himself, then blessed himself again two more times.

"Yes. That was him. The old man. He made the arrangements. He's selling the shipment in Singapore."

"So ... what's the problem? It's medical supplies, right? Going to medical schools, I imagine."

"Yes, yes of course. Medical schools. They pay top dollar for good quality skeletons. Thousands of dollars each." Benny started pacing again.

"So, again, what's the problem, Benny? Why are you so agitated?"

"I know that man, sir. That old man. I know him. I saw his photograph when we once took on cargo in Kolkata. The police were looking for him. For the man who was in cargo hold one.

"His name is Mukti, and he is a grave-robber."

Angell got Benny to calm down and tell him the whole story. It seems this Mukti Biswas had been arrested by the police in India in 2006, but he was let out on bail and then disappeared. But he remained in control of a lucrative trade in black market skulls and skeletons, many of which were robbed from cemeteries, from charnel grounds where they had been partially cremated, and in some cases scooped out of the Ganges. The bodies would be defleshed, the bones subjected to various acid baths, and then prepared for shipment to medical supply houses around the world.

In some cases, people would sell him their own bodies for cash upfront. Upon their death, their corpses would become his property to do with as he wished. His "bone factory" came to the attention of the authorities once neighbors began complaining of the smell.

So it seemed that Mukti was still in business. It was known that he had a network of dozens of other bone dealers and grave robbers throughout India. But when it got too hot for him there, he moved up the "corporate" ladder to act as a middleman for others in the same business, brokering deals from China to Singapore, from India to Europe and the Americas. The demand for bones was high, for complete skeletons even greater. Some of his trade wound up in Buddhist monasteries in Bhutan where the bones were used to make ceremonial implements, such as skull cups and *kangling*: trumpets

made from thigh bones. *Damaru* were also in demand: drums made
from skulls, often the skulls of children.

Benny was terrified of being on a ship that was transporting
bones. He was more frightened of the fact that he had seen a wanted
criminal on board, with all that implied. It meant that the bones in
the cargo hold might very well have been robbed from their graves.
Visions of horror movies about the undead, searching for their
tombs, ran through his mind.

"Where did the shipment come from, Benny? I didn't see those
crates being loaded when I came aboard in Shanghai."

He shook his head. "No, not from Shanghai. Our first stop was
in Dalian."

"Dalian? In northern China?"

"Yes, sir."

Angell thought for a few moments. Could it be that the bones
were Chinese in origin? If so, how were they obtained? This guy, this
Mukti, couldn't be that well-connected to enable him to rob graves
in China. In any case, in a country like China, any such attempt
would be noticed quite quickly. Unless …

"Do you know if the freight arrived in Dalian by truck or some
other type of vehicle? Another ship, maybe?"

"No, I don't know. The shipment was already on the dock when
we arrived. We loaded quickly and then left for Shanghai."

"Do all of the crates contain only bones?"

Benny looked up at him, a question in his eyes.

"What do you mean? What else could they have?"

"I'm not sure, but China has had a problem with tomb raiders
for the past few years."

"Tomb … not grave?"

"Well, they are almost the same, right? But in this case the tombs
are often centuries old. Or older. It's possible some of those bones are
archaeological artifacts. It's also possible that the other boxes contain
actual antiquities, being smuggled out of China for the black market.
In which case, Benny, none of this is our business."

Benny was clearly uncomfortable with that conclusion, but could think of no other option. He knew that the ship smuggled occasionally, but nothing too lethal. No drugs, no weapons. Electronics, sometimes. Even people. But a hold full of the mutilated dead ... that was something else.

"I suppose you are right. And they are going to a medical supply house, anyway."

Angell had his doubts about that, but kept them to himself.

"Sure. The paperwork must be in order. This ... this Mukti guy is probably just an employee now of some Chinese company. They hired him because, well, he knows bones."

Benny's face wrinkled in disgust, but he nodded.

"I am sorry for disturbing you, sir. Dinner should be available now, even though most of the crew has gone ashore."

"Thanks, Benny. I'll be there in a minute."

Benny backed out of the door, and Angell could hear his footsteps recede in the distance. He waited for a few more minutes, then decided he would take another look in cargo hold one.

CHAPTER THIRTY-SIX

CARGO HOLD ONE WAS DESERTED at this hour, and the crewmen were still ashore. They would not leave port until early in the morning. Angell imagined they would start turning up in another hour or so, giving him plenty of time to examine the shipment.

As before, he crept down into the hold and took the electric lamp from its hook beside the door. The hold was silent and dark, but he waited for a few moments anyway, standing completely still and listening. There was nothing to hear.

His eyes grew gradually accustomed to the gloom and while he still needed the lamp he aimed it at the floor and let its light spread out on either side.

The crates were all marked the same way, with the same destination. There had to be more than forty in all, which was a lot of bones no matter how you calculate it. There can't be that much need in Singapore, so Angell figured a lot of this was going to the black market in skeletal material, and would probably wind up in Europe and in the Americas.

For the sake of security, he did not leave his knapsack with the Book in his room, but was wearing it on his back as he crept through the hold. He became aware of its weight with each step he took, as if he was carrying an infant on his back instead of a single book. He adjusted the straps slightly and that is when he heard the sound.

It was faint at first, and he thought it had come from outside the hold. But then he heard it again, a little louder and more insistent. It was a tapping noise, and he remembered the same kind of noise from last night only this time it was louder and obviously coming from somewhere in the hold.

And there it was again. The pattern. The tapping was the same as before, rhythmic and steady. It seemed to be coming from a specific crate, and he made his way down the pathway created by the piles of boxes and towards the source of the sound.

Ahead of him one of the crates seemed to be vibrating. It was shaking slightly, as if it contained something alive. Angell knew that could not be, unless a rat or something made its way into the box, chewing through the wood in search of a bone. Did rats eat bones? He wondered.

He shone the light directly on the crate. It was identical to all the others. He hesitated about getting too close. What if it was a rat? Or maybe something else, something larger or poisonous or something?

The crate continued to gently vibrate, and it did seem as if the tapping was coming from within it. That didn't make sense, thought Angell. How would he have heard it in his cabin, all the way above the hold? Not possible.

The tapping got louder. And now it seemed to be coming from more crates.

This was insane.

He got over his trepidation and went straight to the first crate, the one vibrating. He set the lamp on top of another crate to give him some light and free his hands. There was nothing on top of the crate, it was sitting by itself on the deck of the hold, which itself was unusual. He knelt down next to it and tested its lid.

It lifted right off.

And in the crate he saw the hideous grimace of a foul idol, a bodiless visage composed of a mass of entrails.

It was dark, probably made of clay, and could be described as lifelike if anything like that was ever truly alive. He recognized the creature from his undergrad days. It was Huwawa, an underworld god who was sometimes linked to the use of organs for telling the future. And its face was, indeed, a mass of entrails. It had been slain in a forest, by Gilgamesh he thought. Sometimes a figure of Huwawa was used as a kind of cheat sheet for fortune-tellers to trace the coils of the intestines of sacrificed animals. According to the Sumerians, Huwawa was a giant and a guardian of the Cedar Forest.

"Sons of God," he said to himself. "Daughters of men."

The tapping noise had stopped, he realized, just as he had opened the crate. But that was not the only strange thing. This crate was marked the same as all the others, as medical supplies. But this was clearly not a medical supply, not in any modern sense anyway. It was a valuable artifact, probably stolen from some museum for sale on the black market.

He was about to close the crate when something occurred to him. Huwawa was Sumerian. The book he was carrying on his back contained references to Sumer and even words and phrases in what seemed to be Sumerian, or at times possibly Akkadian. The odds of that seemed inordinately high. But then he became aware of the spookiness of his situation. He was in the hold of a ship carrying smuggled cargo composed of the bones and skulls of the recently deceased, along with the head of a Sumerian monster. And in the middle of all that? The Book that was supposed not to exist.

He wanted to laugh at loud. From respected scholar of religion to murderer and now tomb raider. His life was *really* going to shit.

He turned to go back topside when he realized that he had not solved the mystery of the tapping sound.

"Do I need to?" he asked himself. "It was probably an insect of some kind, some beetle or like that. Let's just get out of here." He nodded to himself, took a last look around, retrieved the lamp and headed back towards the metal stairway that led out of the hold.

And came face to face with Mukti.

"What you do gentleman?" he asked. "You want?"

Angell saw that Mukti was barefoot, which accounted for the silence with which he was able to move in the hold. He also saw that Mukti was holding a large knife with a curved blade. He held it casually at his side, against his thigh, but moved it back and forth in a way that could only be understood as threatening.

"I was just … I heard a noise. I thought someone was down here."

Mukti looked at Angell with a quizzical expression. It was possible he did not understand much English.

Angell gestured to his ear. "Noise. Sound."

The Indian man nodded in sudden understanding.

He brought up the blade of the knife and started tapping on the crate nearest to him, in the same pattern as the tapping Angell had just heard.

"Yes?"

"Yes! That's it. You heard it, too. Where does it come from?"

"Which?"

"The sound. *That* sound. Where does it come from?"

Mukti turned and beckoned to Angell to follow him. Angell hesitated but then decided to do as he was asked. If they got close to the ladder leading topside he would take it and run. Mukti was a grave robber and a smuggler. He would take his chances with the crew.

Mukti padded silently ahead and turned a corner. Angell swallowed, and turned the same corner. At the end of the row, the Indian man bent over another open crate. He pushed the lid aside and waved Angell over to take a look. As he did so, the tapping began again, softly at first like always and then increasing in volume and frequency.

Mukti moved over and beckoned to him once more, a grin spreading across his features. Angell shrugged, and then moved to the crate and peered inside as requested…

…and then backed away immediately in horror, even as Mukti raised his knife for a killing blow.

CHAPTER THIRTY-SEVEN

ANGELL HARDLY HAD TIME to register what he saw in the crate when the loud report of a pistol being fired caused him to drop to the floor. That is when he saw Mukti drop the knife in his hand and stagger towards him as another shot rang out—extremely loud in the close quarters of the hold—and Mukti fell to the floor. He had been hit twice in the back, center mass, and was bleeding and still alive, but not for long.

Behind him, Angell could see the Indonesian captain with smoke rising up from the muzzle of his handgun.

"*Selamat malam, pak.*" He said.

Angell managed to stand up on wobbly legs, and swallowed first before answering.

"He was going to kill me," he said, more like a question than a statement.

"Yah, *pak*. He a bad man. Very bad."

"But ... but you work with him."

"I work with many people. Good people, bad people. This was bad people."

"Yes, but ..."

"These boxes? They are all *haram*. I would not transport, but money is good and the bones are of the *kafir*. You know *kafir*? Unbelievers. So, no shame."

Angell nodded, more to himself than to the captain. The world was a seriously fucked up place, he thought. Seriously fucked up.

"What will we ... you ... do with the body?"

"No problem. My crew. We take care. You go topside. Go *makan*. You know *makan*? Go eat."

Angell didn't think he would be able to eat, but was grateful to get out of the hold in any case. But before he did, he took a last look at the contents of the open crate; the one Mukti said had been the source of the tapping noise.

Yes, there it was. A mummified body. An elongated skull and long, tapering fingers. Maybe a child. Maybe a deformed adult. Angell couldn't tell, and didn't want to know. But the long, tapering fingers ended in long, tapering fingernails. Each of them had been scratching into the wood of the crate, the marks long and deep. Probably due to some mistake in preparing it for shipment, the motion of the ship causing it to ... *ah, hell,* thought Angell. *A logical explanation at this point would be as fantastic as an imagined one.*

And its eyes. Its eyes. Were they real, or glass? Irises pale, almost pink.

They were open, and staring at him.

CHAPTER THIRTY-EIGHT

Monroe never seemed to leave his office.

He knew all the cleaning people by name, including their histories, families, names of their children. He knew them better than he knew the staff. With the staff there was always the danger of saying too much or being exposed to secrets he'd rather not know. With the cleaning people, he could treat them—and be treated by them—as just people. Of course, they had all been vetted and cleared repeatedly over the years and God alone knew how much they really heard or learned while on the job. But what they knew about him was just what everyone knew: he was an old-timer, lived alone, should have retired decades ago. The important stuff was all in his head. He committed nothing sensitive to digital files and much less to paper. The only exception to that rule being the Lovecraft Codex.

It was an enormous file, crammed with odds and ends of papers, reports, analysis, and the all-important timeline. He had biographical data on all the critical players, from military and intelligence officers of various countries to artists, writers, religious leaders, cults, terror organizations, organized crime figures, serial killers, and the like. These were cross-referenced using his own system of color-coordinated inks and dots. It was like a Kabbalah for the conspiracy theorist, a way of systematizing disparate chunks and pieces of information into a somewhat coherent whole. The timeline was the backbone of the system, for its chronological nature gave a kind of skeletal form to the slabs of meat that were the dossiers.

It was named after Lovecraft because the Lovecraft stories and Lovecraft's own life were the key to understanding how all of these events and personalities hung together. Lovecraft provided the lens through which the major determinative facts of the twentieth century—and now the twenty-first—could be understood. Within the Lovecraft oeuvre you had politics, race, war, the paranormal, the extraterrestrial, genetics, quantum physics, and astronomy (to name but a few) all interrelated and strung together like beads on a wire. Monroe had witnessed some of this first-hand, with Bluebird and Artichoke and MK-ULTRA through to Vietnam and the assassinations.

In his more gloomy moods, he saw the body politic as an organism covered in boils. What the conspiracy theorists called the Deep State, Monroe knew was nothing of the kind. The Deep State meme implied some degree of cooperation and cohesiveness between competing entities, and there was none. What there was, was a diseased body giving rise to eruptions of pus in various of its limbs and organs. What they called the Deep State was really the dark, unseen core at the heart of reality itself. The pus-filled buboes—the wars, the assassinations, the tortures, the oppression of peoples, genocide—represented the symptoms of an underlying condition that most humans refused to confront or even recognize:

The planet—the whole planet—was possessed.

Fanciful, maybe. Paranoid, certainly. But as Anatole Broyard once remarked, "Paranoids are the only ones who notice anything anymore." And now Aubrey had supplied him with more data, more meat to stretch out on the bones of the timeline and this ratcheted up the paranoia to a whole new level.

The two old witches in Wales presented him with a piece of the puzzle. They had been in contact with the Order of Dagon since 1970. That was important, because it enabled him to pinpoint the appearance of the Order to a specific point in time and to follow the ripples from that contact in all directions. They had also been in contact with the Order as recently as one month ago. That was important, too, for that was *after* the ritual had taken place in the underground cavern in Nepal, the one that Gregory Angell had been sent to stop. Monroe saw how the Order was manipulating groups in the US as well as in other regions around the globe, and how they were always a step or two ahead of whatever Monroe was doing to stop them.

He flipped through the pages of his Codex, some of them yellow with age, others with ink that was fading. He found the page for the year 1970 and it was revealing, indeed.

2/16 The Jeffrey MacDonald "Green Beret" murders take place at Fayetteville. It was claimed that the murders were the work of a cult linked with Charles Manson.

3/7 Linda Kasabian gives birth to a child while in prison for the Manson killings. She names the child "Angel." The father was Manson Family member Bobby Beausoleil.

4/17 The Apollo 13 crisis takes place.

4/20 Robert Salem is murdered by the cannibal Stanley Dean Baker in San Francisco. Baker is a member of the Four P cult. Baker later arrested on 7/13.

5/26 Joel Rostau, associate of Jay Sebring, murdered in New York. Manson Family suspected.

9/18 Jimi Hendrix dead in London.

November Cathedral of the Fallen Angel founded in Cincinnati, Ohio.

11/6 Attempted murder of Barbara Hoyt by Manson Family member Ruth Ann Morehouse, in Honolulu, Hawaii

11/25 Howard Hughes disappears

11/28 Manson attorney Ronald Hughes disappears. Found murdered in March, 1971.

December Nixon bombs Cambodia

Also that year: Zodiac killings 8 through 16. The Kent State massacre. Crowley follower Kenneth Anger's film *Lucifer Rising* is released: an "Anita Pallenberg presentation" featuring Marianne Faithfull with music by Manson Family member Bobby Beausoleil.

While the listed events were certainly compelling, he could find no immediate relationship between the timeline and his current goal of identifying the operations of the Order of Dagon in 1970. One could make the argument that the Manson Family represented the activity of the Order; or that the Cathedral of the Fallen Angel—a Satanic cult that eventually disappeared, to be replaced by the Brotherhood of the Ram—was connected; or even the Four P cult that was probably another incarnation of the Process Church of the Final Judgment—whose symbol was four "Ps" in a circle, reminiscent of the swastika emblem of the Third Reich. All that was possible, even likely—knowing how the Order worked through existing organizational structures—but what captured Monroe's attention was the last notation in the file for 1970:

Members of the Solar Lodge surrender to the authorities.

This brought Monroe back in time. The Solar Lodge was an occult order based in California in the 1960s that came under fire from the authorities because of an episode known as the "Boy in the Box." The Lodge claimed to be a branch of Crowley's Ordo Templi Orientis, or OTO, although its legitimacy was strongly denied by the OTO hierarchy when news of the Solar Lodge hit the media. The story was that a small boy had been chained inside a box outside in the desert sun for weeks, as a punishment by the Order. It was probably apocryphal, but it was the time of the Charles Manson murders and that was enough to have the authorities raid the headquarters of the group near Vidalia, California as the leadership fled to Mexico and then to Canada.

Disregarding the claims and counter-claims that flew around the event like bats in a belfry, Monroe focused instead on the idea that children were involved with the occult Order in some fashion. This seemed to be consistent with what Calvin and Hywen would publish in 1972, the idea that children could not be excluded from participation in the type of secret society that most Americans would find objectionable on some level. He recalled that children were specifically included (although not required) in the Gnostic

Mass: a relatively tame public ritual of the Crowleyan group during which—in some areas—the high priestess was nude, and which at times could include the consumption of bodily fluids: the "blood of the Lion" and the "gluten of the Eagle" to use their alchemical equivalents.

In middle-class America it was impossible to conceive of any kind of religious movement that didn't include kids. But the esoteric movements of the 1960s and 1970s were focused on adults, drugs, free sex, and transgression. These were movements focused on young adults. Young, unmarried, *childless* adults. Children were an afterthought. Those movements that included children did so at their own risk. Nudity, sexuality, the use of drugs and other intoxicants, indicated that children would not be welcome or if they were they would open the movement to accusations of perversion and immorality.

But the actual practice of occult technology recommended the use of children in some cases as seers, as mediums, and quite frankly as tools. It was an old tradition, going back to the medieval grimoires and even earlier, to ancient Egypt, Greece and Rome. Children, especially those on the cusp of puberty, were believed to possess special powers of clairvoyance and clairaudience. Like some animals, they could see what adults could not see. This might have been due to hormonal changes that took place at puberty, or to the innocence of youth that had not yet been burdened with the cynicism of adulthood, the willingness (or the ability) to see what adults could not see. But all of that was still a far cry from the cynical and criminal abuse of children by some secret societies in order to achieve contact with the world of demons, spirits, and shades.

There were too many instances of children being exploited by adults, either for slave labor or, more frequently, for sex. There was the Franklin Scandal, the Grey Nuns of Montreal, the Marc Dutroux scandals in Belgium, Jimmy Savile in England ... the list went on and on. But evidence for the *ritual* abuse of children was scant.

Pedophiles don't need rituals (they are already pedophiles and don't need an excuse to abuse kids) but some rituals did require children.

The *Grimorium Verum*, for instance, specified that a male child be used to make contact with the spirits evoked during rituals of ceremonial magic. That wasn't accidental or incidental. It was deliberate, and based on experience. Some adults were natural channels, like the medium Edward Kelly for the magician Dr John Dee during the Elizabethan period. But children were almost universally prized as conduits or vehicles for the appearance of supernatural forces. The famous possession case that was at the heart of the William Peter Blatty novel, *The Exorcist*, was based on an adolescent who became possessed by the devil. The case that was at the foundation of the movie *Poltergeist* involved teenaged children. Monroe knew this, but had considered it an antique idea, an artifact of the Middle Ages.

If children were being used as vehicles or channels—mediums—for the evocation of Kutulu, then it would go a long way towards explaining how the Order of Dagon was able to keep their operation below the radar. Nothing was quite so secret, so clandestine, as the traffic in children. The pedophile networks were buried deeper on the web than any satanic cult, terror organization, or traditional organized crime operation.

NSA was doing a good job tracking them but they changed their internet providers, their email addresses, their chatroom IDs constantly. They used proxy servers, VPNs, and all manner of subterfuge to keep from being identified or tracked. No modern occult Order or secret occult society had that degree of sophisticated masking. Monroe knew that the Order of Dagon was an exception in that it had no internet footprint at all. Nothing they did involved electronic traces or social media profiles. It was possible, though, that individual members may violate security protocols and have private access to the Net. So far Monroe had only some of their Order names: names given or assumed upon initiation that were not traceable to their birth names, such as "Dark Lord." But now he had the name Vanek, which seemed to be a genuine patronymic and Monroe could work with that.

And, incredibly, Vanek had used the phone. With any luck the NSA computers would be able to trace the call back to a user somewhere in the world or, failing that, there could even be a recording of the call itself. He had the phone number of the Georges in Wales, so all they would have to do is backtrack from there and list all calls received during the timeframe. Monroe guessed there would not be many.

He bent down to examine the file he had sent Aubrey more carefully, in light of the information Aubrey had uncovered. The son in the mental institution was disconcerting, to say the least, and he had been there since the ritual abuse in 1970, almost forty-five years ago. That would make him about fifty-eight years old now. That was certainly an unusually long period of time to be institutionalized and meant that he suffered from a severe mental handicap. He wondered if he could somehow access the medical files, just to see what the diagnosis was and if there had been any progress, or perhaps an amendment of the original diagnosis.

At the same time, he looked at the scant information they had on the twin.

Vinnie—short for Vinnulus, an odd name to be sure—was born a few minutes before his brother and was therefore the older of the two. They had been born on February 2, 1957. That raised an eyebrow. February 2 was the Christian holiday of Candlemas, but represented the older pagan holiday of Imbolc. Surely that was nothing more than a coincidence.

Making a rough calculation, however, Monroe came up with April 30, 1956 as the probable date of conception. April 30— nine months earlier than February 2—was another pagan holiday: Beltane. He wondered if the twins had been conceived as a result of a ritual that took place on that day. In any other case, the suggestion would be absurd but they were dealing with neo-pagans who called themselves witches, and they would certainly have been sensitive to the pagan calendar of sabbats, quarter days, and cross quarter days.

The quarter days were the two equinoxes and the two solstices. These four divided up the year into quarters. The vernal equinox was the first day of spring, followed by the summer solstice, the autumnal equinox, and the winter solstice. The cross quarter days were those that occurred at halfway points between the quarter days: February 2 or Imbolc; April 30 or Beltane; August 1 or Lammas; and October 31, the infamous Halloween or Samhain.

April 30 was also known as Walpurgisnacht: the night that witches supposedly met at the top of Mount Brocken in celebration of their greatest sabbat, the one involving fertility. April 30 had another relevance for Monroe, however, for it was the day that—according to the *Necronomicon,* the book now in Angell's possession—the "Great Bear hangs from its tail in the sky," thus signaling rituals for "opening the Gate."

All of these dates were mentioned specifically in "The Dunwich Horror."

Was that what Calvin and Hywen George were attempting to do back in 1956? Was their act of ritual sex—assuming such had been the case—an attempt to open a "Gate" between this world and the next, much the way the Keepers of the Book and the Order of Dagon had attempted to do more recently, in the bowels of the Himalayas?

And where was Vinnulus "Vinnie" George? How had he been able to disappear from the face of the earth?

And why?

CHAPTER THIRTY-NINE

FOR THE FIRST TIME IN YEARS, Monroe knew he needed to see a specialist. An expert. He usually relied on himself, a handful of care-fully-chosen agents, and the vast knowledge in diverse disciplines he accumulated over the decades. But he once had needed an expert in Vietnam—the musician who had provided him with the recording of the ghostly chant—and now he needed one again. He needed to bounce his ideas off of someone who would understand exactly what he was talking about without a lot of explanation, and who would help him determine the reason for the fear he felt lurking all around him: even in the hallowed halls of Fort Meade.

Over the years he had consulted with a variety of women and men who had expertise in areas of research and development that would be considered off-the-wall by the casual observer. He thought back to the 1970s and his discussions with the folks over at SRI in California, the ones doing the remote viewing experiments and testing Uri Geller and Pat Price. Then there was Stargate on the East Coast: the military ran that one. Well, the military and the spooks. He thought back to some of the crazier shit they had done at CIA in the bad old days of MK-ULTRA, and that damned little clubfoot Dr Strangelove: Sid Gottlieb the mind control freak and his folk dancing fetish. Monroe never forgave Dick Helms, who was DCI at the time, for destroying all their research. Helms and Gottlieb shredded some of the most important studies on the capabilities of the human mind ever accomplished so they wouldn't be indicted for crimes against humanity. They were nuts, those two. Little better than serial killers themselves. But not all of that research involved unwitting subjects or children or prisoners. Monroe never even knew about it until it was too late and he was the beneficiary of the data without realizing how it had been obtained. He would never have supported it if given the choice.

But that was then; this was now. He had a situation that was gradually growing to the point where he could no longer control the outcome. He had rolled the dice with Angell and won, but now ... now, he wasn't sure. He was out of his jurisdiction, out where the buses don't run. Angell was in the wind, and with him the Book that everyone from Baghdad to Bali was looking for, but it didn't seem to matter. It looked as if a schedule had been set in motion, even without the Book, and that made him very nervous. That, and the kids. He had to talk to someone who could put all of this in perspective and maybe give him a lead or at least something he could work with, a way of looking at the improbable that connected the dots so he could use them as breadcrumbs to find his way out of the dark forest.

It was almost 4 am. The sky was dark and the parking lot was quite empty. There was always a night shift at NSA, working around the clock, but most of the day staff had gone home. It was chilly, and Monroe saw his breath form little clouds of moisture in front of him as he made his way to his car. He would have to pass through some gates on his way out, and then take the side streets for awhile to lose any possible tails. Not that there would be any. The kind of people who would target him would not need to follow him to take him out. But it was nice to keep in practice anyway.

Eventually he got on Waugh Chapel Road for the drive south to the town of Crofton, a trip of about twenty minutes or so. He drove carefully, and got to the condominium he was looking for just as light started to tint the sky to the east. Crofton itself was not far from DC, and the man he wanted to see sometimes had business there. He knew he would be up this early, because for Simon it was not really early, but late. The old man did not go to bed until after dawn.

Monroe got out of the car and sniffed the air. It seemed to have rained a few hours ago, for the streets were slick and the air was fresh. He walked over to the condo entrance and found Simon's buzzer and rang it.

A moment later the outer door opened, softly as if by magic, and Monroe entered the building.

It was clean and secure and quite modern. One would have thought that Simon would live at the very least in a cottage in the forest, if not in a ruined castle overlooking the Rhine—or in a bunker below the New York City subway system—for Simon was one of those rare personalities who could claim to be a magician with a straight face—and yet he never did.

Monroe took the elevator to the top floor, walked down the hall and almost knocked but the door swung open, controlled electronically.

"Come in, Dwight. You're just in time for dinner."

Monroe walked into the apartment and closed the door behind him.

"Dinner? It's almost five am."

"Breakfast, then. Have a seat. I'll be with you in a moment."

Simon still had not appeared, but Monroe was used to that. The aromas wafting out from the kitchen area were enticing, regardless of the time or the appropriate meal. Simon was adept at making curries and *laksa* and other Southeast Asian dishes, such as *roti canai* and *nasi lemak*. His *rendang*—beef cooked in nearly twenty different spices and coconut milk over a low heat for more than twenty-four hours until the beef had soaked up all the flavor and was nearly dry—was legendary among those few who were fortunate enough to have been invited to share it. Monroe, needless to say, was one of them.

He took a seat in the living room and looked around at the familiar surroundings. The colors were all black and grey for the most part, with recessed lighting showcasing a few pieces of religious art from Asia, Africa and Europe. Even though he had not been here in more than a year—and then it was only to try Simon's vaunted *kari kepada ikan* (a fish head cooked in a spicy broth with okra, served with rice cooked in coconut milk, cloves, and pandan leaves)—he knew every inch of the bookshelves that surrounded the living room area and could tell at once if there were new additions. There often were, and some of the titles were familiar to Monroe from his reading in psychology, archaeology, anthropology, paleoastronomy, genetics, and the like; other titles were not so recognizable, particularly if they were in dead languages. Most of the books were non-fiction, but for fiction Simon seemed to have a fondness for the detective novels of Ian Rankin and the classic political works by Graham Greene, as well as the thriller genre represented by Jack O'Connell. A few books by Christopher Farnsworth and John Crowley were in a pile next to the leather couch. In a smaller bookcase under the window was a good selection of Garcia Marquez, Borges, Cortazar and Vargas Llosa. He was an eclectic reader, the type who read voraciously in all genres from many countries—writers that often Monroe had never heard of or knew existed—as if afraid to miss something, something essential. The missing link, maybe, or the clue that solves the crime. In fact, Monroe didn't know when Simon had time to read fiction, considering his work ethic and the amount of effort he put into his craft.

The host finally appeared, dressed casually if exotically in a wine-colored batik sarong and a white Cuban guayabera: the ensemble looking perfectly matched even if the cultures clashed.

"You're going to be accused of cultural appropriation," Monroe observed.

Simon shrugged. "I've been accused of worse." His appearance was youthful, in his movements and his manner of expression, but his hair was gray to white. He was neither tall nor short, his features average. Monroe often told him he was so invisible he would make the perfect field agent. That, and the languages and foreign exposure. Simon always demurred, but was secretly pleased at what he saw as a compliment.

They shook hands and Simon pressed Monroe to take a seat and try some of the *sambal* he had prepared, along with the *ikan bilis* he had fried with peanuts and chilies. The tiny anchovies were crispy and hot, the perfect sort of appetizer, or something to snack on with a cold beer on a warm tropical night.

"How have you been, old son?"

It was Monroe's turn to shrug. "I've been better."

"It's been a long time since II Corps. Are you still getting flashbacks?"

"No, nothing like that. It's just what's been going on recently that has me worried. Boko Haram in Nigeria, the Islamic State in Iraq. Plus an operation that's been ongoing for awhile."

"Anything you want to share?"

Monroe shook his head. "Not in so many words. It's classified, of course, but that's not the reason. I would appreciate a fresh look at something, your take on some bits and pieces that have come my way that are forming up into some pretty hideous patterns."

Simon's smile took up most of his face.

"It's not an operation that's been ongoing for awhile, Dwight. It's been going on for, what, *sixty years*? It's the same operation. 'Same shit, different day,' as we used to say in the tall grass. You know that. It's one of your special projects, so that means it's the one project. The Codex."

Simon was one of the few individuals outside the intelligence community who knew about the Codex, but that was because he had known Dwight Monroe since the Vietnam era. Monroe initially had come to him because of his expertise in Asian religions, especially the more esoteric practices and beliefs, and soon came to realize that Simon seemed to possess stores of information on much more than that.

There was a lot he didn't know about Simon, and that was a little disconcerting for a man in his line of work. He didn't even know the man's real name. Simon, as he once told Monroe, was not a name, it was a title. That made no sense to Monroe until he did some research of his own. 'Simon' comes from a Hebrew root which means 'to hear' but also 'is heard.' Someone who listens, then, but who also talks: is listened *to*. It is a Janus-faced term that represented his function as a kind of gate-keeper, like something out of *The Magic Flute*. You called him 'Simon' the way you might call a military man 'Sergeant' or 'Major.' It was a rank, a position, and nothing more. In fact, Simon wasn't even Simon anymore. He told Monroe that one did not keep that position forever, that one had to move on to new responsibilities.

Monroe respected his friend's requirement for privacy on these matters, especially since he was so forthcoming on everything else. And at that moment, Simon was forthcoming with a platter of chicken curry, cooked Thai style with basil leaves and stewed in coconut milk, accompanied by fragrant jasmine rice. He set it down on a table in a small dining area next to the living room and beckoned Monroe to help himself.

"No chopsticks, of course. Forks and spoons. No self-respecting Thai—or Malay, for that matter—would eat this with chopsticks. We have Singha beer, if you like, appropriately enough, or if you'd prefer something stronger?"

"No, thank you. It's a little early for me, but you go ahead."

"Actually I was about to make some *café da*. Care to join me?"

"Excellent. Just what I need, actually."

The strong brew was sweetened with condensed milk, which gave it a double punch that would help keep Monroe awake for awhile longer. In the States it was called Vietnamese coffee, but in Vietnam it was just … coffee.

After a few minutes, Simon came out with two tin filters over delicate porcelain cups and a pot of hot water. They fussed a bit with the preparations in a fit of nostalgia for old times, adding a tiny drop of *nuoc mam* (fish sauce) on the point of a toothpick to the coffee to reduce its bitterness, and then savored the richness of the coffee itself before setting upon the curry.

"You know, I eat better here than I do anywhere in DC," Monroe said, between mouthfuls. While perfectly true, he was being courteous to his host rather than interrupt the meal with his more immediate concerns. They would get to it soon enough. "At my age, that's a big deal."

"I go to DC myself infrequently, but often enough that it makes sense for me to keep an apartment here. It's far enough away, but also near enough to get to when I need access to the Library of Congress or the National Archives." He looked over at his friend, who was obviously in some sort of distress. Obvious to Simon, anyway.

"Look, why don't you tell me what's on your mind? Something is bothering you, and it's possible I may be able to help. That's why you're here, right?"

Monroe set down his fork and spoon, and leaned back from the table. He wiped his lips with the cloth napkin Simon had provided and took a deep breath.

"You're right, of course. It concerns the Codex. In fact, I am up to my neck in it, if you must know. We received a lot of chatter the past six months or so, mostly from the Middle East but not exclusively. And then, through other methods we employ, we confirmed the chatter. There was an operation being undertaken by our enemies to obtain an actual hardcopy of the Book."

"You mean the *Necronomicon*."

"The same."

"And for what purpose?"

"The purpose for which it was written in the first place. To open the Gate."

Simon was silent for a moment.

"There are certain conditions that have to be met before that can happen," he said.

"I know. And it seems they were meeting them."

"Were the stars right?"

"A supernova, in the appropriate constellation at the appropriate time."

Simon nodded to himself. "Yes, I knew about that one. I wondered ... and they had the Book?"

It was Monroe's turn to nod. "Yes. The operation was taking place in Nepal."

Simon's eyes grew wide. "At a *beyul*?"

"A hidden site, yes. In the Himalayas."

"I take it the operation failed."

"Only because we had an agent in place. He foiled the operation, and killed a man in the process."

"And the Book?"

Monroe sighed. "He has it. The agent. And he's disappeared. The last I heard he was in Beijing, at the Lama Temple, and then in Shanghai, but we lost the trail after that."

"Aha. So, what now? It seems you foiled the plot. All you need is to locate your agent and retrieve the Book. There's nothing I can do to help you with that."

Monroe was uncomfortable, both with sharing what possibly might be considered classified information and with the subject matter itself. In a sense, Simon was a loose cannon. He had not taken any oaths, either to the state or to the various secret societies and lodges with which he was acquainted. He was a kind of CI—confidential informant—but that was usually as far as it went. He never violated any confidences, that was a fact, but one never knew what he did with the information he did possess.

He made a decision, to tell what he could and withhold the rest. For now.

"There has been another development. While we were searching high and low for our ... agent ... we were made aware that the cult would try again, this time using children. We don't know when or where, or how many are involved, but we know they don't have the Book so we are at a loss as to how to proceed in stopping them."

Simon became serious, and lost a lot of the casual attitude he had affected so far.

"How do you know about the children? Can you tell me?"

"It has to do with kiddie porn."

"Ouch."

"Yeah, but the tamer variety, if one can call it that. Child erotica, I think they call it. No nudity, no sexual contact at all, but suggestive poses in a variety of costumes."

"Popular in Japan for some time now, as I recall."

"Right. They call it a variety of terms, *kawaii* or *imouto*, for instance. Words meaning 'cute' and 'little sister.' The models have their own fan clubs, DVDs, magazines, etc."

"But loathsome, nonetheless. So how do you know there is a connection here?"

"Our analysts picked up on the fact that a tattoo appears in some of the newer photos that have appeared online. It's usually found on the back of the model, near the waist."

"Like a tramp stamp?"

Monroe was a little startled to hear the popular term used by Simon, and forgot that his old friend had wide-ranging interests and access to dark corners of the culture.

"Yes, in a way. But more discrete, usually on one hip or the other. Barely visible in some cases, in others visible but slightly blurred."

"And the models themselves? And ... by the way ... let's not call them models. They're victims."

"Right. The victims are all races and ethnicities. A preponderance seems to come from Eastern Europe, based on incidental evidence such as the type of electric outlets or power points we find in some of the photos, plus the occasional print media that's visible, like an old magazine in Cyrillic lettering for instance. Others are Asian. There's a Latin element, possibly Brazilian. Some seem Central Asian."

"So there must be a human trafficking angle."

"We're following that up, of course, with the Bureau and CIA. But they have other things on their plate right now. This may take a back seat to the terrorism threat."

"And you don't have that much time, I take it?"

Monroe shook his head. "No, we don't. This has something to do with our previous operation, the one I mentioned. We prevented a cult from conducting their ritual in the Himalayas. There was a gathering of leaders from the various Orders, and it threatened not only our national security but the security of many of our allies. This new development is probably an act of revenge, if nothing else."

"And the tattoo itself? Is it always the same one?"

Monroe nodded. "You would recognize it. It comes from the Book."

Outside the window, the sun had already come up but the light did nothing to dispel the gloom in the apartment.

"The *Agga*?"

"The same. In combination with the *Arra*. It is so unique that it is unmistakable as anything else. And only those who had access to the Book would know what it meant. I've used it as an illustration in my presentation on Middle Eastern terror groups, and a sharp-eyed analyst who works the pornography desk recognized it without knowing what it was. It was brought to my attention, and here we are."

"But not the *Bandar*? At least, not alone?"

"No. The *Bandar* has not appeared yet in any of the examples we've seen. Just the first two. "

Simon got up and started pacing, back and forth, until he wound up in front of the window, facing the rising sun of dawn: in that weird outfit looking like a muezzin from space about to begin the call to prayer.

"The *Agga* is the symbol of the Old Ones, the gods or entities or whatever you want to call them that were here before humanity evolved. The *Arra* has to be there for the *Agga* to work; they're like two parts of one sentence, an object and a verb, say. Together, it means our race—the human race—invites the Old Ones in: preparing the way, so to speak. They're making a statement. They're saying they're ready, and that they are going nuclear."

"But a statement to whom? We only came across this because an eagle-eyed analyst in the bowels of the Fort had remembered an obscure fact from my presentation."

Simon was silent again, wondering who would see the pictures and what they would be expected to do once they saw them. This was obviously part of a pre-arranged communication system.

"Who receives the images? How did your analyst get them?"

"He downloads them off the internet. The dark web. He's

monitoring child porn traffic, trying to identify where the images originate. It's time consuming and tedious, even for NSA. Fake IP addresses, VPNs, Tor browsers, massive encryption protocols … there's more security with child porn than there is for nuclear silos or bomb-making instructions. Our guy's in the basement *of* the basement at Meade, for chrissakes. Nobody at NSA really wants to get involved with this, so they shunt it over to a low-level analyst. He just happens to be good at what he does."

"They could have used almost any medium to communicate their instructions, Dwight. In the first place they're using child porn because it's surrounded by so much encryption and security, but the fact that they're using images of children is part of the message. It's a command prompt. It's a specific line of code that takes you to an area embedded deep within the system."

"Now you're scaring me. Does any of what you just said actually mean anything to real world gents like myself?"

Simon turned to look at his old friend with a crooked smile on his face.

"Sorry about that. I tend to wax poetic when confronted with this degree of organization and intensity. What I mean is the children *are* the message. It's an old method, rarely used anymore except by those who can evade scrutiny because it's so costly in so many ways. I mean, you can't even mention a term like 'altar boy' without conjuring up all sorts of unsavory associations. But the method is the same."

"Altar boy? Now I'm really confused. But before we get much further along, I should mention that I had a couple called Calvin and Hywen George interviewed …"

"The name rings a bell. Something from the Seventies? Witchcraft movement, that sort of thing?" Simon went off to one of the bookshelves, and pulled down a cheaply-produced paperback.

"Yes, exactly."

"I didn't know they were still alive. They created something of a scandal back then. The initiation of children by adults in sexual rituals? Well, your instincts were certainly on the right track. The Georges can lead you deeper into the Tunnels, but you might not like the trip."

He handed Monroe the paperback. It had a lurid cover, red ink on a black background, and purported to be the *Horned God's Handbook*. It was by Calvin and Hywen George, and was copyrighted 1970.

Monroe started flipping through the book, a copy of which he already had seen, but was fixated on something Simon had said.

"You mentioned 'tunnels.' I heard that before in this context. I think the Georges mentioned it to my agent. What does that mean?"

"It's a reference to the Tunnels of Set. They were proposed—or discovered—by the British magician Kenneth Grant some time ago as a kind of back alley of the Tree of Life in Kabbalah. You know there are twenty-two paths connecting the ten spheres on the Kabbalistic Tree, right? Well, the Tunnels of Set correspond to a different set of paths. Dangerous, populated by nightmarish presences from the darkest regions of the unconscious mind (if that's the way you prefer to think about this), and accessible through forms of magic that are so far outside the realm of what the medieval magicians thought possible that to enter the Tunnels is to risk not only one's sanity but one's soul."

"That sounds like something you would see on a horror movie ad."

"Except for these people it's their reality. I can see now why you are so worried. The combination is certainly suggestive of the Dagon crowd."

"It's a relief to hear you put all this together so quickly. I was worried I was seeing things."

Simon was silent for awhile, lost in thought.

Monroe knew better than to interrupt, so he finished his Vietnamese coffee and wished he had another cup. The lack of sleep and the intense focus of his efforts the past few weeks were taking its toll.

"If Dagon is using children now, they're desperate. At least it means they don't have the Book. But they know what's in it, and how to open the Gate. Or, at the very least, they have a good idea. They're going to force the lock. Or pick it."

He looked over at Monroe.

"There's good news, and bad news."

"Go ahead."

"The good news is that these children have not been sexually molested yet. Dagon needs them untouched. The photographs, the child erotica as you called it, is bad enough but the children have not been subject to actual sexual contact."

"And the bad news?"

"Very soon, all that's going to change."

CHAPTER FORTY

THE SHIP LEFT HONG KONG early the next morning. Mukti's body had disappeared sometime in the night, probably dumped into the harbor waters, and the cargo hold locked up and secured. No matter, Angell had no intention of going back down there again. And the tapping noise had stopped. He didn't know what the cause and effect relation was, but he was grateful anyway.

The captain had become a little friendlier. Never asked Angell what he had been doing down there with the Indian grave robber. Never asked him what he was doing on his ship in the first place. Instead, he offered one of his *kretek* cigarettes: an Indonesian specialty, made with cloves. Angell politely declined. He did not smoke, he explained, but the captain was welcome to light up and he would enjoy the aroma secondhand.

Their next port of call would be Singapore. There, he was told, Angell would leave the vessel and be presented with a passport arranged by his friend. Angell assumed he meant Hine, but didn't want to create any confusion by asking.

The seas were calm and the *Silver Star* plowed through the South China Sea like a Clydesdale. They passed Hainan Island and were soon on their way along the coast of Vietnam. The farther south they sailed, the warmer it became, and Angell spent more time on deck, enjoying the sunlight and trying to get some color in his complexion instead of his usual deathly pallor. He also let his hair start to grow back, and stopped shaving for a few days. He was feeling better every day. Healthier, and more energetic. Even Benny noticed the difference, and told him so.

"You looking good, man. How you feel?"

"Better now. When do we get to Singapore?"

"Oh, maybe another thirty-six hours or so. Why? You in a hurry to leave this fine vessel? Or maybe you got girlfriend in Geylang, is it?" He laughed and walked away.

Angell shrugged and went back to trying to decipher the Book.

He was translating a section that was headed "Invocation of the Four Gates from the World between the Spheres." Even the heading was causing him headaches. What "world between the spheres"? What spheres? And why were there four gates?

Reading further, he had to admit that the section heading was more intelligible than the actual invocations themselves. There were moments when he thought he was getting closer to understanding the underlying assumptions that had created this system and then had to realize he was just going around in circles.

Part of the problem was his training. He tended to read and decipher ancient Middle Eastern texts like this one from the vantage point of his academic background. There were identifiable strains in many of the documents that had been discovered in the past eighty years or so, from the Nag Hammadi texts to the Dead Sea Scrolls. Christianity, Gnosticism, ancient Jewish mysticism ... these were things he could understand and place along a verifiable timeline of sorts. Of course, there was much that was still unknown about even these important subjects. Where was Jesus during the years between his bar mitzvah and his preaching just before his death, for instance? There were those who claimed he had lived in northern India during this time, perhaps in Kashmir where there is a tomb purported to be Jesus's own. Mysteries spawned more mysteries, but with the right documents and the right technology some of these could be solved.

Then there was Neo-Platonism, a philosophy that gave rise to a lot of mysticism in that part of the world and which began in the third century after the death of Christ by a man known as Plotinus, and which was further developed by Porphyry, Iamblichus and Proclus. These ideas saw a rebirth during the era of the Florentine Academy and the works of Marsilio Ficino, for instance, who contributed to the study of astrology as well, and Pico della Mirandola, a scholar of Hebrew and Aramaic.

All of these are well-known—almost exhaustively so—to modern academics. What is not so well-known is the immediate pre-Islamic period among the cultures of Arabia and Mesopotamia. Much that is known about that period, including the pagan religions of that time and place, comes from Muslim historians and from Greek sources as well. Some of these are considered suspect, just as Christian sources on Gnosticism are suspect because the Gnostics were considered rivals to Christianity. Paganism, Christianity, and Judaism were considered rivals to the early Muslim historians. So, basically, it's a minefield of questionable data and unverified assumptions only some of which can be supported by archaeological evidence—such as statues of Arabian deities or burial practices.

What Angell was working with, though, was an actual text that had very little resonance with Islamic writings in term of style, substance or even context. The fact that most of it was in Greek did not help matters. Perhaps if he had the original in Arabic, called *Al-Azif*, he might have a better handle on what all of this meant.

In the meantime, he would work with what he had. He found a blank notebook in the officers' mess and a felt-tipped pen and was writing down translated sections of the Book he felt comfortable with. It was a nice feeling, as if he was back doing what he did best. Reading, translating, interpreting. The Book was a challenge in so many ways, but for awhile he forgot all about its provenance and the effect its very existence had on radically violent groups the world over. Right now, it was only a puzzle to be solved and his head was thoroughly in the game.

He felt refreshed.

Just at the horizon another vessel could be seen, a dark silhouette of a speck to the east of the *Silver Star*. And it appeared to be heading their way at full speed. The captain picked up his binoculars and scanned the horizon, trying to see what type of ship it was and wondering if he should raise it on the radio. His instruments showed it making a beeline for them, but it could be at least an hour before it made any kind of contact.

Benny was watching the radar screen intently. The South China Sea was dangerous at times. The Chinese had claimed the Spratly Islands, and there was always some confrontation over that. More importantly, there were pirates; and while the Straits of Malacca were the target of much piracy, the sea lanes between Vietnam and Borneo were also subject to raids. It had started with the Boat People who had fled Vietnam after the war to find sanctuary in other countries of Southeast Asia, and whose small, unarmed craft were easy prey for pirates and criminals.

The *Silver Star* was well-equipped to defend itself against pirates, but only in skirmishes using small arms. They had six AK-47s in a locker on the bridge, and an assortment of handguns. They had never had to use more than the threat of return fire to convince pirates to find other prey, and the captain had no reason to suspect this time would be any different.

He pulled at the ring of keys on his belt, and handed them to Benny to unlock the gun cabinet. Benny did so, checked the action on each weapon and ensured that they were all locked and loaded.

He nodded to the captain.

"We are prepared, sir."

"*Kasih*," he replied. "Alert the crew."

Benny hit the button that sounded the klaxon from the roof of the bridge, and the captain felt on his waist for his sidearm, the one he had used to kill the grave robber.

The sound of the klaxon made Angell jump out of his skin.

"What the hell?" He grabbed for his Book and his papers which were in danger of falling overboard. He put everything back in his knapsack and looked around the deck, but there was no one there.

Instead, he heard dozens of footsteps pounding down the gangways and heading up to the bridge.

Angell followed the crew members and saw Benny.

"What's going on?"

"Pirates, maybe."

"*Pirates?*"

"Yes. Sometimes there are pirates."

That's when he realized Benny was carrying a nine-millimeter pistol, just like the one Angell had back in Brooklyn.

"Jesus."

The other crew members started filing out from the bridge, holding an assortment of automatic weapons. Angell hadn't seen an AK since Nepal.

"Maybe nothing. You should wait in cabin, though."

"Sounds good to me," he replied, turned, and headed down the gangway towards the lower deck.

It was only when he reached his cabin that he realized he was the only one on board who was unarmed.

"Plausible deniability," replied Max Prime. He was on an encrypted call to Aubrey who had just returned Stateside. "This way we don't have to file a lot of requisition paper for helos and Special Forces. Anyway, we're running out of time. They'll be in Singapore soon and we will have lost him again. Hey, these guys were in the area and they owe us a favor for not having them put out of business a year ago when they attacked that pleasure craft out of Kaohsiung with our Chief of Station aboard. That would have been embarrassing for all of us, right? I mean, we're not supposed to have a COS in Taiwan."

Aubrey felt his anger rising, but he kept it in check.

"How do you know Angell is on that boat?"

"Ship, actually, and the guy at the last temple I checked (it's always the last temple you check, right?) just happened to mention something about a tramper doing the run to Singapore…"

"Just happened to mention it?"

A moment of silence from the other end. Then, "Well, he may have been encouraged to cooperate."

"Goddamnit, Prime! You're a NOC in fucking China! You have Non Official Cover. You can't be pulling that cowboy shit over there. You'll jeopardize our other assets in-country!"

"Cool your jets, man. No one knows nothing about nothing. The guy I flipped? He's Tibetan. Works for the Lama. He has more to lose than us, that I can tell you. He was on his way to Gansu Province on another op when I picked him up. That's how I knew. Anyway, don't worry. He'll be back in service in no time. The guy you wanna see is that Hine guy. He had to have been in on this from the get. If anyone knows where Angell is going, it's him. Pull him in and sweat him, is my advice."

"Agent Prime, I don't need or want your advice. We need our target apprehended, not killed, and any assets he's carrying brought into custody as well. If your pirates go off on that vessel and deep-six it, we're just as good as drowned ourselves. Do you understand?"

"No need to worry. They have their orders. They know they don't get paid if they lose the target."

"Paid? Who said anything about paid?"

"I may have mentioned it. You know. In passing."

"Prime, I'm pulling your ticket. You're ordered to return Stateside, immediately."

And with that, Aubrey hung up the phone and cursed for a solid minute.

Maxwell Prime was in the somewhat unusual and enviable position of knowing his own worth and value. He knew that the threats coming from Aubrey had no teeth, because Prime knew more than anyone wanted revealed. The only way to deal with Prime would be to kill him, and he knew that his people didn't do that. They didn't off one of their own. Arrest him, throw away the key, sure. But Prime had insurance, and if it ever came to that he could walk out of federal custody with an admiring escort. Prime had his sights set on something better than a G-scale job within the bureaucracy. He had been singled out for this mission because of his expertise and his graveyard-like silence and imperturbability under stress. He was also creative and entrepreneurial. These were qualities the intelligence services claimed they liked, but didn't really. Thinking for yourself in these situations was usually frowned upon. Follow orders, there's a good boy.

Maxwell Prime had other ideas about his future. And one of those ideas involved getting rid of Dwight Monroe.

A lot of the younger types in the community thought of Monroe as a crazy old bastard, but one they had to deal with since he was so tight with "management" and wouldn't ever retire or die. The only way to get rid of him would be to discredit him, to show that he had lost his mind and was a security risk, a real liability. This campaign to locate a disaffected university professor should have been proof enough of that, but somehow Langley, the Pentagon, and the Bureau were all okay with it even though his berth was at NSA and he didn't seem to punch a time card anywhere. Hell, Prime didn't even know if Monroe cashed a paycheck. The whole thing was so bizarre that if it ever made the papers the entire intelligence superstructure would crack.

Prime had his own contacts with the *Times*, with *Politico,* and *The Daily Beast*. He could call on them as a last resort, but only if Aubrey got in his way. In the meantime, he had to leave China so that Aubrey thought he was obeying orders. But he would schedule a flight out of Shanghai that stopped over in Singapore.

Just in case his "pirates" fucked up.

The klaxon sounded again.

Angell sat in his cabin and thought desperately of where to hide the Book. If they were boarded they would almost certainly ransack every room looking for goods to steal. A rare book might be just the thing.

He finally settled on that old standby of a loose ceiling tile. As he stood on his chair and started pulling at the tile, he realized that it would be the first place they'd look.

The last place they'd look would be somewhere outside of the cabin. Somewhere else on deck.

He opened his cabin door and looked in both directions.

The captain kept his eye on the approaching vessel, and Benny on the radar screen. The other ship was closing on them fast. The rest of the crew members had gone to their assigned stations, weapons at the ready. They were under orders not to fire until they heard the order. They had been through this drill several times before, and were confident that once the approaching crew saw that they were armed to the teeth they would think twice before attempting to board. And there was no sense in trying to sink the vessel for a sunken ship was worth nothing to anyone.

Through his binoculars the captain could make out the name of the vessel. It was flying a Panamanian flag and bore a plaque with the name *Stella Matutina* on the hull.

Moving his binoculars further up so he could see the bridge, he saw that the crew of the *Stella* were as armed as his were. They appeared to be Southeast Asian, which was to be expected for this part of the world, but there was a white guy on the bridge who seemed to be giving orders.

"Figures," the captain thought to himself. "Why am I not surprised?"

He turned to Benny.

"Try to raise them on the radio once more. If that doesn't work, we use the semaphore."

Benny nodded, and once again tried to radio the *Stella Matutina*.

Satisfied, Angell went back to his cabin. If pirates boarded the ship, he was probably looking at becoming a hostage. Great. Another chapter in his life. Another line item in his non-existent bucket list. Professor, murderer, hostage. What does he do for an encore?

That is when he noticed the ship's engines come to a full stop and suddenly they were sitting dead in the water.

Topside, the captain and Benny were staring down the barrel of a 30 millimeter cannon.

This caused a change in the power differential. It was a Bushmaster II, probably "sourced" from the Singaporean or Malaysian navy. It was a lot heavier than the captain was used to seeing on a pirate vessel in the South China Sea. It could blow a hole in the hull of the *Silver Star* without any doubt. The question remained: why?

The crew of the *Star* still kept their AKs trained on the crew members of the *Stella*. His crew was cynical and seasoned. They knew the *Stella* would do anything it could to avoid sinking the *Star* because a fallen *Star* was worth nothing to them. They, and their captain, realized that this was merely an opening gambit. The terms of the deal had not been revealed yet.

The captain turned to Benny and asked him to semaphore the questions: "Who are you?" and "What do you want?"

After a minute, they had their response.

"We want the angel," was their reply.

The captain looked at Benny, who simply shrugged as if to say, "I don't have a clue, either."

"What angel?" they semaphored back. "We are the *Silver Star*. We are not the Ship of Peter."

"Give us the angel," was their reply. "Or we will sink you."

At that, the 30 mil cannon rotated slightly and leveled so that it was aiming for the hull. The gesture was unmistakable. The next movement would be a shell piercing their skin.

"These people are crazy. *Gila*," said the captain. "Why they don't just steal and go away?"

Benny said nothing, but he understood what the pirates were

asking. He prayed to the saints that they would somehow intervene. He promised he would throw his stash of beer overboard if their lives were spared.

That's when they heard a voice over a loudspeaker talking directly to them.

"Oh captain, my captain!" came the cry, laden with sarcastic intent. "Your fearful trip is done, I'm afraid."

It was the white guy from the *Stella*, using a bullhorn. He had a British accent, and seemed somewhat cheerful under the circumstances. Through his binoculars the captain could see a florid-faced man in a white uniform, white hair, and paunch. He held the bullhorn in his left hand, and what appeared to be a gin–and–tonic in his right.

"Commander Arthwaite here. Formerly of the British Royal Navy, the Secret Intelligence Service, the Metropolitan Grand Lodge of Free and Accepted Masons, and The Grammar School for Boys, Tunbridge Wells. References upon request. Send us your passenger, Captain. A Buddhist monk, goes by the name of Angell when he's at home. Gregory Angell. That's all we want. We don't want your cargo, whatever precious barrels of noxious slime they very well may be, and we don't want your equally slimy lives. Wouldn't know what to do with them, really. Just the passenger. That's all. Give him to us, and we'll be off. There's a good lad. You have five minutes."

The captain turned to Benny in anger and confusion.

"What have you done?"

Benny ran to Angell's cabin and nearly dragged him out of it.

"We must go. Now."

"What's happening? What's going on? Where are the pirates?"

"No pirates. No pirates."

"Who are they, then? What do they want?"

Benny kept a vise grip on Angell's bicep and ran them both up the gangway to the bridge.

"They want you."

On the *Stella Matutina*, the man calling himself Commander Arthwaite leaned out over the rail and watched the *Silver Star* with some amusement. He wagged his empty glass at a steward, who then ran to replace it with another gin-and-tonic.

"Is it five minutes yet, m'Lord?" he asked the executive officer, a Filipino by the name of Rafael.

"Almost four minutes thirty seconds, Commander."

"I think they need a warning shot with the big gun. What do you think?"

"Excellent choice, sir."

"Very well, if you insist. How about one over their bow? Not too close. Just enough to soil their nappies."

"Aye, sir."

The XO gave the order to the gunners and they aimed for a spot about five meters over the bow of the *Silver Star*.

"Sir?"

"Fire when ready, Gridley."

"Aye, sir." He turned to the gunners. "Fire!"

The boom of the shot—fired at relatively close range—caused everyone aboard the *Star* to duck instinctively. The shot went wild, far over their heads, but the intention was clear.

Benny picked himself up off the deck and took hold again of Angell's arm.

"What the hell …?"

"We go now. Up to the bridge. Captain waiting."

The captain knew that the destruction of his beloved vessel was imminent and unavoidable. As soon as they handed Angell over to

the pirates they would sink the *Silver Star* and all hands would go
down with her. The pirates could not afford to leave a trace, or witnesses. If they had gone to all this trouble to find one lonely passenger in the middle of the South China Sea, they would not want
their identity known to the world in case his passenger had friends
in high places. He must have, for why else were they now in all this
trouble?

But Angell was under his roof, as it were. It was a matter of
hospitality. He could not simply hand over the *bule* to the other *bule*
like a side of beef. And the captain had an instinctive dislike of the
British, almost as much as he hated the Dutch.

The crew of the *Stella* was, as he noted earlier, almost entirely
Southeast Asian, like him. Probably a lot of Filipinos, like Benny. And
maybe some of his people, too.

He suddenly had a plan.

"What's it going to be, captain? Angell, or devil?" He laughed at his
own stupid joke.

The captain took Angell by the shoulders and held him so that
the other ship could get eyes on him.

"Come and get him," he said.

"Send him over," replied the Commander.

"No way," challenged the captain. "How I know you no sink
me anyway?"

"I can sink you now, captain."

"And lose your prize? I don't think so."

The Commander turned to Rafael.

"Aim the gun for the bridge. Show them we mean business."

"Aye, sir."

The order was given, and the big gun moved into position so
that the captain could see his fate clearly written down its barrel.

The captain whispered to Angell.

"I will not give you to this man, but you must do as I say. Do not react. Do not nod or make any expression, except maybe look scared."

"No problem," Angell stuttered.

Benny had disappeared, having been instructed by the captain in Tagalog.

"Captain. I'm waiting."

"You come take. We not moving."

The Commander thought for a moment. He had figured this was going to be easier somehow. No worries, though. He would send a lifeboat over to the *Star* and they would lower the passenger over the side.

"Keep the gun on the bridge," he told Rafael. Have everyone train their weapons on the crew. Get two men to take a boat over to the *Star* and retrieve my booty."

"Sir?"

"No, not like that. I mean, the passenger. The prisoner. Whatever the hell he is. Angell."

"Aye, sir."

Rafael saluted and recruited two men to go over the side in a motorized lifeboat.

"I'm sending my men over. Have Angell go over the side."

"Cannot do. Angell has broken leg. Cannot use the ladder."

As they were dickering over how to conduct the hand-off, Benny and three other crew members had smashed open two of the crates in Cargo Hold One. They ran up to the deck with an assortment of human bones and skulls, arranging them artlessly over the deck but just below the sightlines of the *Stella*.

"Christ, what a pain in the ass," the Commander muttered to no one in particular. "Okay," he said through the bullhorn. "I will send my men to your ship to retrieve Angell. They will carry him down to the boat. If there is any funny business, we will sink you at once. Do you copy?"

"Aye, aye, Commander."

"Excellent. Let's get this over with. I'm getting sleepy."

The boat from the *Stella* motored across the distance separating the two ships. Both men were armed. They were dressed identically in black tunics and trousers and had bright red sashes around their waists. They wore round, brimless hats that were also black. They seemed dressed in the traditional attire of Aceh, in Sumatra, as if for a Saman dance. Arthwaite liked his crew in what he called "native togs." Made him feel exotic. They had a stretcher on the boat and life preservers. The sun was starting to go down, and no one wanted to be on the open water once night fell. The area was notorious for sharks.

Angell was busy feigning a broken leg. He had his knapsack with him, but it was curiously light. He had hidden the Book behind a length of fire hose outside his cabin. The captain had another man wrap some cloth around Angell's left leg to simulate a bandage and then sprinkled some chili sambal on it to create the impression of a wound. It was the best they could do in the time available.

The lifeboat bumped against the *Star* where the ladder was suspended. The two men hesitated a moment, then began the climb to the deck to retrieve their prisoner.

More bones were brought up from the cargo hold. The skulls were especially intimidating. Benny crawled along the deck, placing the skulls at strategic positions along the way. By the time the men from the *Stella* came aboard they would think the *Silver Star* was the *Flying Dutchman*.

Every profession has its superstitions. Ghost ships are one of those among sailors. Add to that the religious beliefs of people for whom religion truly is a kind of opiate—a medicine to relieve pain, but also a drug to cause visions—and the sudden appearance of body parts on a ship's deck can be traumatic.

That is what the captain was hoping for.

The two men boarded the ship with stern expressions, carrying the ubiquitous AK-47s as well as the stretcher, so their hands were full. The idea was to strap Angell onto the stretcher and lower him down vertically, with one man below and the other above. As they set foot on deck they were met by Benny who made a slight bow, and then gestured to the bridge.

As the two men walked, guns at the ready, they noticed a human skull balanced against a railing ahead of them. They stopped immediately, looked at each other, then shrugged and kept walking. They turned a corner, and were faced with a deck covered in femurs, tibia, and skulls with the occasional fully articulated hand or foot.

The appearance was so bizarre that the men stopped again, and could not move forward. In order to keep walking they would have to step on or over the bones.

"*Haram,*" one of them muttered under his breath.

"Sorry," said Benny. "*Ma'af.* You caught us at lunch. You know, *makan.*"

At that moment another member of the *Star's* crew came into view, chewing on a tibia and smiling with his teeth stained bright red.

The two men are startled and disgusted, but they lift their weapons as if to shoot at the crew member until they see more men, all sitting down on the deck in a rough circle and appearing to be eating human flesh.

And, in the center of the men and open to view on the deck is the crate containing the humanoid figure that had so alarmed Angell in the cargo hold.

The men drop their weapons and turn to run back to their boat when they are grabbed, tackled and gagged. On Benny's signal their outer clothes and hats are removed and two of the *Star's* crew members put them on. They lift up the stretcher and the two AKs and proceed as if nothing has happened. They appear on the bridge and take custody of Angell, whom they strap to the stretcher, and make their way over to the ladder.

The Commander is not paying much attention to the action on the deck. He is getting bored with the whole process, and knows that his cannon could sink the vessel so he is not worried about a few men with guns. If they don't produce Angell, he will simply write it off as the cost of doing business and report back that they didn't find the *Silver Star*. In the meantime, they would steal whatever they could from the ship as it slowly sank to the bottom.

But a shout from his XO brought him back to the present. There they were, slowly moving the wounded Angell down the ladder and onto the lifeboat. He nodded to Rafael.

"Once everyone is on board safely, I want you to put a round through her hull. Don't aim the cannon yet. I don't want them to get spooked. Wait until the prisoner is aboard. Unless the *Star* tries to make a run for it, in which case sink her."

"Aye, Commander."

They had to send Angell to the *Stella* for he was the only white man on the *Star*. Anyone else would have been too noticeable. Plus, it was always possible that the Commander had some sort of file on Angell that included a photograph. So there was nothing for it but to send him along with the two ringers.

The captain kept his eyes peeled on what was happening aboard the *Stella*. He was angry with Benny for having put him in this position, one in which he could very easily lose his ship and his life, but right now the important thing was to do what he could to save the situation. So far his plan was working. Had they tried to overpower the two men on their own there surely would have been gunfire and bloodshed, and the *Stella* would have fired on the *Silver Star* and it would all be over. This way they had a chance.

Not much of one, but a chance.

When they reached the ladder on the *Stella*, they pushed Angell up first. The crewmembers pulled him up on the stretcher and set him on the deck. Arthwaite came over to look at him and gloat.

"So you're the bloke everyone's been looking for, right? Don't see the attraction, myself. Okay, Rafael. You know what to do."

But Rafael's usual "Aye, sir" was not forthcoming.

The Commander turned to give his order once again when he saw that someone had an AK-47 pointed at his XO's head.

And another pointed at him.

Angell unstrapped himself from the stretcher and stood up on two perfectly good legs. Benny had supplied him with his own nine-mil and it felt good in his hands, like an old friend.

Across the brief stretch of water that separated their two vessels, the crew on the Star were all lined up on deck. In one hand, each member held a weapon. In the other, a human skull. They started a kind of ululation—a tribal cry—that sounded so eerie it rose the hairs on even Angell's neck. The Commander's own crew was obviously more terrified of the ghost ship than they were of their own leader. And, anyway, he was in no position to give any orders.

Except one.

"Tell your men to stand down, Commander."

"And if I don't?"

"That's easy. Your ship becomes the new ghost ship. With you as the captain, lashed to the wheel. Sailing in circles for all eternity."

"How poetic. Here's some prose. My men outnumber the three of you, obviously. They have you surrounded…" he began, trying to brass it out, but in his heart he knew it was pointless.

"Yes, they do. But we have *you*. You'll be dead before you hit the deck, and your XO as well. You were going to kill us anyway and sink our ship, so we have nothing to lose."

The Commander was fuming, but had no answer.

"Tell your men to stand down," Angell repeated. "Now."

The order was unnecessary, as it turned out. The spectacle of the men of the *Star*, shaking skulls and ululating—a sound that carried over the water in an unsettling way—was enough to cause some of the crew members to simply drop their weapons in absolute terror. Some of the men on the Star had smeared tomato sauce across their faces to appear more savage and the entire ship looked as if it was a floating abattoir repurposed as a ghoulish buffet. Not bad for only a few minutes' preparation. Fortunately, they had an almost inexhaustible supply of bones, courtesy of Mr. Mukti.

More men from the *Star* took boats and arrived at the *Stella*, and helped with disarming the crew and locking them into their quarters. They had no interest in scuttling the *Stella* or doing anything further to the crew or to Arthwaite, but Angell wanted to know who had sent them to find the *Star*.

As he rummaged through the Commander's cabin, looking for scraps of information, the crew from the *Star* was busy dismantling the 30 mil cannon. The captain was supervising his crew from the safety of his own bridge, where he remained with a few chosen crewmembers, including Benny.

"Who was this man you brought aboard? I thought he was a monk, escaping Chinese prison?"

Benny's eyes were downcast, his mood solemn.

"He came from a Buddhist temple in Shanghai," he prevaricated.

"Yes. Okay. Buddhist temple. But not monk."

"Yes. Not monk."

"So? American spy?"

Benny looked up.

"No, not a spy. A man the spies want to kill."

The captain was confused.

"A man the spies want to kill," he repeated. "Spies only want to kill other spies. Or politicians. Is he a politician?"

"No, captain."

"So. Not a spy and not a politician. Maybe a dissident? Or some kind of engineer with special knowledge? Computers? Rockets?"

Benny sighed.

"He is a professor, captain. A university professor."

"Ah! Okay. Okay, makes sense. A professor. Everybody always wants to kill professors. They are troublemakers. Make students crazy. Give bad ideas."

Benny's eyes were downcast again.

"What kind of professor? Politics? Sociology? Maybe literature?"

"No, Captain. Religion."

At this, the captain's eyes lit up.

"Religion! Why you no say before? Religion. Ah, we have religion professor on board. This can be very interesting."

The captain was obviously pleased, which confused Benny no end. But at least he was off the hook for not informing him of Angell's true identity. His relief was palpable.

There was some commotion on the deck. Angell had returned to the *Star* with a sheaf of printouts and a satellite phone from the Commander's quarters. He appeared to be agitated.

He ran up to the bridge immediately.

"I can't go to Singapore," he said, breathlessly.

The printouts were from the Commander's PC. They were copies of emails between himself and someone identified only as a number: 191. A prime. But their meaning was clear. Angell was to be apprehended, if possible, or killed if not. But the Book was to be seized at all costs and brought to Singapore where a team would be waiting to take possession of both.

"They'll be watching the port in Singapore, obviously. I can't go in that way. They'll pick me up for sure. I just don't know how they knew I was on this vessel. Someone in Shanghai must have talked."

There was a sudden cheer from the decks of both ships. The cannon had been dismantled and dumped overboard.

"That means no passport, no papers. I'm screwed."

"How much were they paying Arthwaite for your capture?"

"Why, Benny? Thinking of cashing in?" It was meant as a joke, but no one found it funny.

"What I mean, they must have made a down payment of some kind. Did you find cash in his quarters?"

"Not even quarters in his quarters. You're right, though. That doesn't make sense. Look at that operation over there. That's a handsome vessel, and had a mounted cannon besides. The guy must have been running guns, or drugs, or something to pay for all of that. And his crew would be paid in cash, most likely."

The captain chimed in.

"Benny's question. How much they pay for you?"

Angell swallowed.

"Half a million," he whispered.

"*Dollars?*"

"Pounds. Pounds Sterling."

They tried to come up with a plan.

The cost of running a ship like the *Stella Matutina* was considerable. If Arthwaite had taken it out specifically for this mission, the half million would have covered expenses but not much more. Crew and fuel would have eaten up a lot of it. They knew that he probably considered robbing the *Star* of whatever cargo it was carrying and whatever else was of value on board, which would have sweetened the deal somewhat, but what was he going to do with a hold full of frozen seafood unless he had a buyer set up in advance? That didn't seem likely.

A guy like Arthwaite would not have taken the job on spec, so there had to have been an advance of some kind. It was probably done by wire transfer, or maybe even bitcoin, but they didn't have a lot of time to track it down.

Angell could leave the captain and his people to figure all that out. In the meantime, he needed a plan for himself. He couldn't afford to land in Singapore, so he needed another option.

A look at the ship's maps told him the story. There really wasn't anywhere else to go except Malaysia or Indonesia. Singapore was at the tip of the Malay Peninsula; Indonesia was spread out on all sides, across the Straits of Malacca on one side, the Singapore Straits on another. There was Kalimantan, what used to be called Borneo, on another side. None of these seemed particularly desirable to Angell, although it was a good bet they could find somewhere along one of these many coastlines to drop him off without going through customs and immigration, but then he would be in a foreign country without papers and without resources.

As he sat in the bridge, head in hands, the satellite phone began to ring.

CHAPTER FORTY-ONE

JAMILA SAID GOODBYE TO STACEY at the Indira Gandhi International Airport in Delhi when they arrived after 5 pm that evening. Their SpiceJet flight arrived in Terminal 1 and they both had to get to Terminal 3 for their connecting flights, but Jamila's was not due to depart until 6:15 the next morning. Stacey's boarded almost at once, so they hugged and promised to write.

The flight from Dharamsala was packed with young people, mostly foreigners, who had been visiting the city for a variety of reasons and it seemed that Stacey knew them all. It was like a flying party, and Jamila was little uncomfortable with all the strangers talking to her, smiling, asking questions, and trying to maintain yoga poses in their narrow economy seats. But as she thought about it, the idea of blending in with a large group of foreigners might work in her favor.

What she hadn't understood was the fact that she could not enter the gate area without first getting a boarding pass.

A pleasant information clerk in an orange uniform helped her with that in Delhi. She took Jamila's stolen passport and airline ticket and processed it quickly and efficiently, and pointed her towards the security area where she would then hand her passport and boarding pass to an immigration official.

Jamila was a nervous wreck. It was happening way too fast, and she didn't have time to consider any other moves. If they stopped her at immigration, she was done for.

She could wind up spending months or even years in an Indian prison.

There was no other option. She would have to take her chances with the stolen documents and hope that Indian security was not efficient. She would remain at the periphery of the group of foreigners—a few of whom were also going to Istanbul as a connection to other destinations—and hope that their good fortune in the world would rub off on her.

She handed her passport and boarding pass to the bored Indian immigration agent, who simply looked at the documents, stamped her passport and wrote something on the boarding pass, and waved her through.

The Dharamsala group was going to get something to eat at one of the food courts in the terminal, so Jamila tagged along, trying to improve her English since that seemed to be the *lingua franca* of the group. They walked along, without a care in the world, laughing and talking loudly and just being generally excited. She wanted to hold back, but understood that she had to remain part of the group for her own safety, so she tried to act the way they did, force a smile the way they did, and even if she couldn't keep up with their conversation act as interested and involved as possible even if she was sick at heart and longed for a sense of the familiar and comforting.

The strategies of a refugee.

The time passed slowly. They stopped at a restaurant that served local food, and had a number of vegetarian dishes. Jamila was not used to restaurants and the whole experience of the terminal—one of the ten largest in the world, brand new and shiny—was already overwhelming. She was, however, quite hungry.

She had a wad of bills in her stolen wallet, and had counted them out in the ladies restroom so she knew what she had. The amounts on the menu on the wall were given in both rupees and dollars. She studied the menu thoughtfully, trying to understand the dishes from the photographs. When the counter person appeared the others ordered first in a confusing cacophony of sounds. She stood last in the line. When the counter person was finally ready for her, she simply pointed to a photograph and remembered to smile.

Soon a plate arrived piled high with rice and vegetable curry, placed on a tray with a plastic fork and spoon. It was more food than she was used to eating at a single meal (or a single day) and the sight of it shocked her. The others misunderstood, and thought that they had given her the wrong order, but she remembered to smile and started eating. Everyone relaxed and went on with their own conversations, never stopping to wonder why this strange young woman was sitting with them and not contributing to the general *bonhomie*.

Eventually, after eating and hanging out in the seating area of the food court for several hours, the group started to split up to find somewhere to rest in the remaining time before their respective flights. Jamila made sure to stay in the general vicinity of the group going to Istanbul. She wanted to be sure to mix in with the three individuals who were taking the same flight, hoping that the gate agent would not be paying too much attention to the names on the boarding passes. It was a naïve expectation, of course. Jamila did not know how the entire system was computerized and any flag on her ticket would be noticed immediately.

As it was, an agent at the airport in Dharamsala had already entered the information in his computer terminal, flagging the ticket. The problem was the flight she had been on was SpiceJet, a local Indian airline that was experiencing tremendous financial difficulties at the time. The flight she was connecting to was Turkish Airlines, an international carrier and an international flight. By the time the systems spoke to each other, it was too late by about thirty minutes.

As for the Indian security apparatus, the right information did not get to the right terminal in Delhi at the right time. To make matters worse, the family name on the passport and ticket—La Giuffria—was tragically misspelled by the agents responsible. This caravan of errors led the entire process in the wrong direction. It was eventually sorted out, but by that time Jamila was flying at 30,000 feet and she knew she had escaped.

But from what, and to what?

She was in a window seat. Everyone was very kind and helpful. She was offered food by a smiling flight attendant. There were magazines, such as she had never seen before, showing happy people doing incomprehensible things. She just stared at the photographs and tried to imagine the world they lived in. She was flying, but she was not being taken somewhere by someone else. She was not fleeing from, but fleeing to. She would see her people again. Her homeland. Speak her own language, eat her own food. She would find Fahim, the man who had become her father, and she would tell him of the things she had seen and the places she had been, and he would be amazed.

But first she had to get through Turkish immigration.

Without being aware of it, she had not suffered any reappearance by her possessing spirit. She had managed to survive a series of stressful tests, failing any one of which would have seen her arrested and thrown in prison, waltzing through them all. She felt strong, and centered. Maybe it was the techniques that old Rabten had taught her. Or maybe it was her sudden resolve not to be a victim any longer.

The last hurdle had been the airport in Istanbul. The plane touched down in a part of the world that she knew at least a little better than some of the places she had been. The Turkish language was familiar. The people looked similar to her own. As she disembarked and followed the train of people heading for baggage claim and passport control, she became nervous again.

Thankfully, there simply was no urgency in apprehending a possible passport thief. There had been a terrorist scare at the airport as her flight landed, and for once that was a good thing: at least for Jamila. She was rushed through Immigration and Customs and soon found herself standing outside in the Turkish capital.

She had made it. She was free.

Now all she had to do was find a gun.

CHAPTER FORTY-TWO

ANGELL STARED AT THE RINGING SATELLITE PHONE. Benny stared at the ringing satellite phone. The captain stared at Angell and Benny.

"Someone must answer."

"What if it's the Commander's employer? What do we say to him? And can he get a fix on us through a satellite phone?"

"You ask too many questions. Wait forever for so many answers."

The captain picked up the phone and pressed a button.

"*Apa khabar?*" he said politely, rolling the rrrrrrs for about a minute.

"Excuse me. May I speak with Commander Arthwaite, please?"

"Ah, Commander no here. Can speak with me. I am executive officer."

"Put the goddamned Commander on the horn. Tell him it's Prime."

The captain covered the phone with his hand.

"He say his name is Prime."

Angell thought of the email address of Commander's employer, the number 191, and realized it was a prime number.

"That's the paymaster," he told the captain. "The one looking for me."

"What to do?"

Angell could just hang up the phone, but that would be a dead giveaway. He had no idea who Prime really worked for, but he thought he remembered the name from the name card Hine had showed him. Something about counter-terrorism and the FBI. But if Prime was really FBI why would they have contracted this mission out to a renegade sea captain like Arthwaite? It didn't make sense. Prime had to be working for someone else.

He took the phone from the captain.

"I believe you're looking for me?"

There was a moment of stunned silence on the other end, but Maxwell Prime recovered quickly enough.

"Is that you, Professor Angell? Good of you to pick up. I guess old Arthwaite's history, is that right?"

"He's being unavoidably restrained."

"I see. Well, that means I've just saved some money then."

"Have a million British pounds, I understand."

"Ah. Someone's been talking."

"Why are you going to such great lengths to find me, Prime?"

"Not great enough, obviously. Have to do better."

"Why me? How have I managed to find myself on your radar?"

"You really don't know? The clandestine networks of several nations are looking for you, Angell. You're a valuable commodity. You and your book. The Arabs are going positively apeshit looking for that book. I guess they don't have Kindle in that part of the world, right? They don't much care about you, of course. As for your friends back in the States, they are most interested to have you come in from the cold. So why don't we cut a deal, right here and now? You surrender to me in Singapore, and I'll cut you in on that half a million Sterling."

"So you can hand me over to the Arabs for another payday?"

"Oh, no. Not the Arabs. And not your friends in DC, either. I'm getting a little tired of the old farts, actually. Monroe and Aubrey, they're like … I dunno … the Odd Couple. You think either of them ever get laid?"

The captain was looking at Angell and making cutting motions with his hands. He didn't see the need to keep talking to the guy who had arranged the attack on his ship.

Angell nodded to the captain, but kept Prime on the phone for another minute.

"Look, why don't I think about it and call you back?"

"Very funny, Angell. You know there's a schedule, right? A timetable? I have to get you back—to someone, somewhere—in the next three days or the whole project is basically useless."

"What project?"

"Damned if I know. I just follow orders. Well, not orders exactly. Suggestions."

Three days. Angell wondered at that. The last time he had to
deal with a timetable was because of the Keepers of the Book and
their ritual timed for Nepal. Suddenly, the reason for all of this was
becoming clear.

"Okay, Prime. You tell your friends, the Keepers of the Book,
that I am going to be a little tied up for the next few months. Sorry
about that, but I have other plans."

He hung up. He thought about it for a second, then whirled
around and threw the phone into the sea.

"Let's haul ass," he said.

They pored over the maps and considered their options.

The captain had enough fuel to reach Java, his native land, and
knew all the places along the coast where he could send a boat ashore
with Angell and maybe a guide. He could refuel in Jakarta and be on
his way. He might lose his seafood shipment, though, which would
be too bad, but his crew rejoiced in the discovery of a cache of gold
ingots in one of the holds aboard the *Stella*. The price of gold would
more than cover his losses and pay for some additional fuel as well.
Luckily for them, Commander Arthwaite was fussy about how he
was paid. The amount was far in excess of any downpayment Prime
would have given him, so it must represent the ill-gotten gains of a
year or more of piracy on the high seas.

The captain, in a generous mood, went to his personal safe and
withdrew roughly one thousand American dollars in cash and gave
it to Angell. When Angell started to refuse, the captain reminded him
that it was due to Angell being sought by Arthwaite that the captain
now had possession of two vessels and a store of gold.

"You're going to keep the *Stella*?"

"I will send my XO to take it to port in Jakarta. It will be
claimed as salvage. Maybe they believe, maybe not. Anyway, I will
strip it first. There will be nothing valuable left."

Benny looked happy at the thought.

"But ... what about Arthwaite and his crew?"

"We will see. We will see."

Angell was sure that Arthwaite would not survive the voyage to Jakarta, but he hoped he was wrong.

In the meantime, the captain made plans.

He radioed ahead to his brother-in-law in Cilacap, on the south coast of Java, to get a status report on what areas were being policed heavily and which were vulnerable. It was a moveable feast, and his brother-in-law was in the Indonesian Navy, which was only one of several government agencies that conducted vessel interdiction along the coast. One could get very good intel from one agency and think a specific area was safe and then another agency would have its own boats in the water with no coordination with the others. It was a nightmare.

Smugglers, though, had their own way of working around the problem and it usually involved cash. The *Silver Star* was a known vessel, a reputable tramper with no violations, and hardly fit the profile of a smuggler, but that didn't mean anything when it came to dealing with the authorities. The captain didn't seem worried, however, and spent the rest of the day and into the evening trying to arrange a deviation from his planned itinerary that would include getting Angell ashore and in good hands.

Angell said goodbye to Benny, and returned his pistol to him. Benny would take some of his crew to the *Stella* and make for Jakarta. He would release some of the prisoners to work the rest of the ship. Arthwaite, Rafael and a few of the others would be kept in irons for the rest of the voyage.

Benny was in good spirits, and clasped Angell's hands in both of his.

"We keep in touch, man. When you get to safety, you contact me. Okay? I give you my sister's number in Mindanao." He handed Angell a piece of notepaper with numbers and names written on it.

"You don't forget? Good. *Selamat po*, Angell. May God go with you!"

That's what I'm afraid of, thought Angell.

CHAPTER FORTY-THREE

At the same moment, but on the other side of the world, it was already morning.

Lisa traced the architectural firm in Providence that had designed the home in Belle Chasse. William R. Walker was an accomplished architect with many political connections in the Rhode Island State Assembly. His firm at the time—Walker & Gould—was dissolved a few years after the house was designed, and Walker himself died in 1905. There did not seem to be any continuity of his practice after 1936, when the last of his sons died. There was no way for her to locate any documents that would shed any light on why the firm in Rhode Island had been commissioned to design a house in what would have been rural New Orleans at the time.

But she was creative, and this was better than sitting in her cramped forensics lab and writing up reports. She looked up other buildings that the Walker firm had designed over the years and noticed that a few were still standing. The firm had designed a number of churches, but they seemed to have been demolished and had not survived into the twenty-first century.

She began phoning around. Maybe she would get lucky and someone would remember something she could use.

"Hello. My name is Lisa Carrasco, and I'm with the Medical Examiner's office in New Orleans. I am trying to locate anyone who remembers the architectural firm that designed your building by the name of Walker & Gould, and if there is any documentation in an archive somewhere that I could examine?"

She had made this call about twenty times so far, and was greeted with the telephone equivalent of blank stares. The day around her had grown dark and nearly everyone in the office had left. Except, of course, for Detective Cuneo. He was trying to put a rush on the DNA evidence from the crime scene, and also the DNA profile of the boy in the box.

Yes, she said to herself. *It was a boy.* At least, they think it's a boy. The old lady—Mrs. Galvez—had somehow cheated biology and every kind of science she knew to conceive a baby boy, and she was over one hundred years old! A woman, without benefit of man as far as she could tell or at least without benefit of a viable uterus, creating life and it was male. *What a rush!* Lisa had reason to be enthusiastic, for the courts would never allow her to have a child herself.

"Hello? Yes? You do? How wonderful. Can you spell that, please? Excellent. I'm very grateful. Yes, of course. If you think of anything else please let me know. Do you have my number? Great. Thanks again. Bye!"

She hung up in triumph, but a little nervous at the same time. She was glad she had been successful in her quest, but apprehensive that somehow she would be upsetting the apple cart.

"Any joy?" asked Cuneo.

"Yes, actually. That last call. It was for a building on Federal Hill. It used to be a restaurant that was owned by people who had commissioned Walker & Gould back in the day. Evidently it was a famous architectural firm, but only a few people remember it. The woman I spoke with was an architect herself, and she said she would dig up the paperwork."

"Well, that's progress. Good for you, Lisa."

"Another thing," she started to say, then stopped herself. Why did she feel so antsy about this?

"Yes?"

"Well, the year of the blueprint. 1877. Seems there was some kind of scandal back then. In Providence, I mean. That's why this architect seemed to think there would still be paperwork."

"What kind of scandal?"

"Something about a church, and a religious cult. They were clients of Walker & Gould. I don't know yet if there's a connection."

"Jeez, another friggin' cult." He threw down the pen he was using to write a report. "What is it about this job that all I get are religious fanatics? How did homicide become a freakin' sacrament all of the sudden?"

"It is weird," Lisa agreed. "But let's not jump to conclusions. It could just be a coincidence."

Cuneo sighed. "Right about now, I could use a few coincidences, and fewer actual connections."

Lisa tried to smile. "Hey, maybe you'll get lucky. Any news on the DNA front?"

He shook his head in frustration. "Nah. You know how long that takes. It could be weeks or even a month or more before we get the DNA analyzed. We'll have to proceed with the other evidence and work our way around it. We still have an unsolved homicide to work, not to mention the first two from the Nine."

"What do you mean 'we,' Kimosabe?"

Cuneo smiled. "That's right. I forgot. You're forensics. You have your own job to do. And God knows business is good for your department, as it is for mine."

"I can come by from time to time, though. I want to see how this pans out. And, anyway, I'll be getting the call back from that architect in Providence."

He nodded in agreement. "That's great. I was getting used to having you around. We're understaffed around here, as you know, but then so are you. Any assistance you can give will be greatly appreciated, Lisa. I mean it."

"Thanks, Detective. See you around." She got up and made her way to the door. They were the only two people at work that early, and she felt a little nostalgic already. She had her hand on the doorknob when the phone on the desk she had been using started to ring.

Cuneo turned in his chair and was about to get up to answer it when Lisa said, "No worries. I'll get it. It's probably one of my return calls."

He swiveled back around and continued with his own paperwork as Lisa picked up the phone.

"Hello, Lisa here. Yes! Thank you for getting back to me so soon. What? How is that again?" She was scribbling furiously with one hand while holding the phone to her ear with the other. "Got it. Is that everything? Thank you so much! I really appreciate it. Thank you! Bye." She hung up.

"Well?" Cuneo said, over his shoulder.

"You're not going to believe this."

"Try me."

"There *was* a scandal. There was this religious group and they had a church on Federal Hill in Providence, which I guess was a posh place at the time. Anyway, they were run out of town. The whole group. The reasons are a little vague. Before they left, they commissioned Walker & Gould to design a building with specific features. They wanted to duplicate some architectural elements into a new structure wherever they would wind up. Having the firm there, and the church right there, it was easier to have the architect come in and examine the existing structure and then design around it."

Cuneo frowned, not following.

"So you're saying ... what?"

"The building. The house in Belle Chasse, it wasn't meant to be a house but a church, *the replacement of their original church.* Those features, they must have included those boxes in the basement. Why would a church have boxes in a basement, I mean, like that?"

"You say it was a religious group?"

"That's what she said, the architect."

"What was it called? Did it have a name?"

"I have it right here," she said, and read it off from her notes.

"They called themselves the Church of Starry Wisdom."

CHAPTER FORTY-FOUR

IT WAS ALREADY 9 AM and they had been talking for hours.

Monroe had come in with his own ideas about the child porn tattoos and their connection to the chatter concerning Dagon and its intensified schedule, but Simon had filled in a lot of the missing pieces without knowing he was. It was when the conversation turned to the actual ritual itself, how it would be arranged and what to expect from it, that things got a little more arcane.

They made more Vietnamese coffee and wound up polishing off the curry and rice without realizing it. The dining room table was cluttered with books and charts as Simon tried to explain the inexplicable: the theories behind the ritual involving children. So far, Monroe had kept back the information concerning the anomalous DNA and the phenomenon of the twins, and he had not made any direct references to Lovecraft although they both knew they were really working from the information in Monroe's famous Codex.

"The grimoires are full of references to children being used as seers," Simon went on, after at least twenty minutes of giving source material to support his presentation. "Before the onset of puberty and all the hormonal changes that take place at that time, a child is connected more deeply to the Other World than to this one. Once puberty starts, however, the sexual desires serve to connect the child more strongly to the visible world, and to other people more than to 'imaginary friends.'"

"So this is why Dagon needs them to be virgins, untouched?"

"For now, yes. The first part of the rite concerns making contact with the Other, in this case with the beings they call Cthulhu, Shub Niggurath, and Yog Sothoth. There are others, of course, but these are probably the three most important."

"So, once the contact is made, the child is then disposable?" The thought made Monroe, a veteran of many battles and violent conflicts, shudder internally.

"Not exactly. More coffee?"

"Please."

Simon poured hot water into the metal filters and soon the smell of *café da* permeated the apartment.

"The children, once contact is made, are now in a position of even greater importance. They can be sacrificed, of course, and the cult believes that the sacrifice of virgin children is perhaps the most powerful of all. Cults around the world that used to sacrifice human beings were suppressed by local governments until they made the substitution of animals for humans. An animal sacrifice is powerful, but nothing when compared to the sacrifice of a human being, and the blood sacrifice of a child is the most powerful of all. Witness Abraham and Isaac."

"But God stopped Abraham from killing Isaac," Monroe protested.

"Well, yes and no," Simon smiled at his friend's discomfort with the subject. "It *could* be interpreted as God's way of saying there should be an end to human sacrifice. After all, Abraham had no problem in understanding what God wanted him to do. It must have been an acceptable practice at the time, even among the Jews. More significantly, though, is the fact that Abraham and Isaac go up the mountain together for the sacrifice, but Abraham returns alone."

"What?"

"It's true. If you read Genesis 22, where this story is found, Abraham goes up the mountain with two young men and Isaac. He leaves the two men behind and goes alone with Isaac in preparation for the sacrifice. God stops him, and Abraham instead sacrifices a ram. The next we see, Abraham returns to the two men he left behind but there is no more mention of Isaac until Genesis 24. We might understand this as Abraham's attempt to fool the two men that he had performed the sacrifice of his son, perhaps running interference so Isaac could escape."

"Okay. You may be right. But then how does this have anything at all to do with our situation?"

Simon settled himself onto the couch, cradling the coffee in his hand as he got a far away look in his eyes.

"Isaac married Rebekah, and Rebekah was barren, right?"

"Right. I seem to remember that from Sunday school."

"Okay, so … after talking to God Rebekah becomes pregnant."

"Yes, so…?"

Simon turned to look at Monroe directly, fixing him with a stare.

"Rebekah, old son, was pregnant with Jacob and Esau. With twins. *Twins.*"

Monroe sighed.

"What aren't you telling me, Dwight? Dagon, children, the Book, Cthulhu, the Georges and their child initiations …this whole focus on sacrifice, on sexuality and sex rituals … this is Dunwich, isn't it?"

"You're right. Of course. Incredibly. But you're right. It's about Dunwich, in a sense anyway. That's what occurred to me when this started to develop, but I didn't really want to see it. The implications are too … otherworldly. I had enough trouble accommodating the idea that there exists a cult—like a terror network—that traffics in occultism, rare books, and murder. I knew that something was being planned, and I sent a man in to stop it. And it worked. A whole group of cultists …"

"The Keepers of the Book," Simon interrupted.

"The same. They descended on this remote site in the Himalayas for a ritual. My interest was not in the ritual itself but in the participants, how they were organized, how they communicated. What the Book's relevance was to all of that. Why it had become more important to them than politics as usual or their own mainstream religions. It was the type of intel that would have given us an insight into another level of motivation among terror groups. It would also identify key members of the cult and give us an idea as to how it was financed and who was protecting it, and why, and even how it interfaced with groups like Al-Qaeda. The paranormal angle, well … I know about that sort of thing, of course. From the Codex.

And from my work in the community all these decades. I've seen things, I know that the paranormal exists, that there is such a thing as remote viewing and I've used it to good effect. But all the time I was tracking the web of coincidences that reach from Lovecraft the whole way through the twentieth century and now into this one … it was to trace something unnamable, true, some mysterious force in history that operated under our conscious awareness.

"But now I have to take these groups seriously, on their own terms, and not just as criminal organizations or terror groups with some arcane ideologies. And I don't like that. I was much more comfortable with conspiracy theories, historical synchronicities, and esoteric philosophizing. There was some real world context, even for the cabals surrounding the Book. There was a logic to it that I could understand. But *this*, this is … frankly, it's beyond me. And when you involve kids … well …"

"So, I was right. Twins. And the Dunwich scenario. Ritual sex, opening the Gate … Whether you believe in a literal or metaphorical 'Gate' or not, isn't the point, is it? It's about human trafficking, child abuse, some twisted eugenics thrown in, and all in the hands of religious fanatics."

"*Religious* fanatics? This isn't religion anymore. We have to find a new way of describing this kind of phenomenon. What *you* deal with, magic and mysticism, that's the technology behind religion, isn't it? Religion is the cover story, the propaganda arm, for a kind of machine…it's political as well as spiritual, physical as well as ethereal. Body as well as mind …"

They were both silent for a moment—Simon out of respect for his friend's evident distress and Monroe because he had run out of things to say. Monroe lay back against the couch and closed his eyes. He was tired. So damned tired.

In another minute, he was asleep.

Simon quietly cleared away the coffee cups and went into another room where he kept the books and files that he did not want on display. He should have been asleep by now himself, having stayed up all night, but he was restless and wired. He had been aware of Dagon for decades, and knew how they had infiltrated secret societies and occult groups around the world without leaving a trace and, through those groups, managed to exert some influence over exoteric bodies as well, such as social groups, veterans organizations, and local politicos. Their focus, though, was on the practice of ritual magic and they used an ancient form of it as a means of making contact with entities that more "mainstream" lodges did not even acknowledge existed.

Most western occult practices were centered on the standard grimoires: the workbooks that dated to the medieval period. The oldest of these was probably the Picatrix, and that text influenced such authors as Agrippa. There were also old ritual books called by the generic term "Keys" of Solomon. These came in all sorts of varieties, but usually they reinforced the Jewish and Christian concepts of angels and demons, and all subject to the force of God's will.

The Order of Dagon, however, knew no such monotheistic structure. They claimed that their system predated Moses and Solomon; that it was based on the diabolical arts of the ancient Sumerians, Akkadians, and Babylonians. Even then, their rituals were not simple Mesopotamian ceremonies but meticulously crafted rites designed for the express purpose of breaching the thin membrane that separates this world from Theirs.

In other words, for opening the Gate.

The Order of Dagon centers its theology around the concept of the Old Ones: Beings that were on the Earth aeons before the arrival of human beings. The Cult of Cthulhu was one such iteration of Dagon; the Keepers of the Book is another. Some members are charged with keeping the Gate closed, for it would not do to have it swing open at inopportune times. Others are enlisted to practice the rites that would open the Gate when the time has come, when "the stars are right." To Dagon, all the rituals of the European magicians of the last five hundred years or more are derived from these originals—and as such are watered down and inefficient, if not completely worthless. Those few western magicians who employed Afro-Caribbean and Asian elements in their ceremonies come closest to what Dagon does routinely. What the Dagon cult wanted was a way to telescope space and time, to revert the planet to the way it was before human intervention. They wanted to collapse the distance between human beings and the Old Ones: a race from beyond the nearest stars, a race from beyond the remotest calendar. Thus, their awareness of when "the stars are right" (time) and of certain geographical locations (space) where their influence might be strongest.

But there's another aspect to the Rites of Dagon, one that is the inspiration for many whispers of obscenity, transgression, and madness. While the liturgics are followed scrupulously, there is an element of insanity that is nowhere missing in the rites. It involves sexuality, but only in the most generous application of the definition.

This is what worried Simon about Monroe's explanation.

Lovecraft's short story—"The Dunwich Horror"—was one of the most popular of all his works. It even became a film starring Dean Stockwell and Sandra Dee (of all people) as well as a young Talia Coppola in the fictional town of Dunwich with its occultist family, the Whateleys. Old man Whateley's albino daughter Lavinia gives birth at the age of 35 to twin boys, amid rumors of incest. The fact that the birth takes place on the feast of Candlemas in February only adds to the sinister reputation of the eccentric clan, for nine months earlier – when the twins were conceived – was the infamous pagan holiday, Walpurgisnacht.

What foul thing was conjured by Wizard Whateley on April 30 to impregnate his daughter?

At first, Dunwich seems like Lovecraft's snide commentary on the Bible story of the Virgin Mother and the baby Jesus, but it is more complex than that. There is even the fact that Wilbur Whateley is excessively hairy from the waist down, which is an echo of Esau. His twin brother Jacob, of course, witnesses the ladder to heaven on which angels are moving up and down. Jacob utters the famous line "Terribilis est locus iste!" or "How awesome (terrible) is this place!" and calls the spot the "gate to heaven." It is a line that will be reprised in the Rennes-le-Chateau story found in everything from *Holy Blood, Holy Grail* to *The DaVinci Code*.

Before Lovecraft wrote "Dunwich" another author had written (but not published) a novel entitled *Moonchild*. This was in 1917, but the novel did not appear until 1929: the same year "Dunwich" was published. The author was Aleister Crowley, an actual magician, and the novel contains a great deal that is of a practical nature if read with open eyes. In this tale, a woman is impregnated during an occult ritual, moreover one that is intended to attract the attentions of a black magic lodge as a kind of diversion. The woman was discovered by a group of magicians who found her when they visited the apartment of an American performer: one Lavinia King. In fact, Crowley would actually use the name "Lavinia King" as a nom-de-plume for his own writings from time to time.

Lavinia King in Crowley's novel became Lavinia Whateley in Lovecraft's story. Why 'Lavinia'? It's an odd name, not one that is commonly encountered. In Roman mythology Lavinia was the name of the last wife of Aeneas, and as such she was the mother of the entire Roman people by way of Romulus and Remus: the twins who founded the ancient city of Rome, and in whose honor every year—in *February*—the *Lupercalia* was held: young men, naked, ran through the streets with strips of goat skin flailing the women they encounter along the way so that they might conceive. Lupercalia: the "Festival of the Wolf." *Lupus*. The constellation once known as *Therion*, the "Beast." *Therion* was Aleister Crowley's sobriquet, after the Beast in the Book of Revelation.

Lavinia Whateley is the mother of a race of alien-human hybrids, another "new race." It was Lavinia who "opened the Gate"—in the sense that she became pregnant with an alien—so that the aliens had a means of arriving on the planet as organic creatures, composed of both human and alien DNA.

When rocket scientist Jack Parsons attempted this same procedure in 1946 in California, Crowley declared him to be off his rocker. But clearly something did occur, if one is to believe the magicians. The UFO phenomenon began in earnest, and it seemed as if Parsons had opened a Gate and—as Kenneth Grant, the English magician and devotee of both Crowley and Lovecraft wrote—"something flew in."

Simon knew that if he was to be of any help at all to Monroe he would have to divulge secrets that had been discovered at great personal and professional cost to himself. He was aware of the irony.

Monroe spent his entire adult life keeping secrets and being concerned with operational and national security. He had probably never really considered that Simon would be in the same position: having secrets and being nervous about revealing them to someone who was not "cleared." It was the classic case of the intelligence agency meeting the secret society, something that had been going on for centuries. How could they help each other, while remaining faithful to their respective oaths?

The only way, thought Simon, would be to reveal secrets for which he had taken no oaths. In other words, secrets he had discovered himself without ritual obligations to others. In fact, Simon had no such obligations having never accepted initiation into any secret society or occult lodge. Any secret worth knowing, he felt, could be discovered the way the alchemists and magicians of old had discovered them: by observing Nature. For everything else—secret handshakes, passwords, degree rituals and the like—Simon had no patience.

So he collected his thoughts while Monroe napped, and formulated a plan. Monroe was about to be initiated, and he didn't know it yet and would probably not realize it until days, weeks or even years later.

CHAPTER FORTY-FIVE

IT WAS DARK, A DEEP TROPICAL NIGHT that shaded from a royal blue canopy to a pitch black curtain dotted with so many stars; it was like a fantasy of sequins and rhinestones. Angell watched the *Stella Matutina*, under the capable control of his friend Benny, move off to the east. He stayed on deck for a long time, as long as he could still make out the *Stella's* silhouette against the vanishing horizon.

He lifted himself off the rail and went to the bridge to confer with the captain.

"*Selamat malam, pak.*"

"Good evening to you, too, Captain."

"Benny will be okay."

"I think so, too."

"We may have some problems, but I think we will be okay, too."

"Really? What kind of problems?"

The captain sighed in resignation.

"Like this. I think better Benny go one way, we go other. Benny go Jakarta. We go south, maybe to Cilacap. There is a harbor there."

Angell nodded, but didn't really know what to say. One place was as good as another at this point. He would have liked to go ashore at Singapore. It was largely English-speaking and comfortable for a westerner like him, but he knew that was the play most likely to get him picked up and arrested. The Singaporean security services were some of the best in the world, and they cooperated fully with the United States where anti-terrorism was concerned.

"What happens at Cilacap?"

The captain consulted his charts and asked Angell to look at a specific spot on the southern coast of Java.

"Here Cilacap. Maybe we go straight there, but have to deal with *polis*. Maybe pay money, okay. But you are *bule*, a white man, foreigner. Maybe they give trouble. Better to send you ashore separately. At night. Very dark along coast, here. And here." He pointed to several spots on the coast to the east and west of Cilacap.

"I tell my brother-in-law to meet you. He take you to *kampung*, you know *kampung*? Like village. You stay there one, maybe two, days. I arrange passport."

"*You* arrange passport?"

"I am sea captain. Many kind of friend in many port. You don't worry. You *kawan*. Friend. No problem."

"I don't know how to repay your kindness …"

"No worries. I contact my man in Singapore, tell him problem with pirates. Will arrive late. He only care the shipment. No ask questions. So no problem. Anyway I go Java, see family. Eat *bakso* and *opor, Alhamdulillah*. So okay."

"Thank you, Captain. I am sorry I was such a problem."

"No problem. We have one, two days to Cilacap. Talk many religion."

The captain was true to his word.

He and Angell spent every available moment speaking about religion. He was amazed that Angell had knowledge of Arabic and could read the Qur'an in the original. At meals, they spent the entire time discussing Islam, especially the history of Islam in Southeast Asia and the relationship between pre-Islamic practices in Indonesia and Islam. The religions of India were also well-represented in that country, as well as a set of indigenous beliefs that varied from place to place, from island to island. Angell wound up learning more than he expected, and actually started looking forward to his conversations with the captain. But the voyage to Cilacap was short. At an average speed of 14 knots they would make it in two days from where they had left the *Stella*.

When the captain was otherwise occupied running his ship, Angell had retrieved the Book from its hiding place and concentrated instead on trying to translate the rest of it.

Unlike the Abrahamic religions—the monotheistic religions that people in the West had grown up with: Judaism, Christianity and Islam—the religious perspective represented by the *Necronomicon* included female deities, like Inanna and Shub Niggurath. Angell began to wonder if monotheism was really the same as patriarchal religions, and if matriarchal religions were all polytheistic. He had never really looked at it that way before but usually had found himself mesmerized by the texts, the source material, and the archaeology of the Biblical era religions of the Middle East and up to the Islamic period. For a religion to be monotheist, it seemed its god had to be male. That was even true of the religion of the Yezidis.

He was wondering what that meant on the second day when the captain knocked on his cabin door.

"Tonight I will leave you ashore," he said, without preamble. "We are rounding the coast and will follow it to Cilacap. I am waiting for brother-in-law to signal me, then will send one of my men to take you to the land."

He happened to see the Book, open on Angell's small desk.

Angell didn't want him to see it, but had been surprised by his knock. The captain stood over it without touching. It was opened to pages containing some of the mysterious seals for the Gates.

"This is *primbon*?" he asked.

"Sorry?"

"*Primbon*. Like ... ah ... magic book."

Angell swallowed.

"Yes, you could say that."

"You make calculation, of stars and times?"

"You can, yes. There is some of that in there."

The captain nodded, thoughtfully.

"My brother-in-law. He knows *dukun*. He take you to see him."

"*Dukun*?"

"Like priest. Like doctor. Use *primbon*. And al-Qur'an of course," he added hastily. "I think you like this. Very interesting for you."

The bones and skulls had been cleared away long ago and replaced in their crates. The captain would still try to move them in Singapore, and figured they might even be more valuable than his frozen seafood cargo. The men still carried around one or two bones and a skull, just for their own amusement, but usually hid them immediately when they saw the captain—or Angell—approach.

But it was the mummified body in the other crate that had captured his attention. He had seen medical anomalies before in his work, usually at ancient gravesites in the Middle East where some unfortunate children with birth defects had been buried, sometimes in clay jars. But this looked like a fully-formed young adult by its size. The elongated skull could have been the result of deliberate molding of the cranium as was practiced in some cultures, but Angell couldn't help thinking of that movie with Sigourney Weaver, *Alien*, and its hideous monster. He wondered where it had been found, and under what circumstances.

After securing his meager belongings, he decided to take another look in Cargo Hold One to see if there was any paperwork in the crate that would shed some light on the matter. The captain had paper on the entire shipment but it wasn't broken down by individual provenance, only that it had been picked up in China. With the involvement of a known and convicted grave robber, it could mean that there was a tomb somewhere in China that had been plundered of that particular mummy.

Egypt was not the only place in the world that boasted a mummification culture, although it was probably the most advanced. There were mummified bodies in Scandinavia, as well as in the western part of China in Xinjiang Province. But this one did not sport any clothing, and often textiles and jewelry are used to place the body in a specific time, culture and region.

Angell went back down to the hold and remembered the path to the crate. The spot where Mukti had been shot by the captain had been cleaned up. There was no visible blood or other evidence that he had ever been there.

The crate, though, was not in its previous place. It had been moved when they brought it up to scare the men from the Stella. Now he looked around the pillars of crates all over the hold and realized he would never find the one he was looking for and, anyway, it was getting late.

He was just about to climb out of the hold when he heard the tapping again.

Spooked, he nevertheless had to see where the tapping was coming from. He suspected that the strange mummy was once again the source of the sound and that it was leading him to it. He listened carefully and walked down one pathway and up another until the sound grew increasingly louder.

Finally he came to a stop and saw that whoever had brought the crate back down had made a special effort to isolate it from the others. Whether that was for reverence for a dead body or for some other reason—fear, perhaps—it didn't matter to Angell.

It was sitting on a pallet by itself, and the cover recently had been nailed down over it with many more nails than were required. That spoke volumes to Angell. The crew was either superstitious, or had reason to fear the mummy would climb out of the box and murder them all in their sleep.

Angell had no such qualms about a physical threat from the mummy, but he had to acknowledge the eerie and deeply unsettling impression it radiated.

Now he was faced with a decision. Should he try to remove the lid off the crate, undoing all the sailors' work, or should he just leave it there and walk away?

His first impulse had been to check to see if there was any more information about where it had been discovered, but realized that if the mummy—like the bones and skulls—had been stolen in the first place there would be no paperwork to identify its true origin.

But what about the damned tapping sound?

And how had he heard it all the way above the hold, in his own cabin?

There had to be a simple, rational explanation for it. The sound obviously was emanating from the crate, so there had to be something in the crate that was activated—maybe as a security measure—by motion or sound or some other stimulus. A sensor of some kind that was placed with the mummy to alert a guard if anyone tried to steal it. That seemed far beyond the capabilities of most smugglers, but who knew? Advanced technology was becoming cheaper and more available to anyone. Maybe it was something off the shelf.

With these thoughts in mind, and with no desire to find a crowbar to open the crate again, Angell turned and walked away. It would have to be one of those mysteries that would bother him from time to time, but there was nothing he could do about it now.

For a moment he wondered if it was his imagination all along, something triggered by stress, like that Poe story, "The Tell-Tale Heart," where the murderer buried his victim beneath the floorboards of his house but can still hear the heart beating. In that case it was guilt. In Angell's case, it also might be guilt: over what he had had to do in Nepal.

He stood with his hand on the ladder and listened, but heard nothing. He ascended.

When he got to the bridge, he found the captain waiting for him.

He was handed the trusty pair of binoculars and told to look portside. There in the distance was the Javanese coastline. There were tiny lights all over the landscape but it didn't look particularly populated from there. Cilacap was a different story, he was told. A port large enough for their vessel, one of only a few on the southern coast. But they would not put in to Cilacap until Angell was safely away.

The brother-in-law, whose name Angell learned was Salim, would pick him up in a fishing boat and take him to a village that hugged the coastline about halfway between Cilacap and the beach at Parangtritis, south of Yogyakarta. The area was known Gunung Kidul, and the significance of that would not be understood by Angell until it was almost too late.

It was about eight o'clock at night. They had passed a large island that formed a kind of barrier that protected Cilacap from the worst of the tsunamis. The island was notorious, explained the captain, for it was where Indonesia housed some of their worst criminals. The place was replete with prisons, like an Indonesian Alcatraz, except Nusakambangan was a lot closer to the shore than California's famous prison island.

The captain's radio crackled to life. He picked it up and had a conversation with someone in the Banyumas dialect. Angell could not understand a word, but it seemed pleasant enough.

The captain said that Salim was on his way. That there were no patrol boats he could see even though the *Silver Star* must have shown up on coastal radar by now. But just to be cautious, Angell would be lowered onto a lifeboat and sailed out to meet the fishing boat offshore. This way, if a patrol decided to board the *Star* he would be halfway to freedom by the time they got close.

The captain and Angell said their goodbyes. It seemed to Angell that was all he was doing these days: saying goodbye. He wondered if that was what refugees experienced on their way from one country to the next, one sanctuary or camp to the next, making friends and losing them all in the same breath. It affected his own sense of self, his connection to society in general, for he was constantly having to reinvent himself to fit the circumstances. He was forced deeper and deeper within to find the real core of who he was. This was not a comfortable process.

The captain was laughing at the way Angell had been lowered in that stretcher to the lifeboat when they overtook the *Stella Matutina*. He said he never saw another ship captured that effortlessly, with only three men, two AK-47s and a nine-mil. He suggested that maybe they should go into the piracy business together.

"Only joking," insisted the captain, laughing, but Angell could see the calculations in his eyes.

"What would Salim say?"

"Salim would ask for fifty percent."

"So Salim is the real pirate?"

It took the captain a second to get the joke, but then he started laughing uproariously. Angell didn't think it was that funny, but he knew that the captain was just releasing some stress. He would soon be rid of his troublesome passenger and get back to his real world, so Angell joined him in the laughter until the radio alerted them to the fact that Salim was ready and waiting.

Angell hefted his knapsack with its infamous contents, expanded a little with some canned food and bottled water, and said goodbye once again. He took the ladder down to the lifeboat and was motored out to sea in the middle of the tropical Asian night.

He realized he had never learned the captain's name.

A light flashed briefly in the distance, and the lifeboat made directly for it. The sailor in his craft did not speak English and Angell spoke no Tagalog or Javanese so they remained silent the entire time until the fishing boat came into view. Salim was on deck, waving to the boat and urging Angell to board quickly.

Angell awkwardly leapt from the lifeboat to the fishing boat and turned to wave to his escort but he had already started to leave for the *Silver Star* without a word.

"Hi," said the voice on the fishing boat. "I am Salim."

CHAPTER FORTY-SIX

"How long have I been asleep?"

Monroe woke, groggy and stiff, from his prone position on Simon's couch. Daylight was streaming into the windows, which Simon left open as a means of waking his friend gently. He had no idea if Monroe had urgent business that day in the office at Fort Meade or if he could afford a morning's escape.

"About two hours, give or take."

"Sorry about that. I haven't 'crashed' on someone's couch since college."

"No worries. Coffee?"

"Please."

They had had multiple cups of Vietnamese coffee already that night, but Simon prepared a more average—if nevertheless robust—Viennese blend accompanied by real cream. The aroma alone was ambrosia, and Monroe was grateful for the sustenance it offered.

After a few warming sips, Monroe looked up and asked Simon, "Where did we leave off? I'm afraid I don't remember. It's your fault for that excellent curry. And the intellectual overload that accompanied it."

"Are you due back at the Fort anytime soon?"

Monroe checked his watch, and sighed.

"I don't keep regular hours, of course, but I should check in with Aubrey. I really don't even know where he is right now. I must be getting old."

"Getting old? Dwight, that ship sailed a long time ago …"

"Thanks."

"Actually, we were talking about twins. And rituals. And cults that practice nefarious ceremonies, the kind of cults that you are tracking even now."

Monroe nodded, and drank a little more coffee, feeling the caffeine start to work its magic.

"So, then, what is it about cults and twins? And, by the way, I thought no one used the term 'cult' anymore?"

It was Simon's turn to nod.

"It's considered a loaded word, as if one person's religion wasn't another's cult. Cults are basically those religions with which we disagree in some fashion. It's used as a pejorative, usually. But in our case, we are not talking about groups that intend to evolve into what we think of as religions, but groups that desire to stay small, unrecognized, and which are primarily transgressive in some way. They don't think of themselves as belonging to a religion in any normative fashion. In fact, the whole idea of being in a 'cult' is attractive to them."

"Ah. That seems clear enough. So Dagon fits that profile?"

"Oh, for sure. Dagon is basically a terror organization, with robes and candles. Rather than utilize social media the way Al-Qaeda and now the Islamic State do, they remain off-grid and under the radar. They are not looking for converts, have no interest in promoting themselves or attracting public awareness in any way. They work behind the scenes, and instead of IEDs they use complex rituals that exploit sensory systems in an extreme and dramatic way in order to cause changes in consciousness."

"What's their motive then? What do they hope to achieve?"

"By orchestrating a series of rituals in different parts of the world, timed precisely and organized perfectly, they intend to open a Gate. This Gate is … well, it's like computer gates: a binary state of 0 and 1, with 0 representing 'open' let's say and 1 representing 'closed.' In this case a flow of energy across the gate either opens or closes it, depending on its state when the energy encounters it. If it was in 0 state, it's closed; if in 1 state, it opens. The opposite of its state at the time. The ritual generates energy of a specific type and directs it across a closed Gate—in this case—forcing it to open."

"And when that happens?"

"Well, you know the saying 'all hell breaks loose'?"

"Of course."

"Then take it in as literal a sense as you can imagine. As in the Sumerian text of the *Descent of Inanna to the Underworld*, when the goddess Inanna rose from the dead the demons of the Underworld preceded her out into the open, past the seven Gates of the Underworld and into our world."

"So ... Dagon is raising demons?"

Simon shook his head.

"The idea of demons is as culturally loaded as that of cults. It's a way the ancient peoples had of explaining phenomena the best way they knew how. These are not demons in the common sense of the word. But they are 'beings.' Entities, I guess you could call them. Things, creatures with a kind of consciousness, or at least a separate reality as far as we are concerned before science catches up and finds a way to qualify all this without denigrating it. The Old Ones, Dagon calls them. Creatures that existed before us, and therefore before our conception of gods, angels, and demons was developed. They may even be biological in some way, since it is believed that they can procreate with humans to a certain extent, create hybrids of human and ... well, whatever it is they are. In a sense, they are an atavistic force. And potentially very, very destructive."

Monroe set down his coffee cup, now empty. There were a few moments of silence. Simon cleared away the cups and brought them to the kitchen, placing them quietly in the sink. His mind was elsewhere, wondering how much more to reveal to Monroe and coming to the decision that the world was so dangerous that to keep secrets might very well cause more harm—much more—than good.

"In the first place, why would anyone do that? Why would anyone want to? In the second place ... is what you're describing even possible?"

Simon smiled, as he knew what Monroe was getting at.

"You mean, are we just spinning our wheels here?"

"Precisely."

"In the first place, they do it because they can. This ... this technology. It's addictive, in a way. It's a way of understanding and wielding power that is unknown to most of the world, even to those parts of the world that still live with rituals and spells and superstitions and ... sacrifice. Also, they have proceeded so far along this path that they have developed nothing but contempt for humanity, who they see as willfully blind to the reality that exists all around them. Their progress has brought them into contact with the beings—the Old Ones or the Ancient Ones—which has convinced them that the planet would be better off with no humans on it. Including themselves. In a sense, it's really no different from a terror group in that regard, and the rituals are like suicide vests.

"But there's a catch. They also believe that by showing their loyalty to the Old Ones and letting them in they will be rewarded. That their souls or whatever part of them is eternal would survive in the world that the Old Ones will create. It's ironic, actually."

"Why do you say that?"

"The Old Ones. They devour souls. That's how they roll."

"And in the second place?"

"Ah. Is it feasible, you ask? What they do? Well, Dagon has been around for centuries. But then so have the Freemasons. And the Catholic Church, the Jewish faith, Islam, Buddhism, all for much longer. And so forth. That's no guarantee that they know what they're doing. The mainstream religions had the keys to manipulating and expanding consciousness in their hands and lost them, due to dogmas, ideologies, and power politics. When they fought wars, it was caveman style: with clubs and swords and bullets: thus demonstrating that their spirituality was hollow, that their faith was dead. Spiritual crusades, spiritual jihads, gave way to mass murder, invasion, and genocide. They abandoned their core idea, the idea of an immortal soul, and instead sought to destroy bodies. They reverted to a faithless, soulless dynamic paying only lip-service to the spirit.

"Those that kept the sacred knowledge alive went underground, as they always have. They starved themselves, denied themselves, kept silent, removed themselves from society, focused on the invisible, the unnamable, engaged in practices that would have either bored or scared the shit out of the average person, and did them over and over again and at the end they unlocked their own, personal, Gates. And the Gates opened without a sound. And no one heard. And no one knew.

"Dagon was one of those underground groups and slowly they subsumed the others, the genuine Orders, the real shamans, the true magicians. Those who already had divined the secret or were already halfway there. Unlike the Rosicrucians of the seventeenth century, however, their mission was not to heal or to save mankind.

"Consider how much easier it is to destroy than to create. We are reaching a singularity on this planet, a convergence, a tipping point, and it's not the one that Elon Musk is anticipating.

"The real singularity is a mass extinction event, and Dagon is at the controls."

CHAPTER FORTY-SEVEN

MONROE AND SIMON SAT QUIETLY for a few moments as Monroe digested what Simon had been saying about Dagon and the threat it posed.

"You know that the world has now entered upon a new phase, a new normal," offered Simon, breaking the silence. "We used to fight wars between nations, between countries that had armies and ideologies and clear objectives: whether it was money, or land, or other resources. Now, we are faced with asymmetrical warfare. You can have a handful of people in a remote mountain cave waging war long-distance, using cell phones, the Internet, a video camera, and instructions on how to use a car or a truck as a weapon to kill civilians rather than soldiers."

Monroe raised a sardonic eyebrow. "Yes, we know. So, what's your point?"

"What difference is there between a terror cell and an occult lodge?"

"Sounds like the setup for a joke. Something about changing a light bulb?"

"Unfortunately, no. There is no difference, except where the question of violence comes into play. Both the terror cell and the occult lodge are secret organizations, composed of relatively few people, motivated by an ideology that is transgressive. The terror cell uses whatever weapons it has at its disposal to create terror, the end result of which is change in the world. 'America out of the Middle East,' for instance. The occult lodge doesn't use terror and doesn't normally engage in violence to achieve its ends. But it does want to cause change in the world. Both seek to become super-human, to achieve ends that far exceed their position and capabilities in the world. The terror cell takes on political entities like governments or multinational corporations. The occult lodge challenges the very assumptions that underlie those institutions."

"So what you're saying is ..."

"I'm saying that there is little fundamental difference between Al-Qaeda or the Islamic State and the Cult of Dagon. In fact, there is a great deal of similarity. Al-Qaeda is a cult; the Islamic State even more so.

"The leader of the Islamic State, Abu Bakr Al-Baghdadi, is the Jim Jones of his followers, and they've made Mosul his Jonestown."

Monroe thought about that for a moment, but thought he spotted a flaw in the argument.

"Then why should we fear Dagon more than the Islamic State? The Islamic State is heavily armed, with weapons they took from the Iraqi Army and with military leaders who defected from the Iraqi Army, professional soldiers. They are taking physical territory. They are posting videos of themselves beheading people, for chrissakes. Dagon is ... well, virtually invisible. They have no footprint on social media as far as I have been able to tell. They are not out recruiting followers. Not a single car bomb or suicide vest. They are a rumor, more or less."

"And so much more powerful because of it. Groups all over the world whisper about Dagon. They suspect each other of being members. They suspect political leaders of being members. Celebrities. Business executives. All sorts of people. Because they cannot be identified everyone can be a member in the eyes of the public. Their true intentions are unknown; their presence on the world stage is unidentifiable."

"Like the Illuminati. Or the Rosicrucians."

"Precisely. The difference is, Dagon *exists* and *has* an agenda and *has* infiltrated secret societies and occult lodges all over the globe. Their agenda is the gradual erosion of those parts of human consciousness that keep us from going insane. In that sense, terror cells are merely tools in their arsenal, but not the only ones and not even the most important or the most powerful. They infiltrated Al-Qaeda long ago, when it was still a small operation that grew out of the Afghan crisis. Their approach was spiritual, you might say. They had the ideological chops and a deep knowledge of Islamic mysticism so that they were able to virtually hypnotize people like Osama bin Laden, providing him with a message and a means of delivering it. Islamic scholars know that Al-Qaeda does not represent a coherent or respectable form of their religion. It has just enough elements to sound credible but at heart it has an occult character, a chiliastic aspect, that Islam itself does not embrace. Once it was up and running, they moved on to other groups, other parts of the world."

What Simon was saying matched in general outlines what Monroe had always believed and what intelligence experts (and what they used to call Arabists) had suggested. It was his emphasis on the occult character of the group that was intriguing, however, for it verified much of what Monroe had been working on for most of his life: the interface between politics and religion, between political extremism and occultism.

Then he thought of something.

"If Dagon stays off the Internet, how is it possible that they are communicating with their followers using child porn?"

"Oh, that's easy. Dagon is not doing this directly. They are using cut-outs, the actual traffickers. They would pay a premium to ensure that the children are not molested sexually. Dagon would be the source of the tattoos which serve the additional function of letting the traffickers and pornographers know that those specific victims are not to be molested. They were chosen specifically ahead of time; from whom or when I don't know. The pornographers can then photograph them, video tape them, whatever. At a certain time, these children will be returned to the staging area Dagon had selected. Unless, of course, the children in the pornography are not the actual participants in the rituals but stand-ins. That, however, is rather unlikely."

"How so?"

"The other members have to know that this message comes

directly from Dagon and is not a trap. The followers will expect these specific children to be present at the rituals. Some of Dagon's initiates are pedophiles, of course, and contribute a certain level of depravity to the rites that the less perverse cannot pretend to share. That means that these specific children will be at the rituals, and moreover will still be virgins at the time the rituals begin."

Monroe felt a queasy sensation in the pit of his stomach at the very thought of what horrors were awaiting these innocents. He wondered at how they were selected, where they came from, what hell their parents must be going through wondering what had happened to them. These children were far too young to be runaways; some were as young as five or six, the oldest appearing no more than thirteen. They appeared healthy, well-fed and clothed, despite the hollowness behind their eyes and the forced expressions of gaiety and desire.

"Simon, I need to know what Dagon is going to do, and when and where they are going to do it."

Simon got up from where he had been sitting. The daylight was now streaming into the apartment and he had not slept in more than twenty-four hours. If he was going to keep at it, he would need sustenance.

"Give me a minute," he said, over his shoulder. "I'm going to make more coffee, and maybe something more substantial. How do you feel about breakfast?"

Monroe looked at his watch again, wondering what had happened to Aubrey.

"Sure," he said, absent-mindedly. "If it's not too much trouble."

"Not at all. Make yourself comfortable while I cook."

Instead, Monroe headed for the bathroom, bringing his cellphone with him.

"Still in the usual place?" he asked.

"What? Oh, sure. You know where it is."

Monroe walked down the hall and into the bathroom, which also was done in blacks and grays, a little austere but nonetheless handsome as these things go. He closed the door and took care of what he needed to do.

After washing his hands and drying them on a towel that seemed a little too luxurious for everyday use, he opened his phone.

It was a secure cellphone and all calls and texts were encrypted. He dialed Aubrey's number and waited.

After almost a minute the call went through and was connected on Aubrey's end. There was very little distortion, unlike in the movies where encrypted lines always sound encrypted.

"Good morning."

"Good morning, Aubrey. I trust all is well?"

"As well as can be expected. I've just learned that Grothendieck is quite ill, I'm afraid."

"Ah. Well, that is a shame. We could have used some of his advice."

"I've been doing some additional research, at the Warburg Institute. There is a mathematical dimension to all of this, not just from Grothendieck. Numbers, patterns, elaborate tables and charts. There was a Spanish occultist, Ramon Lull, who wrote extensively on a non-traditional way of knowing through using numbers. Something like the Kabbalah, but stripped of a lot of the theology. Actually, it was Grothendieck who inspired me to look in that direction. One of his mutants is Rudolf Steiner, so that directed me to Theosophy, Anthroposophy, and even the German occult lodge the Ordo Templi Orientis, the one that specialized in sex magic."

There it was again. Sex and magic. And mutants. This was truly turning into a Dunwich scenario.

It was Monroe who changed the subject.

"Any word on our missing professor?"

"Nothing, I'm afraid. We're trying to trace his movements on the ground. That Shanghai sighting was the last confirmed one." He left out the conversation he had with his operative, Max Prime, and the possibility that Angell was at sea and would be apprehended by a damned pirate ship. There was no sense in giving Monroe a heart attack, and anyway he had his own feelers out to see if any of that could possibly be true. He had ordered Prime to return to the States, but he knew Prime would take his time coming back. So he had a friend of his in Singapore look for him, because that is surely where he was headed.

"After that, we have him at various places in-country, from Tianjin to Shenzhen. The common denominator is the fact that most of the sightings are on the coast. He could be getting out of the country by sea." Planting the seed.

"That sounds risky. I know there has been no radio traffic, no chatter. No phones, internet. Nothing. Whoever is helping him may be a professional."

"Have we tried more … unconventional methods?" Aubrey was referring to the remote viewing program, which had been successful for them in the past.

"Ever since we lost Miller, we've been flying blind. We've had a few nibbles, but nothing actionable. It's going to take awhile to get another team up to speed. We've burnt through most of them by now."

"Understood. I'm flying back Stateside tomorrow. There's nothing more for me to do here. All the other leads I was working are either dead ends, or just too dated to be of use. Other than the Georges, the best data I have come from Grothendieck and his mutants."

They said their goodbyes, and Monroe left the bathroom to meet Simon at the dining table where he had prepared a humble repast of scrambled eggs, rye toast and yet more coffee.

"The eggs look interesting," he said to his friend. Instead of a bright yellow in color they were a little on the beige side, as if mixed with coffee or broth. "I don't usually like scrambled eggs, but these look intriguing."

"I made them with a bit of white miso paste, whisked into the eggs until blended, and then added the chopped scallions at the end. The miso gives the eggs a kind of earthy flavor and they improve the texture as well."

Monroe started to feel a laugh coming from somewhere. "I must be punchy," he said to himself and tried to stop the chuckle from escaping, but to no avail. He burst out with a guffaw and tried valiantly to recover.

Simon simply stared at him in wonder until he stopped laughing. "What's so funny?"

"You! You can't even make scrambled eggs like a normal person!"

Simon was nonplussed by his friend's mirth, although he could understand the reason for it. He directed his attention towards his own plate and devoured a portion large enough to satisfy a long-shoreman after a twelve-hour shift. He then settled back with his coffee. He was glad Monroe had a good laugh—even if it was at his expense—because he had to discuss some unpleasant details concerning Monroe's purpose in coming to his apartment. The rites of Dagon were not pretty, and they were not to be found in books, but they did work and that made the whole enterprise even more unsettling.

Once his guest had been fed properly and was feeling sated, Simon brought up the subject once again.

"As fun as the past few hours have been, Dwight, we still have to address your central question. Where, when and how will Dagon proceed along its path to opening the Gate, and in what way will that event manifest?"

Monroe finished his umpteenth cup of strong coffee, and nodded. "I just need to know enough to stop it from taking place, whatever it is. I know enough about the outlines of the project to be afraid of it, but not enough to track down the perpetrators and put an end to it. For that, I need your help."

"Right. Well, what I am about to explain to you will seem disgusting and impossible, in pretty much equal proportions. Dagon refuses no technique that would advance its cause. There are two parts to the ritual, as we discussed, plus a third part that I will come to presently. The first part involves making some kind of contact with the Old Ones. These are the forces we discussed, and which your friend Lovecraft limned out in his stories. The three most important are Cthulhu, Yog-Sothoth, and Shub Niggurath. He made up those names, in a sense, but in another sense the names are real, just in ways Lovecraft never knew."

"I have some idea about that. I have lists of possible interpretations in the Codex."

"I imagine you do. Cthulhu is thought by some to be a Sumerian term, *Kutu-Lu*, meaning 'man from the underworld,' which is a fair characterization of the Being."

"Yes, that's the definition I came up with some years ago."

"Well, there's another possibility and that is a Tibetan term, *kusulu*, which refers to a dead shaman who comes back. That would be another—perhaps better—interpretation."

"I agree. Sounds very appropriate."

"But this presents us with a problem. Are his other terms Tibetan? If so, is the Lovecraft pantheon derived from an identifiable Tibetan source? Some source more ancient, perhaps, than the arrival of Buddhism to that country? Something from the land of Zhang Zhung? It's not a question we can answer at once, and may not have much of a bearing on your immediate problem, but we should keep it in mind. You say that the previous ritual to open the Gate was held in Khembalung, in the Himalayas?"

"Yes. That's right."

"Then the Tibetan angle may be more important than we know. Let's leave that aside for now. Without going into too much detail at the moment, I can show that the other two Beings referenced by Lovecraft—Yog-Sothoth and Shub Niggurath—both have Tibetan equivalents. I hasten to add, though, that this may be due more to the Tibetans referencing an older, more ancient terminology and not something intrinsically Tibetan."

"Okay. I understand."

"Good. So, Dagon intends to open the Gate and is making contact on some level with Cthulhu first. Cthulhu, as you know, is the High Priest of the Old Ones which means he is a kind of middle-man to the process. Yog-Sothoth is the one that impregnated Lavinia Whateley in the short story, so we have to assume that this force will be required to do the same once the Gate has been opened."

"Jesus," said Monroe, disgusted already.

"As for Shub Niggurath—the 'Goat with a Thousand Young'—this Being is sometimes considered female. In Tibetan, the word *shub* means 'whisper,' and Shub Niggurath appears in Lovecraft's story 'The Whisperer in Darkness.'"

"That's ... incredible. That can't be mere coincidence."

Simon shrugged. "I don't think so, but then I don't much believe in coincidences. I know in your line of work you don't either. So, these three Beings will be involved in some way in the Opening of the Gate ceremony. Now to specifics."

Simon pulled out a chart that he had been compiling as Monroe lay napping earlier that morning. It was a large sheet of paper on which were drawn various symbols, charts of numbers, and some writing in Simon's indecipherable scrawl.

"The Gate can only be opened when the Great Bear hangs from its tail in the sky, right? Unfortunately, that happens every day. The Great Bear is a circumpolar constellation, so it swings around the Pole Star once every day, losing a degree every once in awhile so that when the tail of the Bear is straight up it may be midnight one month or noon another, and so on. It's a giant clockwork in the sky and the ancients used it for navigation but also for telling time and calculating the seasons."

"So how do we know what day they will use?"

"That's not as difficult as it sounds. The last time they tried this, they timed it with the explosion of a supernova, incredibly one that took place in Ursa Major, in the Great Bear constellation: precisely what they needed. The Gate is not visible from where we are on Earth. The Gate is for the Old Ones, not us. The stars look different in different parts of our solar system, not to mention our galaxy. What I mean is, the constellations with which we are familiar disappear once you leave the Earth. They are rearranged, depending on where you are when you see them. That means the Pole Star, too, is different. That star only appears to be due north from our planet. In space, it's just another star and has no particular importance. In fact, as you know, our Pole Star was not always our North Star due to the precession of the equinoxes, but we are getting lost here. Let's go back.

"The Gate is not visible, as I said. It is a mathematical point that is arrived at by a complex series of formulas involving both algebra and geometry. The geometry involved is non-Euclidean, and the algebra is based on a totally different concept of basic arithmetic which renders the system unintelligible to modern mathematicians. It has no utility at all for anything to do with earthly requirements, but it is an elegant system for the purpose to which it is directed."

Monroe thought immediately of Grothendieck, and of one of his 'mutants,' the mathematician Bernhard Riemann, but instead said, "You're starting to sound like a university professor at an early morning class."

Simon winced. "Sorry about that. I get carried away. Not too many people to talk to about things like this. I'll try to simplify it a little since you really only need the basic concept to work with. Okay, like I said, the Gate is a mathematical point, a point in space. It can't be traced with a normal compass and ruler, for the place in which it appears is in the space *between* the angles we can draw or project using a computer. You have to imagine a kind of fourth or fifth dimensional geometry for this to work, something perpendicular to our own, maybe a dimension in which all triangles are right triangles and the Pythagorean Theorem is a statement of theology and not geometry."

"Okay. Okay, I think."

"Good. We'll get back to that if necessary. Now, using the type of mathematics Dagon uses I can retrace their steps to find out why the date of the last ritual they performed was chosen. As I said, the supernova plus the tail of the Great Bear, but there is a missing element. You need three: time, space, and energy. The supernova supplied the energy, but only if it appeared in the sky at the right place or if the ritual was moved to a spot on the Earth that was in alignment with the supernova. That way you have time, space and energy contributing to the ritual."

He moved the chart aside and pulled out another sheet of paper.

"Lovecraft was precise as to his dates, as you brought to my attention long ago. In his short story, 'The Call of Cthulhu,' he is very specific about day, month and year. And also about place. You have Providence, Rhode Island. New Orleans, Louisiana. And then you have a lot of sea travel from Valparaiso to New Zealand, with specific longitude and latitude given along with the dates. I listed them all out here. After that, our narrator winds up in Scandinavia to find an old sailor who has the rest of the mystery. If we map all of this out, as I have done here on the large chart, you can see a pattern begin to emerge."

Monroe stared at the chart that Simon had smoothed out on the dining room table, but had to confess he couldn't see the pattern.

There were dots on the geographical positions mentioned by Lovecraft and lines connecting them. It wasn't quite a map of the world with which he was accustomed, but something almost surreal, as if Jorge Luis Borges had decided to create a map that satisfied his taste for literary allusions and geophysical asymmetry regardless of whether or not it lived up to navigational standards.

"Yes, I know. Hard to make out after an entire lifetime of looking at traditional maps."

"What is this, then?"

"This was created using both time and space. You know, like those old maps that said 'here there be monsters' when they didn't know what lay beyond the horizon. Except that this one begins *with* the monsters."

Monroe was still confused.

"Remember I said that in order to determine where Dagon will hold its next ritual I had to work backwards from what we know of the last ritual, the one in Nepal?"

"Yes. Right."

"Well, that's what I mean. Our world, our planet, is about the *surface* of the Earth. Our maps are focused on the surface, on countries and continents that we can see. That's natural, because it's focused on *people*. Where people live and work and travel and fight each other and die. But Dagon is *not* focused on people. The map they use is like a photographic negative of our own. It focuses on a continent that is under the Earth, under the Seas. Where Cthulhu is 'dead but dreaming' as the stories tell us. Where there are no people, and therefore no human-created maps."

Something began to click in Monroe's mind. A connection. A thin fiber between two separate dots on the map.

"Dunwich."

Simon's smile acknowledged his insight.

"Precisely. Dunwich—the real Dunwich—is not in Massachusetts. It is, or was, in England, on the east coast. It is a city that disappeared under the waves. It's a sunken city the way that Atlantis is supposed to be sunken. Lovecraft deliberately named his fictional town after another town that is presently under water. What is he trying to tell us?"

"That the story is not about … not about what we can see, but what we can't see. But nonetheless just as real."

"That's one way of stating it. The fictional Dunwich is the twin of the real Dunwich. But, like every identical twin, it is the same but different at the same time. They are identical in time, identical in genes, but different in space. Like the twins separated at birth who live the same timeline but in different cities or even countries."

"So this map …"

"This is a map from the point of view of Dagon and its perception of the world. A legacy of transgressive ritual and constant contact with the Others is an altered point of view, a realignment of the senses, and of the imagination. A map, after all, is a kind of imaginary construction, a two dimensional representation of a three dimensional world. But Dagon's world lies in many more dimensions than ours. Or, to be more precise, it acknowledges many more dimensions than we do. Thus, here, for instance ..." He pointed to a spot on the map. "This is where the underground sarcophagus containing the body of Cthulhu is said to be found. Lovecraft called it R'lyeh. Like the Tibetan *beyul*, it is a hidden city, an undiscovered country if you will. All Dagon's maps are oriented from this point. And since it does not appear on the surface of the Earth, its maps are not reflective of the surfaces to which we are accustomed. You have to adjust your sight, in a a sense, to reconcile the Dagon map with our own. It's tricky, because there are landmarks and other features that are unfamiliar to you. It's hard to orient yourself. And that's the whole point.

"The map is internally consistent with Dagon's ideology. They can use it to travel where they will. Like seeing the constellations from space, the same stars are there just not in the relative positions we know from living on the Earth. It seems illogical to us, even insane, but it's of a piece with their worldview."

Monroe sat back in his chair, closing his eyes.

"I thought I understood a lot of this. I've studied ... well, you know what I've studied. And what I've seen. But this ... this is ... a revelation. It's going to take some time to get this all on board."

"And we don't have time, I know. So I will cut to the chase, as they say. You know that the ancient city of Kutha in Sumer was believed to be the Gate to the Underworld? That assumed everyone understood that a physical location on the surface of the Earth could lead to a non-physical location somewhere else. Like Shambhala to the Tibetans. Even the Dalai Lama says that Shambhala is a real place, regardless of the fact that it's invisible for all practical intents and purposes and cannot be located on a regular map."

"Tibet again."

He shrugged. "Sorry about that. But they have the best terminology for what we're trying to understand. Now, you know that sea coasts are liminal places. In other words, the edge between land and sea is like an initiatory space. One goes from one way of living in the world to a completely different one. We came from the sea, originally, and we are composed largely of water. But we live on land now, and cannot sustain ourselves in the sea without a lot of equipment. Dunwich, the original one, was a town on the coast that eventually was reclaimed by the sea. The mythical Atlantis was an entire continent—or at least a very large island nation—that was completely submerged beneath the waves. What if you had a map in which Atlantis was still on the surface, but other cities along the coasts of other continents were submerged? It would still be the Earth, but you wouldn't recognize it.

"One step further. What would a map of the world look like if it had been created by the cephalopods? By an octopus, say? Let's fine tune that. What if a different *mammal* had drawn the map, for instance a whale? A whale's map is the flow of specific ocean currents. They follow those currents as if they were highways, but they are highways that are constantly changing, like some science fiction movie where the roads shift and turn before your eyes."

"For chrissakes, Simon. I appreciate your profound knowledge of this subject, don't get me wrong, but let's get to the point. I have assets in the field, a timeline that's counting down to God knows what ..." Monroe was rubbing his eyes in frustration. He didn't want to abuse his friend's hospitality but the explanations were getting more and more impossible to follow.

"Sure, sure. Sorry. Okay, long story short, the ritual of Opening the Gate will take place simultaneously at several locations at once. I backtracked from the Nepal ritual and discovered that it took place not only in Nepal but at several other locations around the world including in Africa and Latin America. The major ritual—the 'High Mass' if you will—was the one that took place in Nepal. The others were timed to occur at the same moment. The reason for this is that the underworld lair of Cthulhu is reached by several avenues in several different parts of the world, separated by thousands of miles, even though it's only one location."

"Oh, boy."

"That's why I've been taking so much time with this explanation. It's counter-intuitive. We study religion in a very linear fashion, as if religion evolves over time from superstition to formal scriptures to organized churches. But that's not the case. There is no linearity to any of this. The spiritual force that is the core of religion erupts from time to time and from place to place, but it's always the same. The linearity we observe is a human function, an overlay, not an evolutionary process."

"The timing of the ritual?"

"I believe it will take place sometime during the next few weeks. Astronomers are predicting a meteor storm. Not a meteor shower, but a meteor *storm*. We're talking maybe hundreds of meteors per hour, originating from the debris left over by an ancient comet. The storm will bring enough energy to cause some electromagnetic dislocation on Earth, enough to boost Dagon's 'signal' so to speak. If they cannot perform the ritual at that time, they may try for one of the meteor showers later in the year, but that's pure speculation. That is, unless another supernova is discovered in time and in the right position."

"Okay. So where do the children come in?"

"Children are non-linear creatures, Dwight. They are liminal beings, neither babies nor adults, living simultaneously in our world and in the Other. The Dagon cult will use them as seers in order to make the initial contact with the Old Ones. Then, they will be used as channels to permit the Old Ones to enter through the Gate."

Monroe shuddered involuntarily. "Do I need to know how that will happen?"

Simon's affect became solemn. He stood up and went to the window, where the sun was high in the sky. It was almost noon already. The rising and setting of the Sun was reassuring in the midst of the awful darkness they were discussing.

"No, Dwight. You don't," he replied, speaking in a low monotone, devoid of the animation of earlier when he was discussing purely intellectual concepts. "All you have to know is that these innocents will be violated in horrible ways. Transgression is the central aspect of the rite. The obliteration of boundaries. Social boundaries are part of the human structure they will destroy. The participants need to transgress their own humanity, and to do so they will perform unspeakable acts that will deny their prisoners their own. These acts will lay bare deep, unconscious forces that have been buried all their lives and all the lives of their ancestors going back to the earliest days of civilization. It's consciousness and it's genetics. And when it's over, new organisms will be conceived and new mutations will be born, erasing the boundary between this world and the Other."

He turned away from the window.

"Unless *you* do something about it."

For the next hour they discussed the technology behind the ritual, which was basically a crash-course in some of the most cherished secrets of western esotericism involving sexuality. Simon touched briefly on the influence of P.B. Randolph, an African-American author of books on occultism and his revelation that sex was the essential secret behind the occult. It was partly Randolph's work in this field that inspired the creation and growth of the German secret society, Ordo Templi Orientis, in the early days of the twentieth century. The higher degrees of the Order were specifically concerned with the utilization of sexuality in ritual magic.

However, the understanding that sexuality was at the heart of esotericism—both western and non-western—was nothing new, and common to disciplines as disparate as alchemy, Indian religion and, of course, Tibetan Buddhism. In fact, the mythology and iconography of many of these cultures reflected a "gender fluid" perspective, where the hermaphrodite—for example—was representative of supreme spiritual attainment. In many other cultures, for instance in Siberia and North Asia, shamans were often transvestites.

Children, however, were a different matter entirely. While children appear in some alchemical and Tantric illustrations the deliberate use of children as magical assistants in a sexual sense—as partners or as victims in sexual ritual—was difficult to find. Yet, the example of the Kumari of Nepal is one instance where a young girl of around 6 years of age (or younger) is elevated to the rank of living goddess: a position she will lose when she begins her menstrual cycle at about the age of 12 or 13. This young girl is believed to be "possessed" by the goddess as long as she is pre-menstrual: an analogue to the western occult belief in the ability of pre-pubescent children to "see" spirits. Once menstruation begins and there is an onset of puberty, the ability is lost and the child becomes an adult, bonded to the human community. The period of adjustment is harsh, however, for it is considered bad luck to marry a former Kumari and, in any event, she has not been permitted to learn to read or write or to learn any of the things that would help her transition to human society.

Photographs of past Kumari are somewhat unsettling. They are dressed as adult women, made to wear heavy makeup and elaborate costumes, and are reminiscent of child beauty queens in the United States, such as Jon Benet Ramsey. They are treated with reverence, and are believed to have the ability to grant wishes to the faithful.

However, buried within the Tantras—especially the *Kalachakra Tantra*—there are stipulations concerning the employment of young girls as Tantric partners in the rituals. These are known as the 'mudra consorts,' and the requirement for an 'activity mudra consort' is that she has eyes that are large and well-formed, a narrow waist, and her age is either "twelve or sixteen" and she is menstrual. In this case, the flow of menstrual blood is essential as that means the other *kalas* or fluids are flowing as well. This young girl—who is to be trained in the *dharma* before being employed as a consort—is a partner in the rituals, and she is instructed in the sexual requirements of Tantra, one of which is to maintain her partner's state of arousal without permitting his loss of semen.

As Tantra is concerned with adults attaining contact with the Other and transcending their human bonds—to society, to organized religion, to government, to all of the institutions that arrogate to themselves the ability to interpret reality—the participants have to be biologically adult. The rites are a means of collapsing time: of returning to the pre-pubescent state of awareness where contact with the Other was possible; and of collapsing time even further to the point where Death and Procreation take place at the same moment.

The rites of Dagon, however, employ a different approach because their aim is not spiritual transcendence the way it is understood among the Tantrikas or the yogis and yoginis, but spiritual transcendence as a way of abandoning the Earth to the monstrous Beings who have been here before. It is not so much "transcendence" as "abnegation." The goal is still the collapse of time—and the unity of Death and Conception—but as a means to allow unfettered access to our planet of Beings who need Death in order to be Conceived.

Simon spoke of the rise of child sacrifice in the world, an alarming statistic of which Monroe was well aware from his other channels without being able to contextualize it. The *muti* killings in South Africa—murders of children whose bones or organs are consumed for ritualistic purposes—still take place, as does child sacrifice on a large scale in Uganda. In some cases, parts of the victim's body are removed while the victim is still alive. The victim may survive the experience, only to return to a family that does not accept them and a society that ostracizes them in addition to the psychological and physical trauma they received as sacrificial victims. They often carry large scars across their bodies, have been castrated or otherwise mutilated, and all for profit. The persons who carry out these horrific acts are working for clients who desire to get rich, or destroy an enemy, or succeed in a court case. Clients pay dearly for this service, and the ritual specialist gets rich in the process.

The economic situation aside, the perpetrators believe they are sacrificing these children to the Devil, specifically to Lucifer, and claim—wrongly—that this is their ancient and ancestral practice. Simon identified the influence of Dagon in this tradition, as the occultist who inspired it back in the last half of the twentieth century was one of their French initiates, a man who was central in a famous case involving the performance of the Black Mass in a Paris *arrondissement.* While the shamans believe that they are sacrificing to Lucifer, the style and method of the ritual—or so claimed Simon—was a dead giveaway as an ancient Middle Eastern ritual dedicated to Kutulu.

Yet, with all of this background, Monroe still didn't feel he understood the dynamics of the ritual about to take place. He knew that Simon was distancing himself from the topic, waltzing around it without getting too close, but Monroe had no other option but to be direct about it.

"How does it work, then?" he asked. "How does this ritual take place? How are the children used? I need to know that if I am to find them and rescue them and stop the ritual from happening. I also need to know it in order to round up as many of the perpetrators as possible. The more I know about the logistics of the thing, the better able I am to take the necessary steps. So, I'm asking you again and please be direct: how does all this work?"

Simon was uncomfortable discussing such an arcane and complex subject as ritual magic with someone who had never practiced it and did not have the context to understand it. It wasn't as simple as saying, "first do this, and then do that." It didn't work that way. Anyone can pick up a book on the subject, but that has so little similarity to the real thing that it's the same as reading a travel brochure and thinking you had actually been on vacation. Yet, he knew he had to do it. Knew it as soon as Monroe started voicing his concerns. There was no way out, and Simon hoped that he wouldn't do more harm than good by explaining it to him.

"There are secrets, without which these rituals don't work. The problem is, I can tell you what they are but they won't mean anything to you. It's like … it's like sheet music. If you have never played an instrument before, you can learn to read music theoretically but without actually transferring the music from the sheet to the instrument you won't really understand it.

"Secrets are passed on from adept to adept during the process of many initiations. These are rituals that employ symbolic actions and symbolic language. They set the stage for the transmission of the secrets, without which the secrets are unintelligible and basically worthless. If I tell you that the core secret of the German order, the O.T.O., is sex that really doesn't tell you anything. It's true, but knowing that is next to worthless without the preliminary initiations and instruction. You need the context for comprehending the secret, its value, and its employment in ritual. The ritual initiations provide the context within which the secret safely can be revealed. Without that, knowing the secret is useless."

"Okay. Granted. But I don't need to know the secrets of an occult lodge in order to disrupt its activities, right?"

"No, they pretty much take care of that themselves. Secret societies tend to self-destruct with regularity. Dagon is different, because they don't look for recruits and are happy keeping out of the limelight. New recruits—individuals culled from ads in the back pages of astrology magazines or on the Internet—would also be a real pain to work with, to train and to indoctrinate. Most would-be occultists have expectations that are unreasonable and fantasy-laden, and moreover they lack discipline. Many think they already know a great deal, or have received initiations in other groups, so they won't really do the work required. They are not looking for initiation, but validation. Those individuals are worthless to a serious occult Order. In addition, the intellectual demands of membership in Dagon are considerable. The short answer is: no, you don't need to know their secrets in order to disrupt them but you need to know how they think, just as you would with any terror group or foreign intelligence service. I know you are keeping a lot of information close to your vest and you can't reveal certain things to me, so I am working in the dark a little. Have patience, and I will tell you everything you need to know."

It was getting close to noon by this time, but neither Simon nor Monroe was particularly hungry. Simon made a pitcher of ice tea—regular, unadorned ice tea—and they quenched their thirst as Monroe studied the charts and other documents that Simon had collected and displayed on the dining room table.

"Aleister Crowley was probably the most transparent when it comes to sexual occultism, but that isn't saying very much. While the higher degrees of the O.T.O.—the German occult society of which he claimed leadership after the death of its founder—are concerned with this secret, they were not made part of an actual degree ritual in the Masonic sense. The secret was conferred privately. Crowley, however, wrote it out in various Order documents some of which refer specifically to the creation of a homunculus. With some interpretation, this can be construed as what transpired with Lavinia Whateley in the Lovecraft story.

"Further, one of his rituals—the Star Sapphire—can be construed as a veiled reference to incestuous relations, which is how the people around Calvin and Hywen George understood it. This was the ritual, by the way, that was noticed by the German O.T.O. as having revealed their secret. It was certainly the core of the ritual alluded to by Lovecraft."

"So, what you are saying is that Dagon is a Crowley cult?"

"Oh no, not at all. No. Crowley may have been aware of the secret, but he was not in favor of the type of activity for which Dagon is infamous. While he has been castigated as 'the wickedest man in the world' that is certainly hyperbole. Hard to consider him the wickedest during the era of Stalin, Hitler and Mussolini. But if you combine the Crowley rituals with those of the *Necronomicon*, what you get is quite explosive. It's a little like a satanic interpretation of the Emerald Tablet."

"As above, so below?"

"Precisely. Genetic and neurobiological manipulation in one instance combined with astronomical calculation in another, leading to the Opening of the Gate."

Monroe let that sink in for a moment, before asking:

"At how many different sites will the Opening of the Gate ritual take place?"

Simon pulled the large chart over to himself and pointed at a few spots on the map. "There will most certainly be one in the United States, and based on the calculations I mentioned it will take place in

Massachusetts, the 'classical' location of Lovecraft's Dunwich. Right about here." He pointed to an area in the central part of the state. "I can't say which town for sure as I would need more information and, as I said, the geographical coordinates used by the high priests of Dagon are rather fluid. They will pick a site that has significance for them in some way, but it has to satisfy the other requirements which are mathematical and astronomical. That means that one site will definitely be in central Massachusetts, perhaps up Route 91 which connects two locations known as 'Satan's Kingdom,' but the precise location will be determined by the actual site's more specific significance to them."

"Well, that's certainly a start. Maybe I can get the latest crop of remote viewers to work with some coordinates. Satan's Kingdom? Those are real places, like on a regular map?"

"Yes, actually. Hard to believe, I know. One's in Massachusetts at the Vermont border, and the other is in Vermont itself. In fact, there's also a third, in Connecticut west of Hartford."

"Strange. But maybe too much on the nose for Dagon? At least it will give us a start with the remote viewers."

Simon shrugged. "It might help."

"Where else?"

He turned the chart around so that Monroe would have a better perspective.

"You see that promontory there? What looks like a ridge or an escarpment?"

Monroe nodded.

"That's not actually on the surface of the Earth. It's a few hundred feet below the ocean surface."

"You're not telling me that Dagon has a submarine?"

"No, nothing like that. This promontory is considered to be the classical site of Cthulhu's sarcophagus, the sunken city of R'lyeh. Naturally, the cult can't visit the site to perform the ritual, so they use a set of complimentary coordinates."

"What does that mean?"

"Basically, and again according to their system of geometry which is unlike any of ours although perhaps Riemann comes closest in his idea of multi-dimensional geometry, they can calculate a position on the surface of the Earth that duplicates in a different dimension the location of R'lyeh. It would take too long to explain, so you'll have to take my word for it. That means that the next site will be located along the coast of the island of Java."

"Indonesia?"

"The same."

"Do you have a precise location?"

"As in the Massachusetts example, not yet. I need some more information first, and I'm working on it. When I get the time of the ritual, I will be better able to locate the ritual sites with more precision because they will be linked using Dagon's peculiar geometry. But Java is as far as I can get you right now."

"Are there more sites?"

"Most certainly, and some of them will be blinds. Possibly the Satan's Kingdom sites, among others. That is, they know that other lodges and Orders are aware of what they are up to, at least in general outline, and will try to stop them. In order to throw them off the trail, Dagon will instigate a series of rituals in various places around the globe that have nothing at all to do with the actual Opening of the Gate. Their sole purpose will be to attract the attention of their adversaries while the real ritual takes place in a very few obscure locations. The fact that Dagon uses its own set of map coordinates and its own system of calculations means that none of the other groups—using normal astronomy, planetary hours taken from the old grimoires, and so forth—will be able to anticipate their moves."

"But if you can, then others must be able to do the same."

"Yes and no. I come by my knowledge independently and at great personal cost to myself. Not many others are that committed to this path. One needs a certain strength of mind to stay above the temptation of simply claiming advanced spiritual knowledge when you don't have any more wisdom than your next door neighbor's cat. The problem with many occult Orders is that they are little more than mutual admiration societies. One doesn't need to work very hard—or very smart—to rise high within the degree system. What I am trying to say is that most of the occult groups and esoteric societies you have heard of have no capability of doing what I do, nor the slightest interest in doing so. It's too much like work, I guess."

"So ... how do you know you are right?"

"Ah, now we get to it! Well, for starters, I have been tracking Dagon for the better part of thirty years. They are still human beings, and sometimes human beings make mistakes. They show their hand from time to time, inadvertently to be sure. Also, I track the other lodges and Orders—a relatively easy thing to do these days, due to social media—and can anticipate which ones will be infiltrated by Dagon, or have already been infiltrated, and for what purpose."

"This is the type of information I need, Simon."

"I understand, and you shall have it. Right now, there are at least three secret societies in the United States, Latin America, and Europe that have been infiltrated by agents of Dagon. Some of the newer lodges or chapters of these Orders are actually Dagon fronts, unknown to their members. That is, someone from Dagon joins the Order, rises to a certain level, then sets up his or her own chapter of the parent Order. It all looks quite legal and above-board, but in reality the chapter is a Dagon operation from the get-go. They destroyed the Golden Dawn that way, for instance. Many other Orders today have been similarly compromised."

"Can you write down the list of the Orders you say have been infiltrated by Dagon?"

"Of course. I already have." He handed a small slip of paper to Monroe, who glanced at it, then pocketed it.

"I will work on the remaining ritual sites and let you know as soon as I have identified them to my satisfaction. They won't be obvious places, like Stonehenge or Machu Picchu, though. As I mentioned, they will try to muddy the waters so that everyone goes off in the wrong direction."

"There is only one thing left to discuss now before I get back to my office, and that is the actual ritual procedure. How long does it take, how many participants, at which point does it become dangerous for the victims?"

"The ritual will take place over the course of several hours, even up to eight hours," Simon answered the dreaded question immediately, like pulling off a scab. "It will start at a predetermined time. Once it has begun, the ritual enters into a state of suspended animation you might say. In other words, time as we know it stops. Within the ritual, participants sense the passage of time differently from those without.

"The ritual is conducted within an area that has been consecrated to that purpose, like the old magic circles of the grimoires. It has a boundary, and everything within that boundary is tightly controlled. A magic circle is like a sensory deprivation unit, except that the sensory stimuli have not been eliminated entirely but designed around a single purpose. Anything extraneous to that purpose—any smell, any color, any image, any sound, etc.—has been eliminated so that only the sensory data reflective of the purpose of the ritual remains.

"In this case, the rituals will either come from the *Necronomicon* or are rituals ancillary to it: in other words, rituals that were devised by Dagon for a specific purpose that might not appear in the *Necronomicon* but which have been adapted to be consistent with it. The type of sexual ritual they will employ to open the Gate is not prescribed in the Book. However, the seals, the incantations, the pace of the ritual will all be determined by the Book. The employment of children as facilitators is Dagon's own addition to or expansion of the Book—based on their understanding of sexual ritual as the missing element of the grimoires."

"How much space will they need?"

"Typically, and if the ritual is only being performed with a minimum of operators, they would need a space roughly similar to a large living room. However, this ritual will almost certainly take place outdoors or in a very large hall. They will employ a number of operators, for they have to manage the children in addition to everything else. They will need absolute privacy, of course. Before, during, and after the ritual if they will need to dispose of the victims."

"So, they do intend to kill them?"

"Not necessarily, and not all of them. It depends on when their usefulness has passed."

"Then let's discuss that."

"Very well. There are three stages in the use of children for ceremonial magic of this type. In the first place, as we mentioned, the children are virgin. That is an absolute requirement. The ones used as seers should be pre-pubescent, like the Kumari of Nepal, for the Old Ones will speak to them or through them. I've said earlier that, biologically speaking, puberty brings with it a flood of hormones that complicate matters where this type of magic is concerned. The pre-pubescent are 'pure' hormonally. The others should be just on the verge of puberty as the hormones begin coursing through their bodies; the girls may be in their first year of experiencing their menstrual cycle. No later than that. Liminality again."

"Boys? Girls?"

"That will depend on what we are dealing with. Dagon has no preferences either way as both boys and girls make excellent seers. They may even use both at the same time. Judging from the child porn you mentioned to me, though, it seems as if girls will be the chosen vehicles this time. At least, they are advertising their ritual using girls. This may be an indication of the character of the ritual, whether it is centered on a goddess figure—or perhaps the main celebrant is a priestess."

"Okay, go on."

"The first step is the evocation of the Old Ones. The magicians will be sensitive to their presence, of course, but the children—in this case, the girls—will be made to act as intermediaries, to see the Old Ones or to hear their voices. Questions will be directed to the

Old Ones by means of the children, who will then relay whatever response is given. This is standard practice dating back hundreds if not thousands of years.

"Once the initial contact is made and whatever dialogue has been completed, the central part of the ritual takes place. This is the actual Opening of the Gate. Lovecraft alluded to it in his story. It took place on April 30, 1912 which is Walpurgisnacht (a famous pagan holiday) but also is the day when 'the Great Bear hangs from its tail in the sky' at midnight, according to the Book. Lavinia Whateley became pregnant with her twin sons on that day, due to her father's ritual. What this means for us, of course, should by now be quite obvious. I think it is safe to assume that the invocation of Yog-Sothoth indicates the Old One used Wizard Whateley as the medium through which It impregnated Lavinia."

"They intend to use the children as sexual vehicles for the Old Ones."

"Indeed."

"But they need to be fertile. So the children used as seers will not be the same as the ones used to Open the Gate, as it were."

"No."

"So we are speaking of at least two children per ritual."

"Most likely more. In order to avoid any chance of failure, Dagon will use multiple seers and multiple vessels. That's what they call the surrogates: vessels. As usual, Dagon uses certain terms in more than one sense. A vessel is taken to mean a container, such as a cup or chalice; but it is also understood to mean a ship. The vessel in this case is meant both ways. The girl is a container for the spirit of the Old One to manifest, but she is also the ship It is using to enter our world."

"Twin meanings."

"In a sense, yes."

"So, that covers the first two phases. The children will be used first to make contact and then—through some kind of sex magic ritual—to become impregnated, thus allowing the Old One a physical means of entering this world."

"Briefly, yes. I won't go into the details of the ritual itself. There is no need, and the information would only serve to disgust you. It would be the first sexual experience for these unfortunate girls, and it will not be pleasant. They would be treated as machines, in a way. As objects. As for the third phase, well, that one that is even more worrisome than the first two.

"Dagon will not permit the seers to be used by an adversary. You see—and Lovecraft himself was well aware of this as he described it in more than one of his stories—when you look into the magic mirror, it looks back into you. What I mean is, the seer not only sees the Old One, the Old One sees the seer. Once the seer has been successful and contact has been made, she is no longer necessary for any future ritual. However, another magician may use her to make contact, or she may be used by an Old One to see into this world, this dimension if you will. Dagon cannot permit contact to take place outside of its control. Also, it cannot take the risk that someone may interrogate one of the seers to find out what they witnessed.

"So, the seer will be killed. Ritually sacrificed to the Old One. That ritual will be employed during the same Opening of the Gate in order to provide a blood trail for the Old One to follow. It is an essential aspect of the rite, and the one that provides the energetic medium. Like the *vama marg* rituals in India that take place in charnel grounds, the idea is to bring conception and death together at once. Only in this case, the victim is killed, sacrificed, at the same time as the other victim is being ... impregnated."

"Jesus."

Simon raised an eyebrow. "Not quite. But close. What has upset the faithful of Judaism and Islam is the Christian insistence that God incarnated in this World, became part of human history. It's counter-intuitive, of course, the Creator deciding to appear in Creation as a bit player, you might say. Then what made it worse was the Crucifixion. God—the Creator—murdered by Creation. And that, somehow, was interpreted as the path to universal redemption. The Crucifixion opened the Gate to the Other World so God could return home. The blood trail from the Crucifixion is supposed to lead human beings through the Gate and to the Other World. Is it any wonder that Dagon has understood this mythologem and appropriated it for its own purposes?"

"So ... Cthulhu died for our sins? Is that it?"

"Dead ... but dreaming."

They spent a few more minutes summarizing what they had discussed and preparing an action plan for the next few days. Monroe would work on finding out where the trafficked girls—the ones with the tattoos—were being held or delivered, and would start a surveillance operation centered on Massachusetts. He would also run a trace on the three occult groups listed on Simon's note. He would let Simon look for sites that would have some relevance for Dagon, sites with suggestive names or with some history where Dagon was concerned.

In the meantime, Monroe would activate his Southeast Asian network to find out what they could about a possible religious or occult ceremony due to take place in the south of Java. With all that, he was still trying to find Angell. When asked about the Book, Simon gave the opinion that Dagon already knew all they needed to know to make the ritual effective. They had had the physical Book in their possession until the rite in Nepal, when Angell seized it. However, actually having the original Book seemed to be very important to them.

Monroe knew why, but did not choose to share that information with Simon. It was why he had recruited Angell in the first place, and that was a secret too important to reveal to anyone.

The two old colleagues, both magicians in their own right, shook hands and Simon wished his friend Godspeed. He watched out the window as Monroe waved and walked to his car. It was after noon. Monroe looked up and wondered just where the tail of the

Great Bear was to be found at that moment, and wondered if it was pointing him to the place where the children were being held.

Simon moved his gaze from the window and back to his apartment. He was in urgent need of sleep but had a few quick inquiries to make first. Personal sacrifice was nothing new to him, or to those close friends who worked with him from time to time.

"After all," he said aloud to an empty room that was nevertheless crowded with old ghosts, "*This is who we are.*"

CHAPTER FORTY-EIGHT

SALIM WAS AS GOOD AS HIS WORD. Their boat pulled up to a makeshift dock along the Javanese coast. Angell had no real idea of where they were, other than somewhat to the east of Cilacap. They stepped off the boat and onto the dock, and Salim led the way to a waiting car: a four-wheel drive SUV.

"You know Aji long time?"

"Aji?"

"My brother-in-law. Captain."

"Oh. Well, not long. No."

"He is a good man. Like religion very much."

"I know. We talked a lot about it."

"Ah. That's good. Aji likes to talk a lot."

They drove along the coast road in a companionable silence for a few more minutes and then Salim pulled off on what seemed to be a dirt track.

"We will stay here for tonight. Eat something. I will radio Aji and tell him that you are safe."

"Thank you very much. You have all been very kind."

"No worries."

They drove for a few minutes only and then came into an area of small wooden homes with porches. The interiors were lighted with fluorescent lamps, which cast a too-bright glow over everything, and when the car engine was switched off Angell could hear the sound of bats and insects in the night.

Salim led him into one of the houses, where he was met by Salim's wife—Aji's sister—in a hijab. She was about Salim's age, chubby and cheerful. There were plaques on the wall, green with gold Arabic lettering which Angell saw were quotations from the Qur'an.

He was offered instant coffee and some snacks made from

fermented tempeh. He could hear the sounds of children in another room.

As he drank the coffee he could hear Salim outside on the porch, speaking to his brother-in-law in Banyumas dialect. When he came back in, he looked quizzically at Angell.

"Aji says hello. He is glad you are safe. He says you very much interested in *primbon*, in magic book. Maybe you want to see a *dukun*?"

"Oh, that's not necessary. I'm very grateful, but the captain—I mean, Aji—said something about a passport …"

"Oh, that's okay. Not to worry. Aji arrange everything. I wait for his information first. Then I can pick up."

"Great. That's great."

Salim sat down on the carved wooden chair next to Angell's own, and spoke in a low voice.

"In our family we have one *dukun*. He is a *dukun prewangan*. That means he can talk to the spirits."

Angell was really not in the mood. He had no doubt about Salim's sincerity, but the last thing he needed right now was to go hanging out with the local shaman. He was just eager to be moving, to be going somewhere. He needed time to rest and figure out what he was going to do with the rest of his life.

"He can help you with your book. To understand it, maybe?"

Angell thought fast. The passport would not be ready for one or two days, according to the captain. He would be stuck with this family, as nice as they appeared to be, for another forty-eight hours at least. He could either go and see this shaman, or stick around the house with the wife and kids.

"Okay. Sounds good. When do we see him?"

"I think tomorrow. Tonight we eat, sleep. Tomorrow we go to the next village."

"Thanks again."

"We have room for you, in back of house. Very comfortable. But sorry, no air-con."

It was actually quite pleasant, this close to the shore, so Angell figured air conditioning would not be an issue.

But first, Salim's wife was preparing some food in the kitchen. It was late, but she came out with at least six different dishes. When Angell began to protest, Salim reassured him.

"This is what you call leftovers. No problem. Eat as much as you like."

Salim led the way by example and filled his plate with white rice from a cooker, what appeared to be sautéed smelts of some kind, stewed vegetables, and pieces of some sort of fried meat on tiny bones. There was what appeared to be diced chicken with chili peppers, and a green vegetable that had been sautéed in oil and soy sauce. It was all quite delicious and Angell found himself enjoying the meal immensely. The Salim family ate with their fingers, but they had a fork and spoon that they ceremoniously offered to Angell, who accepted gratefully.

After the meal, Angell was led to his room which contained a narrow bed and a small desk, as well as some children's pictures on the walls.

"My son's room," said Salim. "He will sleep with my other son tonight. No worries."

"Dinner was wonderful. Thank your wife for me, please."

Salim bowed and left Angell to his own devices.

It was silent, except for the sound of insects, probably crickets. It was also warm but not too bad. A soft breeze blew through the window, and rustled what appeared to be mosquito netting. It was almost idyllic.

Angell fell asleep immediately.

At four am he awoke in an explosion of sound.

It was the loudspeaker from the local mosque, calling the faithful to prayer. It was as loud as an air raid siren as they were within a short walk of the mosque, something Angell hadn't noticed when they arrived. Angell was used to this phenomenon from all the time he spent in the Middle East. But hadn't been prepared for it here, in Southeast Asia, although he knew that Indonesia was the most populous Muslim country in the world and obviously his hosts were all Muslim as was the captain.

He lay in bed and listened to the call, and found himself transported back in time to Mosul and the massacre of the Yezidis against a wall in that city. He remembered, too, something he had largely forgotten: the graffiti on the wall near where it took place, the symbol of the cult he now knew was Dagon, or the Keepers of the Book. And the Arabic inscription from the Qur'an, the one that names *al-Qhadhulu*, or Kutulu, the "Abandoner."

Was that what the author of *al-Azif* was trying to say? That Kutulu was a direct reference to a god or divine being who had abandoned the human race? "Spirit of the Sky, remember." Wouldn't that mesh with those ideas of Cthulhu as "dead but dreaming" in a watery grave, remote from his followers but liable to be summoned again?

If the Abandoner was returning to Earth, what did that imply to Dagon? What did they think that foretold?

He shook himself from his thoughts. It was still quite dark outside, but he could hear the footsteps of people proceeding towards the mosque. He knew he would not be expected to go, and could use another few hours of sack time, so he stayed in and tried to reclaim his sleep but after about fifteen minutes he realized it was no use.

He got up, and sat on the edge of the bed, head in hands, trying to orient himself in space and time. He had been on the run for months, and had narrowly avoided capture, first in Beijing and then on the high seas. He thought he should have stayed in Mongolia, where no one was expecting him to be, but that was a dead end. Eventually he would have been found, arrested, and if lucky deported to the States to be interrogated, or to stand trial, or whatever they had up their sleeves. He didn't trust Monroe, and didn't trust Aubrey.

Who else was there to trust?

At that thought, there was a gentle knock on his door. It opened to reveal Salim who said he hoped he wasn't too startled by the loudspeaker.

They had breakfast around 6 am. More rice. More premixed instant coffee with sugar and creamer. Another session with the loudspeaker and more praying. Then Angell and Salim set off to visit the *dukun*.

Angell's first impression of Pak Mahmoud was of a walnut.

The dukun was old and bore heavy wrinkles on skin the color of mahogany. Estimates of his age varied from eighty to more than one hundred. He lived alone in a large traditional wooden house with no electricity or running water: a condition that was by choice rather than necessity, according to Salim. He was barefoot and dressed in a sarong and an oddly-shaped cap, not the usual *songkok* or "Sukarno-style" black cap people were used to thinking of when they thought of Indonesia.

He had a sash around his waist with a *kris*, or ceremonial dagger, thrust into it.

He was about five foot two, but carried himself with dignity and even menace.

Salim and Angell removed their shoes and entered the shaman's home at his invitation. Angell couldn't tell from the man's face or deportment whether or not he was pleased or irritated by their presence, but he let Salim take the lead. In any case, he didn't speak the language and even if he had been able to speak Indonesian he would not have been able to understand a word of Banyumas dialect.

On the way over, Salim had prepared him for the meeting. He said that many people relied on the dukun for medical assistance as well as for spiritual guidance. Like most dukun, Pak Mahmoud did not consider himself a practitioner of *ilmu hitam*, the "black science" or "black magic." However, none of the dukun ever did.

The version practiced by Pak Mahmoud had many Islamic elements mixed in, which was advisable in a country as Muslim as Indonesia; at the same time, however, he was considered an authority on *kebatinan*: the indigenous Javanese form of religion and esotericism. Had Angell been in a better frame of mind and had more time, he would have enjoyed studying this subject for a long time and finding ways to measure it against some of the traditionally Islamic forms of esotericism he had studied in his past, albeit briefly. Today, he was just going along for the ride because the captain had thought it would be "interesting" for him to do so, and he didn't want to insult the man who had saved his life.

They sat cross-legged on the wooden floor of the man's house. They were silent for awhile, and Angell drank in the atmosphere. It was peaceful, the only sound coming from whatever wildlife there was outside plus the occasional roar of a distant motorcycle. A young man, dressed similarly in a sarong, came out with a tray of tea and some plastic bottles of water, and left.

Salim looked at Angell and nodded in the direction of Angell's knapsack. He hesitated a moment, then decided it could do no harm. He opened it, and withdrew the *Necronomicon*.

He held it in his hands for a moment, and then offered it to Pak Mahmoud for his inspection. There was a brief conversation that he didn't understand, then the old shaman reached over with both hands and lifted the Book from Angell's grasp.

He held it for a long moment without opening it. He closed his eyes and seemed to have been transported to another place in his mind. Angell looked inquiringly at Salim, who just shrugged silently.

The dukun then opened his eyes and very carefully opened the Book.

CHAPTER FORTY-NINE

MONROE COULDN'T BELIEVE THAT they had yet to apprehend Angell, after all this time. The man was a ghost, or his people were incompetent. He had to start considering the latter. After all, they probably were embarrassed even to be working with him, regardless of his clout and his reputation. Maybe even because of it. It was a different world, and all the glory was in counter-terrorism. No one was certain what Monroe really did, or what kind of operations he ran. Everything was compartmented to death, so no one had the big picture except him. Even Aubrey was missing a few key elements, and Monroe had to keep it that way.

In the movies, intelligence agents were always depicted as focusing on one operation at a time, like those cop dramas where everyone is working together on a single case until it is solved to the exclusion of all others. Life wasn't like that. Cops, like intelligence officers, always had a number of irons in the fire at any one time. They had to multi-task around dozens of open cases. Monroe was no different. The exception was that all of his cases were part of one, large and all-encompassing, case. The one represented by his infamous Codex.

So as he fretted about finding Angell and the Book, he was also concerned about what he believed was an upcoming operation by the group calling itself Dagon. These were the 'Keepers of the Book' that had possession of the *Necronomicon* until Angell sabotaged their ritual in Nepal. They were no longer Keepers of the Book, however, since that dubious distinction now went to Angell himself. That wasn't stopping the cult from its plans, however. The photos Sylvia had shown him had proved that, if nothing else.

His search for relevant information on the three occult Orders that Simon had given him had so far turned up empty. The one possible lead—a group calling itself the Argon Archon—had come to nothing in the end. It had dissolved; its leader decamped to

Europe and believed to be dissociated. The other two groups were still around, but seemed to have nothing going for them at the time. That could be a misperception, of course, but it would take too long and consume too many resources to find out.

He looked at the calendar. Halloween had already passed, and no developments. A little too obvious for Dagon and, anyway, their schedule had to be a mess right about now. Many of their initiates had either perished in Nepal or had been captured by security forces. Some of them had been interrogated quite harshly, but none of them were giving anything up. Like penny ante Mafiosi, they were more afraid of their *capo* than of any government.

Monroe had distaste for 'enhanced interrogation techniques.' In the first place, they were inhuman and contributed to the overall environment of cruelty and evil they were intended to thwart. Just as importantly, they also were often useless. A man or woman undergoing physical torture will tell you anything to make it stop.

He also knew all about 'extraordinary rendition' and the games the 'community' played to avoid prosecution for holding prisoners in foreign countries and beating the living crap out of them. Such methods, though, were useless with the Dagon initiates. Their training had provided them with the means to escape reality, to withdraw somewhere deep in their own minds so that no amount of pain would affect them. It's as if they weren't even human.

Mutants, maybe.

That's when he got a call from Simon, who told him that he had discovered the time table and that he had better collect whatever resources he could since it was going to get real hairy, real soon.

When pressed, all Simon would say was that it was no longer a two-person operation any more. No way Monroe and Simon on their own could handle all the logistics. He had better identify a few other assets he could trust and bring them together on this. He would need a computer expert at least; while he was good, and he had friends he could trust, he knew that Monroe would be a stickler for regs and would not permit people without security clearances near this thing. The fact that he had already brought Simon in on it was a done deal, but there would be no sense in compounding the matter by bringing in a lot of computer geeks with questionable backgrounds.

Monroe was alarmed by his friend's insistence and realized that Simon's phone was not a secure line so there was a limit to what they could discuss. He agreed in principle and told him he would contact him as soon as he put together a go team on the fly, and hung up.

But who the hell would that be?

Aubrey was in New York, having arrived from Europe and was even now collating the information he had picked up along the way. He could get him to come down, but he might be better off at large so they could send him ... well, wherever they had to send him. He was an excellent case officer, and they would need him in that capacity once they had identified their targets.

Monroe began to realize that the people he knew and trusted he could count on the fingers of one hand. He was old, and many of those he had worked with over the years had already died or retired to somewhere in Arizona or Florida. The younger ones were organization animals, people who would try to see if there was an angle in it somewhere for them: promotion, or glory, or a better pay-grade.

Ironically, he needed people who were as cynical as he was. They were the only ones he could trust to dedicate every last brain cell to this problem without thought of reward, since there was no reward the bureaucracy could offer that would remotely satisfy them.

He picked up the desk phone and called Sylvia.

In the car with him were Sylvia and the man she said would be perfect for the job, the guy from the sub-basement, Harry. He of the child porn. Harry was as excited as a puppy to be involved in some kind of intrigue with Sylvia and Monroe, but tried not to show it. They told him that, although this was not specifically approved by

NSA, Monroe would run interference on that since his connections were "at the highest level." Harry was afraid of losing his job over this, but not afraid enough to decline the offer.

Monroe cautioned them on the drive over.

"We are going to meet a man I have known for decades. He's a little eccentric but brilliant, at least in the ways we need him to be. He's the one who has been cracking this code and he seems to believe that a timetable has been pushed up. Something quite terrible is about to happen, and it involves some of those young children you spotted, Harry. If we are to rescue them, or as many of them as possible, from a terrible fate and do the country a service at the same time, we have to do this my way. Is that understood?"

Harry nodded, and Monroe stared a him in the rear-view mirror until he verbalized it. "Yes, sir."

He looked over at Sylvia, who was in the front passenger seat.

"I wouldn't have it any other way."

Monroe nodded, to himself and his passengers.

"Very well. I hope you both have appetites, because this guy likes to cook."

Simon wasn't happy with having company, especially with two people he had never met, but he understood Monroe's point that they couldn't very well have Simon bring his library of books, papers and charts to NSA. This was the easiest way to do this, plus he wanted to keep the entire project quiet for the time being until he had confirmation—actionable intelligence—that what was about to transpire had implications for national security. He was still under a cloud for having lost Angell after Nepal, regardless of the success of the mission otherwise, and he didn't want to jeopardize his status even further. He still had work to do, and he needed the resources of the US government to accomplish his mission.

As unhappy as he was with the inundation of souls (to Simon, three people were overwhelming) he nevertheless behaved as the perfect host. He greeted them in less exotic attire than when Monroe had visited him recently, and bade everyone make themselves at home. After introductions all around he prepared some of his Viennese blend for anyone who wanted coffee, and he made some Chinese tea available as well. He assumed alcoholic beverages would not be welcomed as they had a considerable amount of work to do.

"Thank you, Simon. But let's get to it at once if we may."

"Right. Well, to summarize, Monroe is aware that a terrorist organization, composed of cells scattered throughout the world, is planning a major event in the very near future. This terrorist organization is motivated by a religious ideology, the same as many others, but its weapons are of a different nature altogether.

"The organization is called Dagon, or the Order of Dagon if you prefer, and its weapons are directed at human consciousness. They involve the weaponization of those technologies that have usually been the province of shamans, priests, and magicians in all parts of the world.

"They have already tried to do this once before in recent memory, in fact only a few months ago, and their efforts were spoiled by a university professor who infiltrated the group and thwarted their ... well, their ritual."

Harry rolled his eyes in the direction of Monroe, as if to ask "do you believe this guy?" but then realized, with Monroe's steely gaze back at him, that he did, indeed, believe that guy.

Simon picked up on the incredulity at once and tailored the rest of his argument to suit.

"We don't have to believe that what they claim is true or real. We only have to realize that *they* believe it, and are willing to take extraordinary measures to insure that they are successful."

"What measures are we talking about?" It was Sylvia's turn to sound dubious.

"The sexual molestation ... well, to be blunt, the rape ... and murder of children."

"These are the ones I found?"

"Yes, Harry. In fact, those photos tipped us off to the whole enterprise. It's why we're here right now." Monroe picked up the presentation from there.

"The children in the photos represent only some of the ones being trafficked around the world as we speak. We know that human trafficking—especially of women and children but including men as well, as slaves—is a scourge that has not gone away. We do not intend to solve that problem ourselves, all at once. What we are doing is focusing on one specific plot to abuse and murder these children as part of a ritual or ceremony that is due to take place, within days or even hours, at different spots around the world. We intend to stop this ritual from taking place, and to rescue these children—or as many of them as we can—in the process. Since there are no nuclear weapons or an oilfield involved, we would not expect the full involvement of our national security apparatus. Due to its sensitivity and the fact that the Order of Dagon has infiltrated police and security agencies all over the world, we cannot take the chance of involving the authorities either. We're basically on our own."

Harry was having a hard time getting this all on board.

"But if we don't involve the security agencies, how do the four of us stop them?"

Monroe nodded, as if expecting the question. Which he was.

"I have my own resources. An informal network of assets who are known to me from decades in service. Sylvia here is aware of some of them. Without giving names away, she can verify that what I say is true."

"Yes, I can. Monroe has been doing this for a long time. Those who support him and his work trust him, and vice versa. They also have their own contacts in law enforcement and security agencies around the world. Thus, they can enlist them when the time is right without giving away too much where the mission is concerned." She was thinking of Aubrey, but she knew there were others.

"Speaking of the time being right, what is the schedule now, Simon?"

Before Simon could answer, Monroe's phone warbled.

"I have to take this," he told the assembled group and retreated to the bathroom to talk in private.

It was Aubrey.

"We've traced your Vanek down to an apartment in New Bedford, Massachusetts."

"That's close to the area identified by Simon as the target for the ritual."

"Well, not that close. A few hours' drive, but yeah, close enough. At least it's not in Nepal."

"Granted. Okay. Where is he now?"

"We put a trace on his car and his credit cards. He does not seem to be home at the moment. I will have a team go in and search."

"Don't we need a warrant?"

"We'll get one from a local judge."

"Don't breach the door until you have it in hand. What's your probable cause?"

"Let me worry about that. In the meantime, I had to put one of our network into custody. The guy watching Angell in Shanghai. I told him to return Stateside but he took a detour to Singapore. I think he was running a personal operation parallel to our own."

"Jesus. Has the whole world gone nuts?"

"Just the part we like. In any case, he's in a safe house and we're sweating him. Seems he sent a pirate ship after our boy."

Monroe wanted to laugh, but the situation was so dire he couldn't muster more than a cough.

"He escaped, from what I understand. We're looking for the vessel he was on out of Shanghai. It was a tramp heading for Hong Kong and then Singapore. From what we know at this point Angell realized he was being tracked and decided not to put in there. The ship never showed up."

"Any ideas where he's headed?"

Aubrey breathed hard into the phone.

"Could be anywhere in Southeast Asia, of course, depending on how much fuel they have. The smart money is on Indonesia. A lot of islands to get lost in there. Thousands of them. Many uninhabited."

Monroe thought for a minute. Simon had indicated that one of the potential Dagon sites was in Indonesia. Was Angell actually headed there? Did he know something they didn't know?

"Send me the data on Vanek and let me know when you have the warrant and what you find. If Vanek shows up, have him arrested. We'll think of a charge later. And Aubrey?"

"Sir?"

"Find Angell. Fast. Find out where he's headed. I'm getting a bad feeling about this."

"Sir."

They hung up.

Monroe left the bathroom and walked slowly back to the group. When he got to the living room he saw that they were all silent and staring at him.

"What's wrong?"

"We have the schedule," Simon replied. "And we've run out of time."

CHAPTER FIFTY

SIMON'S LOGIC WAS PLAIN TO SEE. They had been looking for an astronomical event. Barring the sudden appearance of a supernova—which not even Dagon could have predicted in advance (as far as they knew)—it had to be something predictable and subject to calculation.

As Monroe was talking to Aubrey in the bathroom, Harry had been looking at his secure tablet and trying to see if there had been any activity on the child porn accounts he was monitoring. He could not access the NSA database from there, but he did receive email notifications according to a specific protocol. Instead, he got a news notification from CNN. Seems that NASA was overjoyed that one of their missions was a resounding success. His friend in Human Resources forwarded him the news, knowing he was a space junkie.

It was a little like science fiction. A space probe had been sent to make a rendezvous with a comet. The idea was to orbit the comet and send a lander down to take measurements. What grabbed Harry's attention was the name of the mission: Rosetta. Like the Rosetta Stone. Maybe that had some significance? It sounded, well, cultish.

And the name of the lander, *Philae*.

Simon stopped what he was doing and asked Harry to repeat that name.

"*Philae*," said Harry, reading it off his feed. "The name of an island in the Nile."

"When did this happen?"

"Today. Just now."

Simon ran his hands through his hair, in obvious consternation.

"The word *Philae* is plural. There were two islands in the Nile that were referred to as the Philae. One of them was particularly sacred. In fact, it was considered one of the burial places of Osiris. Two islands.

"*Twins*.

"The ritual will happen today, or at the latest tomorrow, if it

415

hasn't happened already. Within twenty-four hours. They will not miss this event. They will consider it the hand of Kutulu launching the Twins into space, extending their reach to the heavens. Rosetta is obviously a reference to the Rosetta Stone which was found on Philae. The Rosetta Stone means translation: communication, contact. There will be a ritualized form of connection between Dagon and the Philae lander in order to Open the Gate. Do you have the coordinates of the comet?"

And that is when Monroe walked into the room.

The comet's name was the rather prosaic 67P/Churyumov-Gerasimenko, discovered by two Russian astronomers, one based in Ukraine and the other in Kazakhstan, through the observation of photographic plates. In 2004, the Rosetta mission was launched to make contact with the comet but was kept in hibernation in space until January 2014 when it was able to begin the rendezvous, hovering in orbit until it was in position to send down the lander. November 12, 2014 marked the first time in history that a spacecraft landed on a comet.

January, 2014 had resonance for Monroe, because that is when the chatter increased exponentially concerning Dagon and the *Necronomicon*. A few months later, Angell was fighting for his life in Nepal.

"Tell me all about this comet and the NASA mission," Monroe commanded anyone and everyone in the room.

"Well, Rosetta's been orbiting the comet since September. Dagon would have known about it before though, as early as January but no later than August, when the orbiter began its rendezvous with the comet prior to sending the lander."

"No," said Monroe. "They knew about it before April. As early as January, maybe. That means they had a source in NASA. It wasn't common knowledge, right?"

"Correct. It would have been known to space geeks, probably, but it was not newsworthy at the time."

"Okay, go on."

"Rosetta is the name of the spacecraft itself. The lander is called Philae, like I mentioned. They use an imaging system called ..." Harry stopped for a moment as he read the report. "Shit. You're not going to believe this."

"Just tell us, Harry."

"Sorry. It's called OSIRIS."

Monroe groaned. "You've gotta be kidding me, right?"

"No. It stands for Onboard Scientific Imaging System. I kid you not. OSIRIS."

"Dwight," interrupted Simon. "As I am researching the comet itself, I find that there are twenty-six different mapped regions on the comet, each named after an Egyptian deity. There are names like Ma'at, Seth, Nut, Hathor, Geb, Atum, Apis, Anubis ... even Khonsu." Simon put down his laptop and stared at Monroe.

"Khonsu?"

Harry and Sylvia looked confused.

"It's a Crowley reference," Simon explained. "Aleister Crowley. The magician. You've probably never heard of him."

Harry shrugged, but Sylvia knew the name. Probably from all those late night talks with Monroe in his office.

"Crowley called himself the priest Ankh-af-na-Khonsu. It was on a stele in the old Boulaq Museum in Cairo. Translated, it seems to say that the priest was the 'opener of the dwelling place of the stars.'"

Monroe stood up on knees that had seen better days. "This is it, then. It has to be. The timetable was moved up to take advantage of this situation. It fits with the Dunwich scenario of twins, of the Old Ones, in fact with Dagon's whole reason for existence."

"One more thing," said Simon, still staring at his laptop.

"Go on."

"The comet. It has two gates."

The "gates" are called that by the astronomers because they look like gates, and are twins. They are named after two dead women, members of the original Rosetta mission.

Simon had to explain to Harry and Sylvia the relevance of the term "gates" as well as go more deeply into the concept of twins. There was a lot to take in, but as Simon and Monroe needed their help they had to explain as much as possible as quickly as possible. Harry began to realize what Monroe had been talking about during that presentation years ago. He wasn't talking about a terror group; he was talking about an occult group. Had he made that plain during the presentation he would have been retired; gently and firmly, but retired nonetheless.

"The girls you were finding in your web searches, Harry, they are going to be part of this ritual. That is why we have to think like occultists and figure out where they would be holding them. To know that, we have to know what kind of region they would consider important, or sacred, or relevant somehow. It's a tall order, almost impossible, but if we think outside the box…"

"Got it. I think. I'll work on it."

"I'll help you," said Simon. "I have a better computer setup in the other room."

The two left Monroe and Sylvia by themselves in the living room.

"You look like shit warmed over," she said.

"Thanks. As a matter of fact, I feel like shit warmed over."

"I'm not sure what I'm doing here, though."

Monroe looked at her, then looked away.

"You remember that paper that Angell wrote, the one I mentioned back in my office? What was it, a month ago?"

"Only a few weeks, at most."

"Seems longer. Anyway, the paper had a lot of Angell's thoughts on what is actually turning out to be a case similar to that in Genesis."

"Sons of God, Daughters of Men, you mean?"

"Yes. You have a brilliant analytical mind …"

"I bet you say that to all the middle-aged computer scientists."

"Well, not *all*. But it's true nevertheless. And we still need to know where Angell is. It's vital we find out what he's up to. He has the Book, and if he is involved in this thing in any way we could be facing some serious damage. They are either using him, or they are looking for him. We have to find him first."

"Dwight, it's just not possible. If their ritual is taking place today, those girls are our first priority. And, anyway, we don't have the faintest idea where to start looking. Do we?"

"Actually, we can narrow it down a few thousand miles."

"Well … that's a start."

"We think he's near Singapore. Nearer Singapore than, say, California. He was last known to have been aboard ship in the South China Sea and probably heading away from Singapore to Indonesia, best guess."

Sylvia smiled.

"So now I know why I'm here."

Monroe had the grace to look embarrassed.

"I'm from Malaysia. Melaka to be exact. That's practically next door. I have the language and know the culture. Malaysia and Indonesia are always at each other's throats, but they have more in common with each other than they do with the rest of the world. Okay, Dwight. I'll work on this. Tell me where to begin."

Simon was looking at a map of Philae, the Egyptian island, in an old book from his library. It seemed to have all the usual features of a sacred island: temple structures, a promontory of some kind, and several docks for watercraft.

"The Dagon crowd will want something that looks either like the comet or like the lander. They see themselves as the lander, actually: a spacecraft making contact with the extra-terrestrial. Can you access the NSA database from here?"

Harry was uncomfortable.

"Not exactly, no. But what are you looking for?"

"I need to know if there are any locations that match the general physical characteristics of Philae. Maybe not exactly, but in general terms."

Harry moaned. "That's impossible, even for a supercomputer. How do we set up the parameters for a search like that? We don't know size, orientation, configuration, possible locations ... we'd have to go through thousands of combinations and iterations."

"Right, right. It would be better if we determined a general geographic area first."

"Not too general."

"Of course. That means doing a search on names relevant to Lovecraft, his life, his stories, and Sumerian and Babylonian religion ..."

"God, you don't want much, do you? How much time do we have? Like, years?"

Simon smiled. "Yes, I know. It sounds outrageous. But I started the work already. I have a list of towns and cities that appear in Lovecraft's stories and in his life. If we run these and find towns and cities with the same names we might be able to narrow down the field a little." He produced a pad of paper with several sheets covered in names.

"Some of these are pointless. There is no Arkham, for example. No Innsmouth. You can ignore those. Dunwich, we've already found and it's under water in England. I've put an asterisk next to the fake ones, but I'm leaving them on the list in case the real towns don't pan out. Anyway, can you write a program that would go through and identify ... maybe give us an aerial view of each of the towns that shows up? Just in the United States for now. We can expand the search later if nothing turns up."

"I can do that, of course, but it's going to take a lot of computer power. What kind of connection do you have?"

They began a discussion of network speeds and servers that lasted about fifteen minutes, after which Simon left Harry alone to concentrate.

And, anyway, he had to cook.

CHAPTER FIFTY-ONE

THE DARK LORD HAD JUST RECEIVED the last of the reports from his underlings throughout the world, including that idiot Vanek in Massachusetts. Even more importantly, he also had received his final orders from Dagon. Everything seemed to be functioning as desired.

The ritual complex was designed like the clinical trial of a new drug. There would be the actual rituals and there would be a control group. There would be real evocations, and there would be a placebo strategy in place designed to attract the attention of the authorities and of other occult groups, mediums, channellers, psychics, spiritualists, and spoon benders. The Dark Lord was not informed which was which, not officially of course, but he counted on his years of experience in this field to alert him to the frauds.

All the rituals were to be timed exactly and carried out to the letter regardless of their true purpose. There were to be no deviations from the rules and rubrics as set down by Dagon. Failure to perform to specification would be grounds for disconnection.

He poured himself another glass of burgundy and went over the ritual instructions. They were the same as last time, with the exception of the girls. He was proud of the fact that he had been essential when it came to sourcing the breeders and the seers. This was due to all the years and all the money he had spent among the most depraved fleshpots in Europe and the Middle East, in search of the ancient texts, antiques, and human beings that were being bartered and sold in order to prop up one terrorist group or another. The big boys went after the oil and the other commodities too large to stuff in a suitcase. The Dark Lord went after the artifacts, and when the call came out to source children, well that's almost too easy in a war zone.

Not that the Dark Lord ever got that close to a war zone. He used Istanbul as a base of operations for that sort of thing, or occasionally Alexandria. He didn't like to get much closer than that. He didn't go to Israel, nothing much for him there that he couldn't get in Cyprus or Beirut.

But children, they were another story. If it was just kids from families fleeing Iraq or Syria, that was easy. Hell, even Blackwater had an endless supply of underage girls in Baghdad itself. They used to call the Green Zone the Pink Zone, the sick bastards. But Dagon needed virgins, virgins that would pass medical tests as virgins. Usually by the time the kids got as far as the slave markets in Libya, Saudi or Mauritania they were no longer virgins.

That's where he came in. He had excellent connections with the flavor of the month—Daesh—due to his reputation as a buyer of antiquities stolen from the museums and digs of Iraq going back to the first Gulf War. He had an archaeologist on-call, a member of the Order, who could vet the artifacts and make sure they weren't being ripped off. The same procurer of cylinder seals, ceremonial daggers, and cuneiform tablets was also the man to know when it came to human trafficking in the occupied zones.

The Dark Lord made sure never to be in the same room as the transactions going down, just in case somebody was an informant or a police spy. He just made the arrangements and took a kickback from the procurer.

He made a veritable fortune on the last deal: a container full of young girls. Breeders and seers. And word had just come back that they all passed the medical tests, so everybody was getting paid.

He looked at his glass. Empty again. He hadn't remembered drinking it. He poured another.

He was due in Turin early in the pre-dawn morning for the ritual. He had singled out one of the ritual's breeders for himself, a thirteen year-old with jet black hair and almond eyes. Exotic.

Good times.

CHAPTER FIFTY-TWO

SIMON WAS OVERJOYED TO LEARN that Sylvia hailed from Melaka. He was only sorry he did not have enough ingredients to make a real *nyonya laksa* or *asam pedas ikan*. He was, however, able to whip up some *ikan bilis*, *nasi lemak*, and *mie goreng*. They would have to wait for the rice to cook—maybe twenty minutes or so—and in the meantime they chatted about the unique dishes made by the Portuguese community in Melaka. Sylvia was multi-tasking, however, and as she exchanged recipe tips with Simon she was making notes on what she remembered of Malaysian and Indonesian sacred sites. There was no guarantee that Dagon was going to use one of the traditional ones, but if they could eliminate them for one reason or another it might help.

In her heart, though, this seemed like a lost cause. How were they to come up with all of Dagon's far-flung network of cells, and do it all in less than twenty-four hours? She knew they would lose some of the girls who had been trafficked for this purpose and it was killing her, even as she tried to maintain a positive expression. *Who knows?* She thought. *Maybe Dwight is right and finding Angell would solve the whole problem.*

While this was going on, Monroe tried to explain to Harry—who was pounding away at Simon's computer and generating reams of paper printouts on cities and towns he thought might be possible ritual sites—why it was necessary not only to locate the Dagon operations but Gregory Angell as well. He was being a pain in the ass, but Harry didn't have the heart—or maybe the balls—to tell him to leave him alone so he could focus on the job at hand.

Sylvia left Simon to his devices in the kitchen. She walked into the living room and sat down on the couch, studying her notes. There were prehistoric sites in both Malaysia and Indonesia. Since they were settled on Indonesia, she decided to focus on those in that country.

She considered Sumatra as a potential site, as it was closest to Singapore and to Malaysia as well. In Melaka as a child, she had often heard of boats crossing the Straits from Sumatra to come to Malaysia, carrying men looking for work. If Angell wound up in Sumatra, though, there was a good chance no one would ever hear from him again. There were very reactionary groups on the large island, and tribal peoples as well.

No. The most likely destination—if Angell had a choice—would be Java. Java had many modern and relatively diverse cities, some of which, like Jakarta, boasting a considerable expat population as well.

It was generally known that Java Man was discovered on the banks of the Solo River in Java. Java Man was the oldest human fossil ever discovered at the time, in the late nineteenth century, and it caused a great deal of controversy. But Sylvia didn't see how the site of its discovery would make a particularly important ritual site. She made a note of it anyway, just in case.

Then there were the pre-Islamic temples that were scattered throughout the islands, notably on Bali of course, but also almost everywhere in Java as well. Hindu and Buddhist sculptures and massive stoneworks—such as Borobudur—represent the fact that Indonesia was once known as "Far India" to explorers and, indeed, the name Indonesia itself is a reference to its identity as an outpost of Indian culture.

Could Dagon be focused on one of those structures? Borobudur was a famous tourist destination, so that didn't seem likely. Dagon would need privacy. Same with the Prambanan temple complex. In fact, the entire island had temples galore. Where to begin?

But what if it wasn't an actual temple, which would attract attention, but a sacred *place*? The mountains were often sacred in Javanese culture, especially as many of them were also active volcanoes. She had to consider that Dagon might have selected a volcano as a potential site for their hideous ceremony. But how would they manage to move young girls through Indonesia and up the side of a volcano without being seen?

That was the problem. There was no way they could manage

to move a number of young girls in that country unnoticed. They would have to pretend to be a school group or something. Did Monroe know for sure that the girls would all be Eastern European or Japanese? If so, they would be quite noticeable.

Monroe came back into the room after talking with Harry, who was obviously getting frustrated with his constant questions. He saw Sylvia lost in thought, and smelled coconut rice in the kitchen.

Not for the first time he began to wonder if he was finally becoming superfluous. Maybe it was time for him to let go, after all. Most people his age were in nursing homes, or dead. Maybe it was time for him to fulfill his evolutionary responsibility and make way for the younger generations.

"Kids," said Sylvia out loud. It was like she was reading his mind.

"What about them?"

She looked up, a thought taking shape.

"You've been tracking the movement of child slaves out of Europe and Asia, right?"

Monroe nodded. "There is a large and significant trade in human beings, as you know, and especially of children as sex workers and laborers. We discussed this."

"Yes, but this is the vulnerability. I'm looking at Indonesia and wondering how they would move a bunch of white or Japanese kids through the country—or into and out of it—without attracting attention. And of course, they can't."

"I don't see where you're going with this."

"They're not moving European or North Asian kids into Indonesia. It's the fourth largest country in the world in terms of population. They don't have to import children. They'll use their own. And that means whoever is running the Dagon operation in Indonesia is a local."

The implication of that started to dawn on Monroe. *It's true,* he thought. *I am getting old.*

"That means that not all the children we're looking for were trafficked internationally."

"Right. Which means they would never turn up in your search.

But it also means that the children that *were* trafficked were chosen for a specific location and for specific characteristics. Some ... qualities that could not be obtained locally."

"What could those be?"

"Aside from being virgin, what other requirement would make sense in the terms of ritual and ceremony?"

"There's only one, really. I've been blind, I think. I couldn't see what was right in front of me all the time, even though that is all we've been talking about.

"*Genetics.* They are chosen for their race, or ethnicity. Not the ones in Indonesia, most likely. Or anywhere else in Asia. But in Europe and the Americas, yes. Anywhere there is a racially diverse population where any kind of race and ethnic group might be found without anyone taking special notice."

The newspapers and news sites were full of what was happening in the Middle East. The entire Angell mission had begun there, and almost ended there.

There was one man who had the most intimate knowledge of that mission, and he was in New Bedford, Massachusetts, trying to get a judge to sign a search warrant. Monroe grabbed his phone and called Aubrey.

"I'm at the apartment now," answered Aubrey on the first ring. "We've just opened the door. Warrant in hand."

"Excellent. Listen, about Angell ..."

"Still no word yet ..."

"No, no. What I mean is, how all this started. You were in Turkey first, and to that refugee camp, right?"

"Yes, of course. All the details are in my report."

"Yes, I know, but I'm not in my office right now. I just have a question. It's about the Yezidis."

"Go on," Aubrey urged. He had suddenly become quite serious and focused.

"Racially, or ethnically, they are an isolate, right? I mean, they do not intermarry?"

"That's right. The whole reason Angell went nuts in Mosul was due to a series of murders over a Yezidi woman marrying a non-Yezidi man. They have strict rules about that sort of thing."

"You mentioned in your report something about a woman or a girl who became possessed at one point."

"Yes, that's right. We never saw her again, though. Not after the refugee camp."

"She was Yezidi, am I correct?"

"Yes, a woman of about, I don't know, late teens, early twenties maybe."

"And the situation now? With the Yezidis, I mean."

"Well, as you know, they are being decimated. Their homeland is being overrun by the Islamic State."

"And there are many more refugees now than before?"

"Dwight, what's going on?" Aubrey hardly ever used Monroe's given name, so it was an indication that he was worried about his old friend.

"Nothing. Everything. You've been a great help, as always. Let me know what you find, and when you pick up Vanek." And he rang off without saying goodbye.

He turned to Sylvia who was listening to his half of the exchange.

"They're using girls from Iraq. Yezidis. The people that were once said to be devil worshippers. The people who claim they are descended from the Sumerians. The people of the Book. Not that Book, the other Book.

"The *Necronomicon*."

CHAPTER FIFTY-THREE

THE SHAMAN TOOK A VERY LONG TIME, looking at page after page, turning them slowly and carefully. He stared at some of the seals as if in recognition, and at one in particular he gazed very intently. What neither Salim nor Angell could see was that the shaman had entered the seal in his mind and was walking around in it, testing it, pushing at its membrane.

He had become two-dimensional in order to understand the two-dimensional drawing. Then, as he returned to himself in the third-dimension he brought the seal with him so that, in his mind, it became three-dimensional too.

He took a deep breath, then said something to Salim.

"He says that this book was written by a master. That it is older than the *primbon*. He says there are bad people looking for it. That you are in danger."

"No shit, Sherlock," Angell muttered to himself.

"He says those people are here. Now."

"*Here? Now?*"

Salim asked the dukun for clarification. The old man spoke a few syllables, then solemnly handed the Book back to Angell.

"Yes. Here. Now. He says you cannot escape. He says you must ask Lara for help. Only she can protect you. And defeat the armies of … of …?" he spoke again to the dukun, who repeated a word and nodded in the affirmative.

"Of Day-Gone. Does that make sense to you?"

"The Order of Dagon. Yes, unfortunately. But how does Pak Mahmoud know of Dagon?

"And who is Lara?"

Angell wasn't liking this at all. He thought he had escaped the worst of it, and only needed to wait a few days until his fake passport came through and he could decide how he needed to proceed. Now he was back in the thick of it again. This time in a country where he didn't speak the language or understand the culture. And there was this old guy who he didn't know existed until last night, telling him that Dagon was after him. In Indonesia. In the middle of nowhere.

Well, it wasn't the middle of nowhere to them, to be fair. It was their world. Salim and Aji and Pak Mahmoud. But he was there without backup, without weapons of any kind, no JSOC to call in, no air support, no Adnan to cover his six ... This was a time when he could use an Aubrey arranging things, organizing helicopters and Special Forces. But the price was too high.

"I don't know," said Salim. "I never heard of Dagon before. But this dukun, he knows a lot. He talks to the spirits. Maybe they told him."

"Can you ask him again? I'm sorry. I don't speak the language or I would ask him myself ..."

"Hey, man. No worries." He spoke with the dukun and the conversation went on for several minutes, the old man staring off into space as he spoke.

"Okay. It's like this. Years ago there was a strong Dutch presence here. You know that, right?"

"The Dutch East Indies Company."

"Yes, and really a Dutch army, too. A lot of Dutch influence, you might say."

"Nice way to describe colonialism. Influence."

"Well, there were Dutch dukun here too in those days. I mean Dutch ... I don't know what to call them ... witches? Something like that?"

"Well, magicians maybe? Members of secret societies? Like that?"

"Yes, okay. And when the Dutch left after the war there were many graves, many dead Dutch people. Pak Mahmoud talks to them. To their spirits. And to the spirits of the ones who built the temples long ago, before Islam."

"In other words, to the societies that passed away. Dead civilizations."

Salim smiled at Angell's naïveté.

"They are not dead, *pak*. They live within each Indonesian, in one way or another. Some, like the temple builders, are with us every day in our language and our culture. Others, like the Dutch, are with us in our nightmares. Soeharto, too, but Soeharto was a nightmare *we* created. This dukun, he knows this and does not run away from it. So, if he says that this Dagon people are here, then they are here."

"And Lara?"

"You will see."

They started for their car. Angell was surprised to see that the old man, Pak Mahmoud, was following them.

"Yes," said Salim. "He will accompany us to see Lara."

"Oh. I hope it is not too much trouble."

"No, no. Pak likes to ride in automobiles."

"What about Lara? Shouldn't we, I don't know, phone ahead?"

Salim translated his question for the dukun's benefit and they both laughed. It was the first time Angell had seen the old man crack a smile.

"No problem, *pak* Angell. She knows we're coming."

They drove east along the coast road, heading for a beach area known as Parangtritis. Salim explained that it belonged to the Sultanate of Yogyakarta, a city somewhat to the north of the beach and in the shadow of Mount Merapi: a live volcano that exerted a kind of mystical influence over the entire area. Yogyakarta was also the only sultanate left in Indonesia, and maintained a special relationship with the government in Jakarta, the sultan answering directly to the President of the Republic.

A sultan was a kind of Islamic royalty. It was a Muslim title, which made what Salim said next shocking to Angell.

"The Sultan has a wife, of course, who sits on a throne next to his at important functions. But he has another wife, too. A kind of ghost wife. She is the Goddess of the Southern Ocean, and he must meet her at specific times, in private, to ensure the safety and security of his people."

"Wait a minute, Salim. Are you saying that the Sultan—an Islamic king—is married to a Goddess?"

"Yes, but that is because he is Javanese. It is normal."

"And he must meet with this Goddess, and everyone knows about it?"

"Of course. It is necessary."

"And what … I mean, what does he do when he meets her?"

Salim merely raised an eyebrow.

"Oh, come on! That's not true!"

"It is, *pak*. It is an important part of our culture. There is a special dance at the Kraton—the Sultan's palace—where the Goddess sometimes appears. The dancers make a space for her during the performance. It is said that sometimes she will participate and that many do not notice because every place is filled, but at the end of the dance they realize that one is missing. That they had been watching a dance with all dancers, but it was an illusion. You understand?"

"You mean that if they were supposed to have ten dancers they had only nine, but everyone saw ten?"

Salim beamed. "Yes! That is right. The tenth dancer, that was Lara Kidul."

"Wait. *Lara*? The same Lara we are going to meet?"

"The Goddess of the Southern Ocean."

"How do we … how can one meet a Goddess?"

Salim raised another eyebrow at Angell.

"Do you mean, *pak* Angell, that you have never been in love?"

In ancient Sumer, the king would ascend the ziggurat at the New Year celebration. At the top there was a special chamber, and in that chamber the king would meet with the goddess Inanna. They would engage in sexual intercourse, and that would ensure the safety and security of his people for another year. "Spirit of the Sky, remember!"

In modern Indonesia, the same event is held on a day sacred to the Javanese calendar and the Sumerian king becomes the Javanese sultan. Inanna becomes the Goddess of the Southern Ocean, Lara Kidul. Her color is green, like that of the Tara introduced to India and Tibet by the Buddhist scholar Atisha, who learned his religion in the ancient Buddhist kingdom in Indonesia that predated the arrival of Islam.

Angell was putting all this together as Salim spoke, and as Pak Mahmoud sat silently, looking out the window.

The Green Tara. Where had he seen her recently? It was in China, at the temple where the monks were helping him to escape. Her visage shone on him in his mind from that silken thangka on the wall. Was she mocking him, or blessing him?

It was a little after eight am by now. He had been up since the cry of the muezzin at 4, and had not had much sleep at all in the past two days. He started to doze off when Pak Mahmoud pointed to a bungalow nestled between two crags along the beach.

"*Di sini*," he said, in Indonesian. *Here.*

CHAPTER FIFTY-FOUR

"VANEK'S IN THE WIND," said Aubrey into the phone. He was standing in Vanek's apartment with a trio of cops, New Bedford's finest, and they were coming up empty.

"Did you find anything useful in the apartment?"

Aubrey was standing in the middle of what, for all practical intents and purposes, was a studio apartment. One wall was taken up by a bookshelf with the predictable selection of books by Kenneth Grant, Michael Bertiaux, Israel Regardie, James Wasserman and, of course, Aleister Crowley. One shelf had books by Lovecraft and about Lovecraft. The lower shelf was stuffed with books on psychology by R.D. Laing, Wilhelm Reich, and Carl Jung. There was even something called *Tantric Temples,* a heavy hardcover book that had a lot of photographs of weird statues in the Javanese jungles. That one was filled with marginalia in what was presumably Vanek's own hand.

"Nah. There's nothing much here. An old desktop PC. We're taking the hard drive back to their technical staff to see if they can do something with it, but I don't think he would have been that stupid to leave anything incriminating on it. But who knows?"

"So the apartment is clean?"

"Well, I wouldn't say that. It looks and smells like an old cowboy died in here. But there isn't much we can use, I'm afraid."

"Shouldn't *we* take custody of the hard drive?"

Aubrey thought about it for a second, but disagreed.

"I would have to bring it back to DC and we could lose valuable time. I say let the locals handle it. The computer was password protected, so once their technical services people bypass it, they'll let us know what they have. They understand this is an urgent matter of national security. I trust them on this."

"Okay, you're probably right. I'll have someone at NSA run a wire to their tech unit so that we can access the files remotely if possible. What else?"

"Our guy in Singapore isn't talking, but he had a cell phone on him and we traced one of his calls out to a sat phone in the South China Sea. That was either Angell or the pirates who tried to kidnap him. So we have their last location."

"What do you mean?"

"After the call, whoever was on the other end deep-sixed the phone. I mean really deep-sixed it. From what we can determine it's at the bottom of the ocean."

"So it's a dead end."

"Not completely. We triangulated a lot of comms traffic from that general area at the time of the call. There were two ships in the vicinity of the sat phone. One seems to be on its way to the port of Jakarta and should be there in a few hours. The other is also going to Indonesia, but to the southern coast. That ship is too big for a small port. They need something larger if they're to put in anywhere there. There are only one or two possibilities and we're working on it."

"Okay, let's stay on top of this. Can we have someone meet the ship in Jakarta?"

"On it. And we'll keep looking for the other one. Angell has to be on one or the other."

"Right. I have to get back to my team. We're working on the location for the ritual ..."

"You know," said Aubrey, hefting the *Tantric Temples* book in one hand while he used the other to hold the phone. "Vanek has a book specifically about temples in Indonesia. He's written a lot of notes in the margins. Hard to make out, though."

"Bring it with you."

CHAPTER FIFTY-FIVE

By the time Aubrey and the local police were breaking down the door to Vanek's apartment, the man they sought was already on the road.

Vanek decided he needed a head start. He had his final orders from the Dark Lord, and there wasn't any reason for him to hang around New Bedford. The ritual was timed for Wednesday night, so he could take his time and make easy stages across the State. There were one or two places he wanted to see first, anyway. A bookstore in one town. A pub where he used to hang out with his imitation punk band in the other. He would take it low and slow, and be in Whately in enough time to set up the ritual.

He mailed a letter to that kid in Whately, advising him that the Advanced Adepts were on their way to his location and to be ready and at the site by 11:30 pm. He got a kick out of tormenting the newbies. He liked to spook them, make them see things. He loved to assert his authority over people who were more gifted, more intelligent than he was, but he didn't often have the chance. Recruitments were way down. So he had to be satisfied with the lame, the halt, and the blind (as he called them). Not many opportunities for fun in the Orders anymore.

It used to be so easy to get sex and drugs in the old days, especially from the lower degrees. Now everybody was too hip, too PC to be easily manipulated. Too friggin' healthy, too. *Vegans.* Jesus.

He thought back to his parents. Funny; he hadn't thought about them in years. Maybe decades. But they had the right idea back then. Sex and drugs and rock-n-roll. Too bad he had just missed the Sixties.

There was a lot of bad press these days about cult leaders and the like. Everybody was getting wary of them. It was better that they went off-grid the way they were. Dagon and the OTS and the Archon Argon, or Agon, or Aging Assholes, or whatever the hell the

Dark Lord called his group. Off-grid was the better strategy; social media was a cesspool. Everybody claiming all sorts of advanced degrees and enlightenment. The competition was fierce. It had to be more respectable to go retro and handle everything by snail mail. More exclusive that way. Make them work for it. Make them wait for an answer. Make them *think*. Defeats the whole purpose of social media and "instant messaging," and that's the point.

Trouble was, no one did. Just people like that kid in Whately. He was damned lucky to find him, though. Whately was on the list of towns. It was the closest one to him, so he focused on it. Drove down there three, four times in the last few months. To the last remaining bookstore in the area. Slipped those ads in between the pages of the Crowley books, the Dion Fortune books, even the *Secret Doctrine*. Finally got a nibble.

This train of thought went on for miles. Vanek was in no hurry to get anywhere. He was just happy to be out on the road. He was the head of an Order that had fewer total members than a single Theosophical lodge, but that was okay. The ones he had paid his bills. He had that apartment in New Bedford and the VW Bug he was driving. He had more money stashed in various places around the country for when he finally split from America. He had run the odd scam here and there, to be sure. Eventually someone in some government cubicle somewhere would figure it out. In the meantime he hoped this ritual worked and that he would get the recognition he deserved. If not, fuck 'em. He was gone. Italy, probably. Maybe Prague. Some place cool like that.

Not back to England, though. No fucking way. He had to laugh when he remembered his phone call to the old pervs in Wales. He couldn't resist telling them his name. Maybe that was a mistake. He used a burner phone anyway. So that was cool, right?

He hadn't understood at first why he was supposed to make that call at all, though. That old couple had been out of the picture for, like, decades. But the Dark Lord said that we could not assume anything. That they were loyal to the Order. Initiates. They had to be notified in case the Old Ones needed them. In case the Old Ones paid them a visit after the ritual.

The Dark Lord wouldn't do it himself. He never phoned anyone. So it was up to old Vanek to pick up the slack. Part of him hated doing it, of course. He hated fucking England and the fucking English accents. Something visceral. A lot of people, Americans mostly, thought they sounded posh. *He* thought they sounded like little kids pretending to be posh. Ugh.

Well, he went where he was sent and did what they told him to do. He had never had a regular job in his life, so he was grateful for that much and could cut them all a little of that famous Vanek slack.

In the meantime, he needed a drink. It was only 8 pm. He had time. A lot of time.

CHAPTER FIFTY-SIX

"I'VE IDENTIFIED A NUMBER OF THE TOWNS you listed, Simon. Thankfully there are not many, at least not in the fifty states. There were a number of Babylons, especially the one on Long Island in New York. I did come across some chatter about a mysterious group renting a place called the Ocean Castle. That's also on Long Island. It used to belong to a film producer who was murdered."

"I remember that case. Roy Radin, right? Murdered in California?"

"That's the one."

"Okay, that's a start. And a likely one. Any information on who's renting it and for when?"

"It's some kind of shell corporation, but they've rented it for tonight and tomorrow night."

"That's confirmation of the timetable, then. We were right about the Rosetta mission. That could be it."

"There are others, though."

"Go on."

"We have a few from the Lovecraft end of things. Of course, Providence and Boston are on the list but there isn't much we can do with those yet until we have more detail. But he traveled a bit in his life, as you pointed out, and a lot of that was to Florida. I've printed out some city maps of the places that show up, and they're here in this stack. Nothing jumps out at me so far, no ancient sites or occult lodges, but I'm neck deep in algorithms here. You would be more likely to spot something relevant than I would."

"No problem. I'll give these a look while you keep searching."

Simon hefted the six inch stack of paper and walked back to the living room. At the bottom of the pile was an aerial photo of the area around DeLand, Florida.

Monroe looked up as he entered the room.

"What's that?"

"Possible leads. More importantly, though, we have information that a group has rented out an infamous mansion on Long Island's south shore for tonight and tomorrow night. There's cult connections to the mansion going back to the 1980s, including drugs, murder, and murder-for-hire. There's a link to the Son of Sam cult as well."

"Do you have an address?"

"Sure." He handed Monroe the address of the Ocean Castle and Monroe went to a corner of the room to make a call.

As he did so, Simon dropped the sheaf of papers he was holding. He bent down to collect them, hoping that they weren't in some particular order, and saw a sheet with an aerial view of some kind of park or outdoor installation on it. It was stapled to a map of a town in Florida, near Orlando.

Simon sat down and looked at the aerial shot. He turned it a few times, then went into the room where Harry was still working.

"Where's that book I was looking at? The one with the map of Philae in it?"

The desk near the computer was a mess of books and documents, but Simon found what he was looking for and dragged it out of the middle of the pile.

He flipped to the map and compared Philae to the aerial view of the park. He turned it around a few times and tried to overlay the one over the other.

He mumbled a "thanks" to Harry, who grunted in return, and then walked back to the living room.

Monroe had just gotten off the call. "I notified the local police in the Hamptons. They're going to take a look at who rented Ocean Castle and get back to me. They know it's urgent. They just don't know why. In the meantime they're going to have a car stake it out from a safe distance to see who's going in and out."

Simon handed him the two sheets of paper.

"Look at this. Is it my imagination or do these two maps look alike?"

Sylvia interrupted them both.

"I think I've got it," she said, taking off her glasses and letting them swing on their chain around her neck.

Monroe looked up from Simon's maps.

"Got what?"

"A location in Indonesia for Dagon."

But her startling news was suddenly drowned out by a call from Aubrey.

They knew where Vanek was headed.

CHAPTER FIFTY-SEVEN

IN THE SMALL TOWN OF WHATELY, Massachusetts Jean-Paul held onto the envelope with sweating hands. He had to be careful or the ink would get smudged and the stamp would fall off. He wiped his hands on his jeans and flattened the envelope against his thigh.

It was finally going to happen.

They told him he had to be ready at a moment's notice. And now, the letter in his hand proved it. At midnight that very night— November 12, 2014—he had to be standing in the middle of the tobacco field, waiting for the Order to show up. He had been waiting for this for weeks. He thought they would meet him on October 31, Halloween after all, but they were obviously too cool for that. Amateur night, probably. So November 12 it was. A friggin' Wednesday. No matter. It wasn't like he had to go to school or shit like that.

They didn't tell him to bring anything. No robe, no sword, no wand. Nothing. He was just supposed to show up, like Harry Potter waiting for the Hogwarts train. Okay, then.

He stared at the clock. It was only 8:00 pm. A long way to go. Maybe he should, like, fast or something? Do another LBR?

Shave?

Shower. That was it. He should take a shower.

"Bless me, Father, for I have sinned. My last shower was two days ago," he said to himself. He was doing a lot of that lately. Talking to himself, not showering.

He knew there were special prayers you had to say when you performed a ritual shower. It was there in all the grimoires. It took him a few minutes but he finally found the right one.

He went into the bathroom and took of his clothes. Then he put them back on again. He had forgotten to bring fresh ones in with him.

He found a relatively clean set of underwear, a pair of skinny black pants, and a shirt that was almost black. He brought them into the bathroom, and ran the water.

Then left again. He had forgotten the book with the prayer.

Back in the bathroom, he once again removed his clothes. He did it slowly, with intention, but it seemed too much like a strip-tease so he just finished undressing and stepped into the shower, the book open in his right hand so he could read the Latin incantation.

Asperges me, domine, hyssopo et mundabor; lavabis me et super nivem dealbabor.

But it came out as:

"Ass purge me, dominos, hippo et wunderbar…"

Good enough. Whatever an "ass purge" was. It sounded rank. And why should the prayer be in Latin? He hoped it wouldn't be thought of as, like, cultural appropriation or something. He didn't want to piss off any Latin people.

(The demons sat on their haunches over the shower stall, their dripping saliva mixing with the hot water from the showerhead, hissing on the porcelain tiles like acid rain. They were hungry. An idiot would do just fine.)

He finished the shower, taking care to soap up his pits so they wouldn't offend. He had run out of deodorant like a week ago. Okay, two weeks. It's not like he had an active social life.

Oh. Right. Social life. That reminded him.

He logged onto Facebook, Twitter, Instagram, Tinder (well, he could dream), and half a dozen other social media sites on which he posted photos of himself in black robes with his Masonic sword, making mean satanic faces for the selfies. He bitched on there about his former girlfriend who wasn't really his girlfriend but who dumped him anyway. He blocked her, she blocked him, he unfriended her, she unfriended him, he unfollowed her, she unfollowed him. And so it went for a few weeks, played out on social media in front of all their friends. Well, her friends, anyway. He cursed her, using funky language he picked up from some comic book style sorcerer. He called himself Frater Azazel, because that was the cool name of the demon in that movie, *Fallen*, with Denzel.

Okay, now what?

It was about 8:15 pm. He would continue his fast. He hadn't eaten anything since 6:30 pm, and he was feeling it.

He picked up a book at random and tried to read, but almost immediately fell asleep.

Vanek's silver VW bug had seen better days, but before he left he got a tune-up at the garage and they told him it would make the trip, no problem. He would meet the others at the diner in town, and after a quick dinner they would proceed to the tobacco field and wait for the kid. If his car crapped out in Whately, he would hitch a ride with one of the others at least as far as Amherst. He could stay overnight in the college town and take the train back in the morning.

The Dark Lord had told him to be sure to conclude the ritual by 12:30 am. All of the others would be synchronized to the same hour. Dagon would admit of no mistakes, and they would know—they would *know*—if he had screwed anything up.

He was carrying everything they would need. The others were told not to bring anything that could be traced back to any of them. They were to go so far as to remove all labels from their clothing and leave identification in their cars before meeting him at the diner. He would pay for dinner in cash. No cell phones, obviously, or tablets. As for the ritual, they had all done it so many times before they had it memorized.

Vanek started to turn on the car radio, but then thought better of it. Silence was better. He should be focused on the evening ahead. This would be a great day for the Order, his Order, and would ensure its continued existence for a long time to come. And who knows? Maybe one day they would grow to a thousand members, or even more.

Vanek, of course, was unaware of the real dimensions of the ritual in which he would participate that evening. If it was performed correctly—and She always performed the rites correctly, with power and grace—then there would be no "continued existence" for there would be no "long time to come" and most certainly no "thousand members."

The Dark Lord sat back and contemplated what he had accomplished so far. He had arrogated to himself leadership of a defunct occult Order, one whose few remaining members had been fighting over their own claims to legitimacy; he had used it to infiltrate other occult Orders, and had eventually subsumed them all. Dagon was satisfied with his strategy and his leadership. It would be early in the morning on November 13 his time when the ritual in America would be accomplished. After that, who knows? Perhaps a position within Dagon of somewhat higher authority and more responsibility?

Like his underling Vanek, the Dark Lord had no earthly clue as to what was about to transpire.

Her car was ready to have a heart attack, or something. There was smoke coming out of the hood. She knew that was bad. They had just passed the exit for Amherst. She could make it a little further if she pushed it, and decided to wait on the shoulder for the engine to cool off. She had bottled water in the car, and would use it to fill the radiator.

She pulled over and turned off the engine. It was suddenly so very quiet. Hardly any traffic on 91 at this hour. Night was falling, but there was still light in the sky to the west, as if the sun was looking at her over his shoulder. The stars were coming out, like the windows in a huge apartment building in a floating astral city. She imagined cocktails, a nice dinner, some soft jazz in one of those apartments. Someone else reading a book in another. Maybe someone else making love in another. The thought almost made her weep.

She had had to stop so many times on the way across Connecticut and up 91. The crying jags would come out of nowhere; she would start trembling for no reason and would have to pull over and collect herself. She almost turned back once or twice, asking herself what she thought she was doing. She wasn't a kid anymore. She couldn't just take off on a whim and drive around aimlessly. She had kids herself. She had responsibilities.

She stirred herself. Making sure her kids were okay—they seemed to be napping at last—she got out of the car and opened the hood. Just as she thought. Her radiator had overheated. She must have forgotten to do something. Oil or … something. She was usually very good with cars. She had had to be. It's just that she couldn't think. She was still worried about the genetic results and Chromo-Test sending her plane tickets for California. The more she thought about it, the worse it sounded.

Above her, something flew past. A light briefly touched the ground in front of her, then disappeared.

"A plane," she thought, absently. "Piper Cub, maybe. Beechcraft Bonanza." What was that line from the movie? "Cadillac of the skies!"

But she hadn't noticed that there was no engine noise.

In fact, no sound at all.

CHAPTER FIFTY-EIGHT

VANEK TOOK THE EXIT FOR WHATELY, Massachusetts. He still had a lot of time. He would meet the others at the diner as arranged and they would go over their schedule. They would be cautious, of course, and speak only in code. Few people had ever seen him in person, so no one would know what he looked like. He avoided photographs as much as possible, and lived a somewhat reclusive life anyway. The only people he hung out with were other occultists and some musicians he knew from when he was in a band. These days, he tried to maintain an appropriately aloof reputation. It was his brand. And the Order's brand. A certain amount of dignity was required after all those years of drugs and unemployment.

He drove into town and found the diner without any problem. Ahead of him a woman and her two kids walked into the place. He hoped they would not be noisy. He hated children.

He went inside and got a booth. The others hadn't arrived yet, so he would order something and hold the table.

The waitress came over and handed him a big laminated menu. "Coffee?"

"Could you make that tea, please? Black."

"Sure thing. I'll be back."

She walked down the aisle to the booth in the back, where the woman and her two boys were seated. The boys were obviously different ages but they looked very much alike. And how cute they were! The waitress brought their menus and asked if they wanted water.

"Yes, please," answered the two boys, almost at once. Their mother smiled and said she would like a cup of coffee, and how much farther to the Vermont border?

Vanek found it unnerving.

The mother was seated with her back to him, but the two boys were on the opposite side, which meant they were looking right at him. Really looking. Like he owed them money, or something. When they saw that he noticed them, they smiled as if they were old friends.

Kids. How he hated them.

He turned his attention back to the menu.

Gloria noted that the Whately Diner was open twenty-four hours. It had a long, Formica-topped counter with round stools and those little jukeboxes at each booth. There was a neon sign outside that said "Filling Station." It was a little cheesy but the food was hearty and satisfying, and the sense that this was a real diner from the days before fast food ruined the family restaurant industry was comforting to her. She looked around and could almost feel at home, in a way that she didn't back in Providence with all her bad memories and struggles.

The Eggs Benedict and hash browns looked good, even if it was a breakfast dish and it was time for dinner, but she ordered it anyway and the waitress didn't bat an eye. The kids had meatloaf, which looked pretty good, too.

Vanek ordered a salad and drank his tea. It was almost time for his crew to show up, and he was thinking better of it. The diner was small, and he was suddenly a little worried that they would be noticed and remembered. He and the woman and her kids were the only customers so far, and if the place didn't fill up soon he would be too conspicuous. Maybe he should just finish up and wait somewhere outside where he wouldn't be seen by the wait staff.

Or those obnoxious kids.

That's when he saw the kids flipping through the music machine at their table and groaned.

"Oh, crap," he said. That does it. If they start playing bubble-gum he's history. He signaled the waitress for the check. Just pay and get out. They could have their meeting in the parking lot, or somewhere else.

"Anything else, hon?"

"No, thank you. Just the check."

"Right away," she said, and walked back to the counter.

He looked out the window and could see that the first of his contacts was just arriving.

Awkward.

It was already dark, and the parking lot was starting to fill up with people stopping by for dinner or just for some coffee and dessert. The members of the Order were arriving and mixing in with the regular customers, or trying to.

What is it with the occultists I know that they all try to look like bikers? He thought. Leather jackets, shaved heads, goatees, tattoos … it was like a *Sons of Anarchy* road show. And the women were not much better. And for chrissakes, there was one woman with a Baphomet t-shirt! What the hell was she thinking?

Vanek paid the check, left a ten percent tip, and headed out the door, tapping the incoming cultists on the shoulder as he did so and pointing to the parking lot.

They got the message, and signaled each other to meet outside.

Gloria thought the Eggs Benedict was the best she ever had. Her boys were doing some serious damage to their meatloaf, and for once she felt somewhat at peace. She was in a strange town, far from home, and free. The waitress came by, refilled her coffee cup, and smiled at them. The food was good, the place was friendly, and the price was right. It was a beautiful fall evening and the autumn colors were to die for.

She thought of continuing to drive all night, but that problem with her radiator concerned her. She might look for a place to spend the night. It would make a dent in her cash, but they couldn't sleep in the car. It wasn't safe, anyway. She would ask the waitress where a good, cheap motel was and maybe they would head that way and watch HBO.

Vanek met his ragtag group of initiates in the parking lot. All six were present, two women and four men. With Vanek that made seven, which was the number they were looking for.

"We're meeting the kid at midnight at the place we discussed. He's probably so jacked he may be already there."

They laughed.

"You all know your parts. You've made the preliminary arrangements. I understand all is in readiness?"

They nodded.

"It is of utmost importance, and I can't stress this enough, that the ritual culminates precisely at 12:30. That is when the Gate will be opened. We don't know how long it will remain open, so we have to take advantage of this opportunity like never before. You have all trained for this. You all know what to do. There can be no hesitation. The equipment is in my car. You will each take one instrument and leave here. Rendezvous at the site at precisely 11:30 pm. If the kid is there, calm him down and make sure he's in the right frame of mind. We don't want him to start screaming or chicken out at the last moment. Worse comes to worse, just hold him and gag him. Understood?"

They all nodded again, solemnly.

"Okay. Follow me."

They walked over to his VW bug, and he opened the hood of the car—which, in a VW bug, is the trunk—and he showed them the implements.

They were all standard grimoire weapons. Several swords, several smaller knives, some curved and some straight, and one or two others. They reached in to take the blades and at that moment the car was flooded with searchlights.

Monroe had been busy. Aubrey made a few calls and with the license plate of Vanek's vehicle and Vanek's credit card information it took him all of twenty minutes to determine that Vanek had been heading west to Route 91 in Massachusetts. Monroe had an unmarked State Police car pick up Vanek when he turned north on 91 and follow him all the way to Whately. At that point, the Staties waited for instructions.

Whately. Really?

It wasn't spelled exactly the same way, but it was close enough for government work.

Monroe told Sylvia and Harry that Whateley was the name of the old Wizard in "Dunwich" and his albino daughter, Lavinia Whateley and her troubled son, Wilbur. It was the "narrative" that was at the heart of the Dagon cult, the framing of their esoteric philosophy in story form—something that had been intuited or channeled or however you want to call it by H. P. Lovecraft but had also been evoked by Aleister Crowley in 1907. But it was too perfect, and Monroe worried that it was some kind of setup. Then the State cop phoned in to let him know that Vanek was standing around with a group of leather clad losers staring into a car with a cache of edged weapons and what appeared to be leather restraints.

Monroe thought for a second. Follow them to see where they go? Or just pick them up and sweat them? If they split up, it would be a headache. They wouldn't know which ones to tail. Better to grab them all now and hope one of them breaks, and breaks fast.

"Pick them up, officer."

"Roger that."

Suddenly the parking lot was filled with police cars and flashing lights. Seven individuals were arrested for possession of edged weapons in excess of four inches in length. Vanek was arrested on terrorism charges. Three of the others had drug possession charges added to their weapons count. Two had outstanding warrants. And all seven were charged with conspiracy.

The cops knew they couldn't make all the charges stick which meant they probably couldn't hold them very long, but they only needed them in custody long enough for this guy Monroe to get his ass over to Whately and interrogate them.

So off they went to the local jail to await the cavalry from DC.

Gloria got up from her booth after paying the check. She marched her kids to the bathroom first, to make sure they didn't have to go once they got to the car. She had asked the waitress for a good motel and she was told there was one on Route 5. She got the directions, thanked her, and left a good tip.

All fed, washed, and refreshed, they left the diner and headed for their car.

Jean-Paul was too amped to wait much longer. He had to go to the ritual site and check it out. He had, like three hours to go yet, but he wanted to scope it and see what to expect. Maybe they were already there, and would appreciate him showing up early?

He asked his mother for the keys to the car and let himself out of the house. It was a brisk fall evening. Leaves were swirling around. It would snow soon.

Vanek was freaking out. He knew that the others did not have any identification on them. They didn't even have labels in their clothes. As long as they didn't talk, they should be okay. They did have car keys on them, there was no way to avoid that, and those would eventually be traced to their cars in the lot. That, in turn, would reveal their names and addresses. The cops would have the whole crew. He knew that most of the charges were bogus, but he couldn't rely on his people to be smart and keep quiet.

As for him, he was toast.

They not only knew who he was, they had been following him for miles. Terrorism charges? That could only mean one thing. He was on their radar somehow. Somebody was tracking him. Probably for awhile. And now the ritual was ruined. He wasn't as afraid of the police as he was of Dagon. Once Dagon knew what had happened, they would go insane.

Regardless, he would have to let them know what happened. He had to warn Dagon at once, even if it meant he would spend the rest of his life in prison. And if they ever linked him to the other rituals, life in prison was the best he could hope for. In fact, it was probably the best thing that could happen to him, as long as he was safe from Dagon.

Who was he kidding? They would reach out to him inside as easily as outside. If he had ruined the Opening of the Gate … it wasn't only Dagon he had to fear.

The Old Ones had no sense of humor.

Gloria backed up out of the parking lot and headed south, looking for a sign for Route 5. It was really dark now in the small Massachusetts town, and she couldn't make out the street signs.

She stopped at an intersection and opened her window to look out at the mess of signs pointing every which way. She was suddenly very tired and wanted to lie down for awhile.

A light came on from somewhere—maybe a truck?—and shone directly onto the sign she needed. Then it winked out. She made the turn onto Route 5, amazed at her good fortune.

A shadow passed her overhead, not making a sound.

CHAPTER FIFTY-NINE

S<small>YLVIA BROKE DOWN HER REASONING</small> for believing that Angell was headed to Yogyakarta.

"You said you had two ships, one going to Jakarta and the other one to the southern coast. The southern coast of Java is replete with stories about mysticism, esotericism, and the like. Borobudur is there, the largest open-air Buddhist temple in the world. And it's also considered an example of Vajrayana Buddhism, the type of Buddhism you find in Tibet. Somehow that matches with what you've been telling me about Angell in Nepal, and what Simon was telling us about Tibetan terminology being appropriate here because we are dealing with something they understand.

"Then you have Prambanan, which is more traditional Indian—Hindu—than Buddhist. Statues of gods and goddesses, Shiva and Parvati among them. It's also in the same vicinity. And you have the volcano, an active volcano, that you can see from virtually everywhere in that city.

"You also have the Taman Sari, a kind of recreational palace to the south of the Kraton, the Sultan's palace. There are stories that an underground tunnel leads from the Taman Sari to the southern coast. A tunnel. I mean, it touches on all the main points of your theme, right?"

"It does seem to, yes."

She continued, "But there's another aspect which is even more direct. The idea of intercourse between human beings and the Old Ones. You had that at Sumer, in Mesopotamia. You've had that in a lot of cultures around the world. And in Yogyakarta, you have a present day practice of exactly that—the Sultan with the goddess. The Sultan himself cohabits with a goddess on specific days determined by a unique calendar, just like Simon was telling us about the Dagon system of calculating space and time. It actually happens. To this day.

"That is where Angell is heading, and he may be there already."

Monroe asked, "What about twins? Twins seems to be a necessary element."

"Indigenous Indonesian cultures are replete with stories about divine twins, divine siblings, or beings that are the result of human and divine intercourse. There are many to choose from, and we don't have time to figure out which specific myth they will be using. What we do have is a place and time. Granted, the place has to be narrowed down a bit, but I think this is the right approach. And, anyway, you need to find Angell and he can't be that hard to find in the middle of Indonesia."

It was Harry's turn to butt in.

"Aren't we dealing with two separate issues here? Isn't finding these children our first priority? How did this get mixed up with a search for that college professor? No offense, sir, but he seems a little like the white whale in all of this. I mean, why did you need him in the first place?"

Monroe was getting tired, and testy, and he probably had to get on a plane or a helicopter in the next thirty minutes and fly to Whately, Massachusetts.

"I needed him to look for the Book. The one they are all basing these rituals upon. I thought you understood that."

"I don't get it, though. Why was it so necessary to have Angell look for the Book? Why couldn't some cowboy do it? You've got access to all these hard core types with the SEALs, JSOC, all those people. You could've just sent a few of those in and it would have ended quite differently. It seems to me that Angell didn't bring very much to the table."

"Well, in the first place, Angell had the languages, the expertise in the diverse cultures of the places he had to go to, and the experience of being under fire a few times."

"Granted, but you could have had that with any dozen other people from academia."

Monroe raised an eyebrow.

"Okay, maybe not a dozen. Maybe two or three. But I still don't understand. Why Angell? What did he have that the others didn't?"

Monroe frowned and looked away.

Harry went on, "And why that particular copy of the Book? That doesn't make any sense, either. They could have photocopied the damned thing. Put it through a scanner or something. They could have run off a thousand copies. A million! Why that particular Book and that particular professor? In this day and age? It's … it's friggin' medieval."

The silence that greeted the question formed a kind of vacuum into which they all poured their own thoughts, questions, and speculations. The only one who wasn't affected that way was Monroe, because he knew the truth. And it was distasteful.

"He had something no one else did," Monroe finally replied. "Something that—combined with his unique skill set—made him positively unique. And indispensable. The Book, too. Same thing. We needed them both together, in the same place, at the same time."

Harry opened his eyes and his arms wide as if to say "What?"

"His DNA."

Harry looked at Sylvia, who looked at Simon, who had the grace to look out the window.

"His *DNA*?"

Monroe started searching through some papers.

"Are you familiar with the work that has been done in extracting DNA from ancient manuscripts?"

In 2009, a researcher at the University of North Carolina made headlines when he revealed that DNA could be obtained from old books. Since parchment was made from animal skins and even the bindings could be sourced from organic material, DNA would be present in the pages and covers. Similar studies had already been done on the Dead Sea Scrolls. The type of DNA retrieved could be everything from the type of cow that produced the skin to the DNA of persons who handled the books, including bacteria and other sources of genetic material.

Monroe found what he was looking for: a new report in Simon's stack that raised the possibility that non-invasive techniques could be found to date and analyze the DNA from parchments. He passed it over to Harry while continuing to explain.

"This revealed why everyone felt it was so important to have the actual Book in their possession and not merely a copy. At first I thought they were afraid of errors in copying or duplicating. Then I wondered if the Book was really a palimpsest with writing that had been concealed—erased and written over—and they wanted access to the original to have it analyzed under ultraviolet light."

He took a deep breath, and continued.

"It was then that I realized that they needed the physical book for another reason altogether. Of course, they would not have been aware of the DNA angle so clearly as it is a relatively new discovery and the search for the Book has been going on for quite some time. No, it had to be a concept that would have been common a century ago. Centuries, actually, and that's when it came to me.

"Relics. Voodoo dolls. Relics and voodoo dolls."

He sat back with a self-satisfied smile on his face.

It was Sylvia who asked the question.

"What are you talking about, Dwight?"

"I was hoping you'd ask me that question."

"As if we weren't…"

"Churches celebrate their Mass on an altar that has a piece of a saint in it, or under it, am I correct?"

"Yes. Sure."

"It is believed that the relic of the saint carries some spiritual power. Same with pieces of the True Cross, or the Shroud of Turin. There is a subtle connection between that piece of organic substance and the spiritual force of the person from which it was extracted.

"The same is true of voodoo dolls. The old formula requires

that a hair or a fingernail or some other part of the target person be incorporated into the doll. Again, a kind of relic, only in this case the person is still alive.

"These relics are believed to carry spiritual force, a connection with the original person across which some charge is transmitted or received. In actuality, what these items have in common is DNA. If you put a piece of your enemy's skin or a hair from his head, you are potentially holding his DNA in your hand: the actual program that created the entire human being. Something more intimate and much more comprehensive than his fingerprint or his photograph. Him, in miniature. It is a belief that lies behind the saintly relic as well as the scary voodoo doll. Same principle, different execution."

Realization dawned on all their faces. What Monroe was saying was slowly becoming obvious, but raised even more questions.

"Do you mean that the Book contains DNA, and that the DNA is somehow linked to Angell and *his* DNA?"

"Precisely. The Book was originally in the possession of Angell's ancestor, Professor George Angell. It then went through several hands before it finally rested in Gregory Angell's, the man we are looking for. From his ancestor to him, which means there is a good possibility that there is some similarity of DNA between the two."

"So the Book is like a relic, in the way the Catholic Church understands the term."

"Yes, that is what I mean. And Angell completes the circuit, as it were. Angell holding that Book collapses time to the moment in 1926 when an old Nazi known as Tanzler stole it from Professor George Angell during a robbery in Providence, Rhode Island."

"And that means ..."

"That means," said Simon, chiming in, "the moment when Cthulhu was making its presence known to his followers, the infamous 'Call of Cthulhu.' That occurred in 1926, according to the story, which we now know was at least partially true. Lovecraft became aware of the Cthulhu Cult that year, and stole the Cthulhu file from George Angell at that time. This was during the same period that a friend of his, an art school student at RISD, was having visions of Cthulhu."

"For our Gregory Angell to have possession of the Book now is basically to return it to its rightful owner," finished Monroe.

There was silence for a long while as everyone tried to digest what Monroe and Simon were saying. It was Harry, again, who broke the silence.

"Why is that such a good idea? Why should we complete the circuit, as it were?"

"Good question, but it should be obvious by now. George Angell was given the Book so that he could figure out what was going on. He had compiled the file known as 'Cthulhu Cult' because of concern he and his colleagues had over this phenomenon. He never had the chance to start his investigation in earnest, because the Book was stolen from him and wound up with the Nazis in the 1930s."

"So, you're saying …"

"I'm saying that it is now up to his descendant, Gregory Angell, to finish what George had started almost eighty-eight years ago."

Simon looked up at that, stunned.

"Eighty-eight years?"

Monroe looked puzzled. "Yes. Why?"

"I don't know. Call me paranoid, but … eighty-eight? Two 8s?"

"Ah," gasped Monroe. "Why didn't I see it?"

Simon turned to the others.

"Eighty-eight is a Neo-Nazi expression. They use it in place of 'Heil Hitler.' The letter 'H' is the eighth letter of the English alphabet. Two eights, two h's. Heil Hitler. This year, 2014, is the eighty-eighth year since the Necronomicon was stolen by Tanzler and given to the Nazis."

Sylvia groaned. "So on top of everything else there's a Nazi angle to all this?"

"Not necessarily. It could be a coincidence, after all. But the Nazis were deeply concerned with eugenics, and creating a master race, and all that. A ritual of the Dunwich type would play right into that fantasy."

Simon started pacing, and it seemed so similar to the way Monroe paced that Sylvia had to keep from laughing even though the subject matter was sobering.

"A ritual of the Dunwich type. That reminds me. There is a deep connection between the two stories, between 'The Call of Cthulhu' and 'The Dunwich Horror.' It's not something that literary interpreters would have caught, but anyone familiar with a specific occult tradition would have.

"We know that Aleister Crowley underwent a kind of intense experience at the end of October, beginning of November in 1907. He wrote some inspired documents at that time, including a ritual called *The Star Sapphire.*"

"Okay…"

"And Lovecraft set his New Orleans ritual and orgy at the very same date, October 31, 1907 in his Cthulhu story."

"That's … weird, but …"

"Hear me out. The type of writing—the style—of both the Lovecraft story and Crowley's writing of the period are remarkably similar, as if Crowley was trying to imitate Lovecraft's prose."

Sylvia replied, "Or vice versa. Crowley was actually writing in 1907; Lovecraft didn't write 'Call of Cthulhu' until much later."

"Granted. But that's not the point. In 1907, Crowley pens *The Star Sapphire.* That ritual contains some weirdly suggestive prose, along the lines of 'Father and Mother, Father and Daughter, Mother and Son, Son and Daughter,' as if implying a kind of incestuous union. It was this ritual, when it was published, that caused the German head of the OTO to initiate Crowley immediately to the Ninth Degree, which is the Degree that is concerned with the core secret of the Order which—in general terms—is an esoteric interpretation or application of sexuality."

Monroe stood up now, excited because he could see where Simon was going.

"Exactly! In 'Dunwich,' the father has sex with his daughter. Father and Daughter. That union produces twins. One of those twins, Wilbur, grows up to perform rituals with his mother. Mother and Son. But Wilbur is also his mother's brother, because he's her father's son."

"Son and Daughter."

"And since Lavinia Whateley is Wilbur's mother, her union with her father, who is also Wilbur's father, finishes the quaternity. Father and Mother."

"The 'Dunwich Horror' is a *guidebook* to *The Star Sapphire* and to the Ninth Degree. Crowley's own writings on this subject are included under the heading 'Of The Homunculus: A Secret Instruction of the Ninth Degree.' Homunculus: like Wilbur Whateley and his twin brother. The Rites of Dagon: they're about creating artificial life!"

Monroe thought immediately of the test reports from Chromo-Tech. The twins. The alien DNA. It was all coming together, but it was so illogical he couldn't get his head around it. There was a missing piece, a missing *link*.

"Oh, Christ."

"Dwight! What is it?"

"It's not just Crowley's sex magic at work here. Let's not forget the *Necronomicon*. Combine the two, and what do you have?

"A formula for Opening the Gate. A formula for creating *alien* life."

CHAPTER SIXTY

Angell walked behind Salim and the shaman, very aware suddenly of the weight of his Book on his back.

They parked outside a small house, a bungalow, that was nondescript on the outside but inside was painted entirely in green. The walls, the floors, the ceiling. All green. The furniture was covered in green pillows and throws. It was not a rich home by any means but comfortable. It was only a short walk from the ocean.

The old shaman stepped over the threshold and said "*Assalamu aleikum*" to the air. The house was clearly unoccupied. Salim took off his shoes before entering, and Angell followed suit.

It was warm inside the house, and close. The heavy furniture and dusty green cushions all combined to provide an atmosphere of solemnity. On the wall above the overstuffed sofa was a painting of a woman rising from the seas. It was less Botticelli and more *X-Men* in execution, but it conveyed the immediate impression that this was a kind of waiting room for those on their way to meet the Lady.

The shaman did not sit on the couch, but chose the floor. He sat cross-legged on one of the cushions and closed his eyes. Angell was about to ask something, but Salim made a motion for him to keep silent.

As they sat, they could hear the shaman humming. It was a kind of chant, almost sub-vocal, something sensed more than heard. Angell found himself almost swaying to the sound, to the beat.

1—2—3—4. 1—2—3—4.

In the back of his mind he realized that this was the same beat as the tapping sound from the *Silver Star*. But that was in the back of his mind. In the front of his mind he was finding himself getting swept up in the rhythm, like a marching cadence or a dance step. Part of him wanted to stop and shout, to break free of the hypnotic drumming.

Drumming. Salim was drumming. Where did the drum come from?

But to stay afloat in this rhythm was something like freedom. Something like peace. He knew he was tired, exhausted from months on the run, hungry still, and disoriented. It had to be affecting his mind. Making him see things that weren't there. Like the enormous being standing in front of him, the one with the bat wings.

Outside, the weather had grown dark and a wind was picking up. Day was being transformed into night as the clouds rolled in from the south, obliterating the sun.

Inside, devoid of electric light of any kind, the room they were in was getting darker and darker. Angell thought his eyes were open. How else to see that creature standing in front of him?

It was not standing in the room, but on the beach itself. Somehow Angell was on the beach, the clouds swirling around him like the fog in an old English movie from the 1940s. He could almost hear … he did hear … a fog horn in the distance. Or, not a horn exactly. A voice. A ululation. A *cri de coeur*.

Jesus, he thought. *I need a drink.*

A chalice appeared, floating in the air in front of him. *Father, if it be thy will …*

Very funny.

The chalice continued to hover. *Be this wine the Blood of God!*

Hilarious.

He saw the shaman staring at him intently, as if asking him a question. But the shaman's eyes were closed. He saw that, too.

How?

I've been drugged, he thought. Part of him thought. *But how? I haven't had anything to drink since we left Salim's.*

The chalice reappeared.

Someone was trying to tell him something.

He struggled to hear it, but it was all so *sotto voce*. All beneath his hearing.

Then She appeared.

And it all became clear.

CHAPTER SIXTY-ONE

Rituale

THE STAGING AREA FOR THE RITUAL was remote, as per their requirements. It was off the beaten track, miles north and west of the town of DeLand, Florida and bordering Ocala National Forest. It had been the site of a Civilian Conservation Corps camp back in the 1930s; later, in the 1960s, it had been the site of a trailer park, albeit one that did not boast electricity, or running water other than an old artesian well. Squatters had used the place until the 1980s or so when the US Navy decided that they were too close to the Pinecastle Electronic Warfare Range and moved them out. Since then, the place had become overrun with snakes, alligators, poisonous cane toads the size of hubcaps, and other creatures too numerous and too hideous to mention.

On the way from DeLand they passed signs for the town of Astor: a name carrying some resonance for the Cult. There was even a Dexter Island, which some of the more current in pop culture references thought was hilarious, if a little too "on the nose," even though there was a Lovecraft connection as well. A little north of their destination was an area known as Juniper Springs. As juniper is a plant corresponding to the planet Saturn in the old grimoires, this also was considered auspicious.

In general the place served well the requirements of the Dagon elders who appreciated the fact that they were completely off-grid. There still was no electricity anywhere near the site, for which they were grateful. They did not like to conduct these rituals near electric power lines. The paved roads petered out far from the site, which could only be approached on dirt tracks that were barely visible any longer after decades of non-use. Even the meth labs avoided the place, replete as it was with rumors of dead hoboes and serpents the size of fire hoses. It was rumored that notorious coke dealer and suspect in the homicide of a Hollywood film producer,

Laney Greenberger, had buried some of her murder victims in the vicinity.

Several black SUVs followed the lead car into the dense foliage of the former trailer park. A team had been sent out earlier to prepare the staging area for the ritual, and for the possibility that personnel may have to stay there for more than two or three days. In their coded messages, they referred to the actual site as 'Sentinel Hill.'

When they arrived at the staging area, it already was getting dark. The SUVs moved into the camp and parked in a perimeter formation, ready to leave at a moment's notice if necessary. One man from each vehicle's front passenger side got out of the car and swept the area with powerful maglites to ensure there were no unwanted visitors, human or animal. The insects they could do nothing about at the moment.

They set up cell phone blocking equipment so that the participants would not be able to either make or receive calls or give away their location through the GPS units in their phones. (Naturally, the participants had been instructed in no uncertain terms that electronic devices of any kind were not permitted at the site but Dagon never took chances.)

Makeshift shelters had been set up, which were to be used by the participants to prepare for the ritual and to hold the children until they were required. The children were in two SUVs, the older ones separated from the younger ones. They had been drugged on their way to the site and were still unconscious. No one was taking any chances as they had the last time they had been in Florida, when a concerned citizen had phoned in to the police that some well-dressed men were in charge of a dozen or so poorly-dressed children in a park near Gainesville. That incident resulted in the so-called Finders affair, which was carried on national media until the CIA shut it down at Dagon's insistence.

Now the children were well-dressed and well-fed. They came mostly from the Islamic State camps in Iraq and Syria which was how they were able to move under the nose of the authorities. While Monroe and his people had been trying to trace the children shown in the photos of child erotica—going to their sources in Eastern Europe, Latin America and Asia—Dagon had contracted directly with IS, which needed the cash and which had a steady supply of captured women and children. Dagon had no use for the women—they would have taken too long to train and, anyway, testing their virginity would have been time-consuming and fraught with errors—so those became "brides" to the IS fighters.

The children were mostly Kurds and almost all were Yezidi. Dagon liked that element, because the Yezidi were said to be devil worshippers. Anyway, no one else in that part of the world valued Yezidi life. They were reviled by the Salafis who considered them less than human. But to Dagon, they were valuable for they provided a link—no matter how tenuous—to Sumer and to the rites of their unholy tradition. It was a kind of mystical genetics—the type one gets from religious relics of any kind—and Dagon felt it empowered their rituals in a way that was unprecedented. They noted in internal documents that the Catholic and Eastern Orthodox churches require the Mass or Divine Liturgy to be said on an altar over a stone or a cloth containing a saint's relics; they claimed they were doing the same, except their altar was the body of a child, and their relic—their connection to their divine origins in the stars—her DNA.

They were secure in the knowledge that there was no way their enemies could track them. They were in the middle of the tropical Florida forests, which were not much different in some areas from swamps and jungles. While there were many cities in the world that satisfied their need for power centers with ancient pedigrees—Turin, in Italy; Prague; York, in England; Mexico City; Kolkata; Xi'an— they had become overpopulated and over-developed. They were forced to find more remote locations—like the bayous outside New Orleans that they had used back in 1907, or the Himalayas only a few months earlier this year. This time, they set up their satellites well: these were places that would set off alarm bells immediately and would attract the attention of their less-than-imaginative foes. Their most imaginative diversion, a la *Moonchild*, had been to rent the former home of murdered film producer Roy Radin in the

Hamptons for one of the satellite rituals. This 72-room mansion on the dunes fit the popular idea of what a Satanic cult center should look like—the entire point. Radin had, in fact, conducted rituals there himself during the period he was looking to produce a *Rosemary's Baby*-type film in the 1970s. Most of those tracking Dagon were drawn to the carefully-leaked reports that a large sum of cash had changed hands to rent the mansion for the period of the ritual. Dagon might as well have ordered pizza at Stonehenge. Or a fleet of Ubers to Machu Picchu. The fools.

In their Florida swampland, they were surrounded with the emblems and familiars of the Tunnels of Set: the amphibians and the serpents, the owls and the vultures, all in their natural habitats. Their leader was a woman, now in her mid-forties, whose manner of dress and comportment was a deliberate evocation of the goddess known as Babalon to the Thelemites, and closer still to the Ishtar of the Akkadians and Inanna of the doomed Sumerians. She checked her watch, for she still wore a watch—an antique Longines said to have been worn by Jayne Mansfield when she was beheaded in that automobile accident—when everyone else had abandoned them for smartphones. She saw that she had several hours yet before the event that would trigger their ritual. She pressed a button and the window on her SUV rolled down. She stuck her head out and looked up at the night sky. She knew she could not see the comet from there, but it was immensely satisfying to know it was taking place: inexorably, and no one on Earth could stop it. Soon, the Great Bear would hang from its tail in the sky.

She knew that at the same time as their ritual would take place here, another would transpire in dear old Whately, Massachusetts: a town chosen as much for its name and its resonance with the Dunwich story as it was for the fact that the earth of Whately had grown tobacco from seeds brought from Indonesia: one of the very few places in North America where this was so. The very ground had the elements of that same strain buried within its topsoil, where it contributed to the growth of organisms and bacteria. The DNA of the last known land where Kutulu had reigned on Earth, now buried beneath the ocean waves off the coast of Sumatra. The ancient city had briefly surfaced after the famous tsunami of December 26, 2004 which saw temples and cities rise from the waves all over Southeast and South Asia. 2004: coincidentally the same year the Rosetta mission was launched.

The ritual in Whately was an ancillary one. It had a slightly different character, due to the tobacco fields and the Sumatran connection, but as it is on the road to the three Satan's Kingdoms in Connecticut, Massachusetts and Vermont and as its name is Whately, there was no way she could avoid having one of the rites take place there. If she lost personnel in Whately because it was so obvious as to draw attention, so be it. It would deflect the focus of the enemy and waste valuable time as the ceremonial clock counted down.

Her bodyguards gave her the all-clear signal. The area had been swept previously, and electronic sensors installed at waist level (to avoid having them triggered by the wildlife) with a hard-wired connection to a sat phone that was monitored by her people in Berlin. She was the only one in the convoy with a smartphone on-site, and since they were already there she had no need of contact with Berlin or with any of her other lodges around the world.

She opened the back of the phone, withdrew the battery, and smashed it against a rock.

They would not be disturbed for the duration of the ritual.

A shelter had been devised for her sole use, a cabin that was no larger than a suburban living room that had been one of the buildings fallen into disuse and briefly restored by her team. It had kerosene lanterns, a porcelain basin, a few chairs and a single table. She would perform her preliminary rituals there and don her ceremonial robe. She was the main celebrant, but not the only one for obvious reasons. She would be in charge of the ritual's structure and pacing, and would be central to the rites that would result in contact being made.

Her unique contribution was her relationship to Shub Niggurath, a bond that had been developed since her adolescent years and only strengthened with the passage of time. She had been deflowered as a teen by Yog-Sothoth, as had poor Lavinia Whateley, but the results were nowhere near the same. In Shub Niggurath she had reached her apotheosis and was considered by everyone in Dagon to be that goddess's representative on Earth. She was its *tulku*, as the Tibetans would say: the current incarnation of Shub Niggurath. She alone knew the secret meaning of the name.

She dismissed her attendants, and was finally alone in the preparatory chamber. The light was soft, flowing against the cheap wooden planks of the walls like melted butter. The faint smell of kerosene would soon give way to other, harsher odors as she performed the ablutions necessary for the success of the rites.

From the large black bag that went with her everywhere she went—like the famous "football" of the President of the United States—she withdrew her copy of the most important Book in the world. She unwrapped it from its envelope of satin from old *thangkas* and set it upon the table before her. The formulas that were used to rearrange the very structure of experienced reality were contained within its pages. It was a pity they had lost the primary copy at that botched ritual in Nepal, but that soon would be of no consequence.

Removing her clothes completely, standing with legs slightly parted, with both hands she poured the first bowl of water over her head and read the appropriate incantation from the *Necronomicon*.

Outside, the girls were taken from their respective SUVs and brought into two other shelters that had been hastily improvised only a day before. The older girls were brought into the first shelter and given a drug to bring them to partial wakefulness. The men who had served as bodyguards now undressed the girls and began bathing them according to the ritual. They had a set of ritual ornaments for each girl once the bathing rite had been completed.

The younger girls were in a separate shelter, no different from the first. They were similarly stripped and bathed. They would put on robes specific to their task as seers. The bathing ceremony was intended in this case to open their inner vision, to remove the dross of sensory accretions from their "third eye" or pineal gland so that they could more easily "see" the Old Ones when they were called. The bathing ceremony for the older girls had a different function, for they were to be made pleasing to the Old Ones once They had made their presence known.

It was vitally important that the ritual succeed in impregnating at least one of the girls; it was a boon and a sign of favor if all of them were. More than that, it was the signal that the Gate truly had been Opened and that it was only a matter of time—less than a year—before the whole world would know what had transpired. As the Old Ones flooded onto the Earth—and, if they were fortunate, the other, ancillary rituals would result in even more impregnations—then the entire fabric of locality, of space-time, would warp and humans would find themselves either dying in great numbers or simply going insane as the Earth's electromagnetic field went haywire. It would be attributed at first to an epidemic of some kind, a recrudescence of some forgotten plague or collective mania; only with the passage of a few years—two, or three at the most—would the real reason for the end times become known.

She, the high priestess and *tulku* of Shub Niggurath, did not feel joy or elation at this thought. She was not a cartoon character villain, chortling with glee at the destruction of the race. Rather, she felt the weight of the responsibility and the pressure to ensure that every moment of the ritual, so carefully planned for so long, would come off elegantly and cleanly. She was the leader of Dagon, the anointed one, but her burden was heavy. She was well aware of the wholesale slaughter that would ensue, and not only of persons but of entire cultures, civilizations, histories of individuals and of societies going back hundreds and thousands of years. But the Earth had grown sick and had poisoned itself long ago. The Earth was suffering. It needed the tumor that was the human race excised, just to relieve some of the pressure. *Men* ... men like Monroe ... had characterized Dagon as a terrorist cult; in a sense, she allowed as that was true. But it was the human race that was the suicide bomber; Dagon simply provided the vest.

Soon, she would no longer be able to listen to her beloved Mozart, Wagner, or Beethoven. The books she needed as she needed air to breathe or water to drink would all crumble or burn. The *Mona Lisa* would whither into white ash. DaVinci's *Last Supper* would fade in mere moments from its wall. The Forbidden City in Beijing would crumble into loose bricks, something that successive earthquakes could not achieve. The great libraries of Buenos Aires, Paris, and London would dissolve into water and mud. Museums would become brothels; brothels would become churches. People would be reduced to themselves, or to the bonds they had forged with each other. The whole *concept* of music, literature and art would become a distant memory, if at all. Humans would become no more than vessels, vehicles for their basest natures. And then they would die, by murder or by suicide, by disease or by war. And that would be the end of it.

The Old Ones were; the Old Ones are; the Old Ones will be again. That was all that mattered, but she still felt the weight of her task like heavy chains across her shoulders: as in that last initiation so long ago. Like the men who firebombed Dresden, she lamented the loss of all of that architectural beauty but knew it had to be done. They had to follow orders. And so did she.

As she finished her ablutions, she slowly closed the Book. She raised it to her lips and kissed its cover, leather made from human skin. Tears coursed down her cheeks as she trembled at the task before her and its inevitable, hideous result. But instead of saying, with the Christ in Gethsemane, "If it be thy will let this cup be taken from me," she said instead:

"There is no god where I am."

CHAPTER SIXTY-TWO

MONROE ARRIVED IN NORTHHAMPTON, Massachusetts two hours later. He had Harry take him to the airport and then accompany him as they rented a car for the drive up to the State Police barracks. An imposing red brick building that stood aloof from its surroundings, it looked like what it was: the first stop on the last trip.

Harry was thrilled with the assignment, which evidently had been cleared by his superiors before he even knew it existed. He started asking a lot of questions, but Monroe asked him to let him nap a little on the way up. The old man was weary. Harry complied, but his mind was racing.

The Staties didn't expect what came in to meet them. They figured some guy about fifty-five in a black suit, wingtips, and an arrogance after shave. What they got was Dwight Monroe, eighty-five if he was a day, thin as a rail, and sharp as a tack. He flashed some ID at the desk, and was introduced to the man who was in charge of the prisoner known as Vanek.

He had an interrogation room reserved, and Vanek was brought in, in cuffs. Harry was told to sit in the back and keep quiet and observe.

Now, most interrogators at this point might ask the uniform to remove the cuffs, with a "That isn't necessary, officer" but Monroe wanted them kept on. The cop raised an eyebrow, but Monroe waved him off.

"Son, you have a problem," he said to Vanek once they were alone.

"*Son?* I'm fifty-eight years old."

"That makes you young enough to be my son. So shut up."

Vanek sat back in his chair and waited.

Monroe sized him up. He was pushing sixty, as he said, and was wearing nondescript clothing—the kind you would get off the rack in a neighborhood clothing store—and had a shadow of a beard.

471

"Can I take these off?" He motioned to his cuffs.

"You better get used to them, Vanek. They're your new ritual implements."

"You don't have anything on me, old man. A bunch of knives in my car. So what? It's not against the law to carry knives in your car."

Monroe ignored him.

"Your friends are already talking."

"I doubt that very much."

"Good. I want you cocky. Sure of yourself. Stupid. This will go faster that way."

"You don't have anything on me," he repeated.

"None of that is really my concern, Vanek. I'm not with the police."

"Then who are you?"

"My name would mean nothing to you, and anyway you don't deserve to know my name. I work for the US government. I'm in charge of what you might call Special Operations, although we don't give it a title. My job has one focus and one focus only. Can you guess what that is?"

"Busting my chops?"

"See? You're already thinking like a convict. You'll fit right in."

Vanek leaned in to whisper.

"Maybe you won't tell me your name, or who you really work for. That's fine. Do you know who I am? And what holy hell I can bring down on your head?"

"I know who you are, Vanek. I know all about your operation. That gaggle of fools you call an Order. The money you make off your pathetic cult literature, the frivolous lawsuits, the delusions of grandeur that others have to buy into so it becomes real to you, at least until the next check bounces. Am I getting warm?"

Vanek leaned back, as far away as he could get from the man who had yet to look him in the eyes. It was almost as if he was reading from a script, but there was no paperwork in front of him, no file folder with his name on it. Yet, he seemed to know all about the Order.

"I know why you were in Whately. How you drove in from New Bedford, that miserable little apartment you call the headquarters of your boys club in a beat-up old VW Bug. Our people are going through everything you own right now, and I can tell you it won't take long. So stop acting like some kind of Charlie Manson and start acting like who you really are: Charlie McCarthy."

"Who's that?"

"A puppet, Vanek. A marionette. The wooden half of a vaudeville routine."

"Fuck you."

Monroe started to smile.

"Getting to you, am I? See? I told you your arrogance would work in my favor. You were unqualified; even for the limited role they gave you when they made you the king, and you couldn't even live up to that. Ever hear of the Peter Principle, Vanek? No? It says that in a hierarchy everyone rises to the level of their incompetence. You know what that means? It means you get kicked upstairs, and then you die."

"I don't have a damned clue what you're talking about."

"They put you in charge so they could manipulate you. Use you. Convince you of your own greatness. And then pull the rug out from under you."

"Bullshit."

"Is it? Really? Do you really think that they were counting on *you* and your pathetic little band to Open the Gate?"

At Vanek's sudden intake of breath, Monroe knew he had him.

"*You*? Open the Gate? You couldn't open a jar of mayonnaise. You were set up, Vanek, by your own people. You were the fall guy. Don't worry. It was type-casting."

Vanek started whispering again, as if afraid that the interrogation room was bugged. Which it was.

"Do you know what you're saying? Do you have any idea? They'll kill me. And then they'll kill you and everyone around you and everyone you ever thought about. And everyone who ever knew your name."

"You mean Dagon?"

"Oh, Christ!" he yelled, causing one of the uniforms to look into the room. Monroe waved him off.

"Oh, Jesus Christ. How can you say that name? How can you say that *in here*? Oh, God. We're all doomed. We are all fucking *doomed*." He started banging his head on the table. Monroe let him.

"Dagon is even now starting the preliminary rites, aren't they?"

"I'm not telling you anything. I want a lawyer."

"If I was a cop and I was interrogating you, I would get you a lawyer. But I'm not. I can have you dragged out of here and taken to Romania in a C-130 and dropped into an anonymous cell, and the only paperwork they would have on you would be a number. They wouldn't even know your name. And by the time the jailers were finished with you, you wouldn't know it either."

"Oh. I'm scared."

"You should be, but you probably don't have that much imagination. So let me make this simple for you. The ritual. When and where? We'll take care of the rest."

"They'll kill me, asshole. They'll eat my soul."

"Well, we know the 'when.' That's tonight. It's the 'where' we really need."

"It was here. Whately."

"Please. We're not stupid."

Just then, Harry's phone rang. He stepped outside the interrogation room to answer it.

"There are children at stake, Vanek. Young girls. I don't know how many, but a lot. Maybe little boys, too. You know what Dagon will do to them. You've been around long enough."

That seemed to hit home. Monroe saw that Vanek's eyes had gone flat. He found an inner resource that he had only been faking before. It seemed as if he could snap his handcuffs in half, and that made Monroe worried for the first time in the exchange.

"Yes, I damned well know what Dagon does. I know it, chapter and verse, don't I? I've been through the mill, haven't I? Every initiation they had, until I was no more use to them than a bureaucrat with a grimoire." Vanek had slipped into what sounded like an English accent, and at once one of the mysteries that had bothered Monroe was cleared up. Tragically.

"You're the other son. The other twin. Calvin and Hywen's boy. Vinnulus."

"Aye, that's right. You saw what happened with Lucius. They were going to do that to me, but I was too strong for them. They would have killed me right then and there, but the whole twins thing, you know. I was too *valuable*. They moved me out of the country. Taught me what I know. Gave me a new identity, a new start when I was old enough. And then, when I thought everything was fine, all is forgiven, they took me. Over and over, until they got what they wanted. They pushed me until I saw what they wanted me to see. Like a Zen monk who is pushed to his limit by a koan until he gets that moment of illumination, right? Except they didn't use koans on me.

"They're my whole family now. Not the Georges. They can eat shit and die. Dagon. Dagon is all I know. And they sent me to that godforsaken town and made me the leader of a bunch of reprobates. Do I hate them for it? Of course. Do I have anywhere else to go? Of course not. So, fuck you very much, I'm not talking anymore."

Harry stuck his head back into the room.

"They have a location."

CHAPTER SIXTY-THREE

HER SON AND BROTHER APPEARED at the door. He had been
conceived during her initiatory rite some thirty years ago, when
Yog-Sothoth entered her like an earthquake in her loins, a volcano
in her uterus erupting with fire and lava until she screamed and
passed out. He looked like his father, her father. Lovecraft had called
this type of appearance "goatish" but that was unfortunate. Her son
and brother was handsome in a dark and slightly menacing way. His
eyes were what gave him away; gave both of them away if truth be
told. His irises were so light as to almost disappear, devoid of mel-
anin like all her clan who were of Him. But his flanks were thick
with hair and dark. He would not live much longer; there were
too many genetic abnormalities and they were taking their toll. This
was why there had been so many abductions, so many surgeries. So
much intervention in the evolutionary process. The Old Ones had
not evolved on this planet, even though they shared many of the
same basic genetic components. They had a common ancestor, and
a common set of genes.

Well, some of them.

So steps had been taken to prepare the Earth for their Arrival,
but also to prepare Them for the Earth. The planet had changed
considerably since They first walked and swam on its surface, since
they first dwelt below the mountains and the seas. Humanity had
belched clouds of carbon into the air, and changed the planet's
chemical composition over the course of two centuries. Acid rain, the
slow disappearance of eighty percent of the animal and plant species
that had existed an aeon ago, the very oceans clogged with plastic,
the fish and whales dying off: this meant that the Old Ones would
have to adapt to the new environment to survive. Even the sharks
were reduced to eating each other, and here, in Florida, alligators
were attacking the sharks. The Old Ones had no problem with
death and blood, but the alterations in the atmosphere of the Earth

were a concern. They could not wait for millennia of adaptations to take place naturally over the course of hundreds or thousands of generations. So they worked with the existing exemplars and tried to produce survivable offspring.

Her son and brother was one such experiment. There had been many others. Her son and brother … and husband. They had produced two offspring together, ten years ago, but they had died. Genetic anomalies. They knew the danger of incest, but considering that their Father was not from any existing human genetic line they thought they were safe. But the genetic code could not be challenged this way. That is why they had to bring in new coding.

The girls.

Their genetic inheritance was pure. They did not come from the places that were considered contaminated by too many strains to be useful. They had relied on Mengele's notes for that information, the notes he brought with him from Germany when he fled. So they avoided Europe for the most part, except for some remote areas in Eastern Europe where the residents lived an isolated existence. Their focus was on Asia, and on areas of the Middle East where racial stock was subject to strict laws against intermarriage. The Yezidis, of course, fit that requirement perfectly. That young woman who was murdered because she married a non-Yezidi, a Muslim man: that was Dagon. It was vitally important to them that the Yezidi maintain genetic purity, even more than the importance the Yezidi themselves placed on marriage within the clans.

Her son and brother and husband stood expectantly by the door.

"The time is near," he said. "The stars are right."

He pulled his ceremonial robe tight across his chest. It was long enough to cover his legs down to his ankles, thus hiding the long, straight black hair that kept growing back aggressively no matter how much he shaved, applied electrolysis, and lathered creams and ointments. Not because he was ashamed of his appearance, but in order to fit in with human society. In her heart, she was saddened at this gesture. But soon, it wouldn't matter any longer. They had taken the drastic measure of giving up on the careful, excruciatingly slow process of genetic manipulation to the more direct approach of simply seeding human girls with alien genes. Directed panspermia, they had called it. The Sons of God and the Daughters of Men, it was called in the Bible. It was fast, and it worked. Some specimens had to be destroyed due to the action of unforeseen "junk DNA" in some of their targets, but their success rate had been seventy-two percent, which was unheard of.

And it produced twins.

Superfecundation, it was called, according to one authority on the subject. Whatever you called it, it meant that their reproduction cycle was doubled. And when twins mated with twins, it created an exponential population explosion. They didn't need billions of offspring. They didn't even need millions. They just needed enough so that they could dispense with the labs and the abductions and all the other paraphernalia of bio-surgery and IVF and start reproducing on their own. The hybrid spawn of the Old Ones matured quickly: in the thirteen years or less that it took humans to reach puberty, they would only have been on the planet for two or three years. Those that reached puberty first would reproduce others, for their desire to procreate was strong. And in doing so, they would clear a space on Earth for the Old Ones to return.

The schedule was moving up rapidly. The planet would be Theirs in less than ten years from this date. Tonight, the Gate would be opened and the Old Ones would fly through it and begin the process they had abandoned aeons ago.

She looked admiringly at her husband, her brother, her son. "Yes," she said. "It is time. The stars are right."

CHAPTER SIXTY-FOUR

HARRY RACED TO THE CAR AND STARTED IT, talking over his shoulder to Monroe.

"It's just like we figured. That place in Florida, near DeLand. DeLand is where Robert Barlow lived. He was Lovecraft's friend and literary executor. Barlow was also gay. There were rumors that Lovecraft and Barlow had a relationship. He was only a kid in high school when he first met Lovecraft and they spent a lot of time together."

"Yes, Harry, I know all this. What about the site?"

Harry peeled out of the parking lot and headed back to the airfield at Northampton, going eighty miles per hour.

"It's called Pinecastle Electronic Warfare range. It's in a wilderness preserve west of DeLand. It's the only place on the entire east coast that the Navy can do what they call 'live impact training.' But the thing is: it has these strange designs on the ground. It has a six-pointed star in one section and a five-pointed star in another, and between them there is this huge circle made of concentric circles. Simon said it looks exactly like the magic circles in the old grimoires. Somehow Dagon found a site that has occult designs but which is also a match for the original Philae, the island in the Nile."

"You say it is a military base?"

"Not a base exactly. They drop bombs there. It's for bombing practice."

Monroe let Harry keep his eyes on the road while he phoned Sylvia.

"You heard?" she asked when she saw it was Monroe.

"Yes. What can we do now? I can call in the cavalry, but there are going to be children there. We can't start shooting." He sounded anguished, or maybe he was just tired.

"How much time do we have?"

"Not much. These things usually happen at midnight, or later.

But we don't have any guarantees. They could be using some kind of specialized timetable. One of the people arrested tonight told the State cops that they were supposed to meet at 11:30 pm and that the ritual had to be over by 12:30 on the dot. If that holds, that means we have less than two hours until it starts and three hours until it's over."

"We would never get there in time. It's too remote."

"We have to try. Get a hold of Aubrey. He's probably still in New Bedford. Tell him to roust whoever he can in DeLand or at the military base. What's it called again?"

"Pinecastle."

"Pinecastle, right. Wait a minute … isn't there another site for the ritual with that name? The one in Long Island?"

"That's Ocean Castle. But, yeah. The local cops just picked up a gang of weirdos that had started setting up an altar there. We had them watching the place, and when they showed up with a few underage girls the cops had all the probable cause they needed."

"And we picked up the group in Whately. I wonder how many more of these there are?"

CHAPTER SIXTY-FIVE

THE CHILDREN DID NOT CRY.

Not the old ones, nor the young ones. That was probably the most horrifying element of all so far. Children are emotional. They laugh, they cry, they scream at the slightest provocation. But not these children. They must have been terrified, but they did not show it. That degree of maturity—or of resignation—disturbed the bodyguards. They needed these girls to be girls, not women. Not yet.

The drugs, possibly. They had not worn off yet. They were still half-comatose. Even the bathing ritual did nothing to rouse these creatures. The bodyguards hoped that would wear off soon, because the emotional involvement—the *presence*—of these girls was necessary to the ritual's success. The guards had other drugs, other means. They could rouse them with cocaine or some other, less potent, mixture but that would depend on the orders they received from Her.

A bell rang from within Her shelter. That was the signal that the children should be brought to the ceremonial altar. They would drive again, up to a gate in a chain-link fence, where they would be met and escorted part way onto the field.

So the girls were herded into the SUVs once again, just as before. They would precede the rest of the convoy as they had to be arranged in their respective areas at the site before the arrival of her and of her invited celebrants who were just now coming up the dirt road. Their headlights could be seen nearly a mile away.

In just a few hours it would all be over.

There were six older girls, those who had just attained puberty, in one car. They were Yezidi for the most part, torn from their families by the Islamic State from territories in and around the sacred mountain of Sinjar. Some of these girls had sisters and mothers who had been raped, or given or sold in battlefield marriages to IS fighters. These girls, however, had been spared the sexual abuse because Dagon had offered top dollar for untouched girls of a certain age and appearance.

The younger girls were five in number. They were also mostly Yezidi, with one Kurdish girl of about six. Their story was the same.

All the older girls had the identifying (and sanctifying) tattoo—the one spotted by Harry at NSA—on their hips. The tattoos were permanent and their application had been painful, but with the judicious use of drugs the entire process was accomplished quickly and with relatively little drama. The tattoo artists had been promised an obscene amount of money for the procedures.

They were then taken out and shot behind a mosque in Anatolia: a massacre conveniently blamed on Daesh who were happy to take the credit. The girls then appeared in erotica, drawing to themselves and to the image of their tattoos the repressed desires of the sexually transgressive even as their presence announced the imminence of the ritual.

As the two cars containing the girls left the staging area, two more cars arrived. Inside each one were six celebrants, six initiates of Dagon who had passed the necessary tests and trials and who had the seniority and the experience to participate in what would be the most important event of their careers. These were males, and each one would be expected to participate in the deflowering ritual: a version of the Wiccan "Great Rite." The Wiccan rite was intended to represent the magic of the act of creation of the Horned God and Goddess—a European version of Shiva and Shakti. This version, however, had other applications.

There were six pubescent girls and twelve male initiates. She was not taking any chances. She knew this could easily descend into a total orgy, and she had to be careful not to allow that to happen. The control of the ritual was her responsibility: the direction of the combined concentration of all participants and their awareness of the Presence of the Old Ones.

In the beginning, six of the men would be assigned to watch over the five youngest girls. They knew what they had to do, and they understood their roles perfectly. They had enacted the same ritual in the past—albeit under different circumstances and for limited purposes—so this would be no different. One of the six men would be the leader of the other five, and they would assemble the five girls onto a complex diagram known as the five-pointed grey stone of Mnar. A crystal mirror as large as an exercise ball and made of Aztec obsidian would be erected in its center and the girls would make contact with the Old Ones through that crystal.

They would be separated by a path that led to another complex diagram, this time with six spokes instead of five. Between the five-spoked and six-spoked stars there was a larger circle, offset from the first two with paths extending into different angles, and all contained within a kind of octagon made of dirt roads that had been laid out around them. The space between the circles was large, and communication would not be accomplished with any electronic devices but with light reflecting off the mirrors, for another piece of polished Aztec obsidian would be set up in the six-spoked star.

She would stand in the larger of the three areas—in the giant ceremonial circle—and conduct the ritual using implements obtained from the museums of Nineveh and Baghdad, stolen by IS and included as part of her deal for the children.

The lamps would be lit when the stars were right. She consulted her watch and looked up at the heavens. From her training, she could find any constellation—and any visible star with the constellation—without consulting a star chart. But it wasn't a star she was looking for that night. And it wasn't something she would be able to see with the naked eye.

It was a comet.

Her contact at NASA had told her when the comet would be in position where it was needed to be. His timing had always been spot-on before. He had no idea, of course, of just what she was up to with that information. He had no need to know. Dagon was as compartmented as CIA.

The girls. The men. The stars. The rites. The site. The Book. This was a thing of mutants. Of hybrids and homunculi. Of opening Gates and bloody sacrifices.

Of the daughters of men and the *bene hayeshenim*, the Sons of the Old Ones.

CHAPTER SIXTY-SIX

THE CARS STOPPED AT A CHAIN LINK FENCE. There were warning signs about unexploded ordinance, but She knew she had nothing to fear. Everything had been arranged, and as long as their convoy stayed within the lines they would be fine.

They fanned out. One car drove east to the Pentagram. One car drove west to the Hexagram. Her car went directly for the big circle between them.

It was a close replica of the original Philae, the sacred island where Osiris had been buried. Now, OSIRIS was aboard Rosetta and sending images back with Philae. It was delicious. And the last she heard, Philae had landed in the region sacred to Ma'at, the Goddess of Truth, whom one meets on the way to the Underworld.

It was all so perfect it was delicious.

Her son and brother and husband escorted Her out of her vehicle and to the center of the circle. The mirrors had been set up, and she could see the lamps burning at the two other circles. The ritual would begin in only a few minutes.

She opened the Book and set it upon the small podium before her. The censers were lit, the large lamps raised on either side of her.

In the Pentagram, the younger girls were arranged in their proper orientations. Stools were brought out, and they were seated on them like little princesses. Their arms were outstretched and tied to crossbeams. The tension in their arms and back was believed to accelerate the clairvoyant process. It would also make it easier to sacrifice them when the time came. It was dark and scary out there, but the men with them stood behind them like bodyguards. Censers were lit, and a noxious substance wafted across their nostrils.

In the Hexagram, the older girls were restrained—face down—upon slabs of volcanic rock that had been polished to a high sheen. Their heads hung down over the front of the slabs. Their legs were pulled tightly away from each other. Censers were lit, and a different set of herbs and barks was burned, as mildly hallucinogenic as those being used by the seers but with an added narcotic to ensure there would be no drama beyond that which the ritual demanded.

In the main circle, the preliminary ritual invoking the Watcher had just been completed. A sword of great antiquity was plunged into the Earth. At that moment, the shriek of a far-off vulture could be heard.

The invocation of the Fire God was next, another preliminary but an important one. The fire that was invoked was not the terrestrial fire.

From that fire, runners were sent to light the sacrificial fires at both the Pentagram and the Hexagram.

The dedication of the seers was the first phase of the ritual. She, the high priestess and *tulku* of Shub Niggurath, again checked the time. She looked to the right and left, ensuring that Her initiates were prepared, and raised a torch high above Her head.

She threw the torch into the huge brazier set up in the center of the circle, and it burst into flames. At that signal, the ritual proper began.

CHAPTER SIXTY-SEVEN

THE LOCAL COPS DIDN'T KNOW WHAT to make of the request from DC. There was a jurisdictional problem. The Pinecastle Range was military land. Going into the range with a bunch of squad cars was like taking a tour bus into Area 51. They were trying to explain this to the woman on the phone who said she worked at NSA and who had all the right codes, but ...

She said there were kids being held hostage there. Kids who were about to be physically abused. Little girls. That sure was probable cause, if true. But it still didn't mean they could crash the place with impunity. They would have to call the Navy first, but it was nighttime and they didn't know if they could raise the right person in time. Could it wait until morning?

Sylvia screamed at them. There was an imminent peril, she said. You don't need a fucking warrant! They had not heard women in government use that kind of language before.

At the same time, Monroe was on the phone with Aubrey trying to come up with a way to send a Special Forces team to Pinecastle. They had military bases all over Florida: Army, Navy, Marines, Air Force. McDill was the closest airbase to the site, but the site was Navy.

"Okay, then, Marines."

"This isn't like Iraq, Dwight. We had a green light for anything we needed there. This is the continental US. It's a lot more complicated. Listen, what if we got the Navy to sign off on the local cops raiding the place?"

"Sure, but will they? Harry tells me they have unexploded ordinance there. All we need are some squad cars blowing up on military land."

Aubrey and Monroe were frantic. The girls could be killed at any moment. They didn't know how far along in the ritual Dagon was.

"Look, there is one thing we can do. We can get a whole army of squad cars and security vehicles to the perimeter of the range. Lights, sirens, all of it. That has got to put a crimp in their style. And we throw some sound at them. Loudspeakers, bullhorns, whatever we've got."

"You know what you're saying, right? This could be Waco all over again. And that was about the children, too, remember? This could get very ugly, very fast."

"Do we know if they're armed?"

"We have to assume they are. They're going to sacrifice the children. They have to have weapons of some kind."

"That guy we picked up in Whately, he had a trunk full of swords. Think they're going old school?"

"They'd have to be, right? Unless there were Uzis mentioned in the *Necronomicon*."

"But these are fanatics, Aubrey. They may decide to accelerate the ritual just to be sure it's done before we swoop down on them."

"Light."

"What?"

"Light. Searchlights. Big ones. We flood the whole range with light. That should screw up the process and make sure we catch everything they do on tape. Every twitch."

"They won't care about that, but I see your point. How about this: a SWAT team. Two or three. In helicopters. They drop down on the ritual, take out the adults if they have to."

"The jurisdiction …"

"Screw jurisdiction. We're running out of time. We have to authorize this ourselves. If it blows up in our faces, at least we can say we tried. Otherwise …"

"I'll get on the horn. Find the local SWAT commander. Give him the old national security line. Terror cell. That sort of thing."

"You wouldn't be far wrong, Aubrey."

CHAPTER SIXTY-EIGHT

THE SEERS—THE YOUNGEST GIRLS—WERE TOLD what to chant. They were given an easy one, because they were so young and because the repetition of a simple word, over and over, would help increase the sensory deprivation state they were aiming for.

The chant was *Iä!* That's all. Just that one word.

As they began, the leader of the seer group began his own evocation of the Old Ones to visible appearance in the crystal mirrors.

At the Hexagram, the girls were kept in a state of suspended animation by a careful selection of the herbs that were burned in the censer. The men wore masks, which served to conceal their appearance but which also enabled them to breathe clean oxygen. The light of the sacrificial fire cast fingers of shadows on the bodies of the girls. When the time came—once the Old Ones made their presence known—the men had to be ready at once to impregnate them once the signal had been given. There would not be any time for foreplay.

While this was going on, She invoked Cthulhu, the high priest and intermediary between the Old Ones and the human race; then Her own Shub Niggurath; and then finally Yog-Sothoth, Her father. By drawing down Shub Niggurath into Her, She would empower the entire rite. Her husband, son and brother knelt before Her in a precise orientation and at a precise angle with another crystal mirror and drew down the power of the comet into his bride, sister, and mother.

Soon he saw Her eyes grow cloudy and Her visage change. Shub was entering Her vehicle.

Once he saw that take place, the next step was his to take.

He began the charge:

Pater et Mater unus deus Ararita …

At the Hexagram, the men waited patiently for the sign that the Old Ones had been drawn down through the Opening of the Gate. They would then "earth" the Old Ones into the young women strapped to the altars before them, and they would give birth to the New Race.

At the Pentagram, the youngest girls were slipping into trances. Their chant of *Iä!* was becoming garbled and faint. Large cups, like chalices, were placed under the stool of each child. They were there to catch the blood as their heads fell to the earth.

The first child, a Yezidi daughter of eight years, saw a reflection in the mirror but it was not human. She started to tremble. Children in America were afraid of monsters under their beds in their quiet and comfortable and safe homes. Yezidi children knew the monsters were real and could devour them at any time.

She wanted to raise her arm to point, but she was restrained. She was forced to speak her horror directly to the men who held her.

"*I,*" she whispered, for that was its name. "*I, Shub Niggurath.*" Baby talk to her, a babbling of nonsense syllables. But the men knew the name and rejoiced.

Then another child, another Yezidi girl with brown hair and a sad smile, threw back her head and roared, "*N'gai, n'gha'ghaa, bugg-shoggog, y'hah';Yog-Sothoth,Yog-Sothoth!*"

It was happening.

One more. Just one more.

CHAPTER SIXTY-NINE

IT WASN'T LIKE BOTTICELLI AT ALL.

She didn't rise from the sea. She came from the desert. She came *out* of the desert. But she was supposed to come from the sea.

The desert is an ocean, in which no oar is dipped.

Where did that come from? A book? A movie?

The strange tall birdman with the bat wings stood behind him, like his own shadow. He could feel him standing there, menacing, lethal, but was transfixed by the woman in front of him.

He feared the thing behind him, but it made him feel safe. He loved the woman before him, but she frightened him. He knew she was death, but she would protect him.

In his hands, suddenly, was the Book.

Opened to the incantation.

Oh, God. The same one. The one he had to say in Nepal:

> *To the Gate of the Underworld*
> *The Land of No Return*
> *Set thine eyes*
> *The Seven Gates shall open for thee*
> *No spell shall keep thee out*
> *For my Number is upon you ...*
> *Ereshkigal shall have no power over you.*

A voice in his head, in counterpoint to the words from his mouth:

> *To save the Goddess you must slay the God.*
> *To save the Woman you must defeat the Man.*

And from behind him, in a voice that vibrated from the soles of his feet to the crown of his head, a voice whose fingers grasped the chambers of his heart in a grip like a dying man's last breath:

I am, and I am not.
Before Satan was, I am.
Before the Peacock Angel was, I am.
Before Iblis and Lucifer, I am.
Before all the gods you worship, I am.
There is no god where I am.

I am the headless corpse, the faceless bride of darkness. I devour the strong and the weak alike. I march with the armies across my ancient land. My banner is black to those who see. My Caliph is a pedophile, my Sultan a serial killer. They worship me who cannot live their Faith but only die for It. They call on God, but find me instead. They crave purity, but look for it in the filth and offal of the corpses they have created. They seek eternal life, but I chew on their souls and boil them in the tears of their victims.

I am the Man from the Underworld, and these are my Works.

It was spoken in a tincture of hatred and despair that colored the entire speech like a drop of blood in a glass of water.

He was taller than any man, this bird-like creature. His shoulders were not broad, which was unusual except for the fact that his arms were long and drooped past his knees. The overall effect was simian but mixed with something else, something insectoid, like a praying mantis with skin and bones and flesh.

His voice came from elsewhere. He didn't seem to speak with his mouth but the sound issued forth from his torso like the beating of a kettle drum with words that reverberated long after they had been uttered. Watching him, horrified, Angell knew that he was not seeing him as he really was but was looking at an attempt to create a reasonable fiction of a man but without losing any of its own, non-human, nature. The body he was wearing was a mask, an imitation of life, like the result of a plastic surgeon tweaking on crystal meth with a suitcase full of scalpels and knives and a book full of illustrations of chimerical creatures from the Middle Ages: men with faces where their torsos should be, or demons that were half-horse, half-rooster, with long, lolling tongues dripping saliva and acid rain.

Staring, fascinated and appalled, Angell noticed the peculiar quality of light around the figure standing before him. The image seemed to flicker, as if in the tenuous grasp of unfamiliar arrangements of photons that were simultaneously particles and waves. "I am, and I am not." There was a key here, somewhere, to the problem of gravity and the unified field theory but Angell didn't have the physics to figure it out. Instead he realized that he was looking into the eyes of Pak Mahmoud, the old shaman, the *dukun prewangan*, and that he was sitting on the sand in front of the ocean, soaking wet.

The shaman drew in the gaze of this *bule gila*, this crazy foreigner, and saw at once that he had been saved. The Goddess of the Southern Ocean had blessed him. He need fear no longer.

CHAPTER SEVENTY

THERE IT WAS. THE FIRST TO BE EVOKED, the third to appear.

One of the girls, practically a baby herself who, when they found her, could barely speak more than a few words was staring wide-eyed at the mirror. And whatever was in the mirror was staring wide-eyed back at her.

She opened her mouth and, without speaking, a roar of sound erupted from her body.

"Ph'nglui mglw'nafh Cthulhu R'lyeh wgah'nagl fhtagn!"

They had made contact with the sunken city, the *beyul* of Kutulu, the Shambhala of Shaitan. The High Priest himself had torn the membrane between this world and his. The High Priestess, in ecstatic embrace with her husband, son and brother, could hear the roar clearly as her brother, son and husband came in a rush of sickness, lust, fever and death.

No one was ready for what took place next.

The mirrors became portals, gates into this world. What were supposed to be magic circles, mandalas designed to protect the magicians of Dagon, had become doorways through which files of unholy chimeras passed.

These same magicians raised their swords to decapitate the seers just as their counterparts in the Hexagram prepared to penetrate and impregnate the "breeders." But they were transfixed by sights that not even they—with all their experience in ritual magic, sorcery, and forbidden grimoires—had ever experienced.

An army of the damned seemed to pass right through them and out into the world.

One by one they arrived—beings that struggled to maintain some kind of identity within the constraints of the Earth's atmosphere, its dimensional challenges, and the inevitable chemical imbalances. Corporeality was tricky for beings who had never had to concern themselves with it before, who traveled and communicated and fornicated in the dreams and fantasies of human nervous systems designed to propagate a multitude of species, but for whom genetic specialization had condemned them to lusting after the unattainable.

These were mutants, but their physical mutations were simply reflections of the failure of human imagination which seemed restricted to daydreams about sex and love, and occasionally violence. All the illustrations of demons in the old grimoires came alive in the flesh, so to speak, as monstrous images exploded on the retinas of Dagon. The Unspoken—the one fact that even Lovecraft did not explicitly state but which he implied most clearly—was that the interface between human beings and the horrors of his imagination was sex. Orgies were at the heart of every cultic embrace of the Old Ones. Sex was always there, off stage, off camera, and out of frame in his short stories. It was the secret not only of the magical Orders and the esoteric Societies, it was the secret of Lovecraft, too. Teased, hinted, a lifting of the skirt above the ankle, but always there.

And now, here were the Old Ones in complete *flagrante delicto.* All tentacles and tubings, gropings and viscous slimes, the bursting ichor of ancient beings celibate for aeons now let loose upon the brothel of the Earth.

The incubi and succubi of the medieval imagination were nothing compared to an Old One with a hard on. This went beyond mere transgression. This was a full-scale ride through the pornographic hallucinations of a serial killer in Hell. Every psychological, neurological, scatological possibility of which the human organism was capable was meek in comparison. Every bodily function was represented in excruciating detail as being somehow erotically charged. Every neurosis and psychosis—from OCD to hysteria, from schizophrenia to dissociation—was plumbed for its ejaculatory potential.

Advaita, go fuck yourself. We're here to multiply like crazed weasels. Nirvana is for snowflakes. Samadhi is for social justice warriors. Diversity means multiple partners, multiple orifices, all ages, all genders! Sigmund Freud, Jew, will not replace us! *Sex macht frei*, motherfucker.

There was Johann Schwarzer, famous pornographer, fallen in

battle exactly one hundred years ago but now falling all over the girls on the altars, camera running, catching every angle, screaming for more sweat, more erections, more blood of the Lion, more gluten of the Eagle, *Am Sklavenmarkt*.

The whole ritual had turned into a *Herrenabende*, an evening for gentlemen. A diversion. A stag film for a smoker, if the smokers were all doing life without the possibility of parole, featuring Richard Speck in drag.

Something, quite clearly, had gone wrong.

On the other side of the world, the local Dagon chapter—operating in the tunnel between the Kraton, the Taman Sari, and Parangtritis Beach, their own private Tunnel of Set—was frozen in place. The girls, all from villages in East Java, had simply walked away when a woman in a green dress happened upon their ceremony, asking where the swimming pool was. "Hi!" she said, thrusting out her hand. "My name is Stacey. What's yours?"

The Goddess of the Southern Ocean—Lara Kidul, who had called more men to their deaths in her underwater kingdom than Cthulhu in R'lyeh—had been evoked, invoked, and provoked by the words from a Book held in the hands of a man who believed in nothing, who loved no one, but who wanted to be saved nonetheless.

He was, at least, honest.

And he chanted the same incantation that he had performed in Khembalung, to save the world even though it meant his own exile from everything and everyone he ever knew. And it was the incantation that resurrected—not a man, but—a woman, a female, a Goddess from the depths of the Underworld, from the clutches of Cthulhu's Frankensteinian bride, Ereshkigal.

And as she rose from the dead, as she escaped the three days of crucifixion in the Underworld, as she walked through the open Gates

...her demons preceded her.

The searchlights blinded everyone on the field. Swords dropped from hands as heavily armed and armored men descended ropes into the midst of the ritual. One of Dagon's lieutenants rushed the SWAT team with a raised sword stolen from a tomb in Nineveh. He was cut down effortlessly.

One of the other initiates was already inside one of the breeders when the team arrived. The others had begun at the sound of Cthulhu screaming from the mouth of the seeress and were in various stages of penetration. They withdrew roughly and sought their weapons but the tactic of complete surprise overwhelmed their efforts at defense. The stealth helicopters had lived up to their name and reputation. The SWAT team lived up to theirs.

She was getting away. She had no children with her, and it was decided to save the children first and pick up the ringleaders when they could. She and her husband, brother and son ran from the circle to the ring road around the bombing range.

And stepped on unexploded ordinance.

Thanks to the analysis performed by Harry and Simon on the names and places in the Lovecraft world, two more ritual sites were simultaneously breached. Details about those actions are being withheld as local, state and federal government agencies decide if laws were broken, jurisdictions violated, the rights of anyone put at risk.

But in the meantime another twenty-three children were rescued.

And Lucius—poor, demented Lucius—was found dead in his room at the psychiatric institute. They found him with a smile on his face, for the first time in his adult life. The cause of death was undetermined.

Lucius and Vinnulus. Light and Sweet. Castor and Pollux. Twins, but from different fathers. Hywen, well, she got around.

CHAPTER SEVENTY-ONE

CUNEO STOPPED AND WIPED HIS FOREHEAD with his ever-present handkerchief.

"I give up. The service tubes lead nowhere. They dead-end in the walls. It's like the damned pyramids or something."

Lisa commiserated with him, but secretly she was pleased. She believed that this was not a man's mystery but a woman's. She liked that he couldn't figure it out. She liked that she had something of this case to herself.

Of course the service tubes led nowhere. That was the whole point. Just like those mysterious shafts in the Great Pyramid. He had been so close to figuring it out she almost felt sorry for him.

She wanted to tell him they were Fallopian tubes, just to see his reaction and get him off on another tangent for a few weeks, but that would have been cruel. You don't have to attack the enemy, but you can decide not to make it any easier for them.

She had researched the Church of Starry Wisdom. There wasn't much online, and she would have to go to Providence herself and check the archives, but that was okay. What she did discover was enough to make her realize that the Church was involved in trying to seduce a Being to come down from wherever it called home and impregnate a human woman. Lisa, who had been brought up Catholic, found that amazing. (Imagine the Virgin Mother as a loose woman, queer for aliens or angel sex, initiating the Conception herself! How different history would have been if a central mystery of Christianity was not the Annunciation but the Seduction: if it was Mary who had decided when and where and with whom. Mary the Virgin as Mary the proud if somewhat whorish slut, whose tramp stamp read—like Mulder's poster in the basement—"I want to conceive.")

If they were successful, it would challenge every human male in ways it had never been done before. I mean, she thought, how do you compete with *that*? How do you make a woman prefer you to some outer space god who can give her miracle babies that change the trajectory of the planet's history? No more awkward fumblings with clasps and buckles amid protestations of eternal love. No more confusing love with lust, with claims of permanency that were only immediate need. No more men who were only men, mere men, human men, after all their insistence otherwise. Men who were nothing more than their exhausted and disappointed mother's sons. Violent, sick, stupid men who ruined families, destroyed cities, slaughtered millions with bombs and disease, millions who were conceived just as she was with words of rape or love or indifference, men who were gone forever even when they were sitting next to you, staring off into ... into *space*. Why not choose, instead, to give birth to something better, something stronger, something whose difference was a palpable fact and not a lie dreamt up for a quick and dishonest fuck. No more earth men; no more kings, no more generals, and no more Y chromosome-obsessed saviors. No more being told what to do, only *doing*. No more control or manipulation of bodily functions by foreign bodies. The poetry, instead; the sheer poetry of self-regeneration, and the alliance of women with angels to reshape the planet.

For someone like her, it would mean a degree of freedom in this world that she never thought possible.

Cuneo couldn't decide what was going on with Lisa, but he put it out of his mind. He had a more immediate problem. The baby in the ICU was growing too fast, the docs said. Born premature, it was already the length and weight of a one-year old. It was making noises that sounded like words. The DNA had not come back yet, but the docs didn't know if they could hold him there much longer. They were talking about Child Protective Services, which—let's face it—wasn't about to happen.

That's when he looked up and saw a face he recognized. It was the cop from the basement. The one who escaped out the window. The one with the smiley face.

Cuneo got up and reached for his service pistol. Lisa saw the look in his face and followed his gaze. Smiley Face Guy just stood there and looked straight at Cuneo as if to say, "Yep, it's me."

He was about to run away and Cuneo knew he would never catch him, so he just shouted out after him:

"Just answer me one question! Please! Just one question!"

Smiley Face Guy stopped and turned. He opened his hands as if to say, "Go ahead."

"How did you do it? How did you leave the box and the basement without anyone seeing you go?"

He got a huge smile in return. A kind smile, even.

"I never really left," he said.

And disappeared.

CHAPTER SEVENTY-TWO

GLORIA WAS ABOUT TO TURN INTO THE MOTEL parking lot when she passed a young man walking aimlessly along the side of the road. Her kids started asking her to stop. That was freaky. Why would they care? She rolled down her window.

"Hey," she said. "Are you okay?" He didn't appear to be armed or dangerous, but who knew these days?

"I'm good, thanks. On my way to a meeting."

"At this hour? It's pitch black out."

"It's a special meeting," he explained. "Secret."

"Oh, okay." She rolled up her window and turned into the parking lot.

Jean-Paul thought she was pretty, but with those two boys in the back seat his chances at getting lucky were pretty narrow. He wondered what it would be like to make it with an old chick.

He walked on. His car had run out of gas, he hadn't checked the fuel gauge and anyway he didn't have any cash, so rather than call his mother and bitch at her he decided to just hoof it over to the tobacco field. Fuck it. He didn't want to be late.

As he did so, a light passed over him and then winked out. He figured it was a car somewhere. Headlights. Something.

He turned into the field and started walking to the center. The tobacco had all been harvested long ago but there was a sponginess to the soil, a kind of exotic texture, that made him think of tropical islands and long-haired girls in sarongs. Playing ukuleles or some shit. Except that it was fucking cold out.

He had a couple of hours. Maybe he would just wander back to that motel. See if they had a coffee machine.

The demons were restless now. They watched him walk, alone, in the tobacco field. *Marlboro Man. Tobacco Road.* They made pop cultural references among themselves to pass the time. *I'd walk a mile for a Camel.* Jean-Paul tastes good, *like a cigarette should.*

501

He had evoked them to visible appearance once, some time ago, and when he didn't see them he had simply walked away, the lazy bastard, and fell asleep on his couch watching *Dark Angel* reruns. No license to depart. No observance of the niceties. How rude.

But someone had opened the Gate. And now it was their turn.

In the motel she had been able to get the kids to wash their faces and brush their teeth. They were in one of the two beds, watching television and getting sleepy. She went into the bathroom and shut the door.

And peed on a stick.

She knew it. The freak outs. The nausea. The crying jags. She was pregnant. She also knew it was impossible. She hadn't been with a man since her husband left her, and that was more than a year ago.

She sat on the toilet seat and crumbled. What was going on? Why did nothing make *sense*? And how was she going to raise another *kid*?

And how the hell had she gotten pregnant?

She reached into her purse for a Tic Tac and found the notes she had taken during her call to the genetic testing agency.

That's when she noticed it was pretty quiet outside. She opened the bathroom door, but the kids were not in their beds. The television was on, but the sound was turned down. Some religious channel.

Oh, Christ. Now what?

She looked under the beds, just in case they were hiding, and when that proved fruitless she grabbed her keys and went outside.

"Mike!" she yelled. "Bob! Where are you? Why did you leave the room?"

It was dark in the parking lot, the only light from the neon sign over the door to the motel's office and some weak porch lights along the motel's walkway. Once out in the parking lot, you were in a sea of darkness.

"Mike! Bob!"

But she might as well have been yelling "Being" and "Nothingness" for her two sons were gone.

Jean-Paul was also gone. They would find his car by the side of the road, and film an *Investigation Discovery* episode all about him. That was later, though. Right now, he was just ... gone.

Gloria was becoming frantic. She ran to the office and banged on the door, but no one answered. She turned to run to the car, maybe they were there, maybe they started walking along the road—although why they would do that made no sense. But it also made no sense that she was pregnant, and it made no sense that they had genetic whaddayacallit anomalies, and why would they want her to talk to that strange boy; and *where were they?*

"Excuse me? May I help you?"

She turned at the voice which seemed to have come right behind her, where there had been no one only a moment ago.

"Oh! Sorry! I didn't see ... I'm looking for my sons. Two little boys. Mike and Bob. They were in the room with me and now they're gone and I'm going crazy ..."

The young man looked pleasant enough, with a serene expression and a depth to his gaze that seemed to penetrate you when he talked.

"You have to be careful. In your condition you can't afford to get too upset."

"What? What do you mean? How do you ... I just myself found out ... just this minute ..."

"Your boys are fine. Don't worry about them. You'll see them soon. As long as you carry to term. Do you understand?"

Her mouth opened in a frozen scream but no words came out.

"Carry to term, and your boys will be returned to you. They're very special you know."

Then he added, "*Anomalies*. Right? Take care. Have a good evening." And just like that, he was gone, swallowed in the darkness of the motel parking lot.

She fell against the side of her car, shaking like a leaf. She dropped her keys. Picked them up. Dropped them again. Picked them up again, and that is when she noticed her windshield.

Someone had drawn a smiley face.

CHAPTER SEVENTY-THREE

"I WANT TO THANK ALL OF YOU for everything you've done. You should be proud. Children were rescued in four states."

They were sitting in Simon's living room again. It seemed like the most congenial place to be, and Simon's food was better than the NSA cafeteria.

"Did the group in Whately have children, too?"

Monroe nodded. "In a shack in a tobacco field. They had three children tied up there for what must have been two days. They were freezing cold and half-starved, but we found them. One of Vanek's people capitulated and told us. Otherwise we would not have found them until it was too late. And we would not have been able to tie them to Vanek and his crowd. Not legally, anyway. But there is still one missing. A teenager who was supposed to meet them there. He never showed up."

"Or he saw the police cars and decided against it."

"Could be. We don't have a name, though. None of the others knew it, and Vanek isn't talking. All communications were handled with snail mail and Vanek didn't keep copies. Deliberately."

"Did we roll up the entire Dagon operation?"

"Oh, no. The high priestess died in the explosion. And her consort. The others aren't talking, of course. They're trained for that. Better than our intelligence officers. They go through all sorts of yogic training, meditation, and similar programs. They can disappear into their minds for a long, long time."

"The Tunnels of Set," offered Simon.

"Yes. I suppose."

"So there are other branches we haven't stopped?"

"Well, there's that lodge in Indonesia, of course. And several that we know of in Europe. There's one in Chile, another in Argentina. There was a ritual underway in the basement of church in Turin, but when the police arrived their leaders had already escaped. They did rescue some of the girls, though."

504

"And the other girls? The ones we rescued in Florida?"

"The youngest are all okay. They were going to be sacrificed, virtually at the same moment SWAT landed. They were restrained, so there would have been no way for them to escape certain death."

"And the others?"

"More problematic, I'm afraid. The ritual had already progressed to the point where some of them had been violated, but we don't know to what degree. We're having rape kits done on all of them. And then we have to find their families. All of their families. We have more than fifty young women and girls to reunite with their loved ones. If they're still alive, and can be found, and in whatever countries."

Monroe stopped a moment, and changed his tone.

"By the way, a man named Alexandre Grothendieck died today, in the south of France. He was the greatest living mathematician, but left that discipline to focus instead on spirituality, and on an idea he had that the world was being influenced by mutants."

"Mutants? Really? Like our hybrids?"

"The same. He also said that all our dreams come from the Dreamer. I hope he is dreaming now. Not dead, but dreaming."

"And what about Angell?" Simon asked, quietly. "Any word?"

"Oh, I'm sure we'll find him. And the Book. Eventually. None of us is really safe until that Book is in our possession and locked away securely. And Angell isn't safe as long as he has it in his possession. We were lucky this time. Dagon had an exemplar of the Book but they couldn't make it work, even with all their training and preparation going back more than a century. Something went wrong during the ritual, even before we showed up. I don't know what it was, but I'm sure they do. Which means that now they will redouble their efforts to find it. And him."

In a sidewalk restaurant off Malioboro Road in Yogyakarta, Angell is met by Captain Aji. They shake hands, and Aji hands him an envelope containing a passport with an Indonesian visa and his share of the take from the gold bars found on the *Stella Matutina*. It's not a fortune, but it is a sum large enough to finance his travel for the next few months while he finds a place to hide that is not subject to extradition back to the States. Not that such a legal nicety would protect him, now that hordes of pissed-off cultists were after him and the Book, but it was a strategy, anyway.

"Why not stay in Indonesia?" Aji asks him. "Find a wife. Make a family. Forget all this," he said, pointing to the Book in Angell's bag.

"It's too hot here, Captain, and I don't mean the weather. Plus, how can I find a wife and risk making Lara angry with me?"

"As long as she is the first wife, she will be okay with it, I think."

Angell shook his head.

"I am a one-woman man, Captain."

"I think you are a no-woman man, Doctor Angell. But I hope one day you find peace."

"Oh, I found it. I found it on Parangtritis Beach. I just hope I don't lose it, that's all."

EPILOGUE

Mount Sinjar
Daesh-occupied Iraq

THE WOMAN WHO STEPPED AWAY from her cover behind the stone wall checked the action on her rifle, and reloaded. It was a semi-automatic Dragunov, the famous SVD, and it would need another cleaning soon. The sand, dust and dirt were wreaking havoc with it and, anyway, it was getting overheated. Which might be rare for a sniper rifle, but Jamila was nothing if not enthusiastic.

The reporter who was embedded with the Peshmerga thought she was the most photogenic of all the women soldiers who were fighting to rid Sinjar of the Islamic State. She certainly was against type for a woman in that part of the world. She was not dark, did not look like what most people thought Arabs looked like. She was fair-haired and had light blue eyes and a fair complexion. He knew she was Yezidi, which explained a lot, but she was strange in a way he could not identify. Aloof, reserved, introverted. She was dressed in camouflage, and her hair was cut short like her sister soldiers. She seemed ... happy.

She had joined the "jin" (all-female) unit only two months earlier, picked up by a truck on the highway south of Istanbul and headed for what had once been a refugee camp on the border. She was looking for her family, so the story goes, but also looking for a unit she could join to fight Daesh. She had never handled a weapon before, and was put through her paces by the militia she ran into. The refugee camp had been struck, she was told. Some of the refugees had found temporary homes in Europe. Others had gone back: to Syria, or to Iraq.

As for Fahim, the man who had been a father to her, no one had heard anything.

She was still a little too weak to handle firing an AK-47. She had not eaten regularly in a long time. And she had weird fainting spells, or something. Like fits. Not often, but once in a while, and it was scaring the other women. So they put her alone, made her do support work, and kept a watch on her.

That's when they noticed she had a particular aptitude for intense concentration. She knew how to control her breathing, so that she barely moved and could almost disappear, even in a crowd. An alert officer had an idea.

She handed Jamila an SVD. It was the Russian original, the Dragunov, one of the best sniper rifles in the world. Jamila embraced it like an old friend. She had never seen one before, had certainly never fired one in her life, but there was something about it that called to her.

"It is for people like me," she explained, in Kurmanji. "People who should be alone. But people who want to fight anyway." She learned its intricacies quickly. She understood about wind speed, altitude, and the other factors that could influence a long-range sniper's aim. It was like building an architectural marvel in her mind. She imagined the temple in Dharamsala where she trained with Rabten. She remembered every inch, every angle of that building and built it into her mind like a map. She translated altitude into the angles of the remembered temple; wind speed became the way the smoke from the incense bent and curved in the draft.

She took to the PSO-1 optical sight as if she was staring into a magic mirror. She instinctively understood complex technical concepts, such as how to use the reticle with its range-finder and chevrons and stadia.

She volunteered for missions where their intelligence told them women and girls were being held hostage by Daesh. She had no idea that the Keepers of the Book were trading in trafficked girls for their own sick rites, but she didn't need to know. She hated those who had come to her country and taken the innocence of her sisters, her cousins, her people. That they would be forced into marriage at all, let alone marriage to men who were worse than criminals and savages, inflamed her hatred to an impossible degree. That they would force themselves upon her people, "marry" them for a night or two, and then divorce them and pass them on to the next "brave fighter" was an obscenity against all human nature, against all religion. These were not human beings, she thought. These were aliens from another planet: a planet of rape, torture, and death.

She discovered that the Daesh fighters are afraid to be killed by a woman because their leaders tell them they will not go to heaven if they are. She says, therefore, she has proudly sent more than twenty of them to hell. But when she says that to the journalist, there is a catch in her throat. He cannot know that she understands more than most what 'hell' really means.

When they go into battle, the women, they shout and sing, to let Daesh know that they are women and that they will kill them and send them to an eternity in the Underworld. It scares the shit out of them.

She learns from the journalist that the Americans have now joined the fight against Daesh and it was because of the genocide of her people, the Yezidi, that they had done so. But until they get here, it is up to Jamila and her SVD to defend her country.

She didn't know, didn't ever know, that the American news media—something called CNN—had called her and her sister fighters the most inspiring women in the world that year: 2014. All she knew was that she was an expert with the Dragunov. That she could wait for hours, for days, in one spot for the right moment to kill a rapist and murderer at 500 yards. Or run into a house or a mosque where the women were being held and slaughter any man who got in her way.

For the first time in her life, she had learned how to smile. She was no longer the vehicle, not for god or man. She was the driver.

And in her mind, when she sighted through the side mount PSO-1 or the night sight NSP-3, what did she see? Did she see Daesh?

When she loaded the specially-made 7N14 151 grain projectile, did she think of Dagon? Or did she see the man who had come to her camp, the American? The one she saw again in the cave in Nepal when she thought the other men there loved her and valued her, when they had only exploited her? When she slaps the 10 round magazine into the rifle that was now the extension of her third eye, her second sight, does she see the men who had taken her away from Fahim and her people? Who *is* her target? Who is her *real* target? The one she kills, over and over, every day?

She answers that question with her adamantine gaze. "*You*," she seems to say, "If you side with *them*."

The priestesses foretold:

Divinity and humanity in ancient India were twins.

—"The Hoopoe," Mahmoud Darwish

ACKNOWLEDGMENTS

JEAN-PAUL SARTRE ONCE SAID THAT "Hell is other people." As a life-long misanthropist-in-training, I have to agree. But I think there is a corollary, which is "a writer is hell on other people." No one who has a writer in the family or as a friend would disagree, not if they are being honest. Writers are hell on other people because they are anti-social, self-absorbed (or absorbed in their work, which pretty much amounts to the same thing), irritable, absent (even if present, if you know what I mean), passive-aggressive perfectionists for whom the social niceties are torture, phone calls are intrusive, and daily life simply overwhelming.

(I'm looking at you, Kafka.)

So my apologies rather than my acknowledgements to those of family and friends who were exposed to this seething broil of chronic intensity and social dissociation. For me, the kindness of strangers rests in the fact that they are strangers and therefore don't know who I am so they can't bother me. For all the rest, I ask for your forgiveness since it's too late to ask permission.

This is a novel about Hell and other people. It even has a character named Jean-Paul. There are a lot of other Eastern eggs in here, as you will discover. Just don't … like … tell *me* you found them. Let that be our little secret! (insert snarky emoji here)

Oh, but, you know: thanks as always to Yvonne Paglia and James Wasserman! (sigh)

PETER LEVENDA
2017

ABOUT THE AUTHOR

PETER LEVENDA is a well-known author of many published works on esoteric subjects. *His Unholy Alliance: A History of Nazi Involvement with the Occult* bears a foreword by Norman Mailer and has been translated into six foreign languages. *Ratline: Soviet Spies, Nazi Priests, and the Disappearance of Adolf Hitler* broke new ground when it revealed the Far East segment of the Nazi escape routes after the fall of Germany. *His Hitler Legacy: The Nazi Cult in Diaspora: How it was Organized, How it was Funded, and Why it Remains a Threat to Global Security in the Age of Terrorism* explores the pernicious Nazi influence on the modern interpretation of Jihad. Levenda is also the author of the three-volume study of the influence of esoterica on American politics, *Sinister Forces: A Grimoire of American Political Witchcraft.* His Ibis Press book *Dark Lord: H.P. Lovecraft, Kenneth Grant, and the Typhonian Tradition in Magic* explores many of the esoteric themes exposed in this novel.

ALSO FROM IBIS PRESS

The Necronomicon

31st Anniversary Edition of the Schlangekraft Recension

Edited and Introduced by Simon

In the past decades, much ink—actual and virtual—has been spilled on the subject of the *Necronomicon* (also called the "Simonomicon"). Some have derided it as a hoax; others have praised it as a powerful grimoire. Despite the controversy, it has never been out of print for one day since 1977.

The *Necronomicon* has been found to contain formulae for spiritual transformation that are consistent with some of the most ancient mystical processes in the world—processes that involve communion with the stars.

In 2008, the original designer of the 1977 edition and the original editor joined forces to present a new, deluxe hardcover edition of the most feared, most reviled, and most desired book on the planet. With a new preface by Simon, this 31st Anniversary edition from Ibis Press is available in two versions. The first is a high quality hardcover bound in fine cloth with a ribbon marker. The second is a strictly limited, leatherbound edition, personally signed and numbered by Simon. A small number of leatherbound copies are still available.

POPULAR HARDCOVER, BOUND IN HIGH QUALITY CLOTH

$125.00 • ISBN: 978-0-89254-146-1 • 288 pages • Printed on acid-free art paper • 7¼ x 10¼ • Ribbon marker • Sold everywhere

NUMBERED & SIGNED, DELUXE LEATHERBOUND EDITION
Strictly limited to 220 numbered books, signed by Simon.

$275.00 • ISBN: 978-0-89254-147-8 • Three sided silver-gilding • Special binding boards • Deluxe endpapers

Signed edition available exclusively from www.studio31.com

AND MORE FROM

THE LOVECRAFT CODE

PETER LEVENDA

The Journey of Gregory Angell begins . . .

Drawing on decades of experience—as evidenced by his more than a dozen published works on politics, esotericism and religion— non-fiction author and historian Peter Levenda turns to the novel as the best and perhaps only way to tell a story that has to be told, as unbelievable as that story may be.

Hidden within the tales of America's most iconic writer of gothic horror, H.P. Lovecraft, runs a vein of actual terror. Gregory Angell, the present day descendant of George Angell in Lovecraft's "Call of Cthulhu," is summoned by a nameless covert agency of the US Government to retrieve a sacred book from the grasp of an Islamist terror network operating out of northern Iraq, in the land of the Yezidi. Long believed to be devil worshippers, the Yezidi are all that's left of an ancient cult that possessed the key to the origins of the human race ... and of the conflict between that race and another, much more ancient, civilization from beyond the stars.

Angell's quest takes him from the streets of Brooklyn to the deserts of the Middle East, to Central Asia, northern India and an island in the Pacific Ocean where a city that had been buried beneath the waves for millennia comes crashing to the surface after a tsunami. The reader is taken on side trips to Nazi Germany, the laboratory of a South Florida necrophile, post-Katrina New Orleans, and to the origins of the modern science of archaeology in the late nineteenth century.

PETER LEVENDA

THE DARK LORD

H.P. Lovecraft, Kenneth Grant,
and the Typhonian Tradition in Magic

PETER LEVENDA

One of the most famous—yet least understood—manifestations of Thelemic thought has been the works of Kenneth Grant, the British occultist and one-time intimate of Aleister Crowley, who discovered a hidden world within the primary source materials of Crowley's Aeon of Horus. Using complementary texts from such disparate authors as H.P. Lovecraft, Jack Parsons, Austin Osman Spare, and Charles Stansfeld Jones ("Frater Achad"), Grant formulated a system of magic that expanded upon that delineated in the rituals of the OTO: a system that included elements of Tantra, of Voudon, and in particular that of the Schlangekraft recension of the *Necronomicon,* all woven together in a dark tapestry of power and illumination.

The Dark Lord follows the themes in the writings of Kenneth Grant, H.P. Lovecraft, and the Necronomicon, uncovering further meanings of the concepts of the famous writers of the Left Hand Path. It is for Thelemites, as well as lovers of the Lovecraft Mythos in all its forms, and for those who find the rituals of classical ceremonial magic inadequate for the New Aeon. Traveling through the worlds of religion, literature, and the occult, Peter Levenda takes his readers on a deeply fascinating exploration on magic, evil, and *The Dark Lord* as he investigates one of the most neglected theses in the history of modern occultism: the nature of the Typhonian Current and its relationship to Aleister Crowley's Thelema and H.P. Lovecraft's *Necronomicon.*